THERAPY

KATHRYN PEREZ

www.Kathryn-Vance-Perez.com

Cover Design by © Okay Creations
Editing by Megan Ward
Formatting by JT Formatting

Lyrics used with permission.
Bird With Broken Wings ©2012 by Tyler Lenius

ISBN-13: 978-1495421181
ISBN-10: 149542118X

First Edition: February 2014
Library of Congress Cataloging-in-Publication Data

Perez, Kathryn
Therapy / Kathryn Perez – 1st ed

The words on the pages within this book are solely dedicated to victims of bullying, those that ever have or still do suffer from depression, mental illness, and the struggles that accompany it.

You are brave.

You are strong.

You are smart.

You are beautiful.

You are worth it.

NOTE TO THE READER

If you are living with depression or are self-harming like Jessica and countless others, please reach out for help. You can get help by calling any of the following hotlines:

Depression Hotline: 1-630-482-9696
Suicide Hotline: 1-800-784-8433
Self-Harm Hotline: 1-800-DONT CUT

You can also text CTL to 741741 to reach trained and compassionate listeners who are there to help you at any time.

The Crisis Text Line is a toll-free text service available 24/7 nationwide.

People who want to help and are ready to listen are waiting for your call. You are stronger than you know.

Part One

DARKNESS

"Depression is a sneaky, evil bitch. She creeps in when you least expect it and snakes her way throughout the corridors of your mind while feeding on the light of your soul. She shows up during your most difficult times, only making them harder to shoulder. Sometimes, I wish depression was a living, breathing, tangible being, so I could wrap my hands around her throat and squeeze 'til all that's left in her pools of darkness is nothingness, rendering her powerless to ever hurt me again."

—Jessica

"The small words hurt the most."
—Kris Harte

Jessica

GRIPPING MY JOURNAL, I flip through the pages of my written pain. Putting pen to paper is comforting to me; my journal is the only place I can really be myself, the only place I can release my demons and voice my fears. Trying to forget summer break, I push away the thoughts of Brian and the other guys that used me for sex these past couple of months. The heartache they caused is nothing compared to the pain I'll face today.

Senior year. My last year of hell on earth is upon me. This morning I have to step inside the hallways of my own personal nightmare. The fear I feel is almost tangible. Writing will help ease it, but I know it won't be enough. I place my hand over my lower stomach and run my fingers across my scars. I focus on the blank page before me and start to write.

Faces

Familiar places

Trapped within these walls

Taunting me

Trapping me

Laughter filling the halls

Not much longer

It will soon end

Can't let them know

They win

Broken

Beat down

Their derisions

Circling all around

Block it out

Push it down

Keep building these defenses

Brick by brick

My emotions bound

Seeing a stranger

When I look in the mirror

Lost and alone

My soul pleading

Desperate to find a home

I sit in my car, staring at the front steps of Jenson High School as dread washes over me. The drive here was nothing but minutes filled with anxiety.

Only one more year. I can do this. Just one more year and I'll be free of this hell on earth forever.

The past three years were nearly unbearable, and I can't imagine this year will be any different. I grab my backpack and push my car door open. The parking lot's filled with people milling around, chattering about senior year, eyeballing each other's outfits, and sizing each other up. One clique bleeds into another clique, and so on. Keeping a low profile is important to me, so I've chosen to wear a plain pair of skinny jeans and a simple white T-shirt; I don't belong to any of the cliques.

Because I'm invisible.

I barely exist.

A loud engine rumbles as a huge truck pulls up in the parking spot beside mine, startling me. I look over to see that it's none other than Jace Collins, superstar athlete and megapopular boyfriend to my worst enemy. His door opens and he jumps out, throwing his backpack over his broad shoulder. He might be with the biggest bitch in school, but God, the guy is like a huge magnetic force made up of sexual tension and dimples. By the time I realize I'm staring, it's too late; he's noticed me ogling him. A small grin stretches across his face and I blush, snapping my eyes away. I turn and start walking toward the school when I hear her.

"Oh look, it's Jenson High's school slut. How lovely!" Elizabeth shouts, loud enough to draw attention my way.

I clench my backpack strap, keeping my gaze forward. I can feel her eyes gunning a hole through the back of my head. This is the only time of day when I'm visible. When I'm in the cross-hairs of Elizabeth Brant's clique of mean girls, I'm a huge blaring bull's-eye. Engaging with her is pointless. She never gives in or lets up. Now, everyone within earshot stares and laughs at me. Taking in a deep breath, I try blocking it all out. I can hear her spitting more venom my way as she gets closer, and her sidekick Hailey joins in the taunts.

"How was your summer, Jessssssica? How many guys did you add to your list, huh?"

Their laughter fills the air around me, and then I hear him. Jace. He's been stepping in for the past couple of years to shut them up when they talk shit to me. The first time he did it, I was stunned. Why would he care what they said to me?

I'm no one.

I barely exist.

"Okay, enough of that bullshit. It's the first day of school. Do you both have to be such assholes?"

I don't turn around or acknowledge his act of kindness. I'm thankful, but I can never tell him that. If she saw me talking to him, it would be a disaster. I don't know why, but every time I make eye contact with him I get butterflies in my stomach. Of course, he's never flirted with me like so many of the other guys do. I know why they do it, and so does everyone else, but Jace has never treated me like a slut or piece of trash. He's as close to a gentleman as a teenage guy can be.

Last year, when we were paired together in chemistry class, Elizabeth was pissed off. She pinned me down with her stare for the entire hour, but Jace ignored her and rolled his eyes. When class was over, he got up and gave me a small smile before walking away. It was the one time that I hadn't felt like a nobody. For that one hour I'd felt present and not so closed down. It was easier to breathe—it felt like what I assumed school should feel like.

Jace remains a mystery to me. I have no idea why he treats me like a normal girl, but every time he does, my heart beats a little stronger and a little faster. I hope one day I have the

opportunity to thank him. Until then, I'll keep my gratitude safely tucked away.

"Nothing makes us so lonely as our secrets."
—Paul Tornier

Jessica

I CLOSE MY eyes as the blood runs down my stomach, the pain oozing out with it. This is what I want, what I need. Otherwise I'm numb, feeling nothing. The pain and depression stays suppressed until I can release it. It gives me a high and a rush that I crave every morning before I go to school. I know when I walk through those doors each day that I have to flip a switch inside and turn it all off just to make it through. My mom drinks coffee with a shot of liquor to start her day.

I cut myself.

I shove my notebook in my book bag and mentally prepare for day two of dodging Elizabeth Brant and her posse of mean girls. Some days, I wish I could just meet them all somewhere and let them beat the hell out of me; they could spit all of their poison my way and be done with it. If I knew it would make them stop, I'd do it in a minute. My senior year of high school has barely begun, yet I'm already counting down the days 'til it ends. For the past three years, school has imprisoned me.

I just want it to be over.

Every day I pray that they'll forget about me, and I'll really become invisible. But they never do. I do everything I can to keep attention away from myself in order to avoid their radar. It's always futile—Elizabeth is merciless. I've never understood how a girl who is so beautiful on the outside can be so ugly and evil on the inside. How all of her admirers can't see her for what she really is will forever be a mystery to me. But I know better than anyone how easy it can be to fool people and hide your darkest secrets inside.

Because I do it every day.

I head into first period English and sit at the back of the classroom like I always do. I shuffle through my book bag and get my notebook out just as I hear them. Their banter is unmistakable.

"Oh my God, Hailey, did you see him this weekend? Jace was on fire in the game, although he always is. I rewarded him afterward, of course. Then he was really on fire."

The bitch posse giggles as Elizabeth goes on about her boyfriend and the school's quarterback, Jace Collins. They're the "it couple" around the school. Jace is Mr. Popular and, of course, Elizabeth is Ms. Popular. What he sees in her, I have no idea. Well, aside from her long, luxurious blond hair, flawless bronzed skin, perfect body, and crystal clear blue eyes. But she radiates *bitch*, regardless of her appearance.

Elizabeth glances back at me as she takes her seat. “So, Jessica, how much slutting around did you do this weekend?”

I dart my eyes down toward my notebook, refusing to reply to her taunts. Trying to stick up for myself only makes it worse. My long jet-black hair falls down around my face, creating a curtain of defense, and I doodle aimlessly on my notebook, ignoring all of her comments.

Something hits my arm and falls onto my desk, then again, and again. I look up and Elizabeth is laughing as Hailey, her partner in crime, balls up another tiny piece of paper. I roll my eyes at them and look back down at my notebook, swiping the pieces of paper onto the floor.

Brian Wheeler turns, looking at me with an assholish smirk on his face, and waggles his eyebrows up and down suggestively. My stomach rolls along with my eyes as I look away from him. Brian is yet another example of a relationship gone bad. The fact that I've slept with him makes me want to puke.

Elizabeth turns around, mumbling something about what a skank I am just as Jace walks in and sits down beside her. Hailey flicks another balled-up piece of paper at me and he scrunches up his eyebrows, glaring at her. She grins back at him and shrugs her shoulders innocently.

“Hailey, don’t be such a bitch,” he says in an obviously irritated tone.

Thank you, Jace.

You’re a mystery to me, Jace.

Why do you care, Jace?

Jace, Jace, Jace.

“Jace Collins, don’t talk to my best friend like that! Hailey is only warding off the infestation of STDs sitting behind us," Elizabeth hisses.

He looks back at me and mouths the word sorry. I don't reply; no expression, no all-knowing look, nothing.

He's the epitome of male perfection with his sandy, dark blond hair and light blue eyes. He's toned and muscular, but not in a bulky way, and he's tall with wide shoulders. Not only is he the star of the football team, but also the baseball and male swim teams too. He's an athlete and pretty much has a clear-cut future with an athletic scholarship to a major university of his choosing.

The only reason I think he's ever nice to me is because I'm on the girls' swim team. I steer clear of all team sports, for the most part, and I'm definitely a loner. I've been competitively swimming for four years now, and it's the only thing that I really enjoy besides writing. School is a means to an end for me, and I can't wait for it to be over. This place is like a sick form of karmic punishment for something I must've done in a former life.

After English class, we all file out. I walk slowly, allowing Elizabeth to exit first. Hopefully she'll forget that I'm behind her. I make my way to my locker only to find notes reading *WHORE*, along with other expletives in big bold letters, taped to it. I rip the papers off quickly just before Elizabeth walks by, shouldering me hard into the cold metal lockers.

"Oh, excuse me, Jessica. I didn't see you there," Elizabeth jeers. "You should wear a slut warning sign that lets the rest of us know you're there!" she laughs as her followers surround me.

I look to the floor, hugging my books to my chest and shut it all out. This is how I deal with her, with all of them. I lock down, shut it out, and wait for it to be over. She flicks a strand of my hair from my face, and I flinch.

"We all know you slept with Harrison this weekend. You know that Hailey has been seeing him for quite a while. Did you really think you could keep that from us? Huh?" she demands, inching forward. "You better keep your skanky ass away from him. Do you understand me, Jessica?" She's so close that her words spray flecks of spit onto my face. "He doesn't want you! None of them want you, bitch!" She slaps her hand on my locker mere inches from the side of my face, and whispers quietly as she leans in closer to my ear.

"Don't you ever just think about ending it all and sparing us the repulsion of looking at you every day? You'd be doing everyone here a service." She glares at me with hatred burning in her pools of ice-cold blue. My eyes quickly dart back and forth, looking for an out. I feel hot, too hot, and my skin is clammy.

Breathe.

Then I hear his voice.

"Liz, leave her the hell alone already!" he scolds, gesturing for her to make her way to second period. "Remember what I said, skank," she exclaims as she struts off down the hallway.

I look up to see that Jace is still standing here looking at me, his hands shoved into his jean pockets. I feel vulnerable and embarrassed. Why is he causing this awkward, silent moment to happen? I look away nervously and turn back to my locker, opening it quickly with shaky hands.

"Hey, I'm sorry about Liz and her tribe of bitches," he says as I rustle through my locker, stalling so I don't have to turn around and make eye contact with him. My hands are trembling, and I'm trying to regain some form of composure after the face-off with Elizabeth.

Just breathe, Jessica.

"Don't let her rattle you so much. I didn't hear what she was saying, but I promise you her bark is far more scary than her bite."

He has no idea what his girlfriend is really like on the inside.

"Are you ready for swim this year? I hope we kick ass like we did last year," he says, and I wonder why he's trying to carry on a casual conversation with me. The bell rings.

Thank goodness.

I spin around and look at him with my mask of fake confidence. "Thanks, Jace. And yeah, I'm ready for swim team. I really have to get to class, though," I mutter. His mouth turns up into a grin and he walks away in the opposite direction.

What was that all about?

Why do you care, Jace? Why?

If Elizabeth sees him carrying on a full-blown conversation with me, she'll go apeshit. I'm like the plague around here, and the star quarterback talking to me is definitely not a good idea.

The day moves at an arduous pace, but I continue to avoid Elizabeth. I'm not sure what's worse—this place and the way I seem to be the butt of everyone's jokes or home where I'm invisible to everyone.

I go to my car and drive home, blasting Seether out of my speakers. I wonder what kind of day Mom is having. She'll either be drunk, or be Martha Stewart; it's a fifty-fifty chance.

I stopped caring a long time ago. When she's not

drunk, she tries too hard—it's smothering. She overcompensates for her lack of parenting on the days she's drunk as shit. I pull into the driveway and see her sitting on the porch, smoking a cigarette, and holding a glass of wine. There are kids outside playing next door where new neighbors are moving in. Their ball is in my way as I try to park, so I maneuver around it the best I can. A little girl smiles and waves at me as she retrieves the purple ball. I look up as I get out of my car and see Mom smile and wave sloppily at me.

Drunk day today...

"Hi, Mom," I say hurriedly as I walk past her.

"Hi, sweetie. How wassss your day?" she slurs.

"Great, Mom. It was great!" I say, lying straight through my teeth. Telling her the truth is pointless.

I go inside to my room and slam the door behind me. After locking it, I reach over and pull out my hidden box of razors, alcohol swabs, ointment, and bandages. I flip my iPod docking station on and fall down onto my bed. Hinder plays as I pull up my shirt. Unbuttoning my jeans, I pull them down just barely enough to expose the fresh cut from this morning. I have to be really careful not to let the cuts get infected, so I clean and bandage them daily. It's a normal routine for me.

I know I'll have to put on a happy face when my dad gets home. He doesn't really pay me any attention, but I always feel like he has me under a microscope, looking for any imperfection or mistake. I do my best to avoid him like everyone else in my life. The weekend is the only time I socialize, and that usually involves a guy. Sneaking out every night on the weekends is the norm for me. I'm usually cruising the back roads with whatever guy I'm seeing at the time, which changes often. I'm always too clingy, so they always run scared after they get what they want from me. Sex is my way of connecting, another way to feel something. I guess sex equals love for me since I have no idea what love really feels like. It's my version of love and it fills a void, so I continue the vicious cycle of sleeping with every guy I go out with. The fact that guys have never noticed my scars really should tell me that they don't care at all. I know it's usually dark and they aren't that visible, but to this day not one guy has noticed. If they have, they've never said anything.

After cleaning up my cut, I place a bandage on it and button my pants back up. Placing the box of items back in my nightstand, I pull out my journal and decide to write. I rarely understand why I feel the way I feel every day. Writing is my only true form of expression free from the fear of judgment. I can pour all of my feelings, fears, and frustrations into the pages of my journal and know that they're all safe from the bullies that make my daily life a living hell. My secrets must stay hidden, just like my pain.

Pulling the cap off of the pen with my teeth, I chew on it anxiously as I write.

You only know the mask I wear

Who am I?

Do I even know?

Black...White...No gray

I either love or I hate

When I want to hold on, I claw
instead
No sense of purpose
Eyes that are dead
Regret and rejection I swallow
down
I just want someone to love me
Emotional pain creeps all around
When someone hurts me, it hurts
forever
Be. Me. For. A. Day.
Let me walk beside you
Let me look over
See the me you see
Then you can walk beside me
See the you that I see
I'll keep filling the hole in my soul
with IOUs

While you keep filling it with I Hate Yous

I shut my journal and text Harrison. We had a good time this past weekend, no matter what Elizabeth had to say about it. Having someone makes me feel happy, even if it's always short-lived.

Me: *Hey, I had fun last weekend. You want to hang out this weekend?*

He texts right back, and I instantly feel better. Happier even.

Harrison: *Hey, babe. Yeah, I had a blast with you. You really know how to show a guy a good time! I'm not sure about this weekend. Jace and the guys invited me out. It's just some sort of guys' night out thing, but I'll catch you some other time.* ☺

My smile fades along with my happiness, and I instantly feel rejected. I want him to want to be with me, not the guys. Why does this always happen? Why do I need them so badly? Why do I want them so badly?

It's always the same. Every guy I date, I feel consumed by some sort of freakish need. I know it's not normal, but I can't make it stop. In the end it either pushes them away, or causes me to go off on an emotionally charged rant toward them. I regret it every time, but the cycle is on repeat nevertheless. I usually talk with them online because they don't speak to me at school. No one really does—I'm bad for everyone's reputation. Elizabeth makes sure of that. One day last year, Brian sat with me at lunch and Elizabeth and her group made him sorry he ever did.

My phone buzzes and I see that I have fifteen notifications on Instagram. That's weird. I never get much action on any of the social media sites. I have no real friends to speak of. I tap the icon and open the app. I touch the little notification bubble and fifteen comments or likes pop up. It's a picture of me. Shock freezes the blood in my veins as I scroll down. SlutPics123 posted a picture of me hanging myself. A quote bubble above my head says

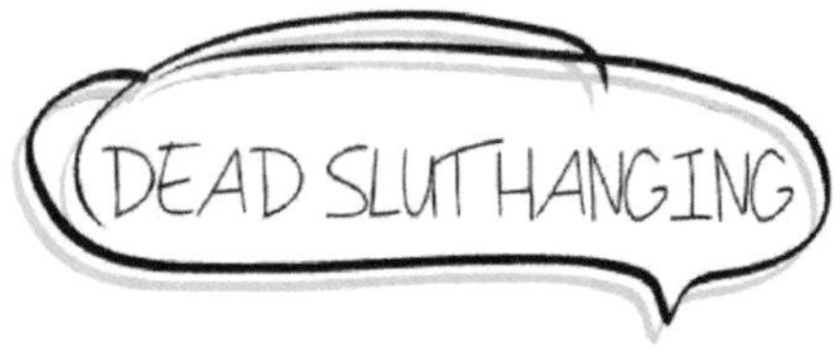

They follow me everywhere I go; I can't escape them! I know Elizabeth and Hailey did this, but this is a new low. Their weapons aren't illegal, yet they cut me deeper than a blade ever could. Hiding behind electronic shields, they use their words like swords. I wonder what's worse—the invisible scars they leave or the visible scars I inflict upon myself?

"I have no one. I need someone."
—Amanda Todd

Jessica

ANOTHER WEEK OF school has inched by and I've done my best to ignore the picture they put up on Instagram and the ridicule that's followed it. Being silent may seem weak, but staying silent takes more strength than they'll ever know.

I'm hoping Harrison will be able to see me this weekend. I've tucked a note in his locker, letting him know I'll be home waiting for his call if he decides he wants to hang out.

He doesn't really talk to me much at school, which I guess I understand. It would only cause him unwanted drama. Elizabeth and her minions have everyone at school convinced that I'm an infestation of STDs.

Mom is Martha Stewart today, which means a cooked meal for dinner. She's humming and prattling around in the kitchen like we're the Cleaver family. Dad will be home soon. He's having a business partner over for dinner, which also means Mom will be on her best behavior. I'll stay huddled up in my room for as long as possible until I'm forced to smile and interact with everyone.

My brother is the star of the family and can do no wrong in Dad's eyes. Jeff always gets the attention from Dad that I crave. I had hoped that when he left for the University of Texas Dad would finally begin to see me, but that didn't happen.

I hear my phone buzzing and grab it, hoping it's Harrison. I swipe the screen, revealing his sexy, tan face.

Harrison: *Hey, you wanna hook up tonight after all?*

Me: *Sure! Where and what time?*

Harrison: *Meet me down at the parking spot by the water tower at 9 p.m. C you there.*

I'm instantly excited, and start rummaging through my closet to find something hot to wear for him. I grab a black miniskirt, red halter top, and my laciest underwear. He never has condoms, so I'll have to stop and get some at the 7-Eleven on my way there. It's a given that we'll have sex. I know it sounds horrible, but I don't feel bad about it. Guys want it, and if you don't give it to them, they don't want you. I want him to want me, so sex is necessary.

I just want to be wanted.

Loved.

After a painstakingly boring meal with Mom, Dad, and his business partner, I change and head out. I tell my parents I'll be back by curfew, but they won't notice if I'm late.

I go to the 7-Eleven and buy a pack of condoms. A few get shoved in my purse and I toss the rest in my glove compartment. I check my makeup in the mirror and run my fingers through my long dark hair. I stare into my hazel eyes and wonder what other people see when they look at me.

Do they only see a slut?

A weird girl?

Are they really even looking at all?

I shake the thoughts away and save them for a later time when I can write them in my journal.

I put my little Honda into drive and head out to the town water tower. It's always been a popular parking place for the local teens. As I get closer, I notice a couple of different cars and wonder why there are people out here so early; it's usually later before anyone starts showing up. I pull in farther and park.

I scan the area and see a couple glowing cigarettes, but can't make out who the people are smoking them. My heart rate kicks up; I hope they aren't *I Hate Jessica* club members.

Me: *Harrison, where are you? I'm here.*

About five minutes pass by, but I hear nothing back from him. I decide to wait a little longer, because I really want to see him. I jump when I hear a knock at my window, and turn to see Elizabeth staring back at me with a smug grin on her face. My heart jams into my throat, and my breathing speeds up into high gear. At least when she corners me at school there's usually an out. It's a crowded, public place with adults around to prevent any serious situations. But this? This is very different. I have no idea why she's here, how she knew I was here, or what she wants with me.

She beats on my window as her friends circle around my car. I quickly start my engine and throw the gear in reverse. I need to get the hell out of here. Just as I start backing up, Harrison pulls in right behind me, blocking my exit. I'm now completely boxed in. Maybe this is best, like I've always wanted. She can do whatever she wants to me and be done with it.

I really don't care anymore.

"Get out of the damn car, whore!"

I turn and glance toward the front of my car just as Hailey pours a beer all over the hood. Harrison walks up puts his arm around Hailey affectionately, and my stomach clenches in anguish.

How could he do this? Did he trick me so that I'd come out here and they could torture me? Why would he be so cruel? I've always done everything he's asked of me. I've always tried to make him happy. How could he do this to me? Tears start to well up in my eyes, but I quickly get myself under control, not wanting them to see me break. I reach over and open my door, step out, and am instantly shoved back against the cold metal of my car.

"I told you earlier this week that Harrison was Hailey's. You just wouldn't listen, would you, skank? Hailey saw your texts to him. Did you really think he was going to keep seeing you? He's not going to lose the captain of the cheerleading squad for the captain of the blow job team," Elizabeth hisses sarcastically.

Everyone laughs as I stand there. Just before I open my mouth to antagonize her, Bentley comes up behind her and wraps his arms around her, kissing her neck. Has she broken up with Jace, or is she being the whore that she always claims me to be? Bravery finds its way to my tongue, and I do the stupidest thing I could ever do.

I poke the snake when it's ready to strike.

"Where's Jace, Elizabeth? Does he know you're out here screwing around on him with Bentley? Maybe I'll let him know and he can be my next fuck. I bet I can show him things he never dreamed of when he was with you." I smirk and cross my arms over my chest. Adrenaline courses through my veins as I await her response.

Her eyes grow wide and she gasps as everyone starts laughing and heckling her over my comment. "Bentley and I are just friends, you stupid bitch. Mind your own damn business. Who the fuck do you think you are anyway?" She slaps me with all her strength and heat creeps across my face. Grabbing me by the shoulders, she slams me into the car even harder.

"All of a sudden you've got some newfound courage tonight, huh? You're going to regret ever saying that shit to me. And if you insinuate that I was doing anything other than hanging with friends to Jace, tonight will feel like a walk in the park compared to what will happen to you next."

She grabs me by my arm and yanks me away from the car.

"Hailey, get your ass over here and help me. This shit is all your damn fault anyway. Your boyfriend's the one that can't keep his dick in his pants!"

I look into her evil eyes defiantly, practically begging

her to beat the hell out of me.

Don't do it, Jessica. Don't make it worse.

"Go fuck yourself, Elizabeth," I reply in a raspy, nervy voice. I make it worse.

I feel like I'm moving in slow motion as I let her manhandle me, not trying to defend myself at all. I don't care, so I just let her and Hailey do whatever they want.

Maybe Harrison will feel sorry for me and want me afterward.

I squeeze my eyes shut at the pathetic thoughts rolling through my equally pathetic mind. Their laughter ebbs away slowly as I slip into my locked-down world of numbness. I open my eyes, and despite my efforts to block it all out, my stomach twists in anticipation of what will happen next. Harrison glances up at me, his eyes full of mockery and disgust.

"Act like a whore, Jessica, and you'll keep getting treated like one," he spouts.

How I thought he liked me, I don't know. Hailey and Elizabeth are dragging me along while everyone else hoots and hollers. I look back at Harrison with hatred in my eyes, in my heart.

"I hate you, Harrison!"

He laughs and grabs his crotch. "You sure weren't hating on this last weekend, baby," he mocks. Joe Fitzer, another guy from the football team, pats Harrison on the shoulder and laughs. "Hey, Jessica, I'm single. Maybe you can show me the same TLC you showed my homeboy Harrison." Joe winks at me as he takes a draw from his beer.

Hailey grips my arm tighter, hearing the guys' words. "Shut the hell up, you horny bastards! No one cares how you let this skank-ass tramp blow you or how you want to get into her STD-infested panties!"

Elizabeth spins me around, grabs my wrists in her left hand, then rears up and slaps me on the left side of my face again. The only fight I put up is the one to gulp down the sobs trying to escape my throat.

"How's that, whore? You like that?" Hailey hisses. "Think about that next time you want to fuck someone else's man!"

She spits in my face, and they shove me to the ground. I can feel the sand and rocks dig into the flesh of my bare knees. My neck cranes, and I grimace at the pain before my head is jerked back violently by Elizabeth yanking me by my hair.

"Apologize, you slut! Tell Hailey you're sorry for screwing around with her man!"

The thought of me owing her an apology is such a joke. What about him? He chose to be with me over her.

"Do it, bitch!" Elizabeth screams as she tightens her grip and pulls my hair harder. Hairs are ripping out of my scalp, but I don't answer. I won't give her what she wants. Not yet, at least. Then she reaches down and rips my earring from my left ear, throwing it to the ground in her rage. I let out a small cry at the pain as warm blood from my earlobe trickles down my neck. Things are no longer comical—not that I ever thought they were—and I know they're far from finished with me.

I glance up and see the lights of several phones all pointed in my direction. They're videoing all of this like I'm some freak show type of entertainment.

"Get your phone, Hailey. Take some pictures of this bitch getting what she deserves."

Closing my eyes, I try to keep myself under control before looking back up at them. The unspoken challenge in their eyes taunts me; it begs for me to antagonize them further. I shouldn't, but I do. I say words that mean nothing to me anyway.

"I'm sorry for making your man come more times in a few weekends than you ever will in his lifetime!" I shout smugly.

I know I shouldn't have, but I couldn't help it. My impulsivity won over. All I want to do is hurt her; humiliate her in front of everyone, even if it means putting my promiscuous ways on display.

I hold back the tears that want to come, realizing just how humiliating all of this is for me.

Hailey kicks me in the chest, forcing me backward onto the dirty ground. She holds her phone out, taking pictures of me as I try to gain my bearings. I hear my heart pulsate in my ears, and anxiety rushes through me. My instincts say to get up, but I don't. Any bravery I had is long gone, but, to tell the truth, I don't think it was ever really there.

For once, I wish I were invisible. I don't want this. I know that now. I thought if they could have their way with me that they'd somehow lose interest, but looking up at them I can plainly see that this is only adding fuel to their fire.

Elizabeth reaches down, digging her nails into my arm and screaming wildly at me as she struggles to pull me back up. "Get the hell up, you whore, and fight back! You're making this way too easy. Where's the fun in that?" She laughs, looking back at the small group crowded around us.

Grabbing another handful of my hair, she lifts her right hand up and backhands me again with all the force she can garner. I fall to the ground, bracing myself with my hands. My face is inches from the dirt and rocks, and before I can push myself back up her knee digs in between my shoulder blades, pinning me down. My face collides with hundreds of little jagged edges, and the metallic taste of blood fills my mouth.

Giving up, I don't struggle under her or try to get away. I completely detach from all the pain, all the degradation, and lie there in defeat. For the moment, the humiliation and shame I should feel is absent, but I know it will come. It always does. Searing blows to my ribs on both sides rock my body and I realize they're kicking me. After long minutes of pain my body goes still, and I hear the rocks crunching beneath their feet.

"Next time you think about fucking someone's man, remember tonight, whore! We'll happily kick your narrow ass again any day!" Elizabeth shouts as car doors slam shut. The sounds of wheels kicking up dirt and gravel as they rev their engines and speed out onto the dark blacktop road fill the air. The grit slides beneath my nails as I dig my fingers into the dirt. With shaky arms, I struggle to push myself up, but my body rejects my efforts. I cough and the pain that seizes me is too much to bear. Allowing my body to drop back down heavily, I close my eyes. The dim light from the moon disappears slowly, bleeding into blackness behind my eyes.

My eyelids begin to flutter open when I hear a soft male voice. I hear words, but my brain can't register their meaning. I can focus only on the pain shooting through my entire body and the taste of blood in my mouth. Gentle hands roll me over, warm arms envelop me, and soft fingers brush the hair from my face. I breathe in intense warmth and the smell of peppermint. My eyes can't focus, but even in this foggy state the immense pressure of his gaze upon me is undeniable. My body wants, but fails to respond to the embrace.

"Hey, open your eyes. Look at me, Jessica. I'm going to help you, okay? It's me, Jace," I hear him whisper as my mind starts to resurface from the depths of darkness. He pulls me up, supporting me when my knees buckle. "Come on, it's okay. I can carry you."

I feel his arms beneath my knees as he lifts me up into his strong hold. My head rests on his chest and I can't help but moan in pain from the pressure on my ribs. I force my eyes to open and look up at him staring down at me. The concern on his face is obvious. His eyes flick back and forth, and I can almost see the questioning thoughts moving behind them as he traces every inch of my face.

"You're badly hurt. We have to take you to the hospital now. Damn, what the hell happened?" He pleads.

My words are lodged in my throat, so I only nod. Despite the confusion of why he's here, or why he's helping me, I relax in his arms as he maneuvers us into his truck. He shifts me out of his arms to his right side, gently sitting me down before reaching across to his glove box. He pulls out a container of Handi Wipes and closes it. He has a Sigg water bottle in his cup holder and he reaches down to grab that as well. He holds it up to me, gesturing for me to take it.

"Here, drink some water. I have some Advil in my backpack," he says as he leans down and pulls it up from the floorboard. "I always keep it for after games and practices." He takes the bottle out from the side compartment and flips the cap off, dropping two capsules into his hand. "Here, take these. It will help the pain a little until you can see a doctor."

I reach out for them, my fingers slightly brushing the palm of his hand. When we touch, an odd energy flows between us—warmth and hesitation mixed with attraction; the intensity of it is nearly suffocating. My eyes dart up to meet his as my heart slams in my chest. Seconds feel like hours as unspoken words flow effortlessly between us. I forget my pain and hurt; everything else fades away but the two of us alone in his truck. I nervously break away from his stare, effectively ending our holy-shit-what-the-hell-is-that-feeling moment, and open my mouth, taking the medicine. I gulp down the water, washing away the taste of dirt and blood. Suddenly I startle, feeling coldness against my cheek, and turn toward him.

"It's okay. I won't hurt you, but we need to clean some of these scrapes up," he says softly as he gently cleans away the dried blood on my face. "I'm sorry, Jessica. I think I know who did this and I'm so damn sorry." He lets out an exasperated sigh, looking away momentarily and creasing his brows. "When I heard there was a get-together at the water tower, I had no idea they had some sick shit like this planned. I got held up at home and left late, so I didn't make it out here until they were all tearing off down the road."

He drops his head, shaking it slowly back and forth.

"If I'd been here, I would've stopped them. I almost turned around and followed them, but I saw your car and had a bad feeling, so I came to see if you were okay." He pauses in trepidation for a minute. "When I saw you on the ground, it scared the hell out of me." He takes another big breath, shakes away his thoughts, and continues. "We need to head to the ER now, make sure nothing's broken."

Why does he care? No one else cares, so why should he?

"Why do you care, Jace? Your girlfriend did this to me, so why are you concerned?" I choke out, speaking for the first time since he helped me up.

He winces at my words, dropping his hand from cleaning my face. He looks away, and his fists clench.

"I'm not them, Jessica. I don't treat people badly just because they're different or because they have a shitty reputation. I'll never be that way even if the people around me are." He looks back at me with sincerity in his eyes. "Elizabeth is a royal bitch most of the time, but her parents are best friends with my mother, and us being together has always been part of their grand plan. It just sort of happened that our families pushed us on each other. Once I go to college, I'll be free to make my own decisions about who I date."

He looks back into my eyes, piercing me completely. "I'd never be a part of something like this, no matter the reason. I don't know you, Jessica, or why you are the way you are. I don't know why you stay so closed off or why such a beautiful girl would repeatedly give herself to these asshole guys. Only you know those things; nevertheless, it doesn't mean that you're worthless or that you deserve this."

He reaches out, gently cupping my chin. "You're worth more than you think. You just have to believe that; then everyone else will too."

I shakily bring my hand up and softly place it over his. Closing my eyes, I feel a tear escape. In this moment, I realize how vulnerable I really am.

"Keep reaching out because you may help pull someone out of darkness and guide them into light."
—Caroline Naoroji

Jessica

I'VE CONVINCED HIM that I'll be fine. I don't want to go to the ER. The last thing I need is to deal with my parents getting involved. My dad would never understand and my mom would just fall apart and make it worse. I'm sore and it really hurts, but the pain is bearable.

"Are you going to be all right to drive?" he asks, still concerned.

I get into my car slowly, wincing in pain. My rib cage is throbbing and my head is pounding. He leans down, propping his elbows on my window, and I feel so pathetic. I'm still shocked beyond belief that he's here helping me, caring about me, and showing genuine concern for my well-being.

"Jessica, I still think you need to go to the ER. I really

don't feel comfortable letting you just drive home, but I can't force you to do anything you don't want to do. I just feel terrible."

I look up at him, and his stare infiltrates my well-built walls. Why do I feel like I can't hide from him? My darkest fears, secrets, and pains seem to all be vividly displayed for him. Right now, my feelings are equivalent to a burn victim, but my burns aren't physical. My emotional skin is raw, and every word, thought, or gesture that falls upon it sends waves of pain throughout my body. His kind, caring words and actions provide a healing, therapeutic effect; an antidote to the daily pain caused by people like Elizabeth.

"I'll be fine. Thank you for helping me. I know you didn't have to. I promise I won't tell anyone."

He looks me square in the eyes. His stare is heavy, and my breath hitches under the weight of it.

"I don't give a damn what people at school think about me, Jessica. High school isn't the be-all-end-all of my life. All I care about right now is that I helped you, did the right thing, and made sure you were okay. Everything else is irrelevant," he says, pushing back off of my car.

He puts his hands on his hips and looks at me. I need to say something, but what? Anything I say is inane and trivial compared to what he did for me here tonight.

"Thank you, Jace," is all I can muster before rolling up my window.

He lifts his hand, giving me a slight wave as I pull out onto the road. My mind is racing, and for some reason the pain seems to be a second thought to all of the others plowing through my mind. No one has ever helped me like that, cared about my feelings, or acted like I truly mattered. I look in my rearview mirror, seeing lights blinking on and off. It's Jace.

I wonder what he wants now.

I pull over and watch as he opens the door of his F150 and jumps out, walking toward me. I roll down the window and he hands me a receipt.

"Here's my cell number. You can call or text anytime if you need anything, or if something like this ever happens again and I'm not around. Okay?"

I look at the wrinkled receipt that has his number scrawled across it, and then back at him. He must see my obvious confusion and surprise because he steps in closer to my car.

"It's fine. You really can call me if you ever need anything." He gives me a genuine smile, then backs up and heads to his truck.

His loud truck roars as he passes by and I just sit here, stunned. Is the star quarterback of the school my friend now? Is that even possible? Why? Why would he want to be my friend and could I even do that?

I've never been just friends with a guy before. I don't even know how to connect with a guy without having a physical relationship with him. I pull into my driveway, hoping that Mom and Dad are in bed, though I doubt they'll even notice my scratched face or bloody knees if they are awake. They hardly ever look at me, and when they do they don't really see me.

The house is quiet and dark as I make my way to my room. I shut and lock my door before I peel off my dirty clothes. I drop them into my laundry basket and look in the mirror, examining the damage from the fight.

My cheek is slightly swollen, my lip is busted, my

earlobe is throbbing, and I have a few scratches on my face from the rocky ground. My knees are all scraped up, and my ribs are already starting to bruise. The bandage covering the cuts on my lower stomach has peeled nearly all the way off, and the wounds have dirt matted into them now. Thank goodness my room has an adjoining bathroom.

I go in and turn on the shower, knowing that the agony of washing my scraped and bruised body is going to be its own form of torture. I step out of my underwear, feeling the pain radiate through my sides as I stretch my arms back to unhook my bra.

I step into the water, turning it up as hot as I can tolerate it. It scalds my skin and I welcome the burn; the thin line between pain and pleasure always sits just beneath the surface for me. My instincts war with my desires and I fight to keep my body under the burning hot water plummeting down onto it. I feel the stinging pain skittering across my flesh and I lean forward, placing my hands on the shower wall as the torrid water washes away the dirt and blood.

The scars from years of cutting tingle and come alive, so well hidden from anyone, regardless of my attire. Being on the swim team has left me with very few places that can be concealed.

Too much pain that time will never erase bleeds through my mind, flooding my memories, reminding me that no matter how clean I am, the grime and disgust will always remain within.

Wrapping a towel around myself, I grab an old vintage Mötley Crüe T-shirt from my dresser, and pull it on over my wet hair. I finish getting dressed for bed and pull out the box from my nightstand.

The weight of the night sits heavily on my shoulders and I feel numb. Numb to the pain, numb to the humiliation. I want to feel something; to know that I'm here, that I'm alive. With this I'm in control; I can control the depth of the cut, the length, and the blood flow. It belongs to me and only me. Here, in the privacy of my room, I can break through the deadness that is my life. It brings me calm, resolve. I bury myself alive on the inside every day just so I can shut everything else out.

The scarlet liquid oozes from the cut as I drag the razor across my flesh. Despite the physical pain, I'm comforted by the familiarity of the act, the internal release. I squeeze my eyes shut tightly and exhale, ignoring the sting and bite of the blade, because at this very moment, the pain is what I revel in. I press down a bit harder, needing to feel more in order to feel anything at all.

I pull it away and wipe it down with alcohol, placing the razor back in its box. Drawing my eyebrows together, I wince as I rub the alcohol swab across the fresh cut and apply pressure. Grabbing a bandage, I place it over the cut, concealing a wound that will leave yet another scar.

I pull out my journal and begin my other form of release—writing.

Drowning in my thoughts

I wear a mask

I'm a facade
I'm okay, I'm strong
Masquerading lies
Beyond my defenses
Beyond the layers
Behind the walls
Beneath the chains
There's a broken child
Fighting a battle
It's a daily war
Confusion and pain
Playing tug-o-war
Love, hate
Yes, no
I really never know
Watching life go by
An outsider
Absence of self

Screaming in silence
Fearing this is a battle
One that I'll never win
Regrets
Loss
I continue waging war on myself
Wishing for
Someone, anyone
To stop the fight...

I close the journal and put it away. I reach for my phone, scrolling down to Harrison's contact. I press delete and store him away with the rest in the back of my mind; with all the others who used me, left me, and never looked back.

My phone buzzes with a text notification from a number I don't recognize. I open the message and it's just a link. I tap it and I'm taken to a video on YouTube. As soon as I click the play button, I know what it is. They recorded me being kicked, beaten. You can't see their faces, only mine. I sit here and relive it all over again. I scroll down to the comments and there it is—all of their hate. One comment after another trashing me, and there's nothing I can do about it. I exit out of it and sink back into a numb, comfortable place. A place where they can't hurt me. I should cry, throw something, scream, or break something, but I just sit here with two thoughts circling round and round.

They're never going to stop.

This is just my life.

I grab my iPod and put my earbuds in. I can never fall asleep in silence. My thoughts scream, flashing behind my eyelids, unless I have music playing in my ears. Music is a form of therapy that brings me comfort. I press play on my Amy Lee playlist and close my eyes. The lyrics of "Sweet Sacrifice" flow into my ears and I write a little bit more before drifting off to sleep.

Squeezing as hard as you can

You've ensnared me

Into your web I've fallen

Your words hurt me

Berate Me

Every day you imprison me

Within your walls of anger

I stand all alone

Confused and beaten down

Will it ever end or am I forever bound?

Peering into your cold evil eyes, I realize

You'll never stop

You'll never go away

Your words

Your hate

How will I ever escape?

Tell me, bully

What would you do if you were me and I were you?

It's Monday morning and I have the awful task of facing everyone at school today, knowing they all know about what happened this weekend. I walk down the hallway and I hear the whispers, see the stares. I reach my locker, thankful that there aren't any notes splayed across it.

Without turning around, I know someone's behind me. No, not someone. It's him. I can feel his presence, the strange vibration between us.

"Hey, Jessica. How are you feeling? Better than when I last saw you, I hope," he says quietly.

I can't believe he's standing here in the hallway in front of everyone talking to me.

Is he crazy?

Apparently he's out of his ever-loving mind. If Elizabeth sees him talking to me, she'll have a complete shit fit. I shut my locker and pull my notebook up into my chest. I do my best to avoid his eyes as I try to walk around him.

"You're going to make things worse if Elizabeth or Hailey or anyone, for that matter, sees you talking to me. Please, just go away. I'm thankful for what you did, but please don't let them see you with me," I say, low enough that only he can hear.

I walk quickly toward class, and though I don't look to confirm it, I can sense him keeping up beside me. God, he's insane. Does he want me to get the shit beat out of me again?

"What the hell are you doing, Jace?" I hiss as I meet his eyes. "Do you really want them to see?"

"I told you, I don't care what anyone thinks. I'm not Elizabeth's puppet like the rest of them."

I stop staring at him, confusion circling around in my mind. "What about the risk you're putting me at? If they see me talking to you, they'll go batshit crazy in two seconds flat," I say, frowning.

He lets out a chuckle, and my mouth drops open. "What? Are you really laughing at me right now?" I ask.

He crosses his muscular arms across his chest and smiles at me.

"Yes, yes I am, actually. What is *batshit crazy* exactly, Jessica? I'm curious to know," he teases.

He's making fun of me, laughing at me. I cock my head to the side and glare at him. My anger gives way to confusion and—I can't help it—a smile finds its way to my lips. I feel a blush tiptoe across my cheeks.

This is a nightmare!

I can't stand in the hallway of the school and flirt with Jace Collins, boyfriend to my archenemy. This is a death wish in the making.

"See, I made you smile! Don't you feel better now? You can't be mad at someone when they're making you smile. It's a fact!" His blue eyes glitter, and the white of his perfect teeth kills me. He's so handsome, beautiful, actually. Not in a feminine way, but in a totally masculine, virile way.

"I think that's the first time I've ever seen you smile. You should do it more often," he says as he swaggers off in front of me.

I can't wipe the smile off my face the entire rest of the walk down the hallway. Dropping my head, I try to conceal my happiness. I pray that no one saw our little conversation take place. I think he's right; this may be the first time I've ever had a reason to smile within the walls of this school. I make my way to first period English and sit in my regular seat toward the back of the room. I walk past Jace as he grins up at me and winks.

What the hell?

He's totally flirting with me. Or maybe it's just his way of being friendly. I can't decipher his intentions and it's driving me crazy.

Elizabeth and Hailey enter the room, drawing all eyes in their direction with their loud and obnoxious voices. I look down at my notebook, avoiding eye contact with them. I slump down into my chair and shrink away from them as much as I can.

"I see that you survived your ass kicking, Jessica. How are those ribs feeling this morning?" Hailey says, but I don't look up. Hoping Mrs. Alcott will come in soon, I just keep my eyes down.

"Leave her alone, Hailey! Do you really think being such a bitch is attractive?"

I lift my eyes just enough to see Jace defend me. Elizabeth's mouth drops open in shock and she scowls at Jace. My stomach lurches as he rips his eyes away from hers to meet mine. I can feel heat bloom across my face and I hope like hell no one can see the unspoken exchange between us. Just then, Mrs. Alcott comes in and clears her throat, drawing the attention away from us.

"Okay, everyone, please take your seats and get your homework from the weekend out," she says as she pushes her glasses up on the bridge of her nose.

Jace gives me a weak smile and turns around in his seat. I pull my homework out for our poetry assignment. We had to write a poem and bring in a quote from a famous person to share with the class. Thank God we only have to share the quote in front of the class. I don't think I could handle putting my poetry out there for everyone to scrutinize and judge. My palms are sweaty at the thought of having to speak in front of everyone as it is.

"Who wants to share their chosen quote first?" Mrs. Alcott asks. Of course, Elizabeth's hand shoots up. She always has to be the center of attention.

"I will, Mrs. Alcott," she says in her high-pitched, energetic, perky voice.

"Okay, Miss Brant. You may go first."

Elizabeth pulls her paper out and flips her hair over her shoulder as she stands up. She's wearing skintight jeans, a fancy lace top, large chandelier earrings, and too much makeup. Nothing new—she always dresses like a Barbie doll.

"The quote I chose is by A.J. McClean: 'I look good, and, not to sound conceited, I sound good too,'" she says with a little giggle toward the end.

God, how rich is that? Yeah, real deep, Elizabeth.

Several of her minions clap like she just cured world hunger or something with that shit-for-an-excuse quote. No matter how ignorant she makes herself out to be, they all salivate over her every word and action. It's pathetic.

"Okay, Miss Brant. Thank you for sharing...that insightful quote," Mrs. Alcott says, obviously not fooled.

"How about you, Miss Alexander? Can you go next and share your chosen quote with the class?"

I chew on my lower lip as I slowly rise from my chair. I take a deep breath, briefly close my eyes, then exhale. I unfold my paper, trying to keep my hands from shaking.

"Um...my quote is by Lao Tzu: 'Man's enemies are not demons, but human beings just like himself,'" I mutter before sitting back down.

Feeling everyone's eyes upon me, I want to be invisible at this very moment. I know people understand the implied meaning behind the quote.

"Miss Alexander, that was very moving. Thank you for sharing. Who wants to go next?"

Jace raises his hand. "I will, Mrs. Alcott."

"All right, Jace. Please, go ahead."

All six feet of him stands and turns slightly, half-facing my direction. My eyes dart back and forth between him and my desktop.

"My quote is by Albert Einstein: 'The world is a dangerous place, not because of those who do evil, but because of those who look on and do nothing.'" He slowly looks up, directly into my eyes, and then sits back down.

I feel utterly exposed staring at Jace, completely immobilized. As he turns back around, everything in the room feels fuzzy. Elizabeth's eyes pin me down, and I know her next explosion is coming soon.

"It's amazing and sad what we have to do to survive sometimes."
—Corey Taylor

Jessica

THE BELL RINGS and my impending doom settles heavily on my shoulders. I feel like Elizabeth can sense that Jace is befriending me, and I know she's going to be furious about it. Why is it that the first time a guy seems to genuinely give a shit about me and my suck-fest of a life, he has to be the guy that the most evil bitch in the school lays claim to? Just my luck, I guess.

I sit in my chair and wait for others to leave the room ahead of me, taking my time to put my books away just right, hoping she'll leave without trying to start some more shit with me. Sitting here, I really just want to claw my way out of this room and get away from her and the judgment that she always bestows upon me.

I watch as Elizabeth prances out of the room, clenching onto Jace's arm to prove her ownership of him—like he's some dog and she's his dutiful master. I'm completely relieved knowing that I don't have to face her right now. I leave the classroom feeling like I can breathe again. Word has seemed to travel quickly, because I see more and more people stare and laugh at me. Is getting beat up really that fascinating? If they only knew how my life really was... It would probably give them nightmares.

I make my way to my locker, continuously scanning the hallway for the Barbie squad of bitches. As I look farther down, I see Jace. He has his back to me, but I can see Elizabeth standing closely in front of him with a serious frown on her face. There's no way I'm going that way during some verbal smackdown between the two of them, especially when it may have something to do with me. I turn in the opposite direction and go into the girls bathroom, a place that I usually avoid at all costs unless it's an emergency. Being trapped in here with one of them is the last thing I want to add to my growing list of things I never want to be faced with.

I anxiously wait for the bell to ring, and realize I couldn't care less about being tardy as long as I don't have to get caught up in the argument Jace is having with her. I poke my head out of the bathroom and see that the hallway has cleared. I make my way to class and accept my tardy slip without guilt.

The day drags on and I continue to hide in plain sight. The stares and whispers have seemed to dissipate due to the new gossip floating around. Apparently, Erin Simpson was knocked up by one of the football players and it's the new big news. Thanks to her lack of condom usage, my story has become the lesser of the gossiping evils today.

PE and the locker room, lunchtime and the cafeteria—these are the worst times and places of my day. Unfortunately, they're back-to-back. I suppose I could try to see the upside to this scheduling nightmare and be glad that it's all over in one fell swoop, but nothing can make me happy about these times of day.

As I make my way to the gym, dread seeps from my pores. The girls locker room is a battleground. There are two main groups in here: the girls who are someone and the girls who are no one. My problem is that I don't belong to either group. I'm in between them, in the purgatory-type space between being on top and being on the bottom. This is the worst space to be in when the entire reason you're here is because you're hated. I have a target with a huge bull's-eye directly on my back, and the biggest group of somebodies in the school put it there.

We have to play volleyball today in gym and I do everything I can to be unnoticeable. Elizabeth and her crew prance out with their T-shirts tied in knots in the back, because they couldn't possibly wear a baggy gym shirt without showing off their perfect bodies. They whisper and snicker while cutting their eyes my way, but I ignore them the best I can throughout class.

Finally, it's shower time. I move quickly to my locker, gathering my shower stuff and towel. I choose the farthest shower and turn on the water. I hang my towel on the hook outside the shower curtain and step inside. Suddenly, I hear laughter and immediately recognize Hailey's voice.

"That slut deserves it. She likes to be naked anyway. Might as well force her to show the entire school what she shows all the guys every weekend."

More laughter and sneers flood the steamy, clouded

locker room air and I close my eyes, not wanting to know what they're up to this time. I pull the curtain back slightly and peek out. Immediately, I see the bare towel hook and realize that they've taken my towel. My heart races and my stomach drops. My locker is far from the showers. This means I have to walk naked, exposing all of my scars that no one knows about. It's the one thing that belongs to me and only me. My secret. My physical scars that represent my emotional wounds.

I look down at my wet, scarred body and back up under the water. It cascades down over me as tears escape my eyes. My tears blend with the water and my misery becomes camouflaged—sadness and desolation that never goes away. I back up against the tile wall and slide down to the floor, pulling my knees to my chest. I quietly sob, not wanting them to hear, and wait 'til I know everyone's left the locker room.

My skin has wrinkled from the water and I tremble as the cold air attacks my skin. I cover my scars with my hands the best I can and pad across the cold tile floor to my locker. As soon as I see my locker, I feel sick. It's wide open and my clothes are gone. A sign on the inside of my locker door reads *SLUTS DON'T NEED CLOTHES.* My eyes desperately search back and forth, looking for anything to cover my body with as panic sets in. I start pulling on locker doors, frantically trying to find one that will open so I can find something—anything—to hide myself with. Then the locker room door flies open and Elizabeth walks in, holding up her iPhone and snapping photo after photo of me.

"Pose, Jessica. Show us what you've got. Show the world what you give the boys on the weekends—that nasty

STD-infected snatch you hand out like Chiclets. Show everyone what the school slut has to offer."

Hailey pulls out her phone and begins to snap photos too. They both laugh as they grab my clothes and throw them at me.

"Here, bitch. Get dressed; you're making me sick. Nasty ho, walking around naked, like anyone wants to see your disgusting shit."

Their laughter echoes off the walls, reverberating around the room and through my heart, as they turn and walk out. I quickly scramble for my clothes, now wrinkled in piles on the floor. My hands are shaking and tears are running down my cheeks. I tremble on wobbly legs as I pull on my panties and pants. My T-shirt and bra are wet, but I don't care. I throw my wet hair up into a ponytail and put my shoes on.

I have to figure out what to do about the photos. In all these years, I've never told on them for anything, but I can't let them put those photos up on the Internet. I quickly make my way to the coach's office and gently knock on the door before entering.

"Excuse me, Coach Hines, can I talk to you?"

She raises her head from her work and examines me up and down. "Sure, Jessica, but first I just want you to know that Elizabeth and Hailey were in here after class and they told me about the issues they are having with you."

What? She has got to be kidding.

"I won't get involved in boyfriend girlfriend drama, but I will tell you that if you're sending inappropriate pictures of yourself to Hailey's boyfriend while at school, it will be grounds for expulsion."

Of course they came out here and told her some big lie to cover their asses. My eyes drop to the floor in shame as I nervously pick at my nails.

"Now, what is it you want to talk to me about?" she asks, as if she's irritated with me about what they told her.

"It's nothing, Coach. Never mind."

I knew there was a reason I've never told. It's pointless. No one cares, and no one sees the hate that passes through these hallways each day. They're blind to it all.

The dismissal bell is the sweetest sound I've heard all day. I can't wait to get to my car. I walk across the parking lot, but stop dead in my tracks when I see Jace leaning up against my Honda smiling at me. I look around nervously, scanning the parking lot to see if anyone else is seeing this. Maybe it's a mirage, which would mean I'm dying of thirst and he's my only drink of water. My feet feel like they're superglued to the asphalt beneath me as I stand here looking like a damn fool.

Jace pushes off my car and starts walking in my direction. What on God's green earth is he doing? Suddenly, a car pulls up beside him. It's that jackhole Harrison whom I now hate with a passion.

I pick my feet up, forcing them to move forward and hoping that Pencil Penis will distract Jace long enough for me to get to my car before he has a chance to approach me. Ignoring the fact that he's waiting for me seems like the best plan in this situation.

As I close in on my car, I rustle through my ginormous purse, which has more shit in it than an episode of

Hoarders, and look for my keys. If I'm ever in an alley or parking lot with a kidnapper lurking late at night, I'm completely screwed. It always takes me forfreakingever to find my keys!

"Hey, Jess!" I hear him call as his footsteps make their way toward me.

The fact that he just called me Jess makes me feel an odd sense of belonging. I try regaining my composure—as if I ever really had any to begin with—and turn around.

"I broke things off with Elizabeth, and I told her to leave you alone from here on out."

My eyes widen and I grapple with a mixture of happiness and excruciating fear. For the millionth time, I wonder why he's doing this for me. I really can't comprehend it; it makes no sense at all. He could be friends with any girl in the entire school, so why me? Why the weird, quiet loner girl that everyone loves to gossip about? He's popular, good-looking, and his family is loaded. Being friends with me is like some sick cliché.

We stand here with a ton of unspoken questions streaming between us. Whether or not he understands my questions, I can't be sure. I know for a fact his answers aren't coming across, though I think we both have an implicit want, maybe even need, for the other to get it, to hear the words we're too afraid to speak. I don't know what to say, so I say nothing. The sides of his lips curl up and he sticks his hand into his pocket, pulls out a toothpick, and flicks it into his mouth. He starts rolling it back and forth across his lips, chewing on it.

My God.

"I'm trying to stop smoking and this helps."

"Okay," I say flatly.

I really have no idea what to say or how to carry on a conversation with him. He's so foreign to me that saying anything just seems all sorts of stupid and wrong. I feel like an idiot standing here staring at him like a deer in headlights, so I turn to unlock my car door. The urge to run and escape this awkward moment tugs at me. I'm accustomed to understanding what a guy wants from me. I usually always know what they expect from the get-go, but with Jace it's like navigating in the dark without a flashlight.

"Hey, um, you maybe wanna come hang out at my house? We have a huge pool, so maybe we can do some laps or something? Get an early start on the swim season? If you're game, that is."

My hand starts to shake as I try to get the key into the door. His question catapults me into some freakish parallel universe where popular hot guys ask extremely unpopular outcast girls to hang out. I know I should stop obsessing over his intentions, but I can't help it. Of course I want to hang out with him, but I know how I am. I attach myself to every guy who comes along. I turn into a chameleon of epic proportions and lose myself in each and every one of them. I try to be who I think they want me to be, clinging to the hope that they'll love me in return. Ultimately, it always ends in disaster.

For some reason, the thought of hating Jace or him hating me breaks my heart a little. I have a lot of regrets, but things ending badly with Jace might be a regret that I'd never recover from. It scares the hell out of me. My lungs expand as I take in a deep breath before answering his invitation.

"Sure, Jace," I reply simply.

His expression goes from hopeful to happy as soon as he hears my answer. "All right, then. You can meet me there in about half an hour. Go grab your suit and head over. If you text me, I can text back with the address."

An address is not necessary—everyone knows that he lives in a gargantuan mansion of a house just outside of town.

"I know where you live. I think everyone knows where you live, Jace," I say with a hint of sarcasm in my voice.

He rolls his eyes and keeps spinning that damn toothpick back and forth across his lips. It's incredibly sexy, and I wish he would stop it.

"Jess? Are you with me, or are you going to keep standing there admiring the view?" he says with a flirty laugh.

I start to respond, but my voice seems to have left me. My attraction to him is causing me to act like an absolute idiot. God, I'm in trouble here.

One of his eyebrows arches and draws my eyes to the blue in his. Then he drops his head a little, so he's looking right at me. "Do you wanna stand here all day or do you wanna come over and get your butt smoked in a race?"

I straighten my shoulders and raise both brows at him. Is he seriously challenging me? I may be quiet, and I may be a loner, but I am a damn good swimmer. I can hold my own against most, even guys.

"Are you challenging me, Jace Collins?" I ask.

"Yep! That's exactly what I'm doing. Why? You scared?" he asks with a little chuckle.

I want to be excited about his interest in me, about going to his house and hanging with him, but knowing those pictures are probably going to fall into his hands very soon, I can't help but feel a little apprehensive. Not to mention I'm mortified that those bitches took things this far, yet again. I don't want him to see my weak or broken side again, though. He has seen plenty of that Jessica.

"Nope, not scared. Just worried about your ego is all," I retort.

"My ego?" he says, obviously intrigued by my comment.

"Yep, because after I beat you it will be all sorts of bruised. I hope you can recover from that, being the star athlete that you are and all. I'd hate to mess with your mojo!" I say, taunting him. My mouth turns up into a slight smile and I realize that for the span of our conversation I have actually felt kind of normal for once. Two minutes of feeling like any other girl just because of some playful banter.

Interesting.

"There's a little smart-ass inside that shy personality you fool everyone else with, huh? You don't fool me, Ms. Alexander, but I'll gladly let you try to bruise my ego—even though it ain't gonna happen. See you in thirty."

He pulls that damn toothpick out from between his teeth and walks away, glancing at me over his left shoulder one last time before climbing into his truck. I exhale, realizing I barely took a breath the entire time he was standing here. My skin feels flushed and my heart is racing. I pull open my car door and practically tear out of the school parking lot toward my house. I pull into the driveway, get out of the car, and plow through the front door to my room.

"Heeeey, sweetie. How was school today?" Mom

asks, slurring her words and letting me know that Martha is long gone today.

"Good, Mom. Just great," I say before shutting my door behind me and locking it.

I strip out of my school clothes and yank open my dresser drawer, searching for my swimsuit. I see the red material stuffed in the bottom of the drawer and pull it out. It's a Nike Fast Back suit and I love it. I grab my swim team bag, which has my Speedo goggles and swim cap, and head out the door. I'm going fully prepared, determined to kick his ass.

I pull up the long driveway at Jace's house and instantly feel the nerves ripple through my body. His mom is used to him being with someone like Elizabeth. She's everything that I'm not. Elizabeth is like a bright and shiny expensive toy while I'm plain with no bells and whistles. My family doesn't have loads of money or a membership to the local country club. I'm not the type of girl she'd want around her son.

The double garage door starts to open, revealing a very hot Jace. He's in regular swim trunks and a white tank top, grinning that mischievous smile that's steadily growing on me. I'm wearing my suit under a vintage Beatles T-shirt and black board shorts with black flip-flops on my feet and my hair pulled back in a high ponytail.

"You ready to get blown out of the water, Jess?" he smirks.

Every time he calls me Jess I light up inside. He could say nothing else from here on out and I'd be happy with just that. I give him a timid smile and sling the strap of my bag over my shoulder.

"I'm ready, Mr. Collins. Let's see what you've got!"

I follow him along a stone walkway that winds around the side of his giant two-story brick house, and we approach a wrought iron fence and gate. He reaches over and unlocks the latch, and as we step around to the backyard area I nearly gasp.

It's absolutely freaking beautiful!

The pool is huge, just like he said, with a Jacuzzi area and an amazing waterfall that cascades water down into the pool. The deck area is adorned with beautiful plants, flowers, and fancy outdoor furniture. There's a fire pit and a big seating area adjacent to the largest stainless steel grill I've ever seen.

I scan the area further and see a breathtaking pergola with ivy vines intertwining through it, perched above even more outdoor furnishings. It's like a little hidden piece of paradise back here. If I lived here, I'd never need to go on an actual vacation. He has a vacation spot in his own backyard!

"Damn!" I say, realizing too late that my inner thoughts just came out of my mouth.

He smiles knowingly. I mean, c'mon, even he has to know that this place is badass as all get-out.

"I take it that you like the pool," he says.

"Ummm, yeah, I love it. Shit, Jace, why do you ever leave your house? If I lived here I'd never leave!"

He shakes his head as he reaches down and curls his fingers under the edge of his tank top, pulling it up over his toned abs and chest, and then, finally, over his head.

God, this guy is fine!

I avert my eyes so the fact that I'm practically panting over him isn't so obvious. He tosses the tank top onto a poolside chair and stretches, raising his arms up over his head.

"It's nice out here, I agree, but things aren't everything you know. Sometimes too much gets to be, well, too much."

I have no idea what he means by that, but I get the feeling there's a hidden meaning there somewhere. I don't dare ask, but I'm beginning to think that there's much more to Jace Collins than meets the eye. A splash snaps me out of my deep thoughts as he dives into the water. I set my bag down on one of the chairs and pause for a second, suddenly feeling anxious about undressing in front of him.

Everything feels different when I'm around Jace: exciting but unpredictable, hopeful but uncertain. I can't explain or figure out why it should be any different with him. He's just a guy. Guys are, for the most part, all the same. So what makes this one stand out?

Who are you, Jace Collins?

I don't know, but I think I want to find out.

I carefully pull my T-shirt off and bend over, pulling my shorts down. Goosebumps scatter across my skin, and my heart is pounding in my chest. The very fresh memory of my clothes being stolen earlier today is almost impossible to push back. Adrenaline starts to course through my veins at the memory, but I force myself to stop thinking about it as I reach in my bag for my goggles and cap. I'm pulling them out when Jace starts talking to me from across the pool.

"You brought your goggles and cap?" he asks, sounding sincerely surprised.

I hold my index finger up, my goggles dangling from it, my cap in the other hand.

"Of course I did. Why? Don't you compete using goggles and a cap?"

He leans back against the pool, propping his elbows up on the side and pressing his lips into a hard line. Did he think I wouldn't come prepared, ready to take him down? He certainly underestimated me, which is not surprising.

"Well, I guess I didn't think you'd come all guns a' blazing. You must really be worried about me beating you, huh?" He laughs as he pushes off the side of the pool, going under the water and swimming toward me.

His head emerges from the water just below where I'm standing. He looks up at me, squinting from the sun that shines bright upon his face.

"Well, get your ass in here so we can do this thing. I can beat you, cap or no cap, goggles or no goggles. I'm sure you need all the help you can get, so you use whatever gear you think is necessary, Ms. Alexander."

I open my mouth and start to respond, but he reaches up and grabs my left leg just behind the knee, pulling on me. I try to pull back out of his grasp, but he tugs harder.

"Hey! Let go of me!" I screech.

"Nope, you're stalling," he says, yanking one last time.

I crash into the water and my skin prickles under the abrupt coldness. Holding my breath, I swim down deeper in the opposite direction of him. I open my eyes under the water and glance back to see that he's right on my tail. Anxious energy jolts through me and I go faster until I reach the far side of the pool, pushing up above the water and sucking as much air into my lungs as I can. I feel the ripples of the water increase as he swims up beside me.

"Almost! I almost caught you, but you had a head start," he shouts playfully as he slaps his wet hand against the side of the pool. "I didn't know you'd bolt on me, so don't be thinking that was any indication of whether or not I can beat you."

He runs his hands through his wet hair and shakes it in a shaggy-dog style. He's adorable. Adorable, sexy, masculine, and sweet.

All rolled into one.

His closeness makes me feel uneasy but needy at the same time. My breathing starts to even out and I quickly wipe the dripping water from my face, because the chlorine is making my remaining scratches burn something terrible. With my movement, a shooting pain races across my ribs and I wince a little at the intensity of it.

"Do they still hurt?" he says. His smile fades some and his blue eyes darken, overshadowed by his creased brow. He seems remorseful about what happened to me, but if it wasn't for him there's no telling how long I'd have laid out there in the dirt and gravel. I smile at him, securing my invisible mask tightly into place.

"They're fine. I'm not hurting that much anymore. I'm fine, really. No worries," I say nonchalantly, shrugging my shoulders and making light of it as much as possible.

He reaches up and ever so softly traces my cheekbone. My breath hitches and I nervously look away from his stare. I nearly whimper at the absence of his finger as he removes it, but then he gently places it under my chin, tilting my face back up so that we're practically eye-to-eye.

An overpowering energy circles around us. He moves in closer and his arm goes around to the small of my back, pulling me into the warmth of his body. My mind's reeling as my eyes flit back and forth between his eyes and his lips. His breathing becomes more rapid, and my chest starts to rise and fall in unison with his.

Is he going to kiss me?

Do I want him to kiss me?

The answer comes instantly.

Yes, I want him to kiss me!

My lips part as we stare at each other for what seems like an eternity. I close my eyes and lean in, wanting to let him capture my lips with his. Suddenly, his arms stiffen and he abruptly pushes me back, putting space between us.

My eyes snap open in surprise. He's looking down with a grimace on his face. He looks pissed off. What did I do? I thought he wanted to kiss me. He pulled me into him, so I followed his lead. What... I'm embarrassed and completely humiliated.

Run.

Run away from the situation; that's what I do. Something goes wrong and I run away. I push my hands down hard onto the side of the pool, attempting to hoist myself up out of the water, but I feel his hands grip my hips, stopping me. I drop back down into the water and stay perfectly still, even though everything inside of me is going crazy right now. I don't turn around. I can't. I have to avoid any and all eye contact; avoid whatever the hell just happened between us. He leans forward and I feel his breath on my neck.

"I'm sorry," he whispers.

Nothing more, nothing less. Just "I'm sorry." We stay there for a minute longer, my back to his front. He leans his head forward and rests his forehead against my wet hair.

"I'm sorry, Jess. I shouldn't have done that. I don't want you to think that I'm just trying to get laid, because I'm not. I'm not Harrison or any of those other worthless, piece-of-shit guys. I want to be your friend, so I shouldn't have almost crossed that line. I'm really sorry."

The heat from his breath continues to assault the delicate skin on my neck with every word he speaks.

"It's just that you're beautiful in a simple, natural kind of way. It's such a turn-on, and you're nothing like what most people think you are. You're strong, independent, and worth so much more than you seem to give yourself credit for." He releases a sigh and continues, "It's hard not to be attracted to the real you."

I turn around slowly and look up at him, forcing back the tears that want to spill from my soul. No one has ever said anything like that to me before. My heart swells and my insides melt. He looks deep inside of me, penetrating the walls I've spent seventeen years building up. Brick by brick, layer by layer, he's breaking through them.

"I. See. You. Jessica Alexander." He cups my cheeks and repeats himself, "I see you. You need to see you too. If you look deep enough, you'll see a strong, beautiful girl who has the world at her fingertips. Don't let this life pass you by because of people like Elizabeth and Hailey. Do you understand me?"

He reaches down and takes my hand. I follow behind him as he leads us out of the pool. He walks over to his chair and grabs a towel, handing it to me.

“Here, dry off. Change of plans,” he says.

What is going on? What is the new plan?

He must see the questions in my eyes, but before I can voice them he says, “I’m taking you somewhere. I want to show you something.”

I nod without a verbal response, because he’s all broody and serious right now, so I’m not quite sure what to say. I’ve never seen this side of him. He pulls his tank top back on and slips on his sandals. He grabs the second towel and dries his hair quickly. Hurriedly, I pull my clothes on over my wet suit, then ring my hair out the best I can. I slip on my flip-flops and grab my bag.

Without a word, he starts for the exit and unlatches the gate. Nervousness crawls down my spine; something feels off, wrong. I don’t know how to explain it, but I have a feeling that wherever he’s taking me, it’s not a happy place. He walks around and opens the passenger door of his truck for me. The warm leather of his seat feels good on my skin as I buckle my seatbelt. He shuts the door before jogging around, hopping in, and starting the engine. His truck is as loud as it is big. I feel like I’m ten feet up in the air in this thing. He puts it in reverse and maneuvers around my little car with ease. When we get out to the road, he heads toward town.

Just before we reach the edge of town, he turns down a side road. As we drive a little farther, I instantly know where we are. My stomach twists and I grasp onto my bag as if it’s a security blanket or something. He turns off the road and pulls in through the entrance, right under a grand archway that reads *City Cemetery* in large scrolled letters.

Why is he bringing me to the cemetery?

This can’t be good.

"Different but not less."
—Temple Grandin

Jessica

"LISTEN, JESS. I know you're probably confused right now, and wondering why in the hell I brought you here. I just need you to...understand," he says, dropping his head to his steering wheel.

Understand what?

He's all over the place. It's actually freaking me out a little, and that's hard to do. This is beyond awkward, beyond tense. The air in the cab of his truck is thick, and my level of nervousness has reached a high point. I need to say something, but what? Why, for the first time ever, do I feel like the strong one while he's the weak and vulnerable one? This is not a feeling I'm familiar with, so I have no idea how to comfort him or how to react.

He saves me from my internal struggle when he opens his door. He gets out, shutting it behind him, and makes his way around to my side. The door opens and he reaches out, offering me his hand to help me out of his monster truck. After I jump down, he closes my door and tightens his grip on my hand as I follow along beside him.

"I've never brought anyone here before. No one knows other than my family. She was always a shameful secret that my parents saw as something that would stain their perfect, upstanding country club lifestyle."

Who? Who's he talking about?

I am so utterly confused right now, but I don't ask questions; I think he just needs someone to listen. So I do. I just listen. He takes in a deep breath as we approach a beautiful headstone that has two cherubs perched atop it on both sides.

GENEVIEVE BELL COLLINS

BELOVED DAUGHTER AND SISTER
MAY SHE ALWAYS
WALK WITH THE ANGELS.

My heart drops into my lower stomach and my jaws clench. He squeezes my hand tighter and I feel a cloud of sadness hanging over us. Releasing my hand, he kneels down in front of the gravesite.

"My sister. She was autistic, and her life was cut short because of people like Elizabeth, because she was different," he says through gritted teeth.

I look down and see the muscles in his neck tense. He reaches up and runs a hand through his hair. I sense his pain and the loss he's feeling, the loss he probably always feels. My eyes glance at the headstone next to his sister's and I see that it belongs to his father. I know his dad passed away years ago from cancer but being here like this just makes it that much more profound. I may not have the best family, but at least they're all still alive. My heart breaks a little as I kneel down next to him and wait for him to finish telling me the story.

"She's been gone for two years. Until recently, I'd done everything in my power to try and forget that horrible fucking day."

He puts both hands on top of his head and grips his hair, dropping his head onto his forearms. I reach over and place my hand on his back, silently comforting him.

"After she was born, Mom had really bad postpartum depression, so she hired a fancy high-paid nanny to take care of her. As she got older, her differences started to make themselves known. By two and a half, her pediatrician told my parents that she was most likely autistic. As she got closer to school age, but was still behaving like a toddler and barely talking, my mom insisted that she be put into a special needs school. She practically hid her away from everyone and allowed the nanny to do most of her caretaking. Mom seemed to be at a loss, and her coldness towards Genevieve was sad. I never really understood it since Mom had always been so focused on me growing up."

He sighs and reaches out, running his fingers across the engraved words on the headstone before continuing.

"She rode a special needs bus to and from her school every day. Like I said, it was as if Mom wanted to hide her from everyone here. Even though Genevieve didn't really express herself verbally, and she didn't like physical affection, she'd always let me hug her. Everyone else thought she wasn't connecting socially, but she connected with me. She'd always reach out, touch my face, and smile. She was so adorable and innocent. I always felt like she was lonely, even though the doctors said she probably would prefer being alone and would need time to herself often. I would go into her room and play with her daily. She loved to line random objects up across her floor, so I'd help her. It seems dumb, but it was our special time together."

A single tear streams down his cheek and my heart cracks for him again.

"One day as she got off the bus, some middle school kids were walking by and yelling stuff at her. Mean, nasty things. It made me so angry; I ran to the end of the driveway, screaming at them to shut the hell up and leave her alone. I was the one who always met her and walked her to the house when she got off her bus, so I had to see those punks every day."

I feel him tense up as he stands quickly, wiping a tear from his face. "One day I was late," he says, breaking down. Painful sobs erupt from his throat, and his body quivers as he covers his face with his hands. He shakes his head back and forth as if he's trying to will away the memory of what happened.

"I was too damn late, Jess. Those fucking kids started throwing rocks at her and she got spooked. She started running. When I ran down the driveway, all I saw was Genevieve running and a trail of kids behind her, taunting her. The damn bus had driven off, even though protocol was for them to wait 'til someone got her. She was probably so scared. She darted out into the street unexpectedly and was hit by a work truck that was speeding by. She was killed instantly—right there in front of my eyes."

His body shakes as he cries the most heartbreaking sound I've ever heard. It's as if he's crying for his loss for the first time. I reach over and put my arms around him, holding him. He drops his head to my shoulder and I feel the wetness of his tears soak into my T-shirt. In this moment, he's like a scared little boy, not the big, strong quarterback. And I feel like the tough girl holding him up, not the weak girl who lets everyone put her down. He sniffles as he pulls his head up and wipes his eyes. He straightens his shoulders and suddenly becomes strong Jace again.

"I'm sorry. You must think I'm some sort of big crybaby or something," he says, raking his hand over his face again.

"No, I don't. If you had told me that story without shedding a tear, I'd think something was wrong with you," I say as my own tears slide down my cheeks.

"After she died, for the first time since she gave birth to Genevieve, my mom acted like a mother. Her death rocked my mom and dad to the core. Guilt and regret plagued them. My mom has never been the same. She spent weeks in her bedroom not eating or showering. Our house was like a tomb for a long time. My mom finally went into therapy for her grief and depression, and the therapist convinced her that the entire family needed to get therapy as well. We started attending family sessions and I learned to stop hating my mom for being the kind of mother she was to Genevieve. Until then, I never really saw how broken-hearted and tortured she was by her guilt."

The sadness on his face is painful to look at. It's heartbreaking.

"Ever since, I've tried so hard to be the perfect son for her, especially after Dad died. I just want her to be happy, you know? It was my fault, after all, that Genevieve died. If I'd been there on time, it would've never happened. I don't want her to see me as the person responsible for my sister's death. I want her to see me as the son they're proud of."

He presses a kiss to the tips of two fingers before reaching down and placing them on top of the headstone. "I miss her every day," he whispers. My heart cracks right in half for him.

"So you see, I can't stand by and let someone bully you, cut you down, just because they have some twisted superiority complex. Just because someone is different doesn't mean they aren't worthy of others' respect. She was different, socially awkward, and odd, but she was a person. A sweet girl who didn't deserve for others to look down on her, tease her, or make fun of her and neither do you. Just think, if only one of those kids would've stepped up and said something, made a stand against their friends, this could've been avoided. But they did nothing. They just stood by and let it happen, which makes them all equally guilty. I won't be that person. I can't be." He shakes his head back and forth in disgust.

All of the pieces of the puzzle that are Jace Collins begin to fall into place for me. I've been so conflicted by his kindness. I'm not sure why he just now noticed how horrible those girls always are to me, but I understand why he feels so strongly about it. Seeing me physically hurt probably brought it all to the surface for him.

I want to ask him a million questions, but I don't because I know how badly I'd hate for someone to pick me apart if I was in his shoes. Why people do the things they do, or act the way they act, almost never lies on the surface. It's always hidden behind fears, anxiety, or a lack of understanding.

I know for me it's unknown. I have no idea why I feel the way I do, or why I think the way I think. It's the biggest part of the problem for me. Sometimes I feel that if I had a real reason, I could find a solution.

Jace had a traumatic event occur in his life that has matured him faster than most people our age. He had to deal with a tragedy that most could never imagine. It makes my problems feel so very small, insignificant. Okay, so my Mom drinks, and my Dad acts as if I don't exist, but I've never had to face what Jace has had to face.

It makes me all the more at odds with my emotions and daily bouts of depression and anxiety. My mood swings of highs and lows, the desperation for acceptance and love; the feelings are so extreme, so strong within my mind that I literally feel like I am on auto-pilot at least half the time, without any control over my emotions at all. The rest of the time, I am completely shut down and numb.

That's why I cut. I control that pain, own it. I can start it or stop it on my own terms. The thoughts that reel through my mind daily like a bad show rerun never stop; they replay day after day. It's a constant struggle, one that I really have no explanation for. That's what frustrates me the most—I seriously doubt that having absentee parents could cause such deep-seated pain in a person. Who knows? I'm not a psychiatrist or anything. Maybe I need one of those, although the thought of divulging the deepest, darkest parts of me to anyone scares the hell out of me.

"I'm so sorry that happened to your sister, to your family, but you can't blame yourself."

I try to stay calm and fight back my tears over his

loss.

"It wasn't you that chased her. You didn't do this, those bullying kids did." I try to relieve some of his guilt, though I'm pretty sure that's easier said than done. Even so, I have to say something and this is what I feel strongest about. He needs to know he didn't do anything wrong. I know my words probably give him little comfort, but I want him to know I'm here for him.

"I know. I spent hours in therapy learning how to say 'It's not my fault.' It's just really hard not to feel that way because I know if I had gotten there on time, she'd still be here today."

"You can't know that. You can't take this on as your responsibility. You were a kid too. It was a terrible tragedy, but it wasn't your fault," I say urgently, wanting him to understand.

He lets out a huge sigh and runs his hands through his hair again. He does that a lot, I notice, and I wonder if it's just an anxious habit of his.

"Let's get out of here. I just wanted you to see, to know this part of me because I never want you to think I'm like them. I know I almost kissed you, but I swear I'm not trying to use you or be a part of some fucking scheme to set you up like Harrison did."

He looks at me with sad eyes.

"I knew something was off when they changed the plans for the night. I'm sure they didn't want me to be there because they knew I'd never stand by and let it happen. Yet again I was too late to save someone from getting hurt."

Regret spreads across his face and he looks so pained.

"The weight of what they did to you was too heavy. I

told Elizabeth it was over and that if she retaliated at all, I'd go to her parents and tell them what she did to you. I meant it too."

I have no idea what to say. He looks at me in earnest and says, "You need to let me know if she does or says anything at all to you. I'm disgusted with myself for giving her the last year of my life. I knew she was a catty bitch, but that night showed me it was on another level. She's different away from school, and I always gave her the benefit of the doubt, because there are things she has had to deal with in her life that fuel her mean streak. But regardless, what she did was inexcusable. I can't look past that bullshit."

Wow.

He answered all my questions with that statement.

I'm happy and sad all at the same time because now he's feeling guilty for what happened to me, when in reality it was my fault. I'm the one who let Harrison use me. I chose to get out of my car that night, to let them have their way with me like some sacrificial lamb. I was stupid. An idiot, really. It's not his fault, no matter when he showed up. The fact that he cared enough to help when he got there is all that matters to me in the end.

"Okay. Thank you for bringing me here, for sharing that painful part of your past with me. I promise I'll hold all of your secrets safely inside," I say.

We walk side by side to his truck and he opens the passenger door for me again, ever the gentleman. After he gets in and backs out of the cemetery, we drive back toward his house. We sit in an uncomfortable silence all the way there. As we pull up the drive, he finally speaks up.

"Thank you for listening. It means a lot, and I hope I

didn't scare you or anything. I don't know why, but I trust you, Jess. I know my secrets are safe with you. If you ever want to talk, know that your secrets can be safe with me too."

A warm smile spreads across his face and I can see life come back into his eyes. Emotions are swirling inside me and I just want to hug him, squeeze tight, and never let him go. But I refrain and just return his smile, nodding.

"Well, I guess you got saved from a good ass-kicking after all, but it's only a temporary pardon, my friend. Tomorrow after school, meet me here and we'll see who reigns supreme in the pool," he teases.

Yeah, the cocky, confident Jace is back. I really like this Jace, but the other one is nice too. I look over, tilting my head to the side, and give him my best sarcastic expression.

"Okay, Mr. Big Shot Athlete. You keep telling yourself that story, but the ending still needs to be written. I'll do that for you tomorrow—with pleasure," I reply confidently.

He chuckles as he slides out of his seat, dropping to the ground. Being the gentleman he always seems to be, he comes around and opens my door for me. He helps me out and we have yet another awkward moment. If I'm going to keep seeing him, I hope these moments stop being weird soon.

He rocks back and forth on the balls of his feet, looking down, and then back up at me. "Um, thanks again. And about what happened in the pool? I promise it will never happen again, Jess. I really am sorry. Friends, okay?" he says with conviction and sincerity.

Why do those words feel more like a sentence rather

than a caring promise? I'm glad he wants to be my friend, but I'm not sure how to do that, or if that's all I want.

"Okay, Jace, but I have to tell you that I've never just been a guy's friend before. I'm not sure how good of a friend I can be to you," I say shyly.

He grins slightly; then he puts his arm around me, resting it on my shoulders casually in a totally non-intimate way.

"Jess, I've never had a girl as just a friend either. We can figure it out as we go. How does that sound?" he asks as we walk toward my car.

His phone buzzes and he pulls it out of his pocket. As he focuses on the screen, his walking slows down to a stop. The light expression he wore moments ago grows worrisome.

"What is it?" I ask. He looks up at me and the worry has morphed into fury. "What? Tell me."

He drops his head and turns his back to me, placing his hands on his hips. He looks up briefly, shaking his head back and forth, takes a deep breath, and turns back around to face me.

"Something terrible has been put online about you. I can guarantee I know exactly who did it, and I promise you I'll handle this today. Just don't even look at these pictures, Jess. Stay offline until I get those bitches to take them down."

I know what pictures he's talking about and I cringe with shame as heat creeps up from my chest to my neck to my face. This is so embarrassing. I just want to fold up inside of myself right now and disappear.

"Okay? Do you hear me?" he insists.

I just nod. My chin begins to quiver and he instantly

comes over and puts his arms around me. "I'm sorry they're still doing this shit to you. I promise I'll take care of this today once and for all."

I hug him back and try to keep it together. He just holds me for a while, letting me feel what I need to without judgment. In his arms, I feel a sense of security that I've never felt in my life. If he wants to just be my friend, then that's what I'll give him. I doubt there's anything that I'll deny Jace Collins. Now or ever.

"What is a friend?
A single soul dwelling in two bodies."
—Aristotle

Jessica

I'VE JUST GOTTEN home from school and Mom and Dad are fighting because of her drinking. I can't take another minute of their bickering, so instead of walking through the shit storm that's going on in the kitchen, I pull my window up and pop the screen off. I swing one leg then the other over and hop out. My feet hit the green grass and I turn, pulling the window back down. My rusty old swing set sits off to the side of the backyard; the swings sway lazily in the breeze. It's hard to imagine that years ago my sober mother laughed and played with me there. When my grandma passed away she took it hard. Something inside of her broke, and she never quite recovered from the loss. Alcohol was her escape. Now it's her prison.

I walk over to the swings and sit on one. I push off

the ground slightly and start to swing. Thoughts of Jace and all of the things that have happened over the past two months since we became friends make me smile. He kept his promise. The photos were taken down that night and never mentioned again, though the stares at school became increasingly worse. School's still not a fun place for me because even though Elizabeth and Hailey stopped taunting me, I still get their death glares. People still look at me like I'm a walking disease, but for the most part no one says anything directly to me anymore. I still get a few notes taped to my locker from time to time, but I just rip them off and throw them away. I can handle the notes and the stares. I can pretty much handle anything with Jace in my life."Hi," a small voice says, startling me. I look over in the direction of my neighbor's backyard and there's a little girl standing there. She's waving at me, so I wave back. A new family just moved in recently but I don't pay much attention to them. Kids are always running around outside. The blond-haired little girl walks in my direction.

"Hello," she says, stopping in front of me.

"Hi." I look down and notice she's wearing purple rain boots and a matching purple jacket. I wonder why she's dressed like that on a sunny day like today.

"Hi. What's your name?" I ask.

"I'm Vivvie."

"Oh, that's a cute name. I'm Jessica. Do your parents know you're outside alone? How old are you?"

"I'm a big girl."

I raise my eyebrows and smile at her. She has little freckles sprinkled across her cheeks and she's absolutely adorable.

"Oh, a big girl, huh? Well I guess big girls get to play

outside alone, then."

"Yes, they do. Why do you use windows instead of doors?" she asks.

"Because I'm a big girl too and sometimes I don't like doors." She sits on the swing next to me and makes herself right at home.

"Do you have a boyfriend?"

This is one very forward and nosey little girl.

"Um, no. I have a friend, but no boyfriend."

"Is your friend a boy?"

"Yes. Why?"

"I don't have a boyfriend. Lots of girls at school have one, but I don't."

She looks a little sad and I feel bad for thinking she was nosey.

"Boyfriends are yucky, Vivvie. You don't need one. You have lots of time for boys. Trust me, they are lots more trouble than they're worth most times."

"What about your friend that's a boy? Is he trouble?"

I smile and shake my head.

"No, he's perfect. No trouble at all."

"You look happier."

Huh? What does she mean?

"Um, Vivvie, how do you know if I look happier?" I ask gently.

"I've seen you before. You always look really sad. Sometimes you even look really mad, but never happy."

"Oh." I don't know what else to say to that. It kind of makes me feel like shit. It's terrible that it's so obvious, even to a little kid.

"Well, I'm okay now. There were mean girls at my school and they made me sad lots of times. They're still mean, but they aren't mean to *me* anymore. My friend looks out for me, which makes me happy."

She turns to look at me. "My school has mean girls and boys. They don't like me much, but I don't care. I don't even let them make me cry anymore. I have a force field now."

"A force field?" I ask.

"Yep, these rain boots and this jacket are my force field. My brother told me they have special powers and nothing people say can hurt me when I'm wearing my favorite color. My favorite color is purple!" She smiles and stands up. She twirls around with her arms wide. "See, lots of purple."

I smile. "Yes, lots of purple. Lots of force fields too. Those mean kids have nothing on you!"

She reaches up to the lapel of her jacket. It has a little glittery purple snowflake pinned to it. She takes it off.

"Here, you can have my special purple snowflake. I have lots of purple stuff, so you can keep this snowflake. My brother says this snowflake will work all by itself if I don't have anything else in my favorite color to wear. So you can just keep that with you and those girls will never make you sad again, ever."

Her small open hand is extended to me and her innocence along with her kindness touches my heart. What a brave little girl.

"Aw, thank you, Vivvie. But you don't have to give me your special snowflake. You keep it."

"Nope, you can't say no. It's rude to say no to someone when they give you a gift. You have to take it."

"Well okay, then. I certainly would never want to be rude to you. Are you really, really, super duper sure?"

"Yep, I'm sure as sure can be sure. Maybe you can just do me a solid someday if I need one."

I laugh out loud at that. "Deal." I smile at her as I take the little snowflake and pin it to my T-shirt.

"Well, I have to go now and tend to Lady Gaga. Maybe I'll see you again, Jessica. I like talking to you."

I laugh again. "Lady Gaga?"

"Yep, my pet pig. She's probably already missing me."

"Vivvie?"

"Yeah?"

"Why did you name your pet pig Lady Gaga?"

"I love music and Lady Gaga is my favorite singer ever, ever, ever. She's my hero. She has the best force fields of all. She has mean girls too, you know, but she doesn't care. She's the best and I love her. Every year, I wanted a pet pig so badly for Christmas. My mom always, always said no. I finally got one and she's my favorite pet. So I named her after my favorite singer. I'll bring her over one day. She has a really pretty collar with sparkles!"

She skips off as she waves good-bye to me. I just laugh to myself. A pet pig named Lady Gaga—hilarious. I raise my hand up to the snowflake, my new force field. I wish it were that simple. How great to be a little kid and have beliefs like that. Again I think about what a brave little girl she is, and I'm thankful she has such a great brother.

It's been a while since I last cut. I know it's because of Jace, but the fact that I don't really have him nags at me daily. He makes me feel safe and loved, even though I've never heard those words from him. My world's a little less dark.

I've never had a true friend before and it's nice. More than nice. He's my escape. Every time I see him, it's like a high, my new drug of choice. Before, cutting and sleeping around gave me a high. Now all I seem to need is Jace's presence. The way he treats me as if I'm a normal girl, like I'm one of the guys, is refreshing and frustrating all at the same time. That day in the pool when he almost kissed me is always at the forefront of my mind, even though it seems that he forgot about it long ago.

We've seen each other nearly every day since then. I go over to his house daily and we take turns beating each other in swim strokes. We've quickly learned that he can beat me in the butterfly every time, but he can never beat me in freestyle.

I still worry about screwing up his reputation, but the fact that he blatantly doesn't seem to care eases my guilt a little. His world is a universe away from mine, although we seem to have so much in common. He likes a lot of the same music I like, and having an actual person to play 21 with is way better than doing it online. He's also taught me how to play dominoes, but he calls it "throwing bones".

Today, he's introducing my bleeding ears to the most amazing stereo system I've ever heard in an automobile, and trying to teach me how to shoot hoops by playing a game like HORSE, only he says he hates calling it HORSE, because that's dumb and horses have nothing to do with basketball. So instead, we play FOUL.

"You aren't trying very hard, Jess. One more letter and I'm victorious once again." I'm already on U, and he hasn't missed a shot yet.

"I'm just letting you win." I suck at basketball, but I don't care because it's fun.

"Jace!" I hear a faint female voice call from behind us. When I turn around and see his mom, I nearly die right here on the spot. We're listening to a band that I've never heard before and, well, let's just say that the band, ever so wonderfully named The Insane Clown Posse, doesn't have the most mom-friendly lyrics. I don't really care for it, but anything that Jace is into I make myself be into.

Like football. I know nothing about it, so I Googled and learned every possible thing I could about football terminology. Now I can watch a game with him and yell things like "Is the ref blind? That was a totally freaking illegal chop block!" or "Do they not see that he was totally roughing the passer?"

My chameleon ways are in full effect, but I like making him happy. I like making him think I'm normal. Cool, even. I just want his acceptance; I want him to validate me. His mom, on the other hand, is a different story. I seriously doubt I'll ever have her acceptance.

I slap him on the arm and motion back toward his mom. He grabs the basketball on a bounce before reaching in the truck to turn the music down. She's wearing a fancy white dress suit and high heels with not one hair out of place. She has beautiful, full lips that would make Angelina Jolie jealous, and her skin is perfect. Not one wrinkle in sight. Her skin looks almost as young as mine.

I gulp down the freaking tennis ball that has formed in my throat and take a deep breath. Jace tosses the basketball into the grass and when his eyes meet mine I'm sure he sees the sheer terror behind them. He tries to make light of the situation, but no matter what he says, it's a heavy-as-hell moment for me.

Mrs. Collins is a socialite who cares more about her family's reputation than anything else. Seeing her son with the unpopular girl is certainly not something she'll be pleased about.

"Hey, Mom. Sorry about the music." He gives her puppy dog eyes with a cute grin stretched across his face. How could anyone be mad at that face? It's such a great face.

Mrs. Collins's facial expression never changes.

Is she made of concrete?

I follow her gaze and realize she's staring straight at my T-shirt. If I could will the ground to crack open and swallow me whole, I would. Jace looks back and forth between his mom's eyes and my shirt and chuckles. I look down at the words scrolled across the front of my pink shirt in big black font: *Music Makes Me Horny*. If there were ever a moment I wanted to be invisible, this is definitely it.

She looks at me like I'm Stephen King's *IT*, about to steal her son away and take him off to a dark cave somewhere. Jace keeps that shit-eating grin on his face as he watches the color slowly drain from mine.

"Mom, this is my friend Jessica. Jessica, this is my mom, Ariana Collins." She steps closer to me and extends her perfectly manicured hand with an obviously forced smile on her very obviously Botoxed face.

"Nice to meet you, Jessica..." She lifts the last half of my name in question. "What was your last name again?" Apparently she needs to find my place on her social ladder.

"Alexander, ma'am," I answer timidly. With those two words, I confirm that my family's last name is not on the country club's member list. My eyes nervously flit back and forth from hers to the ground, and I just want to escape the horrible moment. She looks down at my shirt and then back at me. There's an awkward pause right before she insists on making the situation even more embarrassing.

"Do your parents know you dress like this, Ms. Alexander?" she asks, arching an eyebrow and pursing her shiny lips, which are probably just as fake as her wrinkle-free skin.

She's pissing me off. The fact that she's asking about my parents makes me mad as hell. Little does she know that I'm very aware of how far out of touch she was with her own daughter. She has a look of disdain on her face as if I'm a big bug that she really needs to squash. Before I'm able to answer her, Jace saves me from saying something completely disrespectful and utterly stupid.

"Mom, who cares about the shirt? It's cool. If they had it in a color other than Pepto-Bismol pink, I'd wear one too. Even though boobs and other things make me horny, not music."

I jerk my head in his direction, and then back at his mom, my mouth agape.

Did he really just say "boobs" to his mom? Yes, I think he did.

"Jace Collins! You need to watch your mouth, young man. It's highly inappropriate to talk like that, especially in front of a lad—girl."

"Sorry, Mom," he apologizes. Then he looks to me. "Sorry, Jess." He waggles his eyebrows at me, but his mom doesn't see it. I try to contain my laughter. I've already made enough of a fool out of myself today.

"You're home early, Mom. What's up?" he asks, rolling his soggy toothpick back and forth in his mouth. I'll never look at toothpicks the same way again after Jace.

For Halloween, maybe I'll be a toothpick just to give him the hint that I'd love for him to roll me around in his mouth too.

I shake the toothpick thought from my head as his mom goes into a spiel about a charity dinner they have to attend this evening.

"You're going, Jace. Don't try to worm your way out of it. The Brants are meeting us there at seven o'clock, so make sure you're ready and wearing your nice suit and tie." With that, she turns on her expensive heel and goes inside.

Brant. They're going to an event with the Brant Family, which means Jace, my Jace, will be spending the evening with his ex-girlfriend, the queen bitch herself—Elizabeth Brant. I immediately tense up and my stomach clenches in anger and jealousy. All of a sudden, I feel sick. I turn around and walk over to the fancy yard bench and grab my bag. I toss it over my shoulder and start walking to my car.

"Whoa, wait a minute. Where the hell are you going, Jess?" he says, running up beside me.

"Home," I mutter.

I don't look up at him; if I do he'll see that I'm about to cry, or that I'm so full of jealousy I might explode. I know what's happening, and I have to get out of here. I haven't felt like this in months, and I have to get away from him before he sees the real me.

All I want to do is cry, scream...cut. Because no matter how wonderful these two months have been, I can see ever so clearly now that I'll never fit into his world. The contempt in his mother's eyes was unmistakable. He says he only wants his mom to be proud of him. Well, she could never be proud of him being associated with someone like me. He'll drop me like everyone else has and it will hurt, hurt like no pain I have ever felt.

He grabs my arm and spins me around to face him. He has a confused look on his face as he searches mine for answers.

"Why? We aren't done with our game," he retorts, looking a little dejected.

"You have somewhere to go, Jace. I'm just getting out of your way so that you can go get all dressed up for the charity event." I'm trying to keep the sarcasm and sadness out of my voice, but I'm not sure if it's working.

"Jess, it's only four thirty. I have plenty of time to get ready. You don't have to leave yet."

I look up at him, willing the tears to stay away, and do my very best to smile.

"I know, but I have lots of homework to do, so I should get home and get started on it."

LIAR.

I'm such a liar.

I realize now that instead of completely taking down my walls to let Jace in, I've reconstructed beautiful new ones, ones better suited to his likes and dislikes. He may think he's seen the real me over the past two months, but he's only seen glimpses. I lied to him, lied to myself, and now this shiny new façade that belongs to him, for him, is crumbling layer by layer. Even I don't know what will remain when it's all gone.

His brow creases and I can see he's carefully contemplating what I've said. He doesn't buy my story.

"Jess, all of our classes are together but one, and I don't know anything about a bunch of homework."

I have one class he's not in, thank God.

"Spanish."

Liar, liar, pants on fire.

"I have a ton of Spanish homework," I say, trying to convince myself more than I'm trying to convince him. I pray that he won't see right through me.

"Spanish? Really? Well I guess if you have to get it done, go ahead." He doesn't look totally swayed, but I can't worry about that right now. I just need to leave.

I open my car door and throw my bag in the backseat. As I'm getting in, he leans down with his arms propped up on my door and the rooftop of the car.

"You good? Is everything okay? You seem off or something. I hope my mom didn't rattle you with the shirt remark. Just let it roll off your back. She's just like that. I ignore it, and so should you."

Yes, your mom rattled me, and yes, I'm off right now. So far off that it would make you dizzy if you really knew how much.

"I'm fine, Jace."

Lie, lie, lie.

The lies just keep on coming. I have to get out of here.

"Okay... Well, have fun with your Spanish homework, I guess." He shoves himself off my car, and then closes the door and motions with his finger for me to roll my window down.

"You sure you're good, because I really feel like something's wrong. You know you can tell me if something's wrong, right?" he asks in a voice that drips with sincerity and concern.

Don't do it, don't do it, don't do it.

Then I do it.

"Why would anything be wrong, Jace? Your mom just looked at me like I'm some trashy whore who's dirtying her perfect, popular superjock son, and you're going to some fancy event with the so very upstanding Elizabeth and her family. I have no idea why something would be wrong with me."

The sarcasm in my voice soaks the air between us. The moment the words pass through my lips, I regret them. The look on his face solidifies my remorse and anchors my heart to the pit of my stomach. He crosses his arms over his chest defensively and looks at me in a way I've never seen him look at me before.

I don't like it at all.

"Wow! Perfect, popular superjock, huh? Is that how you see me? Have I ever acted like that guy with you, Jess? I know my mom can be a little judgmental, but I seriously doubt she thinks you're dirtying me, whatever that means. As far as Liz goes, there's nothing there anymore. You know that more than anyone."

He pauses briefly.

"What's odd to me is that I get the feeling that my mom isn't really the issue. Are you jealous, Jess? You do realize we aren't going to be celibate or not date people just because we're friends with each other, right? I mean, you've become like my best friend, but I'll eventually date again, and so will you. But when I do date again, rest assured, it will not be with Liz."

I gape at him, wishing more than ever that I'd never said a damn word. This is a conversation I've been trying to avoid for two months. I know he hasn't dated since Elizabeth, but I grow more and more anxious every day worrying about this topic. The thought of him with another girl makes me physically ill.

I don't have a damn clue how to answer him, so I do the next best thing. A stupid thing. I lie again. Only this lie is a big, fat, Texas-sized lie.

"No, Jace. I'm not jealous. I just hate Elizabeth! Also, your mom does think those things, regardless if you think so or not. I've been getting those kind of looks for years; I know very well what your mom was thinking about me."

I can feel my palms getting sweaty as this nervous, jealous energy poisons my thoughts.

"As far as the dating thing, yes. I'm well aware of that fact, so aware that I actually have a date this weekend. I hadn't told you yet, but there. Now you know. Hopefully that will ease your worry over my possible jealousy and some horrible bout of celibacy-bound friendship. Have all the sex you want and so will I."

I roll my window up without giving him a chance to respond, and pull out of his driveway. Just before I turn onto the blacktop road, I look once in my rearview mirror. He's standing in the very same spot, unmoving and staring at me as I drive away.

The drive home is one hundred kinds of awful. I rock back and forth in my seat, slamming my hand on the steering wheel and cursing to myself. TWO MONTHS. That's all it took for me to screw things up with the best thing that's ever happened to me.

When I get home, Mom's baking cookies and humming to herself.

Hello, Martha.

"Hi, sweetie. You want some cookies? I made your favorite," she asks.

My favorite? Does she even know what my favorite anything is?

I walk over and take a cookie off the pan before walking to my room. After I lock the door, I drop the cookie into the trashcan.

Snicker doodles are most definitely not my favorite.

My phone buzzes, and as soon as I look at the screen, my heart rate speeds up. Jace. I swipe the screen, revealing his text, and his words make this dreadful day even worse.

Jace: *Jess, I don't know what your deal is or why you went all superbitch on me, but I do know that it was bullshit. I have been nothing but a friend to you, and this is how you treat me in return? I don't know why you're so pissed or acting all psycho... And just so you know, I didn't make the comment about dating because I need to go get laid. I just wanted to make sure we were on the same page. I just needed to know that you weren't having feelings for me that would cause you to be jealous. Whatever your deal is, just know that I did not like how you acted today. Friends don't act shitty to each other like that.*

I throw my phone across the room and drop down onto my bed, burying my face in my pillow.

How did I ever think he'd want me like I want him?

It's obviously the furthest thing from his mind. Am I

that bad? That unattractive? Or maybe the problem is the fact that he knows how many guys I've slept with.

Whatever it is, I know that our friendship is never going to be the same after today.

"Second chances are sometimes needed
more than once."
—Kathryn Perez

Jessica

I SIT UP, peeling my face off my tear-soaked pillow, and reach over to yank my nightstand drawer open. I pull my box out and open it. The familiar smell of rubbing alcohol hits my nose, and it triggers me to want this even more than I already thought I did.

I pull my shorts down and my breathing picks up. Adrenaline zings through me the second before I press the razor's edge into my flesh. Dragging it nearly two inches across my lower stomach, I feel the warm blood flow and the endorphins fire off in my brain like bombs on a battlefield. Tears trickle down my flushed face, and I squeeze my eyes shut. I'm so fucked-up. There's something seriously wrong with me and I know it. Suppressing it for the last two months, trying to fool Jace and myself into believing

I'm a normal girl... It was a pathetic attempt to change. Just like putting a bandage over my ugly cuts doesn't change what they hide, putting a front up for the past eight weeks didn't change the mentally disturbed girl that I really am.

I curl up in the fetal position and clutch my journal, running all of the day's events through my head. I can't even dream of sleeping until I do some writing. Tonight's entry will be nothing like the last entry. I run my fingers over my handwriting from a few days ago. I can almost feel the happiness flow from the page through my fingertips.

The cracks
Mending slowly
Loneliness no more
Home is with him
He is what for
Darkness fading
Smiles and laughter
We are creating
Opening my eyes
Seeing for the first time

A reflection

That may not

Equal her demise

Reading this last entry hurts. My heart aches. In the end, I always sabotage the good things that cross my path; it's inevitable.

My phone has buzzed two more times, but I can't force myself to look. I'm too terrified that he'll say he never wants to see me again. I can't handle that. Not to-night.

Pulling the chewed-up pen cap off and grinding my teeth against it, I start to write. Pain and fear burst out of me in the written form of words.

So tired

Can't let go

Can't move on

Standing still

Running away

Can you still see me?

Am I fading away?

Back to that place

Darkness

Did I ever really leave?
Or am I poisoned at the core?
He will never understand
The storms that are raging
His fingers slipping
Through my hands
For too long I've weathered
Violent thunder quaking
Losing him
Only means going under

My phone buzzes again and I push off the bed, irritated that he won't just let me be. I grab the phone and swipe the screen to find three texts from him. I look at the time. Almost seven o'clock. Shouldn't he be on his way to spend the evening with the evil bitch?

I tap the first text.

Jace: *Why aren't you responding? I know you got my text.*

He texted that not too long after the first book-length

text that he'd sent about being pissed at me. I tap the next one.

Jace: *Are you really giving me the silent treatment? Are we in grade school, Jess? This is dumb! IDK why you're acting this way, and it's frustrating the shit outta me. Text me back, even if all you do is tell me to fuck off. Just say something...please.*

Now I feel like shit for not reading the texts earlier. I would have texted him back after that one. I tap the last one and hold my breath.

Jace: *I'm coming over. See you in 15.*

Holy hell!

He's coming to my house. I look at the time of the text and realize he'll be here within ten minutes. I run into the bathroom, wiping the smeared eyeliner from under my eyes as I go.

Shit!

My eyes look like I've been toking up on a ginormous blunt or something. Now he's going to think I'm a psycho and a druggy.

I run a brush through my hair and twist it up in a loose knot on top of my head. Then I quickly straighten my bed blankets, hide my journal, and drop to my bed to take one last calming breath. I hear the doorbell and freeze. He's here, and the fact that I never have anyone come over makes me extremely nervous. I'm so happy that Martha Mom is here tonight and not Drunk Mom.

I make a beeline for the front door, but Mom beats me

to it. She's holding a glass of clear liquid, and I immediately know that Martha is well on her way to drunkenness, if not already there.

Great.

Now he can see my drunken mother along with my bloodshot eyes and know what winners we are here at the Alexander house.

Mom opens the door and the most handsome man—yes, I said man because the person who's in my doorway at the moment is no boy. He has on a solid black suit with a white button down and turquoise tie. I drink in every inch of him as my chin rests comfortably on the floor. His hair is gelled and styled like some Hollister model, and I have the urge to plow straight through Mom and tackle him.

Is he trying to torture me with all that sex appeal?

There it is: the motherlovin' toothpick rolling back and forth between his full lips, lips that I just want to suck on. I feel the heat creeping across my cheeks and I swear I hear my heart beating in my ears.

"Hey," he says, pushing his hands into his pockets innocently.

He looks at me first, and then over at Mom. I freak immediately. The last thing I want is for Mom to do or say something stupid, so I walk past her onto my front porch. I look back at Mom just before shutting the door. "Mom, I'll be a few minutes," I say, and then turn to face him.

"Um, you couldn't introduce me to your mom, Jess?" he asks harmlessly, like there isn't this huge gaping hole between us right now. If either of us takes a wrong step, we'll surely fall feetfirst into it.

"Trust me, you don't want to meet her tonight." Our

eyes meet; the awkwardness between us is uncomfortable. "Aren't you supposed to be at the charity thing?" I ask.

"Nope, I'm where I'm supposed to be," he says, stunning me into a state of disbelief. "Have you eaten dinner?"

I stand there, staring at his mouth and trying to make sure I've heard the words correctly, all the while being totally distracted by the toothpick.

"Jess, dinner—yes or no?" he asks while I stare at him like a love-struck puppy.

"No," I deadpan.

"Well, go let your mom know that we're going to go grab a bite to eat, then. We need to talk."

I don't say anything. I just nod. Then I look down at my clothes and back at him. I feel seriously underdressed, not to mention *Music Makes Me Horny* is still written across my chest.

"Don't worry about what you're wearing. We'll go through the drive-thru."

Drive–thru? Really?

Okay, whatever. I'm hungry as hell, and I know we need to talk if I want to salvage any kind of relationship with him. He's too important to let my warped brain completely screw this up.

"All right, just let me tell Mom and I'll be right out." I feel jittery nerves waving through my body. What if he wants to tell me we can't be friends anymore?

God, please don't let him tell me that!

I walk in the house and peek around the corner to the living room. "Mom, I'm going with a friend to grab something to eat. I'll be back in a little bit."

She holds her hand up and murmurs, "Okie dokie, sweetie." Sounds like she's a happy drunk tonight. I guess that's better than sloppy drunk, so I'll take it.

I grab my phone and purse from my room and walk out to his truck. He has removed the jacket and untied his tie. His sleeves are unbuttoned and rolled halfway up his forearms. The top two buttons of his shirt are also unbuttoned, and he looks even better like this than he did all put together five minutes ago. His lip is slightly upturned, giving me a little grin. It helps me breathe a little easier, knowing that he isn't so pissed anymore.

"Are you okay with DQ?" he asks and I giggle. "What? Dairy Queen is the best. Steak Finger Country Baskets are the shit!" he says, backing out of my driveway.

"Nothing, it's just that you're supposed to be at a fancy dinner eating fancy food and you want to go to Dairy Queen. It's funny, that's all."

"Fancy doesn't always mean good, Jess." His comment is ambiguous, but I don't question him about it.

As we drive, we sit in silence until he reaches over to turn his stereo on. The quiet is replaced with lyrics by Staind, and I gaze out the window, wondering how the night will end. I doubt things will go well if I'm honest with him, but lying won't resolve this either.

We get to the Dairy Queen just as the Staind song fades into one of Hinder's. He pulls into the drive-thru and turns the volume off before rolling his window down.

He looks over at me and asks, "What will it be?"

A small smile stretches across my face. "Well, I guess I'll have the Steak Finger Country Basket since you say it's the shit. And a Vanilla Coke, please." He grins and orders one for each of us. "Oh, and I want ice cream too. A Peanut Buster parfait with no peanuts, please."

He raises his eyebrows at me, obviously confused by my strange request. "You want a *Peanut* Buster parfait with no peanuts? Jess, what's the point of ordering something with peanuts if you don't want them in it? That's weird."

"Well, that's me. Weird," I answer flatly.

I don't want to get into my weird food issues, so I don't elaborate. The thing is, I don't like crunchy stuff inside my food. I like peanuts just fine, but not in my ice cream. Just like I love pickles, but won't eat them on a burger. Biting into something and feeling a crunch inside of it creeps me out.

I have several weird tendencies that I've hidden well from Jace. I don't like my food to touch on my plate, and I won't use the same fork for two different foods. If I have mashed potatoes and green beans on my plate I need two forks. Thankfully, forks are not needed to eat a Steak Finger Basket.

I'm also completely repulsed by dirty dishes. When I have to load the dishwasher at home, I gag repeatedly. Touching old, stuck-on food makes me ill. I know I may seem like some weird OCD germaphobe, but the idea of bacteria or germs really doesn't factor in. It's the dried-up, gross food that bothers me so much. That's just how I am.

I count when I fill the tub with water too. That's another weird thing I do. Not sure why I do it, but I've done it since I was a little kid. Once the water is at the level I want, I stop counting. Sometimes it's a 1,000 bath, and sometimes it's a 500 bath. Weird, I know.

He orders the Peanut Buster parfait—sans peanuts—and we pull up to get our order. I reach into my purse to get some money out, but he holds up his hand.

"No way, I got this." He hands the cashier the money and doesn't even look back at me until she gives him his change.

"Jace, I can buy my own food. It's not like we're on a date or something."

I don't know why I'm such a glutton for punishment, but I just have to go and say that—with a shitload of sarcasm in my voice. He grimaces at me before turning back to get the food. He plops the bag down in the seat between us, and places the drinks in the cup holders. The cashier hands him the ice cream last.

He turns as he hands it to me. "Here's your weird ice cream," he says in a monotone voice.

He's mad again. I can sense it, and it's totally my fault. We pull onto the road and the direction he's driving in tells me we're going to his house.

Why are we going to his house?

"Where are we going?" I ask, even though I already know the answer. I'm hoping he'll elaborate on why without me having to ask.

"My house. My mom's not home and she won't be until late, so we'll have privacy to talk, which we apparently really need to do," he suggests.

God, he is still mad, and he still wants to talk. This won't end well. I can feel it.

We're sitting at the fancy outdoor table on his pool deck. The outdoor lighting reflects off the pool's water, glistening as the sound of the waterfall fills the air.

This is way better than any restaurant.

He hands me my food and starts eating his. I ate all of my ice cream before we even got here, but I'm still hungry.

"I can't believe you ate your ice cream before your food," he says with a steak finger in his mouth.

"I can't believe you talk with food in your mouth," I tease.

Bravery is brimming inside of me, and I just want the dreadful anticipation of this talk to be over with already.

"Jace, what do you want to talk about?" I ask, but I don't make eye contact.

Coward.

"Nope. Food first. Talk second."

I look up at him as I dip my steak finger in the gravy. "Okay," I agree guardedly.

We finish eating and he gets up to throw everything away. Then he goes in his garage and comes back out holding what looks like an empty beer bottle.

What the hell?

"Um, what's that for?" I ask, pointing toward the bottle.

"Spin the bottle," he says, completely serious.

Spin the freaking bottle? Really? *He's got to be joking right now.*

His expression remains thoughtful as he plops back down in his chair. He places the bottle side down in the middle of the table then leans back, staring at me. I can't help but laugh. It's too much.

"It's not what you're thinking. You spin it and if it lands on the other person, you get to ask a question—any question—and the other person has to answer honestly. If it lands on nothing, which is likely since there are only two of us here, you have to tell a truth about yourself that the other person doesn't know." He pauses briefly before reaching out to grab the bottle.

I already don't like this game and we haven't even started yet. I think I like the middle school idea of regular spin the bottle much better.

"Here, ladies first," he says, giving me the bottle. I spin the bottle and it lands on the chair beside me where no one is sitting.

"Truth," he says as he bores a hole right through me with his indigo eyes.

"I'm sorry for making you mad today," I tell him, because it's the best truth I can come up with, and I am really sorry for making him mad.

He reaches out to spin the bottle without replying. It lands on the chair beside him. He has this serious, stern look on his face and it makes me feel uneasy.

"I'm glad you're sorry, but I'm still pretty damn mad," he says, and my lips puff out in a little pout. It's my turn, so I spin again. His eyes are pinning me down as I do so. It lands squarely on him.

"Why are you still mad at me?" I ask pointedly.

He lets out a big exasperated sigh and leans forward, resting his elbows on the table.

"I just don't know why you freaked out. And that crap you pulled by getting all shitty and mean with me was completely out of left field. One minute everything is fine, the next you're furious and bitchy. You drove away after the sex comment, and I was left standing there thinking what the fuck just happened?"

He pauses, opens his mouth, and closes it again. I see the inner struggle he's having, trying to form his thoughts into words.

"I'm just going to ask. If I'm way off base, then say so, but I have to ask. Do you want more than just a friendship with me, Jess?"

His question wraps around my neck and strangles me with fear. This is it. I am at a crossroads. I can lie, or I can be honest, but for some reason both paths seem like they will end badly.

I drop my face into my hands and force the tears to stay at bay. I don't want him to see this sad, broken-down side of me. He saw it after I got beat up, and I never want him to see it again. But all I want to do is cry because I can feel things falling apart with him already. I fucked up by overreacting and that's the way it always starts for me. One overreaction leads to another, and eventually anything that was good is ruined.

"Jess, why are you about to cry? I swear I'm not trying to be a complete ass about this. I just think we need to get on the same page about whatever is going on. Please, just talk to me, dammit. You never open up to me, and I've opened up and told you more stuff than I've told anyone else. Why can't you do the same? You're frustrating the hell out of me."

I lift my face from my hands and the tears escape, unhindered by my desperate efforts to hold them back. When I look at him, I can feel his frustration, his anger, but most of all I can see that he's sincere about wanting to fix whatever is wrong between us.

"Please don't cry. Dammit all to hell! I hate this. It's obvious you're hurting. I can see it in your eyes and not just because you're crying. There's a pain behind them that I can't reach." He takes a deep breath and continues, more gentle now. "You have to tell me what's wrong, or it's going to eat away at me. What's wrong, Jess?"

I've always felt as if he can read me better than anyone else ever has. He's right about the pain, just not the level of pain. The problem is how am I supposed to explain myself to someone else when I can't even explain it to myself? There's no way to tell him what's wrong with me without sounding like the unstable, needy girl that I know I am.

I have to tell him how I feel about him because if I don't it will be yet another regret I'll have to live with. No matter what happens between us in the future, I need him to know how he has made me feel and how much more I want from him. I reach down deep within myself, mustering every ounce of bravery I can, and tell him what I've wanted to say for weeks.

"Jace, I'm sorry for acting like I did. I'm sorry for all of it. I was jealous—am jealous—at the thought of you being with someone else. When you start to date again, I want it to be with me. The next time I feel someone's lips on mine, I want them to be yours."

I pause before continuing to pour my soul out all over this table.

"You've given me more in the past two months than anyone ever has in my life. I trust you. You make me feel like I matter. You're funny, sweet, cocky, sexy, adorable, and you always know how to make me smile. There are things you don't know about me that I'm not quite ready to tell you about yet, but I'm going to do my best to stop lying to you and to myself about my feelings for you."

I pause to catch my breath and gather my nerve to finish what I want to get out.

“I know you’ve made it clear you don’t see me that way, and I know you don’t want me like I want you, so I’ll try really hard to continue being just your friend, because having some of you is better than having none of you at all. I just don’t know how to control my feelings or my actions when it comes to thinking about you being with someone else.”

I suck in a rush of air, trying to regain my breath after spitting all of that out faster than he could probably keep up with. I look up at him, feeling more exposed than I’ve ever felt before in my life. He has no idea how hard it was for me to say those things. Giving him that tiny glimpse of my desperation was incredibly difficult.

He leans back, crosses his arms over his chest, and lifts his eyes to mine. A lone tear rolls down my cheek, but I don’t try to wipe it away because these tears serve a purpose. I just let it fall, allowing him to see me. I can’t help but wonder if my life will always be filled with these kinds of moments, fear, sadness, and pain.

Confusion and worry cloud his eyes. I drop my gaze from his and look down to my lap.

“Jess, I know that was hard for you to say. To be honest, I already knew without you saying it, but I just needed to be sure. First of all, this isn’t about me not wanting you, so please don’t think that I’m blind, dumb, and deaf to the beautiful girl sitting in front of me.”

He leans in toward me and rests his elbows on the table.

“That’s not what this is about. You have no reason to feel unwanted, so just know that right now. Any guy in his right mind would want you, especially if they knew the Jessica that I know. Aside from your body, your eyes, and that damn curtain of shiny black hair, you're funny as hell and I have a shitload of fun with you. You have no idea how many times I've wanted to grab you in the pool, throw you over my shoulder, and take you inside to my bedroom."

He stops to drop his head briefly.

Looking back at me he says, "But what stops me is the inevitable. Think about it, Jess. How many high school relationships turn into something lasting? Few to none. How many people date in high school, have a huge falling out over some stupid high school bullshit, and then graduate never to see or hear from each other again? The answer is almost all of them. I don't want that for us. I don't want to lose what we've built."

His words wrap around me one by one, bit by bit, solidifying everything I already knew. Jace is different from the rest. He's good and true. He's one of the nice guys.

"You're the only friend I've ever shared Genevieve with, and it makes me value this friendship more than my raging teenage hormones. I want to have you in my life for years to come, and the only way to make sure that has a real chance is to take the drama of a physical romantic relationship out of the equation. Can't you see that us being friends is safer than us being something else?"

I know that everything he's saying makes sense. He's so thoughtful, and the fact that an eighteen-year-old guy can put his hormones on the back burner for something he values more says a lot. Guys usually value me based on sexual encounters alone, so I should be happy about this, but I'm not. I can only think about him being with someone else eventually, and I can't stand the thought of it. Thinking about him with another girl breaks me. It consumes me, causing an abysmal hole to open in my chest that threatens to suck me inside of myself, never to be released again.

I have no idea what to say or do. This will never work. Maybe if I was normal and had the ability to regulate my emotions I could agree to everything he said, but the fact that I know he'll fall into bed with another girl someday overshadows our friendship. And it will continue to do so, until the day it finally cracks in half, irreparable. I can walk away from him now and never look back, or I can stay friends with him and take what I can get before that awful day comes. A smart girl would walk away, but the desperate girl that I am will stay.

"Okay, Jace. I'll try harder. I don't want to lose this either. You're important to me, so I'll try to stop wanting more. Just be patient with me, okay?"

He stands up and rounds the table before reaching out and grabbing my hands, pulling me up. His warm arms wrap around me and I drop my face to his chest, hugging him back. He squeezes me tightly and kisses the top of my head. It isn't the kiss that I want, but I'll take it.

"Thank you. I'm relieved that I don't have to lose my best friend. Plus, who will keep me in line if you aren't around?" he says with a hint of laughter in his voice. "It will all work out. We'll figure it out as we go."

He holds me for a moment longer, and I squeeze him back knowing that I won't have many more of these hugs before I screw it all up again and lose him forever.

"Remembering. Forgetting.
I'm not sure which is worse."
—Kelly Armstrong

Jessica

Six years later...

Starving for more
Back pushed against the door
Looking for nothing
Hoping for something
Like a white crayon
Drawing upon white paper
Showing no results

All these years
Invisible...
Where did I go?
Where have I been?
Lost myself
All for him
Relenting
Spending myself
Treading the waters
Being pulled under
Holding my breath
Giving in
Breaking down on the inside
Looking for someone
Looking for more
Wanting to smile
Needing to explore
Exhale

Relax

Just needing

Just wanting

A friend

A place

Where I can be myself

Be free

Just be me...

Looking back on the day six years ago when I lost Jace forever, I know I didn't have a pretty picture painted of my future with him, but I couldn't have imagined what it would become, or how far I'd slip away from any chance at normalcy. I never could have predicted such despair or agony, and I never thought that I'd eventually hurt Jace just as badly as I hurt myself.

In a few weeks, I'll have to face a day that I never want to face—the date that our child would have been born. Every year the day comes, and it rips me to shreds. So many wrong decisions, so many impulsive choices, and so much misguided love and hate brought me to that tipping point all those years ago.

Thinking back on my senior year of high school, I feel an immense weight, intense pain that cripples me in every way imaginable. It rides on my shoulders every single day, haunting my every decision, my every action.

After we had agreed to continue being friends that day so long ago, I really tried hard to keep my word. Every day, I tried to push my urge to have more of him away. I tried to hide my possessiveness and my jealousy. Jace was so considerate of the feelings he knew I struggled with, and he always made a point to avoid flirting, never rubbing it in my face when he noticed other girls.

For a while, I deluded myself into thinking that he would be single from there on out. We still spent tons of time together, and when swim season started we were pretty much inseparable. We watched each other's races, cheered each other on, and practiced in his pool daily. His mom tolerated me, for the most part, but the tension was always there. Jace finally met my parents on one of their better days and it actually wasn't as terrible as I had thought it would be.

Things were going well, despite my pent-up desire for him. He still made me happy, and he still filled the emptiness inside me that I desperately needed filled.

We were near the end of the school year, and everyone was off scouting colleges. Jace was extremely pumped about going to Baylor University, and every time he talked about it a little part of me felt like dying. All I could think about was that he was leaving me. He mentioned several times that I should go there too, so that we could be together, but he knew how I felt about school. It was a place I never wanted to be again, whether it was here or there.

He had gone to Waco several weekends in a row, and had even brought me back a Baylor T-shirt. He was getting familiar with the area and touring different parts of the school's programs. He was undecided on what he wanted his major to be, but was still excited about going. I didn't want to ruin that for him, so I kept my sadness to myself the best I could.

The weekend right after we graduated turned into hell on earth for me. I had always looked forward to the end of high school, but what happened ended up being worse than all four years of high school rolled into one. Jace was going off to Baylor soon and I wanted to spend some time with him. I decided to surprise him that Friday afternoon, knowing his mom would be at work and it could just be us. In my warped brain, I thought there could be a possibility of him finally caving and us moving on to something more now that high school was over. When I got there, the nightmares that I had lived over and over in my paranoid mind came true right in front of my face.

Even now, the memory still haunts me.

I walked slowly around the side of the big brick two-story house, and faced a sight I never wanted to see: Jace and a pretty brunette in his pool. He pressed her up against the side of it and covered her mouth with his. His hand gripped her breast, which was barely hidden under her tiny white bikini top, and both of them moaned as the water splashed around them.

I froze like time was standing still.

I knew I should turn and run away, but I couldn't. I stood there, watching their every move. Jace reached up and untied her top, releasing her breast, and dipped his head down to cover it with his mouth. Her head dropped back, and I heard her mumbling to him as she ran her fingers through his hair.

"God, Jace, that feels amazing. After today, you

won't be able to get to Waco fast enough for me, baby."

My heart slammed into my ribs, and my eyes welled with unshed tears. She was from Waco. He had met someone there, but didn't tell me. And he let her come here—to the place we shared together practically every day. Tears spilled from my eyes and a sob escaped my throat. My sobs must have carried across the water because Jace froze and turned around. His eyes met mine through the gaps in the black iron gate, and we stared at each other for what felt like forever until he snapped into action.

He pulled her top back up, telling her to cover herself, then pulled himself up out of the pool quickly in a panicked state, his obvious arousal very much on display through his swim trunks. He grabbed a towel anxiously, and wrapped it around himself as he ran in my direction. I didn't even attempt to move. It was over, and I knew it.

"Jess, what—" he stammered, trying to form complete sentences. "What are you doing here?" he tried again. I didn't look up. I just stood in front of him like a helpless, worthless shell of nothing. He looked down, bringing our faces eye-to-eye.

"I'm sorry you saw that," he said, encasing my face with his wet hands, hands that only moments ago had been grasping onto some other girl's breast. I pushed his hands away. My fight or flight mechanism finally kicked into high gear, and I was on the run.

As always.

Just before I reached my car, I turned and scowled, throwing millions of daggers at him with my glare. It was all coming out of me at once. When I reached that level of hurt, every emotion I felt was in overdrive and nothing could stop them.

"I HATE YOU, Jace Collins!" I screamed venomously.

His face practically turned inside out with anguish at my vengeful words. He stopped in his tracks, and I saw wetness in his eyes that could have been mistaken for pool water had I not known better. He put his hands on his hips and dropped his head to look at the ground. I turned back to my car and yanked the door open as hard as I could. Whipping around, I spouted one more hateful thing at him.

"I wish you would've never helped me that night! I wish Elizabeth and Hailey would have beat me to death. I wish I would've died that night; that would've been better than you coming into my life!" I yelled as my voice cracked.

I'd never seen such a pained expression on Jace's face—ever. It was tragic, and I was the one to put it there.

Days and days went by.

Every day he sent me text after text, begging me to talk to him, but I never replied. The night before he was supposed to move to Waco, he came to my house drunk. I'll never forget opening my door and seeing him standing there. After not seeing him for so many days after such an awful incident, he looked even more beautiful.

"Jace? What are you doing here, and why do you reek of alcohol?"

He smiled a lazy smile when he answered me. "I'm leaving tomorrow, Jess. I just wanted to say good-bye to my friend."

I looked out to his still-running truck and realized that he had just driven to my house drunk off his ass.

"Jace, you're drunk! You can't drive around in this condition. You're going to kill someone, or yourself. I'm

taking you home. You can have someone get your truck for you in the morning. Wait here while I get my keys."

I got my keys and hooked my arm in his, leading him to my car. He rested his head on my shoulder and inhaled loudly, nuzzling his nose into my hair. My skin prickled and my stomach flip-flopped at feeling him so close to me.

"I love your hair, Jess. It's the prettiest hair I have ever seen, and it smells so good."

"Shut up, Jace. You're drunk and don't know what you're saying," I told him, even though I wanted to hear every drunken thing he had to say about me.

Even if I knew it wasn't true.

I pushed him down into my passenger seat and shut the door, shaking my head as I went around the back to my side. Silently, I got in, started the car, and backed out of the driveway.

"I'm not ready to go home yet, Jess. Just drive around," he whispered, laying his head back on the head-rest.

"Jace, you need to go home and sleep this off. You have a big day tomorrow, plus I don't want to drive around with you. I'm only helping you because I couldn't let you kill yourself driving like this."

He rolled his head to the side, regarding me with sadness in his bloodshot eyes.

"Jess, don't hate me anymore."

I could barely restrain myself from jerking the car to the side of the road and reaching out to hug him. I wanted to say how sorry I was for what I had said, to beg him to forgive me, but I didn't because the vivid picture of him with that girl was still too painful. Forgiveness didn't come easy for me. Actually, it usually never came. Once

I'd cut someone out of my life, there was no going back.

"I'm sorry it couldn't be you, Jess," he said simply, and he reached across to tuck my hair behind my ear. "That it wasn't you in the pool with me. Forgive me, don't hate me anymore."

My heart was thumping, and my mind was reeling. I had no idea what to say to that because I wished I were the one in the pool with him that day too. I gripped the steering wheel tightly, struggling with the tug-of-war in my head. He reached down, grasping my hand and interlocking his fingers with mine.

"My mom is still at the country club. That's where my going away party was," he said as his thumb rubbed over the soft skin on the back of my hand. "She usually stays until close. Come inside with me. I just want to spend time with you before I leave tomorrow." His hand squeezed mine before he continued, "I feel like I'll never see you again once I leave."

His words, his actions, his very presence—it was all too much. His eyes captured mine and it felt like a million butterflies were being released in my stomach all at once. I knew he had been drinking, but I also knew how badly I wanted to have at least one more moment with him, despite my anger over how he hurt me. I knew he didn't do it intentionally, but that didn't make the pain any less real.

"Okay," I whispered, caving to my desires.

I'd never been in Jace's room before. I'd always suspected he never asked me up because he was worried about the always-present fact that I wanted more from him

than friendship. Looking around, I saw that, like the rest of his house, it was huge. A large flat screen was mounted on the wall with every gaming system you can imagine, and across from them was a big queen size bed. Sports posters littered the walls and Baylor University memorabilia was placed throughout. There were two large beanbags off in the corner, and a shelf full of trophies and medals from all of his athletic accomplishments.

I startled when the TV clicked on to a channel that streamed music. "We Belong Together" by Gavin DeGraw began to play and he dropped the remote on the bed.

I looked up to find a new emotion behind the sapphire blue of his eyes: desire. My head swam at the sudden shift in him, in us, in the room. It was everywhere—this need for each other—and it was undeniable, at last. He stalked toward me with determination, searching my face, and as I stood there under his gaze, all of the air in the room seemed to disappear. I could barely breathe. He stopped inches from my body and leaned down, putting his lips tantalizingly close to mine without actually touching them; so close that I could feel his warm breath on my face and smell the aroma of peppermint mixed with whiskey.

It was intoxicating.

"Do you know how many times I've wanted to kiss these lips?" He whispered every word with obvious restraint, putting an emphasis on each syllable. It drove me crazy, and I couldn't help the images that flew through my head of his lips on mine, on me.

He kept his mouth excruciatingly close to mine, but never touched me. I closed my eyes and tried to breathe. I felt dizzy with need, and my legs started feeling unstable. He reached up painfully slow and rubbed the pad of his thumb across my lower lip. His eyes darkened and hungrily flitted from my eyes to my mouth.

"I'm going to kiss you now, Jess," he whispered, so low that I could barely hear the words. "I'm going to kiss you like no one has ever kissed you before."

My God.

He leaned forward and briefly skimmed my lips. A soft moan escaped my throat and my breath mingled with his. Too soon, he paused, moistening his lips with his tongue. "Jess, after I kiss you, which I'm going to do real soon, I'm going to lay you down on this bed and make love to you like no one else ever has."

A bolt of unrestricted pleasure coursed through my entire body and straight to my core at his words. My heart said to stop him because he had been drinking, but the selfish part of me wanted it so badly. This was the side of Jace I'd been waiting so long to see. I'd always loved the kind friend Jace, but the uninhibited, take-charge, incredibly sexy Jace that stood before me set me on fire. Swallowing hard, I looked back into his eyes and nodded, biting on my lower lip and trying to restrain myself from saying anything that might ruin the moment. He hadn't even kissed or touched me yet, but my body was already responding to him in places that normally needed much more one-on-one contact.

He slipped his hand around the back of my neck, gripping it firmly, and in that moment, I completely submitted to him. I wanted to feel his lips on mine more than I wanted the air in my lungs. He captured my mouth ardently, with an eagerness that nearly made my knees buckle. His warm, soft tongue traced the seam of my lips, and I opened for him. When our tongues met, they intertwined in a feverish dance, and the sexual energy between us seemed to intensify with our increased movements, touches, lust. Whiskey and mint teased my taste buds and I wanted more, needed more Jace, but not just physically; I also craved the love he offered up with each caress. My heart raced, my skin flushed, and every single fiber of my body was on edge. That one kiss was the most riveting sexual experience of my life, but it was so much more than that. I'd been with a lot of guys, but that kiss caused every single one of those experiences to fade from my memory. It wasn't just a kiss. It was a promise, a pure, raw display of tangible love. My heart would never forget and it would never be the same again.

I leaned in, wanting to taste more of him, but he pulled back, and a whimper escaped my lips with the absence of his on mine.

"Jace, I—"

"Shhh, Jessica," he said in a low throaty voice. When he called me Jessica like that, my stomach clenched and my mouth watered in anticipation. "Lie down on the bed, Jess," he demanded.

As soon as I felt the backs of my knees hit the bed, I froze. He stood in front of me with unwavering confidence, exuding tons of masculinity. He reached down and curled his fingers under the edge of his shirt, pulling it up over his head. I dropped my eyes to his rippled abs, which I'd always admired. He started unbuttoning his dark denim jeans and the words **Lucky You** *stared at me from the inside of his zipper. Their truth was not lost on me at all. He pushed them down, letting them fall around his ankles, until all he had on was Nike boxer briefs. They hugged his toned legs and everything else perfectly.*

I swallowed, trying to get the lump in my throat to go away, and his voice snapped me out of my ogling.

"Lie down, Jess."

Without a word, I lay down and scooted back, closer to the headboard. He crawled onto the bed and chills spread across my body as he climbed up and rested beside me. With a single finger, he reached over and traced from my lips down over my chin, my neck, down between my breasts and all the way to the edge of my shirt.

He leaned over, barely ghosting his lips over my ear, and whispered, "I'm going to take your shirt off now."

His words sent an anticipatory shiver down my spine and I closed my eyes as I gripped the blanket in my fists beneath me. The nerves ricocheting through my mind intensified, and for the first time I realized I was scared to death to sleep with someone. But not just anyone: Jace. My Jace. He was different. It was different. We were different. This was going to be unlike any other time I'd had sex, and I knew it.

He must have sensed my anxiety because he leaned over and pressed his lips to my cheek. "It's okay, Jess. Just let me make you feel good; let me love you."

I melted at his request. It was more than that, though; there was an unspoken command in his words, an assurance that he would love me, take care of me, make me and my body feel like no one else had ever made me feel. And I was lost then, entirely lost in Jace and his promises. Anything he wanted was his for the taking.

He removed my clothes, piece by piece, with a reverence like I'd never experienced. The fabric was replaced with his lips and skin on mine—sensations everywhere. He moved lower to take my shorts off, kissing his way to my abdomen, and I froze, knowing he was about to see my scars. I took a deep breath and let things play out. It was too late to worry about his reaction. If the scars repulsed him, then they just would, but I wasn't going to let that stop me from enjoying every second that his hands were still on me.

Just after he pulled my shorts and panties down, I saw the surprise and worry cross his face. Below my panty line looked like a war zone from years of cutting. The scars imprinted on my skin revealed years of hidden pain.

He craned his head up, looking at me as he brushed his fingers over the damaged skin, and I could see the questions and concern that swirled in his eyes. He didn't speak a word, but his silence said so much to me. He turned his gaze back to the scars and leaned down, placing his warm lips to them. My eyes filled with tears, but I fought them back. He had just kissed the spot that always reminded me of how broken I really was. He still wanted me anyway, and I loved him for it.

His head dipped lower, and as he worked his magic I threw my head back in pleasure. He did things to me that lifted me to levels of frenzy I had never known before. Every touch was slow and deliberate. When he started trailing kisses up my body, he relaxed on top of me, his flesh molding with mine. He looked down at me hungrily, licking his lips, and I blushed knowing what he was tasting.

"Good, Jess. So good."

I gasped just before he dropped his lips to mine, claiming my mouth in another aggressive kiss. His hand ran down the side of my body as he lifted his hips to remove his boxers. When his body met mine again, currents of warm buzzing energy flowed between us. My breathing was rapid, and my chest was rising and falling quickly. He deepened our kiss and nudged his knee between my legs, spreading me wide for him. He rose up on both hands and looked down at me before asking a life-changing question.

"Jess, are you on the pill?"

A thousand things rolled through my mind... If I told the truth, he would put on a condom, we'd have sex, and I'd never see him again. Or he wouldn't have any protection, and he'd have to stop.

Or I could get pregnant and he'd never leave me.

My answer would alter our lives forever.

"Your outer journey may contain a million steps;
Your inner journey only has one:
The step you are taking right now."
—Eckhart Tolle

Jessica

SITTING IN THE waiting room of a mental health clinic wound tight as hell, and dreading the fact that I've been forced into therapy, isn't the way I want to spend my morning.

But this is a step I know I have no choice but to take.

The memories of that night six years ago, when Jace and I had sex for the first and last time, have replayed in my mind over and over, just like they do now. The way he seemed to sober instantly when he got me in his bedroom, and took control of my body like I was his to possess... It's still the single most passionate night of my life. My awful decision tainted it, though, and turned something that could've been beautiful into something very ugly.

Looking back now, I remember how I cried all the way home after I left Jace's house. I cried for him, for me, and for the lie that I told. I wanted to take it back, but it was too late, and what was done was done. Jace had come inside of me, and I was not on birth control.

I'd always relied on condoms, because I never wanted to tell my mom that I wanted birth control pills. I doubt she would've cared, but I still hadn't wanted to broach the subject with her.

Jace got dropped off the next morning to get his truck, and I was beyond nervous to answer the door when he came to say good-bye. I didn't know what to expect from him after our night together, and I was terrified that I'd see regret on his face.

I remember it as if it were only yesterday.

Opening the door, I took in his faded jeans, white Nike's, and Baylor T-shirt. He had his hands in his pockets and he looked at me with a flirty grin on his adorably handsome, dimpled face. The oh-so-sexy toothpick was in full effect, and he looked nothing like a guy who regretted anything.

"Hey," he said simply.

The moment was awkward, and the fact that we had slept together lingered in the air.

"Hey back," I replied.

"You wanna take a ride with me? I have a couple hours before I have to head toward Waco," he asked, and held his hand out to me.

I looked down at myself and back to him because I was still in pajamas.

"Jess, it's just a truck ride. Who cares about your ug-

ly *pajamas?" he asked, chuckling and shaking his head back and forth at me.*

I had on my black and orange plaid pajama shorts and the T-shirt that went with them. It was an orange T-shirt that said Ugly *across the front of it. It was dumb, but I liked clothes that said weird and funny stuff. I just seemed to wear them at the wrong times.*

I laughed a little, and agreed to go on the ride. "Sure, just let me tell my mom and put on some shoes. I also have a going away gift for you."

I told my mom I'd be back later and slipped on my flip-flops. My hair was down and fell wildly around my face and past my shoulders. We got in the truck and he backed out of the driveway. As he pulled onto the road, he reached over and grabbed my hand. "Get over here, you're too far away," he said, tugging at my hand.

I scooted over right beside him with a smile on my face. I really loved his truck, especially then, since it allowed us to be so close. He pulled my hand up to his lips and placed a small kiss just on top of it. It was sweet, and I knew in that second that I loved Jace Collins. I had never fully admitted it to myself because I didn't think I could possibly know what real love was, but that was real love. The kiss on my hand was love and I knew it. I felt it with every fiber of my being.

I recognized the road we turned down and instantly jerked my head, looking at him in confusion. "Where are we going, Jace?" I asked, squeezing his hand.

"Don't worry. It's early morning, so no one will be there," he assured me.

We pulled up to the water tower entrance, and my heart beat a little faster than normal. That place held bad memories for me and I hated being there. Jace knew it too, and sensed my discomfort.

"Jess, no one is here. No one is going to hurt you. It's just you and me. Just Jace and Jess, okay?" he said, cupping both of my cheeks and giving me a thoughtful smile.

He leaned forward, kissed the very tip of my nose, and placed his forehead against mine before saying, "This place doesn't need to hold bad memories for you. This is where we saw who the other person really was for the first time. This place holds a memory of second chances." He looked out, scanning the place where he helped me that terrible night. "That night may not have had a happy ending, but it paved the way for us to find each other. Their wrong choices brought us to the right place—each other." He was so right. God, did I love that boy. "I know you're probably really confused about last night, Jess, but I don't regret it, not one damn bit of it. I was an idiot for not doing it sooner. I should've given in to my feelings a long time ago. I let stupid fears get in the way and I copped out. I regret that. Last night was amazing and wonderful and incredibly hot, Jess. It makes me all wound up just thinking about it right now." He paused, looking at my mouth.

"And these..." he murmured, leaning down and placing a chaste kiss on my lips. "These are the softest lips I've ever felt and they taste like candy. I could kiss them all day and never get tired of it." He kissed me one more time, softly.

I pulled a bag out of my purse and handed it to him. "Here. I got this for you at the mall. Just don't wear it in front of your mom," I laughed.

He pulled the blue shirt out of the bag and held it up. Music Makes Me Horny *was written in bold black letters across the front of it.*

"You said you'd wear one if it came in a color other than pink, so there you go," I said.

"I love it!" he said with a big goofy smile.

"It's Jace blue."

"Jace blue?"

"Yeah, it's the color of your eyes."

We both laughed, and he held the T-shirt up to his chest.

"Mom will love this shirt. I'll have to be sure and wear it when she comes to visit just to piss her off." He chuckled.

He leaned in and kissed me on the cheek, thanking me again. Then he fell quiet. He looked nervously into his lap, and then back up at me. He opened his mouth as if he was about to say something, but snapped it shut like he didn't quite have the right words yet. His brows creased, and he ran a hand nervously through his hair.

"Hey, let's go sit on the water tower platform. It's nice out." We walked hand in hand over to the tower. We climbed the ladder and I took in the view of the surrounding trees. With his arm comfortably around me, we sat and he asked hard questions that I did my best to answer.

"Jess, what happened to you? Why do you have all those scars?" he whispered with his head hung low, looking at me with worry and concern.

My heart raced and my palms started sweating. I knew I'd be faced with it one day, but I didn't want it to be that day. I just wanted to say our good-byes on a good note. He could see that I was scared to tell him by my tense body language and the apprehension that must've been written all over my face. He reached up and stroked my cheek, assuring me that I was safe.

"Hey, it's okay. You can tell me. Who did that to you?" he asked. The distress in his voice was heartbreaking. The thought that he had never considered that I did it to myself made me even more frightened to tell him the truth.

I shook my head back and forth as my eyes filled with tears. He pulled me into a warm embrace and held me tight. I cried on his shoulder, trying to figure how to tell him the truth. I had lied to him about so many things. I needed to be honest about this, even if he did end up thinking I was crazy.

I pulled away from our hug and looked at him. He reached up with his thumbs and wiped my tears away, kissing me softly on the forehead.

"It's okay, whatever it is. Just let me in, Jess. Let me help you," he said as he searched my eyes for answers.

"I did it," I said in a shameful whisper as I looked down at my fidgeting hands. I didn't want to see his face when I said the words.

He took both my hands in his and pulled them up to his mouth. He kissed each one tenderly before pulling me to him. I buried my face in the crook of his neck, hiding from the truth the best I could. He was going to think I was dirty, damaged, crazy, or worse—not good enough for him. He stroked my hair slowly and we were both quiet for a moment as he processed what I had said.

"Why, Jess? Why would you do that to your beautiful skin? Why would you hurt yourself like that? It doesn't make any sense. I want to understand, make me understand," he pleads.

But I couldn't make him understand. I barely under-

stood it myself. All I knew was that I needed it, wanted it, and the relief it gave me was necessary for me to function. But he'd never understand that.

"Do you still do it?" he asked.

"Yes, but not as much as I used to," I admitted quietly as I picked at the peeling paint on the side of the tower with my fingernail.

"Why is that?"

"Because of you. I don't need it as much anymore since you came into my life. Those girls stopped torturing me and it made things a little less miserable," I told him.

"Then why do it at all? I just don't get it. You're beautiful, strong-willed, funny, you have a huge heart, and when you smile it lights a room up." A sigh escapes his lips and I know he's having a hard time understanding what I'm trying to explain. "Why would you feel that hurting yourself was the answer to anything? You have me now; we have each other. You don't have to do that, Jess."

I'd felt so loved by him that morning, even more than I had the night before. The innocent sweetness that radiated off of him was palpable, and it wrapped me up in a warm blanket of security that I'd wanted to keep forever. I'd promised him that I would stop hurting myself, and he'd promised to never bring it up again unless I wanted to talk about it.

"I have to leave today, but Waco is only four hours away from here. I'm not going to be far at all. We'll figure this out, I promise. If you don't want to go to school up

there, maybe you can find a job and move closer," he said as he rubbed back and forth over the back of my hand with his thumb. "I can come home most weekends and all holidays until we decide how to work this. I want to be with you, Jess. I want you to be my girl. I know I've always said I didn't, but I was a dumbass that's now finally come to his senses," he said. Then he brushed a few strands of hair from my face and looked at me expectantly.

"Say something, Jess. You're making me nervous." He huffed out a laugh and waited.

I looked at him and, with all seriousness, told him I'd do whatever I could to make it possible for us to be together. I didn't know then what an empty promise I was making, but I meant it when I said it.

"I'll do whatever you want me to do. I can look for a job up there and we can see each other on the weekends like you said because I want to be with you too, Jace. So much it hurts. I want to be your girl more than I can say," I said, feeling hopeful, but incredibly vulnerable. We scratched a heart into the side of the water tower with one of his keys.

So sweet and so memorable.

He put his finger under my chin and tilted my head back up. Our gazes met and I could see myself in his eyes. I saw a place in him where I could belong, a place I could call home. Jace was home to me, my safe place.

No matter how much I tainted what we had back then, I've always carried what I saw in him that day with me.

"Jess, we're going to be okay. You're going to be my girl, and I'm going to be your guy, and we're going to be one of those high school couples that don't end up hating each other."

I smiled at him and he at me before we kissed. I want-

ed so badly to believe every word he'd said.

Looking back now, it stings to know how much he'd meant what he said. The sincerity in his voice was pure; it was everything that resembled who Jace was. Tears threaten to find their way into my eyes as the memories flood my mind in waves.

We drove away from the water tower and he stopped back at my house.

"Go inside and get your suit," he said

"Ummm...okay, but why?" I asked hesitantly.

"We're going back to my house for one more race. I can't leave knowing I couldn't beat you in freestyle." He winked at me with that flirty grin on his face.

"Or maybe I just want to see you in that swimsuit again. All this time I've had to restrain myself while we were in the pool, now I don't have to anymore," he said, wiggling his eyebrows up and down and sending a shiver through me. I wasn't used to Jace flirting with me, and I realized how much I was going to enjoy being more than just friends with him.

After stopping by my house so I could change into my swimsuit, we headed to his house for our showdown.

"Why aren't you in your suit yet?" I asked him when we arrived at his house, pulling my hair up into a quick ponytail.

"I'm going. I just wanted to be standing here when you came out of the pool house in that swimsuit," he said with a wicked grin on his face.

We stood on the pool deck and I walked up close to him, rising up onto my tippy toes like I was about to kiss him. Just as he closed his eyes to meet my lips, I shoved him into the water. He made a huge splash and resurfaced moments later with a shocked expression stretched across his handsome face. I slapped my hand over my mouth, trying to hold in the laughter, but I couldn't help it. The look on his face was priceless.

"Damn, Jess, what the hell was that for?" he said, trying his hardest to sound mad, but he wasn't.

"That's for the day you started then stopped kissing me in this pool. Now we are even," I said curtly.

He shook his head, getting the water out of his hair, and then ran his hands through it as he glared at me like a tiger on the prowl.

Shit!

"You know I'm wearing my brand new Nike's and my brand new Baylor shirt, woman. What am I going to wear to Waco now?" he asked in a very cool but calculated voice as he climbed out of the pool.

He took a few squishy footsteps in my direction and I took a few steps back.

"Jace, I'm sorry. Don't get me back, please," I said, sticking out my bottom lip and batting my eyelashes at him.

"That's not gonna work, Jess. You're so going to get it. If you weren't so damn beautiful I'd really make you pay for this." He laughed and pulled his wet shoes off one at a time, followed by two wet socks. He undid his jeans and peeled them off along with his wet shirt and dropped them all into one soggy pile. He was standing in only a pair of black boxers, hands on hips, staring at me like I

was a challenge he'd never lose. Suddenly, he charged at me and I squealed, running from him.

"No, Jace, no! I give! I surrender! I swear!" I yelled, running around the pool and laughing as my heart pounded in my chest.

"Nope. Jessica Alexander, you're going down!" he threatened as he closed the distance between us. He wrapped his arms around my waist and hoisted me up over one shoulder.

"You sure are a lightweight little thing." He smacked me playfully on the butt. "It'll make throwing you into that cold morning water so much easier, though." He threw me straight into the ice-cold pool.

I shrieked as I came up for air; goose bumps covered every inch of my body. He dove in right after me and I took off swimming to the other side. I turned under water once and glanced back, seeing that he was right on my tail. I felt him grab my foot and I knew he had me. I swung around under the water and we were face-to-face. He smiled, wide-eyed, and pulled me into him. He blew all of the air out of his lungs and kissed me square on the lips underwater. It was playful, it was sweet, and it was purely Jace.

He went to Waco later that day. It was the last time I ever saw him. Even though he'd wanted to come home on weekends, he ended up not being able to because of football practices. We talked every day on the phone and texted constantly. We even played around and tried to have phone sex, which always ended up being more of a comedy relief hour than anything else. Then we resorted to sexting with each other, which was equally comical. I remember the day that I was drinking a bottle of water when I got a sext message from him that made me literally spew water out my nose.

Jace: *When I see you next imma lick your hot sexy lady folds.*

All I could think to myself as I laughed my ass off was what the hell is a "hot sexy lady fold" and who even talks like that? I sexted him back with an equally hilarious comment.

Jess: *Well after you lick my hot sexy folds I will lick your hot rod of steel.*

My phone rang immediately and it was him. Laughter roared in my ear when I answered. "Rod of steel" became his new favorite way to reference his man parts after that.

The very next week was the week I lost Jace forever. I started feeling sick and was throwing up every morning. One particular morning was horrible, worse than any that came before that, and when he called he could tell something was wrong. He wanted to know if I was sick and I told him I thought I had a stomach virus. After a few seconds of silence, he asked me the question that had been lurking in the back of my mind since we'd been together.

"Jess, when you told me you were on birth control that night, you were, right? There's no chance you're pregnant, is there? Because it's morning and you're puking, and that's a scary combination."

I didn't answer him right away and he took that for my answer. "Jess, you are on birth control, right? Jess?

Please don't tell me you lied to me!"

Immediately I began sobbing into the phone. That confirmed his suspicion and he went off the deep end.

"Dammit, Jess! How could you? How could you lie about something like that? How could you make a decision like that for me?" he shouted and continued on through my hysterical sobs. "I'm eighteen years old; I'm on a college scholarship living in a dorm. How the hell am I supposed to be a dad right now? Shit, you don't even have that much. You're still living at home with your parents. I can't believe you could do something like this." He paused and all I could hear was his rapid breathing. He was pissed or hurt or both. I didn't blame him. What I did was beyond pathetic and sick. "You knew how much I wanted Baylor, how hard I worked to get this scholarship. Now I'm supposed to give it all away, because you lied to me! God, I can't even talk to you anymore right now. I'm too mad and I'm just going to say shit that I shouldn't." He stopped and went completely silent for what felt like forever before he sighed. "I don't want to be a scumbag to you. I'm angry and I just need to cool off before we talk more. You need to go take a pregnancy test today. Then call me back and let me know what the results are. We'll go from there. Bye, Jess, I love you." He said before he hung up on me.

That day, I cried until I had no more tears to cry. I wanted to cut, but I was too defeated to even do that. I did go get a pregnancy test; it was positive. When I called Jace back, I made a choice and lied again. The second lie that would change my life forever. I told him the test was negative and that I really did just have a stomach virus. He sat quietly for a while. I didn't speak anymore; I couldn't. Then he told me he needed some time to think, and we hung up. I did the only thing I thought I could do. I couldn't ruin his life. I couldn't be the reason everything he worked so hard for got taken away.

Pulling into the driveway at his parents' house was nerve-racking. My hands were shaking so hard I could barely drive there. His mom had never warmed up to me. Hell, I didn't even know if he had told her we were together as a couple or not. I walked up to the front door and pressed the doorbell with a trembling hand. Mrs. Collins opened the door and regarded me with disapproving eyes. My voice shakily found its way to my throat.

"I'm pregnant and Jace is the father," I blurted out. Her eyes grew wide and she stepped to the side of the entryway and motioned for me to come inside. She closed the door and walked toward the front formal sitting room.

"Why are you here telling me this, Ms. Alexander? Jace is obviously not here—I'm sure you already know this. So what brings you here to my doorstep to tell his mother this news?" she said in a cool tone, never wavering from her stoic persona. She stared at me like I was a dirty piece of trash that needed to be discarded with yesterday's garbage. She crossed her legs and straightened out her expensive skirt as I gathered my thoughts.

"Mrs. Collins, I know you don't like me much, but I'm here telling you this because I don't want this to ruin Jace's life. I'm only a few weeks along, but I don't have the means to take care of this by myself. I'm asking for

your help." Deep down I wished she'd talk me out of it, tell me it would all be okay.

I was trying to keep from breaking down right there in front of the ice-cold woman who never showed one ounce of compassion for me, or for what I was asking her for. She simply got up and walked across her pristine hardwood floor—her fancy heels clacked with every step—and reached inside her purse. She pulled out her checkbook and a pen and started writing. When she was done, she turned to me and held out a single check.

"This is enough money to keep you from ruining my son's bright future and then some. I'll give you this money gladly if you promise to never see my son again." The check felt heavy. It equaled the deletion of everything that connected me to Jace. "You're right, Ms. Alexander, I don't like you. My Jace is too good for the likes of you. I never understood his fascination with you or why he spent so much time with you. So take this money and I never want to see you here on my property ever again. You will not speak of this to anyone else and Jace is to know nothing about it. You say whatever you need to say to make him think you are serious about not seeing him anymore." She motioned toward the door. Silently, with the check in hand I walked out of Jace's house and life forever.

I went to Dallas that week and terminated the pregnancy. I spent the night in a hotel and drove back the next day. I lied to my parents and told them I was going to see Jace and tour the college. When I got back home I got into my bed and slept for hours, clasping my stomach, feeling hollow and overcome with grief for what I had done. That night was the night Jace finally called me after days of nothing from him. I answered, only knowing that what I had to say to him was going to break the last bone in my emotional body.

"Hey," he said tentatively.

"Hi, Jace."

"Are you feeling any better?" he asked.

"I'm fine," I said, lying to him yet again.

I heard him breathe out a sigh before he said, "Jess, I'm still really upset with you for what you did and I don't know if I'll ever be able to trust you again. That was all kinds of wrong that you lied about that. I care about you a lot and I can't imagine not having you in my life, but damn, this is a big deal. I don't know how to process this kind of thing. I'm not saying I can't get past it, but I'm saying I need some time. I just can't say how I really feel about this. I just need more time to decide what I want. I don't want to lose you, but I need to be able to trust you."

"Jace," I started, but my tongue and my tears were working against me. I had to get ahold of myself if I was going to get through this and make him believe me. I took a deep breath, willed my throat to remain open so I could get this out, and steeled myself against the agony of losing him, which was already threatening to consume me. "You don't have to take time to decide. I can't see you anymore. We can't be together. I'm no good for you and what I did was unforgivable." I bit my lip hard to stop myself from sobbing into the receiver.

Silence answered me and I blundered on, saying what I had always wanted to say to him. "I love you, Jace Collins. I always will." Then I hung up the phone before he could say another word.

That's the day I tried to commit suicide. I remember

the details vividly.

I locked my bedroom door and pulled my box from my nightstand. I contemplated writing a note, but decided against it. No one would care. In fact, some would be happy to hear I had done it. I pulled the razor blade from the box, clear on my intent, even though the finality of what I was about to do never quite penetrated my reality. I just had a million emotions running through me and I wanted all of it to go away. The loss of Jace, the loss of the unborn baby I was carrying, and an unbearable sense of loneliness plagued my thoughts. I just needed it to stop. All of it. I wanted out. I sat on the edge of my bed and took a deep breath. Tears rolled down my face as I put the blade to my wrist. Just before I pushed down, someone knocked on my window, scaring the shit out of me. I nearly jumped out of my damn skin. I dropped the razor blade to the floor and went to the window. I looked out and there was the little girl from next door again. I hadn't seen her since that day when she gave me the snowflake. She motioned upward with her thumb for me to raise the window. I unlatched it and pushed it open.

"What are you doing here, Vivvie? Is everything okay?"

"Why are you crying, Jessica?" she asked.

I wiped the wetness off my face quickly and shook my head. "No reason. This just isn't a really good time for me to talk, Vivvie."

"Why were you going to cut yourself?"

I gaped at her, thinking she had been watching me through my window.

"Vivvie, sweetie, I wasn't. It's okay. I'm okay."

"Do you have your snowflake?" she asked.

"Uh, yes, somewhere. Do you need it back?"

"No, but I think you really need it right now. You're sad again. Really sad. Why are you so sad again?" Her big eyes searched me, full of concern.

"Vivvie, I can't talk about this right now. Thank you for coming by, but I just can't talk right now. Okay?"

"Okay." She dropped her head in defeat. I felt awful.

"I'm sorry, Vivvie," I told her.

"It's all right. Can you talk tomorrow?"

On any other day her question would've had an easy answer. On that day, I had planned for there to be no tomorrow. But she looked at me with such sincerity that I couldn't say no.

"Sure," I said. A huge smile stretched across her little face and I had the strangest sense of obligation to follow through with what I'd agreed to. That next day, we sat on the swings and she told me stories about her pet pig, school, and her favorite songs. She stopped by every day, if only just to say hi. Sometimes when I look back, I think little Vivvie may very well have saved my life that fateful day.

For days, Jace had called and texted me, but I never answered or replied. After a couple of weeks, he called maybe once a week. Then, after a month, I never heard from him again. Suicidal thoughts lingered, but never did I get back to such an emotionally charged place that I thought to make that decision again.

I got a job in Dallas as a waitress and a tiny studio apartment. Though I didn't want to leave without telling Vivvie good-bye, no one was home when I went to her house. I left a note on their door for her. I hope she got it. I think of her often and still have the snowflake she gave me. I canceled my cell phone service and got a new phone and number to ensure that Jace was never able to reach me again. I spent months in seclusion outside of work. I cut every single day and started drinking. When I'd get off work, I'd head to my favorite spot and the bartender, would slip me shots. Then I'd drive home buzzed out of my mind. With the help of the alcohol, I started being more social and fell back into my old ways. My customers and others at the many different bars I worked at hit on me all the time, and I took many of them up on their offers. I had been fired multiple times by different employers. Meaningless sex had planted itself firmly back into my life. One night recently, after leaving some guy's place, I'd gotten behind the wheel drunk again. I swerved off the road and hit the embankment, hitting my head really hard and bruising my ribs badly. I was knocked unconscious and someone called the accident in. An ambulance transported me to the hospital and during my medical examination the doctors saw the extent of my self-harming. Eventually, I had to face the drunken driving charges, but was sentenced to mental health and alcohol abuse therapy instead of jail. I also paid a hefty fine and had my driver's license suspended. I had hit an all-time low in my life. The person I had become was not someone I ever wanted to be. I didn't call my parents. Oddly enough, I called my brother, Jeff. He was working as an attorney at a small firm here in Dallas and he's the one who represented my case. We'd never been close, but he did what he needed to do to help me.

"Jessica, the judge will not be easy on you if you don't go to all of the appointments he's ordered you to attend. Please keep that in mind," Jeff told me, letting me know I needed to take this seriously.

"I will, I promise. Thank you again for helping me. I really appreciate it," I told him as he left.

Sitting here in this mental health clinic, I know when I go in there to talk to the doctor I'm going to be expected to spill my guts and tell all of my deepest, darkest secrets to some stranger with a bunch of papers framed on the wall saying that they know how I feel. The idea that someone could ever understand how I feel is so foreign to me that I don't even hope that therapy will give me a resolution to my problems. I just hope for a little peace, one step at a time. This can't be as horrible as I'm envisioning it to be. At least I hope it isn't.

"The past is never dead."
—William Faulkner

Jessica

I'M PRACTICALLY READY to bolt out of this whack job place if they don't call my name soon. I've bitten my nails down to nubs and have aimlessly flipped through stupid gossip magazines 'til I'm blue in the face.

Can we just get this show, which is my fucked-up head, on the road?

Just as I'm feeling my frustration boil, I hear my name.

"Ms. Jessica Alexander, please." A stout woman holding a file folder says from the now open door, which I thought probably led to some mental case dungeon of some sort.

"Hi, I'm Veronica, Dr. Ward's intake assistant. We have quite a bit of paperwork for you to fill out. Then Dr. Ward will be in to see you," she tells me as she passes me a clipboard full of forms.

While filling out page after page of personal information, medical background stuff, and many extremely personal questions, such as how many sexual partners have I had, I'm more than over this damn paperwork. To be honest, I have no idea how many sexual partners there have been in my life. All I know is the number is high. I guess with a ballpark figure and leave it at that. Next, it asks if I've ever been pregnant. There are options to fill in the dates you gave birth, or a section to say if the pregnancy was terminated or if you miscarried. Filling this out is painful for me, to say the least. I turn the page to the next form, and it's a questionnaire with multiple choices ranging from strongly agree to strongly disagree with all the other variations in between. I scan over it briefly and blink, looking more closely at each question. The questions have an uncanny resemblance to all of my problems. It's like a Jessica test.

How odd is that?

I read through the questions and statements once more before filling in my answers. I answer strongly agree to all of them with the exception of number seven, seeing as how I don't really have career goals to start with. I've had so many jobs over the years, all of them waitressing, but I either get fired or quit because I can't get along with my boss or fellow employees. Whatever this test is for, it seems very clear that it's practically made for me. The fact that there's a questionnaire like this out there suddenly makes me feel like it's possible that I'm not the only person to have all of these problems. I hope this means there's an explanation, or, better yet, a solution.

"Ms. Alexander, Dr. Ward is ready for you now.

Please just give her the paperwork when she comes in. Follow me," Veronica says before heading out of the room.

"Sure. Thanks," I reply.

I follow her up and around the corner into a large office. I expected to see the typical shrink sofa thing, but there isn't one. There are two large soft sage-green wingback chairs with dark wood end tables beside each of them. A glass-top table sits off to the side with bottled water and a Keurig on it. The walls are neutral and adorned with elegant abstract paintings all in soft colors. The room has a relaxing feel to it, which is a good thing, I suppose. There's a huge mahogany desk with all of the typical desk accessories sitting on it, along with a computer. Behind the desk is a wall-to-wall bookshelf full of different, very organized, books and what looks like awards and certificates in frames. I sit down in one of the big chairs and nervously fiddle with my pen, clicking it open and shut over and over again. I hear the door open and a woman with dark hair walks in. She doesn't look to be too much older than me, and she's classically beautiful. Her slate-gray dress suit hugs her slender body perfectly, which comes just above her knees, revealing long, toned legs. She has on solid black heels and her hair is pulled over into a low side ponytail that swoops down just below her shoulder. She has dark brown eyes and tan skin. Her makeup is perfect and not a single hair is out of place.

"Hello, Ms. Alexander. I'm Dr. Ward," she says as she extends her hand out to me.

We shake hands briefly and I give her the paperwork. She sits down behind her desk and flips through the file, scanning through each page momentarily. She places the file down and reaches in her desk to pull out what looks like a recording device of some sort.

"Ms. Alexander, I prefer to record my sessions rather than taking written notes because I like to look at my patients when they talk to me. If you're comfortable with that, I will start the recorder now. Is that something you are okay with? You'll be assigned a patient number on the recording in order to keep your identity private."

I guess I don't see anything wrong with that. If I have to sit here and talk about all of my shit, I'd like for the person to at least look at me when I'm talking. Otherwise, it will feel like they aren't really listening to me at all.

"I guess, yeah, that's fine," I say in a low tone.

My first session was, more or less, okay, I suppose. It could have gone worse, so I don't want to dwell on it even though I know I will. Dr. Ward was nice enough and seemed to know what she was doing. The fact that she gave me a diagnosis so quickly after just reading over my paperwork and talking to me surprised the hell out of me.

"I can almost come to the conclusion just from your questionnaire that you suffer from borderline personality disorder or BPD. Looking at your answers, you meet all of the criteria for BPD. This is a very prevalent disorder affecting millions of American adults. BPD is even more prevalent than bipolar and schizophrenia. People with borderline personality disorder see people as all good or all bad and have extreme, blink-of-an-eye mood swings. Their fear of abandonment, combined with feelings of emptiness and self-loathing, makes others feel like they're constantly walking on eggshells around them. A person suffers while living with BPD and causes most all of those around them to suffer as well."

Every damn thing she said describes me, all of it. How could I have lived twenty-four years of life, most of it being hell, and never known this? I've never heard of this BPD stuff, ever. Bipolar? Sure. Depression? Yeah. But borderline personality disorder? No, never once have I heard of it. Why? What causes it? And how did I get cursed with this miserable shit?

After hearing more, I learned that even though there are a few medications that can alleviate some of the symptoms, such as depression and anxiety, BPD cannot be fixed with a pill. The most effective treatment is dialectical behavior therapy. The treatment consists of once-a-week individual psychotherapy by an intensively trained DBT therapist, a two-and-a-half-hour skills training session conducted in a group setting weekly, and substantial homework assignments. It's very extensive and requires a lot of determination and dedication on the part of the patient—like I really wanted to be back doing homework again.

Now I have to go through some freaking shrink process that will take forever. Why can't there be a fix-it pill for this like there is for so many other things? This sucks. I guess that place will be my second home between group therapy, individual therapy, and now this DBT shit. At this rate, I might as well just commit myself to a mental ward.

"Jessica, you can do this. Many people who suffer from borderline personality disorder lead very healthy and productive lives after successfully completing treatment. You're young and have a lot of life left to live. You've lived for years in a type of darkness; this is your chance to come out of that. You can claim this life and make it your own. The decision is yours. You may always feel like you have no control, but I assure you that right now you hold all the control in your hands. But you have to really want it for yourself. I can set you up with our DBT therapist and she can start seeing you right away. But, like I said, it's your choice. Our self-harm group meets tomorrow. I strongly suggest you attend."

This is all so overwhelming and confusing. I never expected any of this when I went there. I envisioned lying on a couch, spilling my guts to some pretentious shrink, getting a prescription for some happy pills, and being sent on my way. All of this stuff is deep, heavy shit. Before leaving her office, she gave me a lot to consider.

"Jessica, please think about this. Give yourself a chance to explore the possibilities that are out there for you to heal. You can have anything in this world that you want if you want it badly enough. I'm offering you the resources to do that, all you have to do is take them."

I ponder over her words again as I drop my face into my hands, feeling years of pain and self-doubt, years of questions and blame wash over me. Jace's face flashes in my mind and his words echo like drums of hope within me, vibrating off of every nerve ending in my body.

"I see you. You need to see you too. If you look deep enough, you will see a beautiful, strong girl that has the world at her fingertips."

I remember his words so perfectly.

I lie on my bed drinking a glass of 151 and feel the urge to cut so bad, but I know I have to try to will it away. I finally have answers, the puzzle pieces are finally coming together, and there's a solution, regardless of the effort that I have to put into it. There's something out there that can really help me. All I have to do is take it and do the work to get better. Thoughts of Jace are racing through my head. The pain of missing him never gets easier; it's as acute as it was the day I said good-bye to him forever. If this treatment can help me to finally get over him, get over the past and what I did to our baby, then maybe it's worth it. I need to learn how to let him go. I need to learn how to forgive myself. It's been six years and it's time to stop missing him, wanting him, and wondering where he is and if he's happy. Still, I always hold on to hope that we'll find each other again someday. It's an empty hope, I know, but it's always there.

I run my hand over the bumps on my abdomen and wonder if it's possible for scars on the inside to be worse than scars on the outside. I reach for my journal and decide to write for a while. I'm fighting the urge for a different kind of release, which I know I'll soon give into, regardless of my newfound diagnosis. I put pen to paper and write, thinking of Jace.

Distance

Now my only friend

Looking back

Memories of the end

Imprinted on my heart
Footprints you left
Tears
Sadness
Emptiness
Full of regret
Eyes shut
Eyes wide open
I still see you there
I'm still hoping...

I drop my journal down on my nightstand and go for another glass of Bacardi 151, knowing full well that after my accident I shouldn't ever drink again. But it's been a really rough day for me. I need to relax and wind down.

I think about calling Donnie from the bar whom I've seen a handful of times, but he's getting attached and, for once, I'm not. He's great for a good time, but for some odd reason I've never clung to him like I do most guys. I've told many guys that I loved them over the past years knowing it wasn't real, but I just wanted to feel loved, hear the words. Granted, no guy has ever affected me like Jace, not once over the past six years.

Not being a bullied teen anymore has caused me to be

more forward, more outgoing, and less apt to shy away from things. I've met a lot of great guys, but usually scared them off in one way or another. One guy saw my scars and freaked out on me. That was the last I ever saw of him. Strange thing is, most guys haven't really cared about them or even asked about them, which only reaffirms that they were only after one thing. Ryan was the only guy that came close to giving me the warm fuzzies, but I ruined that too. He said I called him too much, and that I was moving way too fast for him. He was a small business owner and had a really good head on his shoulders. I laugh thinking about how forward I'd been with him and some of the others. It wouldn't be good for me to see Elizabeth Brant these days. I'm a grown woman who is no longer the scared little teenager I used to be. Sure, I have my shitty issues and still feel all sorts of fucked-up inside, but so many years of building walls has caused me to harden—not to mention the liquid courage that fuels my mouth so often.

I hear the doorbell and wonder who the hell that could be before padding across the cold floor to the door.

Donnie knows better than to come by without calling, and no one else comes here, ever. My brother has only been here once and my parents never visit me. A bit buzzed and unconcerned by the fact that I'm wearing only a little white pair of boy shorts and a cami tank top with no bra, I swing open the door, thinking that whoever's there is about to get a nice show.

I gasp, dropping my drink to the floor, shattering glass everywhere. My eyes must be playing tricks on me. The alcohol has finally altered my sense of reality. That has to be it. This can't be real. After six years, I stand face-to-face with Jace Collins.

My throat starts to close up instantly. It's as if the oxygen in the room was sucked out with the opening of my front door. My eyes wide, I scan him up and down in pure shock and awe. He is Jace, but he isn't Jace all at the same time. He's still beautiful, but he's so much more than that now. Jace is very much a man. Before breathing or speaking or acknowledging him in any way, other than dropping my glass, I just stand there in pure astonishment.

"Hi, Jess," he says. His voice is deeper than I remember. Smooth, sexy, kind of husky. The deepest male voice I've ever heard in my life.

My mouth moves, but words don't form. My heart's crashing into my ribcage and my legs are weak.

"You look like you've seen a ghost. Aren't you going to invite an old friend in?" The word friend rolls off his tongue with what sounds like a hint of anger.

Every damn syllable slaps me right in the face. But something's wrong, very wrong. He has a dark, hardened look in his beautiful blue eyes. His face is stern and he seems tense.

I nod, still in a state of shock, before finally finding my voice.

"Ummm, Jace what are you... I mean, how did you? Why are you...here?" I manage to stammer out, my voice cracking as I fumble my words.

I look over at the clock—it's after ten o'clock. I have so many questions rolling through my head right now; it's a whirlwind up there.

Why is he here? And how did he find me?

Those are the two I want answered first.

He points to the shattered glass on the floor and says,

"Are you going to clean that up? It could be dangerous." His tone is stoic. I know things ended badly, but after six years I would think he'd be over it already.

"Umm, yeah... Come in. Just let me get the dustpan and a kitchen towel," I say, nervously averting my eyes from his penetrating stare.

He steps over the mess and walks into my apartment.

Jace is in my apartment.

I want to pinch myself to make sure I'm not in some alcohol-induced daydream. He's wearing the most intoxicating cologne, which follows me as I head to my kitchen in a daze. I inhale surreptitiously and sneak a peek at him as he's looking around. He's wearing snug-fitting jeans with an untucked black button down, sleeves rolled halfway up his arms—the same way he did in high school. I want to reach out and touch him just to be sure he's real.

He's holding a folder in his hands, and his grip is white-knuckled, fierce. My eyes dart back and forth between him and the mess I'm cleaning. With shaky hands, I finish up as fast as I can and return to the kitchen to wash up. He follows my every move with his eyes. I feel like that shy, bullied teenager all over again, but then I snap to reality and realize that, in fact, I'm not that timid girl anymore. Still all jacked-up in my mind, yes, but not as weak on the outside.

"What are you doing here, Jace? It's ten o'clock at night and we haven't seen each other—" He cuts me off mid-sentence.

"In six years. Yes, Jessica, I'm exceedingly aware of how long it's been since you hung up on me and never returned a single call or text." His jaw clenches and I'm one hundred percent sure that he hasn't let go of what happened. “I distinctly remember coming home and knocking on your door, only to find out you were gone and had given your parents specific instructions not to give out your address.” He steps in closer to me and I freeze. “I’m also aware that you turned off your phone and deleted your Facebook account and anything else that I might’ve been able to use to get in contact with you. So, I certainly don’t need you to tell me how long it has been.” He inches closer and closer to me with every word until he’s nearly in my face. I look up into those bright blue eyes, which I’ve seen over and over again in my dreams, and even though it’s Jace, he looks like a stranger to me. My eyes move down to his lips, lips that I have imagined on my body many times. Now, those images replay through my mind, juxtaposed to the real man standing before me. His dirty-blond hair looks like he’s been running his hands through it all day. It’s shorter than what I remember.

I take one step back, putting some distance between us because I’m becoming increasingly aware that he’s not happy to see me. It hurts, but it pisses me off too. Caught in a mixture of emotions, we stand here in an uncomfortable silence. He’s much taller than me, so I have to angle my head to look up at him.

“I think you owe me an explanation, Jess. Why did you do it? Why did you end it when it was barely getting started?”

I start to sidestep him because he’s making me uneasy with the harsh tone he’s using. His hand comes down on the arm of my sofa like a barricade stopping me in my tracks.

“You’re not running away this time. I deserve a hell of a lot more than that from you. So, tell me.” Lowering his voice to an alarmingly quiet whisper, he says, "Tell me, Jess. Tell me why you ran."

I flinch as chills spread over my body in reaction to his breath on my ear. Tears build in my eyes and I blink furiously trying to hold them back. He holds up the hand holding the folder and slaps it down on my coffee table causing papers to fan out across it.

"You know what, don't bother. I just wanted to hear you say it, but you're obviously going to continue your lies and secrecy. I guess some habits die hard," he says with a sneer. I've never seen disgust on Jace's face, but I do now.

My eyes move from his angry ones down to the folder, and the color slowly drains from my face. I can feel his stare boring a hole through me as my mind processes what I'm seeing—all of my paperwork from the therapy session. My name is on the tab of the folder and it has everything in it that I filled out earlier this morning.

How in the hell does he have my file?

"A past left without resolution is surely a past that will revisit you one day."
—Kathryn Perez

Jessica

"I DON'T KNOW how you have my file, but I'm pretty damn sure that's fucking illegal," I say, my eyes never leaving the papers spread across my coffee table. All of my deepest, darkest truths and lies are on display, staring back at me, mocking me.

He knows...

Jace knows about the pregnancy and that's why he's here. I always hoped we would find each other again, but now I wish for the opposite. The disgust I saw moments ago has faded, only to be replaced with a pained expression that breaks my heart. The hurt circling in his eyes makes me want to reach out and hug him like he used to do for me when I was hurting.

"I don't think how I have the folder is the issue right

now. The issue is what's inside it," he growls, reaching down and pulling one of the forms out. "This," he says, holding it up to me, "is the issue! This, Jess, is a really huge issue because if I'm reading this correctly you were pregnant six goddamn years ago!"

My face drops into my hands as the horrible reality of what I did resurfaces and crashes down around me. Right now, it feels like all I've been doing is living a rented life, never owning my choices, or the consequences of them.

"Jessica, please tell me that you didn't lie to me about being pregnant with our baby. Tell me that you didn't abort our child," he shouts with desperate eyes.

I drop down onto the sofa and look up at him. My face is streaked with tears and my chin is quivering as I try to form some semblance of words.

"Jace, I'm so sorry. So sorry. I never wanted to hurt you. You were never supposed to know," I whisper, because I hate admitting any of this out loud.

A cloud of shame hangs over me and I can't even look at him another minute. He balls up the paper furiously and throws it across the room. My heart is breaking all over again as my past surges up, surrounding me, choking me.

"No. No. No. This can't be true."

Tears form at the corners of his angry blue eyes. He runs his hand furiously through his hair and turns his back to me as he drops his head. He stares at the floor for a moment, and then places his hands on his hips. He starts pacing back and forth in my small living room while I just sit there in horror, watching him try to keep himself together. He stops and looks me dead in the eyes.

"I fucking loved you. When everything and everyone told me not to, I fell in love with you anyway," he growls.

"I did everything in my power to stop feeling anything more than friendship with you. I did that because I knew how fragile you were; I just wanted to be a friend. Someone you could lean on, count on, someone like Genevieve never had," he says, shaking his head back and forth. "Relationships are messy; they can change people for the worse. I didn't want that for you, for us. But I did it anyway. When I saw the pain in your eyes the day you caught me in the pool, I knew it was all wrong." He looks right at me and the agony on his face is killing me. "I liked her, but she wasn't you. She couldn't make me laugh the way you could, she hated my music, and she didn't have my secrets. You, Jess, you had my secrets. I gave them to you and I knew that day I should've given you everything else too." He pauses, taking a deep breath, and I can see the soul-crushing torment of the loss in his eyes.

My heart's racing and my stomach is in knots. I feel nauseated and the alcohol-induced bravery I was feeling has ebbed away. I did this to him, to us. One lie on the night that he finally gave all of himself to me led to another lie on the phone that fateful day, which led us here tonight. I'm a terrible, awful person and tonight I see it more clearly than I ever have before. Tears and regret can never fix what I've done to this beautiful, compassionate man that loved me when no one else did.

"I came to you, Jess. I came to you that night ready to give you more than my secrets. I sat at that damn party where everyone was telling me good luck and how I was starting my life for the first time. I sat there and all I could think about was you and how I wanted you there too. I wanted to start my new life with you. The more I drank, the more I fell into a shit storm of thoughts and possibilities, all involving you." He continues to pace back and forth anxiously. "I told myself I couldn't leave the next morning without coming to see you. I needed you to see that I wanted you as much as you wanted me. When we were together that night, yes, I had been drinking, but dammit all to hell if I didn't sober up the minute I had you in my bedroom. I knew you had been with plenty of guys, but that night...that night you looked more innocent and untouched than any girl I'd ever known. I knew no one had ever made love to you. That was just for us: me and you." His words drag me back to that night and the reality of what I had with him slaps me across the face. "You were beautifully flawed, but perfect to me. I've relived that night in my head a thousand times. I was so mad at you when I found out you lied about the birth control. I was furious because you lied to me during something so special, something that shouldn't have been tainted. That night was everything that represented the good and the beauty of what we finally found with each other and you ruined it," he says, dropping down onto my recliner directly across from me.

My mind can't process all of his confessions fast enough. Every word he says crushes me inch by inch. He's right, though—I ruined it. I ruined everything. Jace loved me and I threw it all away. Now he knows the worst of me, and he'll probably hate me for the rest of his life. I don't know what to say to him—no words can make this better. So, for once, I just say the truth.

"I'm sorry. I loved you too. I still do." Tears spill down my cheeks and I stare into my lap. The pain on his face is too much to bear.

"I think your version and my version of love are two

very different things, Jessica."

I glance up at him and he has his elbows resting on his knees, his hands clasped together, and a lost look on his face. Regardless of the heavy moment we're having, I still need to know how he got my file folder and found me. That has to be addressed.

"How did you get that file, Jace? I need to know," I ask him point-blank.

"Where is he?" he asks, ignoring my question.

He? He who? Who the hell is he talking about?

"What are you talking about? He who?"

"Your husband. Is he out? Working? What?" I look at him, clearly dumbfounded.

Me, married? That's a joke if I've ever heard one.

"I'm not, nor have I ever been married to anyone. I don't even have a boyfriend. What the hell are you talking about?" He looks at me confused, stunned. He rubs the tops of his thighs with his big hands and rocks back and forth once before standing up.

"Yes, you were engaged. One month after looking for you myself, I had my mother hire a private investigator to find you." His eyes search mine for answers. "The report she gave me said you were living somewhere in Dallas with a guy, that you were engaged to be married. There were even pictures of you in a bar smiling and drinking, having a good time with him, like we never even mattered." He drags his hand through his hair like he always has. "After that day I never looked for you again. I lost myself in sports and classes. I didn't date for a very long time after you." The sigh that he releases shows just how exhausting this is for him to recall. "I was shut off emotionally and dove into learning everything I could about the human mind—what makes it work and what causes it to break. I kept telling myself if I could help other people that were broken inside like you, that maybe it would make up for everything. That's when I met Victoria," he says, placing both of his hands behind his head. He looks up at the ceiling like the words he's searching for are written on it.

Victoria? Who the hell is Victoria?

Jealously instantly boils inside me, even though I have no right to it.

"Dr. Victoria Ward. She's my fiancé," he says, answering my unspoken question. And my world implodes all at once. My stomach rolls and I think I'm going to throw up. I shoot up off the sofa and run to the bathroom, slamming the door shut behind me and locking it with trembling hands. I drop down in front of the toilet, feeling bile rise in my throat. My eyes are so blurred from tears that everything around me looks hazy. The walls start to spin and my body starts to shake. I grip my arms, hugging myself and digging my fingernails in hard. I squeeze my eyes shut just as I hear a knock at the door.

"Go away. Please, just go. Leave me alone. You got what you came here for. I killed our baby and now you know what a mental case I really am, courtesy of your fiancé. So just leave me the hell alone!" I sob, screaming at him through the door.

"Just open the door, Jess." Anger rises up in me like a raging fire.

"Don't call me Jess. Don't call me that ever again! I hate you, Jace Collins. Just go away and stay out of my life. Go marry your shrink doctor and have a happy, mentally stable life. You don't need anything else from me;

there are no more answers for you here," I say, pulling my knees to my chest. He doesn't reply and I can hear his footsteps walking away. I sit there, waiting to hear the front door shut, but I never do.

What's he doing? Is he rummaging through my apartment? Digging for more ammunition against me?

I drop my head to my knees and squeeze my eyes shut. Thoughts and questions pillage my brain like a hurricane ripping through me.

He's engaged. To her.

He's engaged to a woman that knows every single one of my weaknesses. I try to push the thoughts away and squeeze my eyes tighter, as tight as I can. I grind my teeth and clench my jaw to keep the cries muffled, silent. I don't want him to hear me cry anymore. I know he's still here; I can feel his presence, but I'm not coming out of this bathroom, so he just needs to give up on the waiting game.

I can only focus on the pain shooting through my entire body, and the taste of blood in my mouth. Gentle hands roll me over, warm arms envelop me, and soft fingers brush the hair from my face. I breathe in intense warmth and the smell of peppermint. My eyes can't focus, but even in this foggy state the immense pressure of his gaze upon me is undeniable. My body wants to, but fails to respond to the embrace.

"Hey, open your eyes. Look at me, Jessica. I'm going to help you, okay? It's me, Jace," I hear him whisper as my mind starts to resurface from the depths of darkness. He pulls me up, supporting me when my knees slightly

buckle. "Come on, it's okay. I can carry you."

I feel his arms beneath my knees as he lifts me up into his strong hold. My head rests on his chest and I can't help but moan in pain from the pressure on my ribs. I force my eyes to open and look up at him staring down at me.

My swollen eyes open as I come out of my dream only to realize that it's only partly a dream. My ribs don't hurt and I'm not bloody this time, though there's more twisted blood and muck from years of depression and anxiety on the inside than there has ever been on the outside. Once again, I'm in Jace's arms and he is mending my wounds, but this time I think he's just as wounded as I am.

I tilt my head up just enough to take in his strong jawline and beautiful face. I can sense his reluctance to look down at me so I look away. He kicks open my bedroom door and leans down placing me on my bed. I notice the clock glaring at me from my nightstand, saying it's midnight. I expect him to turn away and leave, but he doesn't. Instead, he stands beside the bed close enough to make my heart skip a bit, but far enough to maintain the leagues between us. I have no idea how he got into my bathroom, but I guess I'm glad that he did.

"We need to talk about everything, Jess. I can't leave with things like this."

The look in his eyes matches his insistent tone.

His eyes are pleading with me.

"I feel like if I walk out that door, you'll be gone again and I can't have things left unsaid between us. Not this way—not again." He crouches down beside my bed and sits on the floor. His head falls back to rest on my blanket only inches from my thigh. I don't know what else there is to say. He knows it all now, except for the part his mother played in it. That bitch fabricated some story about me getting engaged. Just thinking about it makes me so mad; I want to drive back home and whip her Botoxed, high-heeled ass. Everything in me wants to scream out the truth about her, but she's still his mother. There's no reason to tell him what an evil bitch she really is. I've caused him enough heartache; I'm not going to add to it. He twists his head to the side, facing me, and I want to reach out and run my fingers through his soft hair. After all this time, he still takes my breath away.

"Why'd you do it, Jess? Why didn't you want our baby? Was it because of me, because of what I said on the phone that day about school and my future? Did you do it because of how awful I was to you that day? "He shoots the questions off one after the other and in them I hear his heartbreak, how he's beating himself up over a past that neither of us has the power to change. "I just don't understand how you could go through with it. I know I was such an asshole, but I swear I would've never abandoned you or our child. I loved you and I would've loved our baby too."

Every word he says wraps around my heart and squeezes it, ripping me apart. I don't know what answers to give him because the truth is I was scared of ruining his life. He was so angry with me and all I could think about was how I could fix what I did. But that doesn't make it his fault. I was the one who ultimately made the choice to do it, not him. The fault lies with me, no one else.

"It's not your fault. None of this is your fault. I made the decision. I did this."

"But why, Jess? I thought you loved me too. How could you do that? Why would you run away and never look back? How is that loving someone?" he asks, every word tearing off another layer of my resolve.

"I just don't know how to love someone, Jace, and I guess I don't know how to allow someone to love me. How can I when I don't even love myself? I hate the girl I was and the woman I've become. I'm sorry for everything, more than you'll ever know." The hard truth spills out of me, but I know that there's not a single word I can say to fix the broken pieces of our past. "I thought I loved you. I still go through every day loving you, but until I know what love really is I can't proclaim it to anyone. I know I got pushed into therapy, but this morning I finally got some insight as to why I am the way I am." I massage my temples and try to keep talking without crying. "For the first time ever, I finally allowed myself to hope for a better me. Now that can't happen because I'll never go back there again. Your girlfriend or fiancé or whatever—she knows all of my shit. Knowing you're hers, I'll never be able to get past that."

He turns his body toward the bed and rises up onto his knees. He's looking at me and the electricity that was always there between us has stalked us six years into the future.

"Jess, you have to stay in therapy. I know I shouldn't have, but I read your file. I could lose my job for all of this. To be honest, I can't believe I'm here."

He pinches the bridge of his nose and closes his eyes briefly.

"This is all so wrong. All of it," he mutters.

"Then go. Just go and live your life. Don't ruin your career over me."

His expression turns from pain to anger and he sits

up.

"Do you think I want any of this? You left me, Jess. You left me without a single word. Do you have any idea how you ripped my heart out? I spent day after day missing you. I fucking loved you, Jessica!"

This is all too much for me. I can't deal with it. Thinking about him being so hurt crushes me.

"I'm so sorry, Jace. I just wanted to do the best thing for you. A knocked-up girlfriend was not going to help your future."

He shakes his head and sighs.

"You shouldn't have made that assumption all on your own, Jess. I may have a hard time forgiving you for what you did, but after reading about your history, I can see how you came to the conclusion that you did—even though I disagree with your choice." His voice lowers and everything about him looks sad, defeated. He's so hurt and it's all my fault. "I knew you struggled with inner demons, but that's not all this is. You can't control this on your own. You have to get help. You can't stay at our clinic because of this obvious conflict of interest, but you have to find another therapist."

I stare at the ceiling and try to absorb all of the five million emotions dive-bombing my thoughts.

His phone buzzes, interrupting our conversation. He grabs it out of his pocket, looks at the screen, and frowns. It's her. I know it is, because if Jace was mine and it was after midnight, I'd be looking for him too. He pushes up off the floor and walks out of the room. I hear him say hello, but his voice fades away as he walks into the front of my apartment. He's only gone for a minute before he returns. He looks torn, like he needs to leave, but wants to stay.

"Just go home. Go home to your fiancé. I'll be fine." I say, sitting upright. I glance over at my nightstand and notice my journal lying there. Fear shoots through me as I think back to when I was writing earlier. I know I didn't leave it there. He already knows all of my mental shit; if he read that journal he knows every fear, every weakness, and every sliver of happiness I've ever felt. My soul is inside that journal. He follows my stare and immediately I know he read it. That's it! That's enough of him infiltrating my life tonight. I may have done something terrible and awful six years ago, but he has no damn right to read my medical files or my very personal thoughts. I reach out and grab the journal, but it isn't clasped shut so the pages fan out. A single wrinkled piece of paper floats to the ground. We simultaneously reach down for it; he gets to it before I do. I stand up, clutching my journal to my chest.

"You had no right, Jace Collins," I yell, poking him in the chest with my finger. "You had no right to read my medical file and you certainly had no right to read my personal journal! I want you out. Get out of my apartment right now. Get the hell out!"

He is cool and unfazed by my rant as he examines the piece of paper. He reaches down and flicks on the light on my nightstand, looking at the paper more closely.

"Is this what I think it is?" he asks as he squints at the old tattered receipt.

"Obviously you didn't hear me. Get. Out. Now," I scream, reaching out to grab the fragile piece of paper.

"You kept that old receipt even after you put my number in your phone? You kept it all this time?"

Yes, you asshole, I did. It was all I had left of you and

I couldn't bear to throw it away.

"Yeah, so what? Now get the hell out!" He fastens his eyes on me and my mouth automatically snaps shut, because it's a different look than he's given me all night. He's looking at me with the depth of more than six years of loss in his cerulean eyes. They look sad, but needy. For the first time since he got here, I feel the vulnerability of my exposed, barely dressed body. He rakes his eyes from my face all the way down to my feet and then back to my face again. He steps in closer and reaches out, but I recoil.

"Jess, it's me. You don't have to be afraid of me," he whispers. The way he's staring at me right now, he's nothing but a contradiction. He has a fiancé, yet he's looking at me like he wants to consume me in every way humanly possible. I've looked into his eyes so many times before, but tonight, right now, the Jace looking at me is the Jace that made love to me six years ago. I can feel the heat radiating off of his strong body and my heart is beating so hard it almost vibrates throughout the room.

His voice breaks through my memories, "I should leave. I should walk out that damn door and never look back, but... Fuck! I can't. I can't leave and walk away from you without..." He stops mid-sentence and reaches out, grasping my face between his hands. He crashes his lips onto mine. His tongue invades my mouth with a hunger like I've never felt before. His right hand slides down to the lowest point of my back and he pulls me into him. Our bodies mold together perfectly, like two long lost puzzle pieces. Walls that have been built sky-high crumble and begin to fall. I feel every fiber in my body going off like fireworks and every ounce of me feels nothing but love for this man, but I can't be sure that's what it really is.

I don't think I'm capable of it. He begins placing a trail of kisses from the corner of my mouth down my neck, and he slides his other hand down over my shoulder taking my cami strap down as he goes. Goose bumps fan over my body and I shiver. He backs me up to the bed as he licks and caresses my collarbone. I have no idea what we are doing or why, but I can't stop him. I want him, but what about her? He belongs to another woman. I fall back onto the bed and the weight of his body follows. For a moment, our eyes meet; his are glazed over with desire.

He's looking at me like I'm the only woman on earth. But clearly, I'm not.

"What about your fiancé?" I ask breathlessly. "You belong to another woman." I hate myself for reminding him. He leans down so close to my face that I can feel his warm, rapid breaths on my lips. His hand travels up my side, barely grazing the outer curve of my breast before finding my face. He gently takes hold of my chin and looks deeply into my eyes.

"I belong to you, Jess. My heart has belonged to you since I scooped you up off the ground over six years ago. That has never changed."

"In the end we only regret
the chances we didn't take."
—Anonymous

The Past

Jace

Six years earlier...

I TAKE ANOTHER drink of my beer and scan the room. All of these people are supposedly here for me, and I don't even know half of them. Mom always has to make everything so elaborate, and apparently if you're rich and high society your underage kids can drink—as long as it's expensive imported beer and fancy cocktails. This night is supposed to be exciting. I'm supposed to be psyched about going to Baylor tomorrow, but all I can think about is Jess. I hated seeing her so upset. Seeing that look on her face when she caught me in that damn pool with Brittney was awful. I don't know what I hate more—that she saw me or that I did that. I'm such an asshole! I can't think about leaving without seeing her, but I have no idea if she'll even let me talk to her. She was so damn pissed off and hurt. So I'm sitting here consuming as much liquid courage as possible so that I can take my sorry ass over to her house to apologize.

Of all the people that could wander into my line of sight as I sit here thinking about Jess, that prick Harrison has to catch my eye. He saunters toward my table and it's an effort for me to stay seated. I just want to get the hell out of this place. These people are not my friends. They're the people my mom wants me to have as friends.

"Hey, dude! So, Baylor huh? I bet you're stoked. Got any hot chicks lined up over there yet? I bet those college girls are mind-blowing in the sack," Harrison says, patting me on the shoulder. I just want to flick him off like a fly. He's such an arrogant fucktard.

"Harrison, not every guy goes to college to get a piece of ass, you know. Some of us actually want to go and play sports while getting an education." He laughs and pulls a chair out, spinning it around backward as he straddles it.

"Jace, bro, please don't tell me you're still running around with that slut Jessica Alexander? What's your deal over here all mopey and shit? I know it can't be because of her, dude, because she ain't worth it," he says. What a class A motherfucker this guy is. He has no problem screwing her behind his girl's back, but he thinks he's better than her.

"You know what, Harrison? You're a real son of a bitch." I push up out of my chair and look directly at him.

"You screwed her, right? Cheated on Hailey with her multiple times, from what I heard, and you think she's the worthless one?" He grins—the bastard grins. I want to bust him right in his smug face right now. "Did you ever fucking consider that she thought you were a nice guy, that you really liked her? You went into it knowing all you wanted was an easy piece of ass, so I'd say you're pretty fucking worthless yourself." I slam my drink down on the table and look back to him, trying to contain the urge I feel to whoop his ass for what he did to her. "What you did that night, or, should I say, what you didn't do when those bitches beat Jess up makes you even more of a piece of shit than you already were. So don't come over here talking about someone you know nothing about, acting like we're bros. My mom invited you to this charade, not me, so go blow smoke up someone else's ass, Harrison, and save me the condescending bullshit already." I turn and walk away before he can respond, because if he says one wrong word I know I won't be able to control this anger I'm feeling. I head over to the bar for another drink when I see Elizabeth.

Somebody please shoot me now and put me out of my misery.

She sashays over to me in her tiny, barely there yellow dress with her blond hair tumbling down her bare shoulders. She's holding a martini glass, looking like a perfect future candidate for one of those housewife reality shows. What I ever saw in this girl, I'll never know.

"What's up? You look real nice this evening, Jace. Are you here with your good pal Jessica? I don't see her skulking around here anywhere. You still playing the knight in shining armor to the county whore or not? She must be real good in bed for you to keep her around for so long, Jacey," she says as she sips her drink and bats her long, fake eyelashes at me. I roll my eyes and try to hold in all the things I'd really like to say to her. She may be a complete and total bitch, but making a scene isn't worth it. She's baiting me and I know it. I lean in really close so only she can hear me.

"Elizabeth, let me say this once and only once. I don't need to sleep with Jess to know how good she is because she's a genuinely good person. Funny thing is I did sleep with you and all I learned in the end was what a horrible, callous person you really are on the inside." Her smile fades, replaced by a pissed off frown. "So keep calling Jess all the vile things you want, but you might want to take a look in the mirror, for purposes other than checking your lipstick, before you start throwing stones," I hiss. Her eyes widen and her jaw drops as she glares at me.

"Thanks for coming, Elizabeth. It's always such a pleasure," I joke before giving her a chance to say anything. I leave her standing there stunned as I make my way through the crowd.

These people are so self-righteous. Harrison and Liz think they're so much better than Jess. They just don't know the girl I know. She's got a shady past, but, for some reason, I don't care. The time I've spent with her has shown me so much more than I ever thought I knew about her. She comes off as this broken girl, but when it's just her and me she's different. I'll never forget the way she first dove into my pool with an air of confidence like no other. Then she smoked my ass in a freestyle race, like it was a piece of cake. When I beat her in the butterfly stroke, she was immediately ready to go again so she could try to beat me.

"Jace, get your butterflying butt back here. We are doing this again. That was beginner's luck. I'm a little rusty on my butterfly, but you are totally not winning again," I remember her telling me. She stood on the side of the pool, her hand on her hip with an eyebrow arched, looking at me with a flirty grin on her face. She never did beat me, but she damn well tried.

She's also hilarious and all of her funny shirts make me laugh. Even though she's been with half the guys I know, when she's with me, she seems so innocent and shy. I hate that she thinks I've never looked at her as more than friends. If she only knew how many times I've checked out her ass in those tiny little board shorts she likes to wear, or how many times I've breathed in the shampoo smell of her hair when we played basketball. The way her hair falls down all messily in her face is beautiful, and she has the best smile I've ever seen. No one at school ever got to see that smile. She loves my taste in music and even though I know she doesn't really care for football, I love that she tried to get into it for my sake. Liz hated football and bitched constantly when I watched it.

"Did you see that? That ref was totally wrong—that was definitely an illegal chop block!" Jess said one day when we were watching a game in my living room. I nearly spit out my soda when she made that comment. I looked over at her with raised eyebrows and she just shrugged her shoulders saying, "What? You know it was!" I just laughed. She always makes me laugh.

I love how she's naturally beautiful and I like how she doesn't cake makeup on her face the way other girls do. It's refreshing, and being with her is too. I just hope I haven't ruined things with her for good. I pull my cell phone out of my pocket and contemplate calling her, but, more than likely, she won't answer. I shove it back in my pocket and suck down the rest of my beer. I scan the crowd for Mom, but I don't see her anywhere. I decide to text her and let her know I'm tired and headed home. I fumble for the keys in my pocket and shuffle out the back doors to the parking lot. I know I've had too much to drink and shouldn't get in the truck, but I want to see her. I know she won't take my calls, so I'm going over there to make her hear me out. I want her to know how I really feel—no more of this "just friends" thing anymore. She needs to know what she means to me before I leave, and if she'll let me, I'll show her exactly how much I want her.

Driving over to Jess's house, a ton of things are rolling through my head. I'm pretty pissed at myself for letting all of this time go by without seeing things more clearly. I pull over at the gas station to get a bottle of water knowing that I really need to sober up a little before talking to her. I don't want to be a total drunk when I say what I need to say.

I'm sitting in her driveway and I'm freaking nervous as hell. I get out and go to the door, pushing the bell and holding my breath until it opens. It's her. And the look of shock on her face is undeniable. She's wearing little denim shorts and a white fitted T-shirt with a picture of a cat on it that says *You've Cat To Be Kitten Me Right Meow* in black writing. I nearly chuckle out loud as I read it, but I'm here for a serious reason, so I hold it back. I really do love her funny shirts and she looks so damn adorable right now. She's going to make me crazy. I just know it.

Why do you have to be so adorably beautiful, Jess?

"Jace, what are you doing here and why do you reek of alcohol?" she says, and I immediately feel bad for coming here after drinking so much. She's never going to take me seriously now.

"I'm leaving tomorrow, Jess. I just wanted to say good-bye to my friend," I tell her, trying to sound as sober as possible.

She peers over my shoulder toward my truck. "You're drunk! You can't drive around in this condition. You're going to kill someone else or yourself," she huffs. "I'm taking you home. You can have someone get your truck for you in the morning. Wait here while I get my keys."

Shit! She's mad, but at least she's going to be alone with me long enough for me to get out what I need to say to her. She comes back out, hooks her arm in mine, and leads me to my car. I rest my head on her shoulder and inhale loudly, nuzzling my nose in her sweet-smelling hair.

"I love your hair, Jess. It's the prettiest hair I have ever seen and it smells so good," I tell her. She's warm and sweet and trying to take care of my drunken ass. I really like it.

"Shut up, Jace. You're drunk and don't know what you're saying," she snaps. Man, she's feisty tonight. This could be a good thing or a very bad thing. She pushes me down into her passenger seat and shuts the door. I can't let her take me home yet. I need to talk to her first.

"I'm not ready to go home yet, Jess. Just drive around," I tell her.

"You need to go home and sleep this off. You have a big day tomorrow, plus I don't want to drive around with you. I'm only helping you because I couldn't let you get yourself killed driving like this," she says, sounding really irritated with me. I have to make her hear me, listen to me. I can't leave tomorrow with her pissed off at me with no idea how I feel about her.

"Jess, don't hate me anymore," I whisper as I roll my head to the side. Her jaw clenches and her knuckles whiten as she grips the steering wheel tighter. As we approach my house I know my minutes are limited.

"I'm sorry it couldn't be you, Jess, that it wasn't you in the pool with me." I reach over and absently tuck a dark lock of her beautiful hair behind her ear. "Forgive me, don't hate me anymore."

There I said it.

Now it's out there and she knows I'm no longer in friend territory. Before she has time to say anything, I take her hand in mine and boldly ask her to come in.

"My mom is still at the country club. That's where my going away party was. She usually stays until close. Come inside with me. I just want to spend time with you before I leave tomorrow. I feel like I'll never see you again once I leave," I say, looking deep into her stunning eyes as I reach over and intertwine my fingers with hers.

"Okay," she replies, and I want to pump my fist in the air I'm so happy.

Once we get up to my room and I put on some music, I don't waste any time. I look at her, feeling a raw, deep-seated desire like I've never felt before. My alcohol-induced haze lifts in a rush, and I take in just how beautiful she is—perfectly petite with swimmer's curves and tone. She's looking back at me with the innocence of an untouched girl, and all I see is a girl that's mine. Right now, she seems so fragile, so pure. I step toward her and everything in the room falls away. It's just me and her, nothing else. My heart's pounding and my blood is rushing through my veins fiercely. I stop only inches from her body and lean in, putting my mouth close to her full, pouty lips. I can feel her warm, rapid breaths on my face. Nothing can beat this moment for me. I've wanted to kiss her again countless times without guilt or trepidation.

"Do you know how many times I've wanted to kiss these lips?" I whisper, never taking my eyes off of hers.

She sucks in a breath and closes her eyes. I reach up and brush her lower lip with the pad of my thumb, tracing her softness with my skin and my eyes. My gaze lingers there until the need I feel threatens to consume me with every second that passes. I need her mouth on mine.

"I'm going to kiss you now, Jess," I murmur, letting her know I'm not stopping myself this time. "I'm going to kiss you like no one has ever kissed you before."

I lean forward and close the tiny space between us, just barely brushing my lips against hers.

"Jess, after I kiss you, which I'm going to do real soon, I'm going to lay you down on my bed and make love to you like no one else ever has," I tell her, making my intentions clear and leaving no doubt about how much I want her.

Her body tenses at my words and nervousness flits across her face. Her teeth sink into her bottom lip and her green eyes fill with heat and passion. My confidence starts to mingle with fear because I'm realizing that I'm about to make love for the first time in my life. Sex is one thing, but love...well, love brings things to a whole new level. It's exciting and terrifying at the same time.

Calm the hell down, Jace.

Don't screw this up.

I slide my hand around the base of her neck and brush my lips against hers, savoring the kiss before it turns desperate. My tongue glides against hers and I feel her body tremble as I pull her in closer.

I want more.

I want to feel her skin against mine. I want to touch it, memorize every inch of her before I leave tomorrow. I pull away briefly and back her up toward the bed. She tries to speak, but I stop her.

"Shhh, Jessica," I say, drawing out her full name. "Lie down on the bed," I tell her firmly.

She's standing against the bed frozen and unsure. I reach down, gripping my shirt and pulling it up over my head. I slowly unbutton my jeans as her eyes follow all my movements. My jeans fall around my ankles and I tell her again, "Lie down, Jess."

She doesn't say a word, but does exactly as I told her. Her eyes are wide and her cheeks are flushed. I can see the rapid rise and fall of her chest and I know she realizes that I'm not stopping tonight. Crawling onto the bed above her, I hold my weight with my arms just close enough to feel her breasts brush against my chest.

I roll next to her and prop myself up on one elbow,

tracing my finger over her soft lips, down over her chin, then neck, and finally, slowly, between her breasts. My bulge stiffens to a painful length as I watch her nipples grow taut under the thin fabric of her shirt. I want to feel her, to take her funny T-shirt off and feel her soft skin under mine.

I whisper to her, and can hear the love and lust dripping from my words.

Her eyes squeeze shut, concealing the want in them, as I run my hand beneath her shirt, gently kissing her on the cheek.

"It's okay, Jess. Just let me make you feel good; let me love you," I tell her. With that, her body relaxes into my touch.

I love you.

You love me too, Jessica.

I drag my fingers across the top of her bra, grazing her nipples, and she gasps. Her responsiveness nearly breaks me apart. I reach around with one hand, unclasping her bra and releasing the heaviness of her breasts. I slowly pull her shirt over her head and she reaches out to grasp my shoulders, digging her fingernails into my skin. My hands glide down and unbutton her shorts. I gradually pull them down, revealing her smooth olive skin, which contrasts perfectly with the little white bikini panties she's wearing. The sight of her makes my heart thump even harder in my chest. Her eyes meet mine just as I run my fingers beneath the thin, white fabric. She looks worried, maybe frightened, and her body tenses. I don't know why she's freezing up on me, but then I see the scars. So many of them lined all along the area above her pelvic bone. My eyes dart back to hers, searching for answers to questions I don't even know how to ask. I brush my fingers across the scar tissue, wondering who did this to her and why. It breaks my heart. When I don't say anything she looks relieved. I lean down and press a kiss against her warm skin, tracing each scar with my lips to show her how I wish I could kiss the pain away for her.

I'll fix you, Jess.

Let me make it better.

I grip her hips as I slide my tongue along the curve of her inner thigh—I can't wait any longer to taste her.

The scent of her arousal drives me crazy as I dip my head to the wet heat between her thighs. My hands slide up and down her body, taking in every damn inch of her. I bring my hand down to explore her before sliding one, then two fingers inside her. She tightens around them, and it feels so good, too good. Fuck, I've never been this turned-on in my life. I need to be inside her, join my body with hers, and make her mine. I curl my fingers up, bringing her closer to the edge before sliding them out. I don't want her to come on my hand; I want that to happen when I'm buried deep inside of her. She whimpers as I begin trailing kisses up her body slowly and deliberately. I allow my weight to press onto her as I lick her taste from my lips. She blushes, seeing her wetness on my face, and I lick my lips again giving her a wicked grin.

"Good, Jess. So damn good," I say before dropping my mouth heavily on hers. I pour every ounce of my heart and soul into this kiss as I remove my boxers. I can feel her entire body shake with nerves and I can't wait to feel the heat of her wrapped around me when I push inside her for the first time. I move her legs apart with my knee just as I realize that the only condoms I have are in my truck.

Dammit! Please let her be on birth control.

"Jess, are you on the pill?" I ask as I search her eyes and hope to God she says yes so I don't have to stop myself. She nods and relief washes over me. I grip my fingers around her waist and slowly press my body between her thighs.

Incredible.

Her moans, her heat, her hands on me, my hands on her, the feel of her; everything about this moment has me on the edge. I lean down and capture her nipple between my lips, grazing it with my teeth. She pushes her hips up, wanting more, as she moans.

This girl...oh my God, this girl.

I look up at her and ask her to open her eyes. I want to watch her as I make love to her for the first time. I want her to feel me and know that this is different from anyone else she's ever been with.

"Open your eyes, Jess." Her eyes flutter open and meet mine as a charge of energy hums between us.

Silky, black hair is fanned out all around her face, and, in this moment, she is the sexiest girl I've ever set eyes on. Staring at her as if she were the last girl on earth, I thrust into her slowly, deeply. A moan escapes her throat and I circle my hips to give her as much pleasure as I can, not caring about my own. Her eyes are wide and glossy before she squeezes them shut again. Desire overwhelms us both, and I pump faster as she throws her head back in ecstasy. It makes me crazy—I need more of her. I lean down and kiss her, dragging my teeth along her bottom lip, nipping and sucking it into my mouth. My body moves in an unrestrained rhythm and she meets me thrust for thrust. Pent-up breaths and moans pass through her lips as her breathing increases. The sounds she's making will forever be music to my ears. Our bare skin, slick with sweat, slides against one another and everything in my mind goes foggy as her warmth clenches tight around me. She's getting close. Knowing this, knowing that I'm the one making her feel so good has me close, so close. The softness of her skin and the roughness of her nipples grazing my chest ignite all of my senses, making my body tingle. My heart is slamming into my ribcage as I rock back and forth harder. Her legs clench around my waist and she unravels beneath me, crying out my name. Watching her lose control is the most beautiful and amazing sight I've ever seen.

"Jace... Oh God, Jace."

I've had sex many times, but this is different. Watching her come completely undone sends a need to claim her all the way up my spine. Looking down at her writhing beneath me, I'm lost, completely lost in her. I'm hers in this moment and all those that will follow. I drop my full weight upon her and thrust deeper, burying my face in her hair and inhaling the scent of shampoo and lust and love—inhaling Jess. Finally, my body finds its release and I'm overtaken, completely and irrevocably overtaken by Jessica Alexander.

"Missing someone you love never gets easier. Those that say it does have never truly loved."
—Kathryn Perez

The Past

Jace

HEARING THE PAIN in her voice when she hung up on me was terrible. I feel like my chest has been ripped open and my heart's fallen at my feet. It's been two weeks since that phone call, since I was a total asshole to her. I can't believe she just broke things off like that. It doesn't make any damn sense at all. I've called her a hundred times, sent multiple text messages, and...nothing. I can't go home for two more weeks because of this damn football camp, but when I do I plan on going to her house and begging her to forgive me and take me back. I miss her so damn much. A football hits me in the chest unexpectedly, knocking me out of my daydream.

"Hey, man, are you still pining away over your girl? There's a big frat party tonight. Are you coming or are you moping?" my roommate asks.

Trent is a big, burly guy. He's a linebacker on the team and he's a brick with big, broad shoulders and enormous traps. He practically lives in the gym.

"Nah, bro, I don't much feel like going to a party. I'm just going to hang out here."

"Whatever, man. Your loss. These are the only college years you're going to have. Piss them away if you want. Chicks aren't worth it. That's why I walk the single line. I let them know right off the bat that I'm not looking for anything serious. You may want to consider doing the same. Otherwise, this room is going to get pretty damn boring after a while."

"I love her. I can't just let it go. I screwed up and I have to fix it. Going out and getting trashed isn't going to make things any better. She's mad, but she'll come around. She has to."

"Suit yourself, dude."

He gets ready and leaves for the party while I sit here going stir crazy. I send her another text—even though I know it's pointless, but it's my only connection to her right now.

Jace: *Please call me. I hate this. Please talk to me. I'm coming home in two weeks and I'm coming to see you so we can work this out. I'm so sorry for being such an ass. Please don't shut me out. I miss you, Jess.*

I wait and wait for a reply, but as usual, there's nothing. I throw the football across the room in anger and grab my iPod. I put my headphones on and turn the music up as loud as it will go. I lay here for what seems like forever until I fall asleep. I wake up to a rattling and banging noise only to see Trent falling drunkenly through the door with an equally drunk girl on his arm.

Great, now I get to listen to them grope each other.

Screw that, I'm out of here until he's done with her.

"Room's all yours, man. Just stay off my bed. That's all I ask," I tell him, grabbing my ball cap and cell phone.

I walk through the dorm hallways and pass by several groups of people that were obviously out having a way better time than I did tonight. I head out to my truck with no idea where I'm going. I just want to fast forward to two weeks from now so I can go home.

I wake up full of nervous excitement knowing that today I'm driving home. I know it won't be easy, but I have to convince Jess to forgive me.

"Take it easy, man. Good luck with your girl. I still think you should rethink the relationship shit, though."

"Thanks, man. When I come back I'll be in a better mood. I may even go to one of those parties with you. I'll see if Jess will come up to go with us."

"Sure, man. Whatever you say. Drive safe."

The drive feels like it takes more like a thousand hours rather than a few. When I pull into town, I go straight to Jess's house before I even go home. Her car isn't in the driveway.

Shit!

I still get out and go to the door so her mom can let her know I was here. She'll get that I'm serious and call me. Shortly after I knock, her mom swings the door open. She's wearing pajamas in the middle of the day and she looks like hell.

"Hi, Mrs. Alexander. Will Jessica be home anytime soon?"

"She's gone, sweetie," she mumbles, and her words, coupled with the smell of alcohol, hit me like a ton of bricks.

"Yes, ma'am, I see her car isn't here. When will she be back?"

"She ain't coming back, sweetie. Can't tell you where she went either. My daughter hasn't ever asked much from me, but she made me promise not to say a word about where she went if a good-looking young man such as yourself came looking for her. All I can tell you is that she moved out two days ago."

I shake my head in disbelief. This can't be true; she'd never move away and not tell me.

"Why? Why would she not want me to know where she went?" I ask, crestfallen. "This makes no sense at all."

"I don't know what to tell you. All I know is she was sure in a hurry to get out of here. I'm real sorry, but I can't tell you where she went. I promised and I'm keeping my promise," she tells me with a sad smile on her face and a shrug. Then she shuts the door.

I stand here staring at the closed door like a fool. None of this makes sense. I yank my phone out of my pocket as I go back to my truck. I punch in her number to call her again. If I have to leave her a million voicemails and send a thousand text messages, I will. The phone rings once; then I get a recording saying the phone number has been disconnected.

"Dammit!" I throw my phone across the cab of my truck. It crashes and falls as I slam my hands down on the steering wheel.

Driving to my parents' house, my blood is boiling. I just want to scream. I can't believe this is happening. She's just—gone! I have to find her. I *will* find her. This is all my fault; I was a prick to her on the phone about the birth control thing and she's just totally closed me off. I'm running every scenario of ways to find her through my head, when immediately I know what to do. I pull up at home and practically pull the handle off my door as I get out. I go inside, calling out for Mom as I do.

"Honey, what are you so frantic about? Come here, give your mother a hug. It feels like you've been away for ages. I had Bernadette make some of your favorites, since I knew you were coming. What on earth's the matter, Jace? You look pale. Are you ill?" She says, looking me over.

"Mom, I need your help. I need a private investigator. Can you hire one for me?" I ask her, hoping to God she's not going to think I've gone crazy.

"Son, why do you think you need a private investigator? What's this all about?" She asks impatiently. "Come sit with me in the sunroom and have something to eat. You look like you haven't been eating well at all." She turns and starts walking away from me. I follow, but don't miss a beat.

"I'm not hungry, Mom. I need to find Jessica. She's gone." That word kills me.

Gone.

"She moved and her mom won't tell me where to. I need to find her. I know you know people who do this type of thing. Can you please help me find her or pay someone to help me find her?" I say desperately, giving her the irresistible eyes that I know she can't say no to.

"Jace, honey, what is it about this girl that has you so enamored? You and Elizabeth made a perfect couple. I always envisioned you two marrying one day." She's calmly making me a plate of food and I just shake my head, frustrated. "Then this girl comes along and you just walk away from a relationship that was good for you. From what I understand, this Jessica isn't a very good girl." She pulls a glass from the cabinet shelf and begins pouring me some tea. "Maybe not finding her is for the best. You're in college now, just starting your life. You should just focus on your studies and football," she says, holding the full glass out to me.

I knew she would argue, but dammit, I have to convince her. If I don't try—at least make an effort to find Jess—I know I'll never forgive myself. It will haunt me forever.

"Mom, please. I don't ask you for much, but I'm asking you for this."

My hand grasps the cold glass of sweet tea and she slowly takes a sip of hers. She's killing me with the suspense, but Mom never does anything without weighing all of the options and possible outcomes.

"Sure, honey. Let me see what I can do. Just write down anything you think will be helpful and I'll pass it on to Jason. These things can take some time, though, so don't expect a speedy result."

"Thanks, Mom. Thank you so much. I love you.

You're the best. Jessica is a good girl, Mom. She's not like what everyone says she is. She's a good person and she's important to me."

I put the glass down without ever taking a drink and hug her tight, and for the first time since I arrived in town, I feel an ounce of relief. The hold on my throat is still there, but now it's a little easier to breathe than it was when I felt I had no options.

"Hey, man, how long are you going to be on that thing tonight? Aren't your eyes bleeding by now?" Trent's sprawled out on his bed and has been quiet, for the most part, while I continue my search for Jessica.

Where are you, Jess?

"No, they aren't. She deleted her Facebook account, but she has to be on some network somewhere. I know if I keep looking I'll come across it some way or another. It's just that Jessica Alexander is a pretty damn common name. I've been scrolling through one Jessica after another for what seems like forever."

I rub my temples and huff out my frustration as I lean forward on my desk.

"I thought your mom hired a private investigator or something. Why not just wait 'til he digs something up instead of driving yourself crazy staring at that damn computer screen?" He's got a point, but—

"Because sitting here doing nothing to find her...doing nothing feels fucking wrong. Even though she doesn't know I'm trying, *I* need to know I'm trying. One day when you love someone, maybe you'll get it. I can't explain this shit, I just know I can't give up."

I slam the laptop shut and rub my blurry eyes.

"It's been too long since I talked to her last. The more time that goes by, the further she slips away from me. I can feel it. I'm losing her before I even find her."

"Dude, I'm sorry. That blows. I hope I never fall in love 'cause from what I can see, it sucks," Trent says as he moves his hands behind his head, as though he's contemplating the validity of his "love sucks" statement. I know he's trying to help, but I just can't deal with him right now.

"Loving someone doesn't suck. Losing the person you love is what sucks." I grab my keys and gym bag and head for the door. I need to get out of here and think, work some of this aggression out before I explode. "I'm going to the gym to hit the treadmill. I'll be back later."

I can't believe how much time has gone by. It's been a month since Mom said she would have her friend look for Jess. I hate to keep bugging her, but the wait is excruciatingly painful. I pull up to the gym and grab my bag out of the back. I need to run—hard and fast. I feel so much pent-up frustration and anger that it's eating me from the inside out. I did this; this is all my fault. If I had been more careful with her that day about the lie, maybe things would be different right now. I always saw her as a much stronger person than anyone else did, but maybe she wasn't. Maybe my cruel words broke something inside of her that day. She struggled with so much pain, so many inner demons. Those scars were proof of it. I should've handled things differently. I may have pushed her too far. Now, I may never get the chance to say I'm sorry.

Practice today was brutal and my body's aching from head to toe. I see a package sitting in front of my dorm room door and I suddenly forget about all of the pain I'm currently feeling. It's from Mom's private investigator! I unlock the door as fast as I can and rip open the large envelope. A document and several photos spill out across my bed. My eyes and brain can't take in everything all at once. I scan the pictures and all I see at first is her face, her smile. All I see is my Jess. Then my chest opens up and everything inside me is ripped out. She's not alone in the pictures. Photo after photo shows her and some guy hugging, laughing, kissing, touching. I flip through them over and over again just to make sure my eyes aren't playing tricks on me. I flip to the last one and she's looking up into his eyes with her arms draped over his shoulders, and she's smiling at him.

That's my smile.

She's smiling my smile for someone else.

"Fuck!" I scream and hurl the stack of pictures across the room.

I drop onto the bed and pick up the document, forcing myself to hold back angry tears. I read each line. The only address found for her turned out to be vacant. There is no phone number, no email, and no alternate address listed. The information says that she's engaged to be married. I drop the paper to the floor and fall back hard onto the bed. I run my hands through my hair, gripping it tightly, and squeeze my eyes shut. I want to cry, scream, beat the shit out of something, but I do none of these things because I can barely breathe. It hurts. It hurts. So. Damn. Bad. She's gone for good, already with someone else, like we never even mattered.

Why, Jess?

Fucking, why?

The door opens and Trent comes in. He stops abruptly, taking in the mess of pictures scattered all over the room.

"What the hell, bro?" he asks.

"It's over. She's moved on." I clear my throat and throw my arm over my face before going on. "Sorry for the mess. I just can't look at them anymore right now."

"Damn, dude. Sorry it didn't work out. You want me to trash them?"

Do I?

I don't want to see her with some asshole, but I don't want to throw them away. She looks beautiful, even if she is with someone else.

"No, I'll get them picked up," I say. I take a deep breath before rising off the bed to clean up the mess I've made.

"Man, you can't possibly be planning on keeping pics of her with another motherfucking guy. That's just a little twisted, don't you think?" Trent asks incredulously.

I grab them one by one, and the images burn into my mind, forever to be replayed like some terrible movie.

"I don't know what I plan on doing with them. I just can't throw them away right now," I say, shoving them into my desk drawer.

"She's engaged," I whisper to myself, trying to wrap my head around the finality of what that really means.

"Okay, enough of this whiney bullshit. You're coming out with me tonight, you're getting wasted, and forgetting all about this girl for a little while. Get your mopey ass up, get a shower, and get dressed."

I really don't feel like going out, but forgetting sounds pretty damn good right now because remembering hurts like hell.

Yeah, forgetting sounds really good.

I'm sitting at the bar watching people practically have sex out on the dance floor. The strobe lights are flashing and the smell of smoke nearly makes me gag. The club scene has never really appealed to me, and tonight is no different. People are crowding all around the bar trying to get drinks, so I move and find a table toward the back, away from all the commotion. Trent finds me and puts another drink in my hand. "Drink up, man. Loosen up a little," he says.

I just nod and take the drink. It's the third one he's given me so far and whatever it is, it's really strong. I can feel a buzz coming on already. I'm swirling the tiny straw around in my cup when a girl walks up to my table. She's smiling and looking down at me with big doe eyes. Long bone-straight ebony hair falls low beneath her shoulders. It reminds me of Jessica's; I always loved her hair. I can't make out the color of her eyes due to the flashing light in contrast to the darkness of the club, but when she smiles, the extreme whiteness of her teeth takes me by surprise. She's striking, older-looking.

"What are you doing back here all alone? A good-looking guy like you should have an equally good-looking woman by his side." She's cocking one eyebrow, exuding an air of confidence. She seems cocky, but not bitchy. Interesting is the word that comes to mind.

"I'm not alone. I'm here with my roommate. He's just conveniently indisposed on the dance floor at the moment, that's all. It would seem that you're just as alone as I am, though," I say, looking up at her. She's pretty, but she's not Jess. Too elegant, too proper.

"You mind if I rectify our mutual problem? Can I have a seat here with you?" she purrs in that confident tone again.

"Sure, why not?"

I gesture toward the chair across from me.

She leans over, putting her cleavage on display as she sets her drink down and pulls out the chair.

"I'm Victoria, and you would be?" she asks, offering me her hand.

I reach out and shake it briefly.

"Jace."

"Nice to meet you, Jace." She beams at me like she's won the lottery.

Awkwardness settles between us and I have no idea what to say to this girl. She's attractive, obviously carries herself well, and seems nice enough, but I'm just not interested. I've only just realized that I lost Jess for good. Getting caught up with another girl right now isn't even close to being on my list of priorities.

I miss you, Jess.

"Why so sad? Some girl must've done a real number on you." She leans back in her chair casually and crosses her long legs.

“What makes you think I’m sad?”

“Your eyes. You have terribly sad eyes. They make me wonder whom you could’ve loved enough to make you so sad. Why don’t you tell me about it? I’ve got all night. I’ve been told that I’m a good listener.”

“It’s been a long day, a long bad day. I don’t really want to talk about it. Let’s just say that I’m not looking for a serious relationship for a very long time,” I mutter and take a sip of my drink.

“Fair enough! What about fun? You have any aversion to fun?” she asks, and shoots me a small, teasing smile.

“Fun is okay, I guess.”

“Great. Then get up and let’s go dance. I’ve got moves and they’re all kinds of fun,” she laughs as she stands up, shaking her hips from side to side.

What the hell? I’m nearly drunk, Jessica’s getting married, and my heart feels like someone pulled it out of my chest and beat it with a mallet. I guess a little fun and dancing can’t hurt.

"True love will always find a way to come back."
—Unknown

Jessica

HE'S JUST TOLD me that his heart belongs to me. I want to believe that, but the fact that he's engaged really kills the sweetness of the moment. Suddenly, the warmth of his body feels too hot, wrong. I can turn off my emotions for other guys, but not with Jace. I can't do this, not now, not like this. I bring my hands up to his chest and push him back.

"No. Your heart doesn't belong to me. You've given it to someone else and that can't be ignored." I roll out from under him and stand up off the bed quickly. I pull my cami strap back up and act on my sudden need to cover myself, reaching over to grab my robe.

"Why does it always come to this with us? You're hot, you're cold. No matter what I do I've never been able to figure you out," he says as he sits up.

"Maybe you need to stop trying to figure me out, Jace. I mean, you come knocking on my door late at night after not seeing me for six years, and then you drop this bomb on me that you're engaged to my shrink! You come here armed with all of my personal, very private information—which, again, I'm pretty sure is illegal—and expect me to just fall into bed with you? Seems like I'm not the only one experiencing a little crazy around here."

He drops his head. "I didn't come here intending to get you into bed. I'm sorry if that's what it seems like." He exhales and pinches the top of his nose in frustration.

"It's just that when I picked you up and held you in my arms, I couldn't help but be pulled back into the past. Losing you was hard for me. It took me a long time to finally accept that you weren't ever going to be a part of my life again." He stops, seeming to search for words to explain what I put him through. "Then, finding this file, finding you, coming here, going through a myriad of emotions just overwhelmed me. I've thought about, dreamed about seeing you again for so long. So having you in my arms made my resolve crumble, to say the least."

He looks up at me and I hug my arms tightly around myself. I have no idea where we go from here, but wherever it is, he needs to leave. I can't think with him this close to me and the longer he stays, the more likely I am to not give a shit about him being engaged.

"You should go. You being here isn't good. You wanted to confront me about the pregnancy and you did. I can't tell you enough how sorry I am, nor can I change what I did. You should just go live your life with your fiancé and forget all of this, forget me."

The walls of my bedroom feel like they're closing in

on me, so I turn and walk back to the front of the apartment, away from Jace. I hear his footsteps behind me and with every step my heart beats faster. Saying good-bye this time will have a finality it's never had before. I reach out for the doorknob, making sure he realizes I'm really ready for him to go. I feel his hand on my shoulder and I flinch.

"Jessica, right or wrong, you and I will always be under each other's skin. I've walked around for six years holding all of this underneath the surface. Finding that file was a tear in that surface and I'm positive I can't just cover it back up. Everything that's been pent-up inside me for all these years is flooding out. If I walk away from here and never look back, it will burn like an iron in the back of my mind forever."

With every word he speaks I lay down another brick, building my wall higher and higher. He's engaged, engaged to a successful doctor—a stunningly beautiful, successful doctor. I can't compete with that and I won't compete with that. Too much time has passed, too many bridges have been burned, and I'm not stable enough to deal with this. No matter how much I want him, it just feels off. Before, when I was with Jace it felt so right, but standing here with him tonight, it feels more wrong than I can even explain to myself. Plus, I think he still sees me as this shy, weak teenage girl that needs to be fixed.

"I can't deal with any of this right now. I just found out today that I have a serious mental illness. I'm under a court order to attend therapy because I had a drinking and driving accident. In the hospital, they saw all of the years' worth of scars and the judge took pity on me. Now I have to find a new doctor because I'll never go to Dr. Ward again since I know she's engaged to the only guy I've ever loved." The reality of everything hurts so badly. As the words leave my throat they burn. "In the very same day, that guy walks into my apartment after six years and waylays me with a ton of emotional shit. We aren't teenagers anymore. I'm not a bullied and beaten-down young girl that needs you to come pick me up every time I fall," I tell him, straightening my shoulders and trying to look strong. "You couldn't fix me back then and you can't fix me now. I'm just as broken now as I was then, only now I'm trying to find strength in my pain." He's looking at me with pity swirling in his eyes and I hate it. "Back then, I tried to be invisible; I hid from everything and everyone. Now, I just wear my pain for everyone to see and don't give a shit what they think. I'm a grown woman and even if I'm seriously delusional about many things in my life, I have enough self-respect not to hop into bed or do anything else with a man that's engaged to be married to another woman. Not even if that man is you. Please, just go." Tears fight their way into my eyes, but I refuse to let them fall. I can't allow him to keep seeing me as a weakling. He lets out an exasperated sigh and I see years of regret pool in his bright blue eyes.

"I'm not trying to fix you. Even though the therapist in me wants to do that, that's not what I'm trying to do. I just... Hell, I don't know what I want or what I'm doing. I just know how I feel. I love you, Jessica. I've never stopped loving you. I just thought being with you would never be a possibility again, so I convinced myself to try and love someone else, even if it was a different kind of love." We stand facing each other, silently volleying our words back and forth, and I do everything in my power to stop him from penetrating my defenses. But the more he talks, the weaker I get.

"Jessica, trust me, if there were a button I could've pushed years ago to turn off my feelings for you, I probably would've done it, but there wasn't and there isn't one now. All I could do was disguise it and put it in the back of my mind like it wasn't there anymore," he says, drawing his brows together and dropping his head. "I put a fortress around the love I felt for you and kept it hidden because that was the only way I knew how to move on." He looks back to me and our eyes connect. His are red and the dark circles under them show how draining this has been for him. "But seeing you, knowing where you are, you being so close by...I won't be able to hide it anymore. It'll be a lie. And the way I see it, now that I know where you are I don't have much choice in the matter. Not knowing where you were, thinking you were happy and married was the only way I could convince myself that we wouldn't be together again." He reaches out and gently tilts my chin upward. "I love you, Jess, and I know you love me too. There hasn't been one day in the last six years that I haven't loved you. I'm not letting you go this time. I can't."

I love him too, or at least I think that's what I feel for him. I don't know what he wants me to say. He's engaged. That keeps running through my mind.

"You're engaged. Are you saying that you're going to go tonight and break off your engagement with Dr. Ward to be with me? Is that what you're saying to me?" He stands silently as I berate him. A selfish little piece of me wishes he'd say yes, that he *is* going to go shatter her heart, but I know that wouldn't be right. "You don't even know me anymore! I keep telling you, I'm not the same girl you used to know. Why would you break off something as serious as an engagement for someone you don't even know anymore, someone that you haven't seen in six years? That doesn't make any sense."

Disappointment and defeat are written all over his face as he looks down, shaking his head.

"I don't know," he says, looking back at me. His eyes roam over my face like he's searching for the magic solution to this situation in it.

"The wedding is in four weeks," he blurts out.

"What?"

"We're supposed to be married in four weeks back home. Her and Mom have everything all planned down to the very last stupid detail."

Married. Thinking about Jace being married to someone else puts a crack in my armor. It hurts; it burns my throat as I try to swallow the acidic thought of it down.

"Well then, in four weeks you should get married. Buy a big fancy house and go to charity dinners with your mother and wife. You can have the white picket fence and everything. It sounds like a perfect happily ever after, Jace. Don't give it up for some broken girl you slept with once." I bite out. I'm doing my best to keep it together, but I'm slowly unraveling. I love him; I hate him. I want him to stay; I need him to go. My contradicting thoughts circle my mind like vultures.

"Jessica, falling in love can't always be a happily ever after or a once in a lifetime kind of story. Those happen in books, in movies. This is life and it's real. Life has no script, no outline. We broke the rules of love long ago. All I know for sure is that with you, the rules will never apply."

Before dejectedly walking out, he stops to look at me

once more.

"And you weren't just a girl I slept with once. You're a girl I've loved—always." And then he's gone.

I wake up the next morning with a headache from hell. I massage my temples and start replaying everything that happened last night. My cell phone is chirping at me at an annoyingly loud volume and I fumble for it, not even opening my eyes to see who it is.

"Hello?"

"Hey."

"How'd you get this number? Actually, never mind—don't answer that. The file, right?"

"Yes, the file. How are you this morning?"

What is wrong with him? Has everything that happened last night flown right out his proverbial window?

"Fine, I'm just fine. Peachy, actually!" I remark.

"No, you're not. I can hear it in your voice. You're lying."

"Jace, it's too damn early in the morning for this. What do you want?"

I'm mad—pissed off, actually—that he's acting so normal, like we can just pick up right where we left off six years ago. He's getting freaking married in four weeks!

"I forgot the file at your apartment. I need it back before Vic—I mean Dr. Ward realizes it's gone."

What in the hell? He has lost his mind! Like I give a shit about him getting into hot water with his head-shrinking, soon to be wifey!

"That's not my problem. Wait a minute; does she not

know about me, about you coming to see me last night? How did you know about the file if she didn't give it to you, Jace?"

"I took it. We were leaving the clinic and she'd left her keys in her office. I told her I'd get them for her. They were on her desk, and when I grabbed them I saw your name on a file folder that was sitting there. It shouldn't have even been left out like that. That was a huge screw-up on her part," he says, trailing off at the end.

Wow! So this doctor chick doesn't even know about me. This is an interesting turn of events, for sure.

"I'll deliver the file back to the clinic myself. I'm supposed to attend a group thing there today anyway," I say, silencing him. Let him chew on that for a while. She might be the one marrying him, but he was mine first and I want her to know it.

"Jess, don't do that," he warns. "She isn't one to play games."

"Wow. That's rich coming from you, Jace! You're engaged to her and you're playing games, you're playing with fire. Maybe you should be honest with her; you are marrying her. Don't you think you should go into this thing with a clean slate?" I say, being a total sarcastic bitch.

"Stop. Just stop talking about me getting married like you're okay with it, like you don't care."

I do care; I hate it. Every time the words roll off my tongue, I want to gag. But if I have to keep reminding myself that that's the reality of his future to stop myself from having some deluded idea of a happily ever after with Jace, then that's what I'll do. He's never seen this side of me before. He only knows shy, weak Jess. Not mean, cold, shut down, bitch-on-wheels Jessica.

"I am okay with it. I am perfectly okay with the fact that you're getting married. So okay with it, maybe I'll even buy you guys a wedding gift," I snap.

"What's happened to you, Jess? You're not a bitch. That's not the person you are. Why are you doing this?"

It's who I am today. It might not be me tonight or tomorrow, but right now, yes, I'm a bitch. An hour from now I may be curled up on my bed crying my eyes out, or drowning my sorrow in a glass of 151 or maybe I'll be bleeding out the pain, but right now, I'm a brick wall that he's not getting through.

"I told you, I'm not the same person I once was. You need to accept that."

I've spent years making sure I'll never have to endure other people torturing me ever again. I'll never be someone's verbal or physical punching bag again. If that means being a coldhearted bitch on the outside, so be it. It's a defense mechanism and it works, regardless of the method.

"What group are you supposed to attend today?" he asks, ignoring my last statement altogether.

"What, you mean you didn't get that from my file when you were breaking the law getting all of my other personal information?" I say, raising my voice now.

"Just tell me the name of the damn group you're going to, Jessica," he barks back.

"I don't know the name of the group. It's for self-harmers or something. It's for fucked-up people like me. What difference does it make?"

"That's exactly the type of group you need to be in, but like I said, you need to find one at another facility. I can help point you in the right direction if you'd like."

Oh God, now he sounds like my fixer again.

"Whatever, Jace. Are we done now?"

"No. I really need that file back, Jess." His voice is insistent, but I'll be damned if I'm going to give in to him right now.

"Well you aren't getting it. Push me and I'll report you, for taking it, and your fiancé, for leaving it out in the first place."

"Fine, Jess, have it your way. But confronting Victoria won't solve anything, trust me," he huffs. I just smile and wait him out. "Good-bye, Jessica," he says, and hangs up.

Every time he uses my full name it sends chills up my spine, but I shake it off and pitch my phone on the bed. I get up and start the shower, letting it get hot before I hop in. I stand under the water with my eyes closed; memories of him touching me, kissing me last night, flood my mind. These thoughts are trying to rob me of the strength that I'm so desperately grasping for. I need to Let. Him. Go. I have to.

With the infamous file folder in hand, I walk through the doors of the clinic. I strut with false confidence to the front desk and ask for Dr. Ward. I have on a pair of dark denim skinny jeans and black boots, and my very fitted black top shows off my body in all the right places. I also put big loose curls in my hair this morning. It falls down past my chest, and I almost hope Jace sees me—he always did love my hair. Last night, I looked like shit. Today, I have makeup on and I look good. That's the one thing I've never had reservations about—I know I'm not ugly. As I've gotten older, my confidence in my looks has grown and I've been able to embrace that about myself.

"Excuse me, I need to see Dr. Ward briefly. I have something to return to her," I inform the squatty receptionist behind the glass window.

"Do you have an appointment with Dr. Ward today?" she replies.

"No, I don't. I just need to return something to her, that's all. Is that possible?"

She regards me from under her eyeglasses and punches in a number on the phone as she picks up the receiver.

"Doctor, we have a young lady here that says she needs to return something to you. Do you have a moment or would you prefer I set up an appointment?" She seems satisfied with the answer before she hangs up and looks back up at me. "She says to send you on back. She has a few minutes before her next patient."

"Thank you."

I make my way through the winding hallways until I get to her door. My heart's beating so fast that the blood in my veins can barely keep up. I suck in a breath and knock on the office door.

The door opens and there she is in all her elegant doctor glory, dressed in an all-white pantsuit. Doesn't she know it's after Labor Day?

"Oh, hello, Ms. Alexander. What can I do for you this morning?" she asks with a polite smile on her face.

I hold out the file folder and make deliberate eye contact with her in order to keep from staring at the very large ring on her finger—the ring that should be on my hand.

"I believe you may need this back," I say coolly.

She looks down at the file and back to me, confused. "How did you get this?"

The answer to that million-dollar question is sure to knock the good, proper doctor on her narrow, high-class ass. She has her hair up in a flawless French twist and I just want to reach out and muss it all up. She reminds me of Jace's mom, all prim and proper.

Fake!

"You should ask Mr. Collins that question. I'm just here to return it," I tell her, trying to maintain my composure.

"Excuse me? Mr. Collins? What's this all about?" she asks, and I can see her defenses go up as she narrows her eyes at me.

Funny you should ask.

"What this is all about is your fiancé, my ex-boyfriend, stole that file from your office last night. Then he tracked me down to my apartment," I say, dropping the bomb right down on top of her flawless head.

For the first time since meeting her, she looks taken aback and rendered speechless.

"What are you talking about? Forgive me for saying so, Ms. Alexander, but there's no way the man I'm engaged to was at your apartment last night," she retorts snottily.

Bitch!

I knew it was in there. I knew she was a dirty bitch from the get-go. No way does a person dress like that and not be a bitch. She's a cookie cutter of all those socialite women that care more about their social status than anything else.

Jace is marrying a clone of his mother.

With that thought, I have to fight the urge to throw up in my mouth a little. Just as she's mentally sharpening her claws, I stop her dead in her tracks. I'm a pro with bitches like this. I can predict her next move before she can even think it. I guess I should be thankful to Elizabeth Brant for one thing—she gave me Bitch 101 training for years.

"You're probably right, doctor. I'm probably delusional and imagined the whole thing. Jace was never at my apartment, he never stuck his tongue halfway down my throat, and he never told me he still loves me. None of that could've possibly happened because I'm just a borderline having a mental breakdown, right?"

I flip my black mane over my shoulder and turn to leave. Before I do, I have to give her one last thing to think about.

"Oh, and doctor, when Jace says 'I do' to you in four weeks, just know that in his mind he's really thinking 'I don't.'"

"The heart will break, but broken live on."
—Lord Byron

The Past

Jace

I HAVE NO idea what I'm doing at a club and I especially have no idea why I'm on the damn dance floor. This girl says she's okay with just having a good time, but I don't think I've ever met a girl that doesn't eventually want more. More isn't a factor in the equation for me right now, at least not for a very long time. Her arms are draped over my shoulders and she's smiling like a Cheshire cat. Even though I can't deny that she's gorgeous, I also can't deny that she's not Jess. The song ends and as it starts to fade into another one I back away, putting some considerable space between our bodies.

"Well, I think I'm gonna call it a night. Thanks for the dance," I say, giving her an unconvincing smile.

"Okay, your loss. Maybe I'll see you around campus sometime. And maybe next time I see you those eyes won't be so sad."

I just give her a polite nod and weave through the crowd of sweaty bodies until I find Trent. He's in the middle of two blonds as they rub their bodies up and down his. The grin on his face only widens as he sees me approach. He holds up his drink in a prideful gesture, obviously pleased with the situation he has himself in. I just shake my head at him.

"I'm heading out, man," I tell him.

"Well, as you can see I'm a little busy at the moment, so I'll catch you later, bro. Are you sure you don't want to join in? Maci or Staci would be more than happy to accommodate," he chuckles.

I look between Staci and Maci, unsure and uncaring as to which one is which. "Nah, man, you have fun with all that. I'm going back to the room to crash."

"Suit yourself, J."

I give him a backward wave as I turn and walk away. Before I make my escape, I see Victoria back at the bar chatting up some other guy. She turns, giving me a wink and a little wave. I wave back and leave.

What's wrong with me?

I'm nineteen years old, in college, and I can't even go out to a bar and have a good time.

The winter break sped by at lightning speed. I did my best to avoid places that reminded me of Jess, but it wasn't easy. I even drove past her house a few times on the off chance that her car would be in the driveway. No such luck. She's still on my mind daily and it's an effort for me to live in the present, but I'm doing it.

Now, it's the first day of the spring semester and I'm actually a little nervous. I'm still undecided on a major, but I did sign up for a psychology class because the more I think about what happened to Genevieve and how tortured Jessica was, the more I think I may want to pursue something in a field where I can help people. I could get a degree to be a counselor in four years. I'm still not positive, but I'll see how I like it anyway.

After going to a couple of basic classes, like math and science, I head over to Psychology 101. I find a seat and get my notebook out. Other students are filing in the room and I see the professor walk in. He's a tall, skinny man wearing thin-rimmed glasses and stereotypical sweater-vest professor clothes. He flips on the smart board and the class syllabus pops up on it. As all of the students get settled I see a woman come in holding a briefcase in her hand and a laptop case over her shoulder. She almost looks familiar, but I can't quite put my finger on it because I can only see her side profile. She hands the professor a few folders from inside her briefcase and they exchange words. She looks like she may be a professor or maybe a teacher's assistant. Maybe that's how I recognize her. The skinny professor makes his way to the front and center of the room and begins introducing himself.

"Good afternoon, everyone. My name is Professor Andrews and this is my TA, Victoria Ward. Welcome to Psych 101."

Victoria Ward!

Bells go off in my head and when she smiles during his introduction it hits me. Son of a bitch, it's the girl from the club last semester. She looks totally different, but it's definitely her. She's wearing gray dress pants and a white, tailored button down. Her hair's up in a high ponytail, and her lips shine with some kind of gloss. She continues assisting the professor with whatever it is he's preparing for class, and then he hands her a stack of papers and she leaves. My eyes follow her as she walks out the door.

The professor drudges through the syllabus and by the time class is over, I'm already mentally bogged down with information. After only one day of classes, I have more homework than I ever imagined I'd have. I grab something to eat and head straight for the library. I have to be at the gym in two hours, so I guess I should make the most of my time.

Our first assignment for Professor Andrews is on psychology in history. I let out an exhausted breath and flip open my textbook. I'm deep in thought, reading the text, when the chair across from me pulls back. I glance up and it's Victoria. Our eyes meet briefly and I clear my throat before looking back down at my book. She most likely doesn't remember me, which is probably for the best. Then again, there are a ton of empty tables and chairs, so why sit at this one with me?

"Hi."

I look at her and half smile.

"Hello, Victoria," I respond. Then I dismissively look

back to my homework.

"Wow. You remember my name; I'm impressed. How do you like Baylor so far?" she asks, as if she doesn't want the conversation to wane.

"It's good, no complaints."

She sits there, with what I consider to be a confounded expression on her face. She looks like she expects me to offer more, but I don't.

"You're in Mr. Andrews's psychology class, correct?" she prods.

"Yep, looks like it."

She studies me for a few more seconds, roving her eyes over my face before refocusing back on my eyes. With my lack of eye contact and obvious *I'm not interested* vibe, you'd think she'd back off.

"Are you still brokenhearted, Mr. Collins?"

I harrumph and glance up at her quickly before looking back to my book.

"I'm fine, Ms. Ward. It's all good."

Whether I'm still sad or not is irrelevant at this point. Jess has moved on and I have to do the same—eventually. Regardless, I'm still not interested in starting up a relationship with someone else.

"Well, that's good to hear. Are you up for coffee later?" she asks with a streak of confidence that demands my attention. She isn't afraid to go after what she wants, that's for sure. I have to give her that much. She's noticeably older than I am and even though that doesn't intimidate me, it does tell me that she's a woman—a woman that, sooner or later, will want more. Silky pearl earrings dangle from her ears and her long ebony ponytail swoops down over her left shoulder. She's classy, intelligent, and probably comes from money.

Definitely a woman who will want more.

The fancy job, fancy house, perfect straight A kids, and a tiny lap dog are probably all on her checklist. I'm a Ford F-150; this girl is a Mercedes. We are not compatible. She'd be totally compatible with my mother, though.

"Sorry, but I'm not much of a coffee drinker," I say nonchalantly as I avoid her stare by flipping through the pages of my book. She's trying really hard to get my undivided attention while trying to remain cool and under the radar at the same time. It isn't working.

"Well, all right, then. If you ever need help with your psych class, let me know." She pushes a piece of paper across the table. Then she gathers her things and leaves. Her tight ass and well-curved hips saunter in the opposite direction.

Yep, you could've had that, but you're a damn fool they say, mocking me as they fade from my line of sight. I shake the temptation away and focus my attention back on my homework.

Women are evil, evil beings!

I check the time and realize I need to get to the gym to meet the guys for our workout. I shove my books and the number Victoria gave me into my bag and leave the library. I see Trent and some girl pressed up against my truck, and roll my eyes. This guy is the biggest player I've ever met; I can't believe girls are into that shit. Why do us nice guys always get shit on while guys like Trent have sweethearts falling all over them? They have to know that his dick has been in half the female population around here. But either they just don't seem to care or they're too dense to realize it. As I get closer, I can see that the girl he's with doesn't look all that pleased. In fact, she looks a little pissed. She's petite and has shiny shoulder-length brunette hair, toned, tan legs, and pouty lips. She's cute, not all blond and big-chested like most of the girls Trent usually gallivants around with.

"Hey, what's up, man? What's going on?"

"Hey, J. Not much. Bree here is just being moody, that's all," he says, with a shitty smirk stretched across his face.

She pushes into his barrel chest and retorts, "I'm not being moody. You're an asshat and you're a whore. I'm not going out with you ever again! Do you understand me, Trent Bailey? Never again!" she shouts and she curls her fists and stamps her little foot, as if to punctuate her words. "I'm not a tramp, nor am I one of those football team groupies. I liked you, but then I hear from Chelle that you screwed her roommate last night. What the hell is that? I'm not playing your bullshit games," she screams, and then ducks under his large arm and stomps away, leaving a trail of expletives in her wake. I raise my eyebrows at Trent and shake my head.

"Looks like you got a lively one there. You might want to start keeping track of who rooms with whom if you intend on keeping up the pace you've been going at. Otherwise, there's gonna be a pack of pissed off chicks with pitch forks at our dorm room door one day ready to tar and feather your big dumb ass."

"Yeah, yeah, yeah. Whatever, man. She'll come around. I actually feel a little bad that she found out. I like her, she's not stupid, and she doesn't get on my nerves when I've been around her for longer than ten minutes." For a second, I see a flash of regret on Trent's face, but it's gone just as quickly as it came. “Plus, she won’t even let me get past second base. It’s a little refreshing now that I think about it. I like a challenge.” He laughs and throws his bag in the back of my truck.

“You suck, man. That’s shitty to just see her as a piece of ass. You should try getting to know her. You might actually enjoy the company of the opposite sex for reasons other than screwing,” I tell him as we head toward the field house.

“I don’t ever want to be you, man, so I think I’ll stick to what I know. Watching you sulk around for all this time has been some depressing shit,” he says, wiping sweat from his forehead. “You’re nineteen years old and you live like a damn hermit, always huddled up in the room moping. How long are you going to let that chick keep you in a chokehold? I’m not saying you need to go out and get laid every weekend, but fuck, don’t you want to get some ass? You do have needs; lefty and righty can’t handle things forever you know.”

I glare in his direction. “Screw you, man! Unlike you, I actually have some damn respect for women. I’m not going out and getting action from anyone unless I can give them more than that. Otherwise, I don’t want anything to do with it—needs or no needs. So, get off my jock about it already. I’ll move on when I’m ready to fucking move on.”

“You’re a damn sap, J. I hope I never let a chick have me by the balls like that! No pussy is that good, dude.” Trent shrugs and I roll my eyes at him.

“Whatever, man. You just don’t get it.”

Even though I wish I didn’t, I do still love her. I hate that I do and with every day that goes by, the sting of it remains. But I have a feeling I'll never stop missing her. Soon enough, I'll have to wake up and realize that some people can stay in your heart, but not in your life.

Team workouts haven't been too bad lately, but this one was brutal and I'm drenched in sweat. Trent stayed afterward to lift some more, but I said screw that. I'm beat. I wipe the sweat from my brow and walk through the parking lot. I look up to see Victoria leaned up against my truck with her hands shoved into little jean shorts' pockets. She's got a Baylor shirt on and aviator sunglasses. She's relaxed, ankles crossed, and looking at me with a flirty grin on her face. What is it with this girl? Every time I see her she looks different. Club Victoria was hot and dripping with sex appeal, TA Victoria is always smart and professorial, and library Victoria was cool and composed. The girl so casually propped up against my Ford is refreshingly cute and easygoing. She looks like a girl, not an older woman.

"Looks like you had a demanding workout today," she purrs.

I walk around her and throw my bag in the bed of my truck. As I pass, the sweet smell of her perfume makes its way through my not-so-well-built barrier. She smells good, too good. This girl's going to make me crazy; I can already feel it. She just won't take a hint, and why does she have to smell so good?

Shit!

"They're always pretty damn demanding, but I like it

that way. What can I do for you? Seems like you're following me."

"Not following, just persisting," she taunts, and the corner of her mouth turns up slightly. She purses her shiny lips and then deliberately bites her lower one. Yep, this girl has *danger* written all over her. Big yellow caution lights are flashing all around her tight little body, which I can't stop my eyes from roving over like a horny teenager.

Don't do it, Jace, just walk away.

"Some girl did a real number on you, huh?"

I'd like to reach out and unlock my door, but she has her ass leaned up against it. No way am I putting my hand anywhere near that. So, I just stand here trying to figure this girl out.

"Yeah, something like that," I say, shuffling some gravel around with my foot as I stare at the ground.

"Well, how long do you plan on allowing her to keep making you miserable? Just so I can have some sort of timeline, you know."

I look up at her and notice the way the sun reflects off her skin, the way the light breeze gently lifts her shiny black hair. The skin on her neck is creamy white and smooth, and, for the first time in a long time, I feel a sudden twitch behind my zipper.

I need to get the hell away from this girl, like yesterday.

"And you need a timeline, why?" I ask as I pull my keys out. I push the automatic unlock button before she responds, hopefully giving her the hint that she needs to move her ass off my door.

"Oh, just because I need to have a general idea of when you're taking me out. You know, so I can be fully prepared."

I raise my eyebrows in reaction to her forwardness. She gives me a cute, crooked smile and I shake my head, smiling back and letting out a little laugh. She definitely deserves credit for self-assurance, that's for sure. It's sort of sexy. She's confident, but she doesn't come off as bitchy. Not like Liz. Liz was a bitch because she was insecure; I always knew that about her even though no one else ever did. Mrs. Brant treated Liz like a trained poodle, always insulting her, telling her she wasn't good enough, how she needed to be perfect. So Liz just created that mean girl shit to block out the insecurities she felt from home. At school, she wanted to be the queen bee; unfortunately, she went about it all wrong. Victoria just seems genuinely sure of herself, even though I sense a little spice in her too.

"You're pretty cocky, aren't you Ms. Ward. Who says I'm gonna ask you out? You're my TA; I'm pretty sure that's frowned upon. And shouldn't you be hitting on juniors or seniors anyway?"

She leans forward. "I won't always be your TA," she whispers. I feel her breath on my skin and I'd have to be dead not to react to her close proximity and the promise in her words. Thankfully, she straightens up again, giving me some room to breathe. "Plus, I didn't take you for a guy who'd be scared of an older woman, Mr. Collins. But maybe I've been all wrong in my assumptions about you." She pushes off my truck and slants her sunglasses slightly down the ridge of her nose, looking up at me with those chocolate brown eyes. I have to blink a couple of times to snap myself back to reality.

"You have my number. When you stop licking your

wounds, give me a call. You could learn a thing or two from an older woman. And who knows? You might just enjoy the education," she jeers. Then she strolls across the parking lot, never looking back. I rake my hand down my face and lean up against my truck as I look up to the sky.

Damn!

"The only impossible journey is
the one you never begin."
—Tony Robbins

Jessica

AFTER VICTORIA MADE her little insulting comment to me, I matched her barb with equally venomous remarks. I'm not in high school anymore, and not even some snooty, well-educated doctor is going to bully me. I have gone from floor mat to raving bitch over the past six years and I have no shame about it. Six years of building defenses, six years of emotionally fortified walls have been built and the good doctor was certainly not going to scale those walls today. On the inside, I felt inferior standing there in her grand office, which was adorned with her prestigious accomplishments, but she'd never know I felt that way. Never! My words were emotionally charged and impulsive, but it was my way of putting her in her place. It wasn't the most tactful way to do it, but, then again, tact was never my forte. My last boss told me I needed to get a filter for my mouth, so I tactfully told him to fuck off. That was my last day at that job. My angry defensive mechanisms are firmly in place, and have been for a while now. Every time someone attempts to lash out at me or hurt me, I respond accordingly—by overreacting.

Black and white—no shades of gray anywhere in between.

I can go from zero to one hundred in an instant. The guy I've been seeing, who's not my boyfriend, says I'm emotionally volatile. I can't disagree with Donnie on that point. Keeping my emotions in check at this group thing will certainly be a challenge.

I walk into the therapy group room and all I keep thinking is how bad it might be if someone says the wrong thing to me. I could end up thrown out of this place before it's all said and done. I slowly glance around the room. This entire process is terrifying and intimidating. There are chairs in the center of the room set in a semi-circle with one chair facing the others set in front. Off to the side is a table with water, coffee, and a fruit bowl sitting on it. There are a few people already here that obviously know each other. They chat and several more people enter the room as I walk over to grab a bottle of water. My throat feels like it's drying up and I feel the nerves as they attempt to uncomfortably settle into my body.

"Hi. You must be a newbie," I hear a voice say. I look over to see a petite girl with black-tipped blond hair that falls just below her neckline. She has on a tiny miniskirt and a white tank top. There must be more necklaces and bracelets on her right now than I have in my entire jewelry box. The diamond stud in her nose twinkles and her left ear has a small black spacer in it.

Great. I'm in the punk rock, goth group.

“Yes, it's my first day here,” I reply unenthusiastically. “Well, I'm Mercedes. It's not my first day. It's my 267th day, but who’s counting, right?”

I gaped at her trying to fathom how in the hell she's endured coming here that long—and why. “Wow. Um...that's a long time. That sucks.”

She grins unapologetically and says, “No, not particularly. I mean, yeah, at first I hated it, fought it every inch of the way, but then I met people who got me, who understood where I was coming from. No one in this group buys the crazy I'm able to sell to everyone else in my life. These people call me on my shit. Ms. Robin and the others in this group have never turned on me, abandoned me, or rejected me like everyone else I know. So I keep coming back.” She shrugs, and then turns to pour coffee in a large Styrofoam cup. “Plus, there's free coffee!”

I’m actually surprised by her admission, but it eases my nerves slightly. Maybe I won't be such a freak in here after all.

“My name is Jessica. I'll be honest, I'm not here of my own free will and I'm not even close to being happy about it. But, nonetheless, I'm here,” I sigh.

“It's cool. Everyone always feels that way. So, whatcha in for? Binging, purging, fucking, starving, cutting, spending, or all of the above?” God, she says all of that like it’s a choice between caffeinated or non-caffeinated coffee. She just casually asked this personal question like it's no big deal. I have to admit, it takes me completely by surprise. I raise both eyebrows, but avert my eyes as I aimlessly spin the lid on my water bottle back and forth. "Oh, come on! This is a self-harm group. If you're in this group, we all know why. It's not a secret here like it is everywhere else in our lives. So, spill it." Damn, this chick is a trip. No-holds-barred.

"Cutting," I say in a low voice.

"See, that wasn't so hard, was it? Now, come, let me introduce you to some of the other crazies," she jokes. I frown at her not-so-funny remark as she grabs me by the arm. "Don't be so sensitive. We're all a little crazy! If all the so-called normal people of the world were to come here and lay out all the bones that are hidden in their proverbial closets, I can guarandamntee you that you'd find they're all a little crazy too! At least we can joke and be honest about it."

I don't reply, but I must admit, in her own bold and quirky way, she makes a shitload of sense. Most people are able to hide the ugliness in their life and succeed at it. I've tried for so long to hide mine, but have failed miserably. It's as if I've been using a white crayon on white paper all my life. I've had no results, nothing to show for my efforts. We make our way over to the seats and she introduces me to some other group members.

"Jessica, this is Aimee and Chris. Ladies, this is Jessica. It's her first day and she's a bit on the shitty side, so you'll have to forgive her." Both girls look at me with genuine smiles.

The blond-haired girl pulls earbuds out of her ears and sticks out her hand. "Great to meet you, Jessica! I'm Chris. The first day is always the hardest, but it gets easier.

I promise." She puts an earbud back in one ear and relaxes into one of the chairs close by.

"I'm Aimee," the petite girl says, tucking a piece of flaming red hair behind her ear. "It's not so bad, really. Just give it a chance." She smiles again, and in it I see reassurance, warmth.

"Come on, you can sit with us. Ms. Robin will be in soon," Mercedes says as she gestures to the chairs.

I sit down between Chris, who's lost in her e-reader while listening to music, and Mercedes, who pulls a doodled-up notebook out of her bag.

"Ms. Robin always gives us homework, plus she always posts a quote or something to set the mood for each session. I'm a quoteaholic, so I write them all down."

I didn't bring anything with me except my purse and I don't carry a notebook around in it. I guess I'll just listen for today. More people file into the semi-circle and take a seat, and even though I know they aren't, I feel like all eyes are on me. A short, middle-aged lady enters the room carrying an easel, a variety of folders, and a notebook. She has a pen tucked behind her left ear and she's wearing red-rimmed glasses. She has a calm about her that seems to fill the room. She places her armful of items on the floor next to the center chair and sets up the easel, placing a white board on it. She pulls a dry erase marker from her pocket and writes something across the white board, which reads *An error doesn't become a mistake until you refuse to correct it.* My eyes scan over the words repeatedly as I attempt to soak up their meaning and how they apply to my life.

"Good afternoon, everyone. Hope y'all are doing well. We'll get started in a few minutes, so please take your seats."

From the corner of my eye, I catch a glimpse of a tallish guy and turn my head slightly to the side to get a better look. Low-slung, old, faded jeans rest on his hips and a fitted, gray shirt stretches across his broad chest. He's wearing black Doc Martens-type boots along with a black beanie on his head. Strands of his chestnut hair poke out from under it, falling just above his well-defined eyebrows. Small light brown freckles are sprinkled across his nose and his incredibly strong jawline meets with jaws that clench repeatedly, like he's tense. Suddenly, he glances up and his dark blue eyes meet mine. A deeply creased frown stretches across his well-structured, golden-brown face and I quickly look away, planting my eyes in my lap. I nervously tuck a strand of loose hair behind my ear and wonder why in the hell he glared at me like that. It was as if I'd pissed him off in another life or something. He isn't familiar at all, but in that short-lived second he looked at me like he knew me, and it wasn't a happy kind of recognition. It was a look of disdain.

I keep my eyes focused anywhere other than in his direction. I hear the legs of a chair pull out as he takes his seat to my left. I can feel eyes burning a hole through me, and I strain to maintain my resolve not to look back in his direction. Keeping my head down, I shift my eyes to the side just to make sure I'm not being paranoid. Nope, not paranoid. He's staring directly at me, leaning back with his long legs extended and crossed at the ankles, mirroring the way his arms cross over his chest. His expression is stoic and his lips are pressed together in a hard line.

"That's Kingsley Arrington. He's semi-new here," Mercedes says, apparently picking up on the weird tension in the air. "He's been coming for about a month now, but so far he hasn't participated in any of our discussions. He hasn't spoken one word yet. He just sits over there, all mysteriously broody and moody, and then he gets up and leaves each week."

"Oh, well I didn't really even notice him," I lie.

"Suuure you didn't. Girlfriend, I may prefer the female sex, but I'm not blind to male sex appeal when I see it. And, clearly, neither are you." I look at her, surprised by her comment, and she laughs.

"Please tell me I'm not your first lesbian acquaintance. You just looked at me like I grew horns out of my head or something."

"Oh God, no! I mean, well, yes, you are, but I didn't mean to look at you like that. It's just I haven't had any female friends—ever, gay or straight. And you don't *look* gay." She laughs a little louder.

"And what exactly does *gay* look like to you?" she asks, leaning back and quirking a brow at me.

"Umm, I don't know. I guess I pictured a lesbian as more tomboyish or something. That, and you're wearing more makeup and jewelry today than I own."

"Typical."

"I'm sorry, I—"

"No, really, it's totally cool. By the way, you're not my type, so you don't have to worry about me hitting on you. So relax. I'm just a girl, just like you—only I have a girlfriend instead of a boyfriend," she says, seemingly not bothered by my reaction.

Thank goodness. I don't have anything against her or the fact that she has a girlfriend. I'm just surprised, that's all. She's very nice and treats me like a normal human being. She's funny and seems to be completely nonjudgmental—nothing like most of the people I've met in my life.

Except Jace.

I shake his name from my thoughts and focus my attention back to the front of the room. I can still feel Kingsley's eyes on me and I almost want to look right at him and yell "What?" but I can't do that. I have no idea what his major malfunction with me is, but it's starting to piss me off.

"Okay, people, let's get started. We have a few new group members today that I'd like to welcome and to everyone else, thank you for continuing to come back. We're going to talk about impulsivity today—what drives it and how it leads to errors in judgment."

I draw in a deep breath and gently pinch the ridge of my nose. This isn't going to be easy for me at all. Talking in front of strangers isn't appealing to me in the least. I fidget with my water bottle and peel the plastic wrapper off in strips.

Mercedes leans in and whispers, "Don't stress. You don't have to talk if you don't want to. It's one hundred percent up to you when you decide to share or not." I relax into my chair, thinking her words are the sweetest ones I've heard all day.

Thank God!

"Chris, if you could remove your earphones, I'd appreciate it," Ms. Robin says with a winning smile. Chris quickly pulls them out and stuffs them in her bag along with her e-reader.

"Sorry, Ms. Robin."

"Okay, who can tell me what impulsivity means to them?" Ms. Robin asks and her eyes dart around the room expectantly. I do my best not to make eye contact with her. I do not want to get pinned down for an answer.

Mercedes shifts beside me and calls out, "I'll go, Ms. Robin." I slink down into my chair a little more now that all eyes are facing my general direction.

"Okay. Thanks, Mercedes. Go ahead, dear."

"To me, impulsivity is like a magnetic force pulling you in a direction that you wouldn't naturally go in. You know, like for me, I can see the tub of ice cream in my freezer and know that I shouldn't want to grab it and eat the entire thing because I'm having a bad day, or because Leila has pissed me off, but some force pushes me to do it anyway. Then afterward, I freak out and run to the bathroom, shoving my finger down my throat to get it all out. I guess it just feels involuntary."

"Great, thank you so much, Mercedes. Anyone else want to share? How about you, Kingsley? Would you like to share this week?" My eyes reluctantly dart in his direction and I curse them for being traitors.

"Nope," he says, expressionless until he cocks his head to the side and looks at me. The disgust is back and I'm starting to get a complex. Do I look like ass today or something? Do I have a huge zit on my face that I'm unaware of? What? I have no idea why this asshole keeps looking at me like this.

"All right then, Kingsley. Just know you're safe talking here any time." He nods and goes back to brooding.

Surprisingly, the hour flies by and Ms. Robin is already wrapping things up. "Okay, I'd like to thank all of you for participating in our discussions today. Your homework is to jot down times when you feel impulsive over the next week. Write down why you're feeling it, and then attempt to use some of the distress tolerance skills we learned here today. Remember the distracting method, self-soothing, improving the moment, and thinking of pros and cons about the choice you're facing. Write down whether you were successful or not using these methods. We'll discuss the possible whys in one of our groups next week." I pull out my cell phone, open up my notepad app, and type in the homework assignment. If I'm going to have to write down every time I feel impulsive, I'm going to need a big notebook.

"See, not so bad, huh?" Mercedes asks.

I nod, "No, not so bad, I guess."

"Okay, so I'll see you next group, then?"

"Yep, I'll be here with bells on," I quip sarcastically. She laughs and shoves a torn piece of paper at me.

"Here's my number. Call anytime. We all need support systems; sometimes a friend is all you need to get through a rough patch." She smiles.

A friend.

The only friend I've ever had was Jace and that turned into a total disaster. I like Mercedes, but having a friend isn't familiar ground for me.

"Sure," I nod. "And thanks, Mercedes. Thanks for being so cool." She smiles and meanders out of the room with a bounce in her step. I reach down and grab my purse. In my peripheral vision, I see someone walk through the door and look up instinctively.

Jace.

Of course it's Jace. In black slacks and a baby blue

button down that accents his ice-blue eyes perfectly. My throat tightens as if someone's strangling me and my jaws clench. His eyes are fixed on me and I fumble with my empty water bottle and all of the label scraps, inwardly cursing myself for making a mess that I now have to take the time to clean up instead of being able to run out of here. Grabbing a handful of the small scraps and the bottle, I stand up and our eyes meet once again.

God, he is still so gorgeous.

He shoves his hands into his pockets as he approaches me. Then, just before he says anything, Kingsley passes by us with a backward glance in my direction; I blink and chew at my bottom lip, feeling like I'm suddenly trapped in a pressure cooker full of hot guys and angst. The small exchange isn't lost on Jace. He raises a brow and turns in Kingsley's direction.

"You know him?" he prods.

Is that jealousy I see on his face?

He has a damn fiancé and he's asking me questions like this. What a prick! A sexy prick, but a prick, nonetheless. He infuriates me with his self-righteous posture and tone; with that little turned-up side grin and that motherlovin' toothpick—it's come back to haunt me. Good. God.

"Whether I know him or not isn't really any of your business, now is it?" Sarcasm rolls off my tongue, but he just smiles back at me.

"No, I suppose it isn't," he reaches up, scratching his head. He seems to be at a loss for words, but he stands here blocking my path anyway.

"What do you want, Jace? Shouldn't you be off picking out napkin patterns or something with the good doctor?"

Bitch.

I'm such a bitch. He winces at my words and sighs.

"Why are you back here? I told you that you have to find a new clinic. I know you went and saw Victoria too. You've caused quite a stir, Jessica."

Me? I've caused quite a stir? Is he serious? *He's the one who stole my damn file!*

I lean in closer, so that my voice can't be heard by anyone else, and I look him dead in the eye. The aroma of his cologne captures my attention, causing me to pause momentarily before speaking.

"Listen to me," I say, using my lowest, most dangerous voice. "You took my file from her office. You are the one who caused a stir, not me. I could get you both in some serious trouble if I wanted to, but I'm not out to hurt you, Jace." I take a big breath and straighten up, letting my cheeks pucker out as I exhale. "Just leave me alone. Marry your doctor and leave me the hell alone. I can't just drop out of these group sessions or I'll be in trouble with the judge. I'll request a new clinic today. Just leave me be, okay?" Each word slices through my heart and the pain of them burns my throat.

"You don't mean that and you know it," he whispers fiercely, and his intensity is almost too much to take. "I don't buy your show, Jess. I. See. You. I always have and I always will. No matter how hard you try to hide inside yourself, I'll always see you. Those walls may be up, but I see right through them," he finishes. Then he turns and walks away.

My chest rises and falls quickly as I try to regulate my breathing. I sling my purse strap over my shoulder and push through the exit door breathlessly. I have to stop letting Jace Collins affect me so powerfully. He's like a drug; every time I'm around him I go into some involuntary inebriated state. It's pathetic.

I get to the parking lot and see a big Harley Davidson sitting off to the side with none other than Kingsley straddled upon it.

Great.

Was he waiting for me to come out? Was he about to abduct me and commence cutting me up into small pieces somewhere? What the hell? I turn on my heel in the opposite direction toward my bus stop. Then, suddenly, I hear footsteps crunching the gravel of the parking lot behind me. I pick up my pace as my heart hammers in my chest. Right then, I stop abruptly in my tracks. I will not let him scare me. Thoughts of being terrified in high school flood my mind and anger roars through my veins. I turn around and face him.

"What's your deal? Why are you following me and what the hell did I ever do to you? Why did you spend the last hour looking at me like I was dirt on the bottom of your boot?" I shout in a rush, practically out of breath by the time I get it all out. He scowls and pulls off his beanie. He rakes his hand through his disheveled hair as his eyes shoot back and forth between the ground and me.

"I'm sorry." He has the most sexual, raspy voice I've ever heard from a guy's mouth. It's like sweaty, hot sex on gravel.

"Oookay. Thanks for the apology, and forgive me for saying this, but you creeped me out in there and you're creeping me out now," I say as I defensively cross my arms over my chest.

"You just remind me of someone, that's all. It sort of threw me for a loop, you know? I didn't mean to freak you out," he says roughly. Although his voice is kind of gruff, his stature is apologetic, and his eyes, though they won't meet mine, reflect the truth of his words. "It's just that...," he starts, and I admit it; I'm intrigued by him, curious to know what he has to say. "You know what? Never mind. I just wanted to apologize, that's all." He looks back at me and I see something other than contempt in his eyes. I see sadness; a raw pain that's all too familiar to me.

"It's okay. Already forgotten," I say. What I don't say is that even though I have no idea what it is that's torturing him, I know. I understand. I relate.

He just nods and pulls the beanie back onto his head. I watch him walk back to his bike, put a helmet on, straddle the big motorcycle, then look in my direction once more before he cranks it and drives away. I have a feeling there's a lot more to that guy than meets the eye.

Who is Kingsley Arrington?

And who do I remind him of?

"The way to love anything is
to realize it may be lost."
—Gilbert Chesterton

Jace

I SIT AT my desk, aimlessly flipping through papers. I'm lost in thought, thinking about Jess. I know that any minute Victoria will walk through my door with more questions than I care to give her answers to.

I've never told her about Jess in detail. I've always kept the specifics locked away in a vault within me. Victoria knows I went through a tough breakup, but whenever she pressed me for more information, I always changed the subject.

Once, years ago, when she'd stayed over at my place, she had grabbed a T-shirt from my dresser drawer to throw on. It happened to be the blue *Music Makes Me Horny* T-shirt Jess had given me.

"You can't wear that," I'd told her.

She'd looked down at it and laughed. "Umm, why not? It's funny, and now that I know this bit of valuable information about you, I'll be sure to play music every time you're around."

"Take the shirt off, Vic," I'd said with clipped words, brokering no argument.

"Fine, geez. It's childish anyway," she'd said, obviously irritated, as she tugged it over her head.

She'd asked me later what the big deal was and I told her I didn't want to talk about it. I still don't want to talk about it, but it's inevitable now.

So I just sit here and wait.

The doorknob begins to turn and I brace myself. Victoria steps into my office and I can see the anger plainly on her face.

"We need to talk. I've canceled all of my appointments for the day." She sits down in the chair across from my desk and crosses her legs. "Who is Jessica Alexander? And how does she know we're getting married in four weeks?" I lean back in my chair, place both hands behind my head, and look toward the ceiling.

"Well, spit it out, J," she snaps. "Please explain to me why my patient walked into my office this morning holding her file—a file she says I should ask you about. She also claims you were at her apartment last night. Is that why you didn't come over? Did you lie to me about where you were when I called you?" her voice is rising, and though Victoria doesn't get hysterical—ever—she looks and sounds as close to it as I've ever seen her. "Please tell me that some mentally disturbed whore isn't the girl from your past that had you twisted up for so long." Her tone is condescending, patronizing.

I drop my hands to my desk and lean forward, pissed. I've been wrong about a lot of things in the last couple days—taking the file, lying to Victoria, and kissing Jess last night even though I'm engaged—but that's all on me. I'll be damned if I'm going to sit here and let her talk about Jessica that way. As I look at her sitting across from me right now, I can't help but see Elizabeth in her posture, hear Elizabeth in her judgmental words, which are soaked with superiority. How she can say something like that and be in this profession blows my mind. I know this is a special case, but I've never heard her say anything about a patient with such ugliness in her voice before.

"Don't, Vic," I warn.

"Don't what? Don't ask my fiancé where he was last night? Don't ask why some mentally unstable borderline slut claims you don't want to marry me? Don't what, Jace?" she says, raising her voice again.

"She said that?" I ask, focusing in on what Jess must have told her. I'm right. Jess does care. Vic glares at me and I can see she's seething. I sigh and decide it's time to put it all on the table and let the cards fall where they may. I'm a terrible liar anyway and, regardless of everything, she deserves the truth.

"Yes, she's the girl. But, despite what your initial opinion is from the couple of hours you've spent with her, she's not what you think she is," I say, cutting her off before she can start to argue. "And you should be ashamed of yourself for saying such things about one of your patients. You're acting like you're better than her, stronger than her, but Vic, strong people don't push other people down. They help them up," I scold, still pissed off that she just verbally bashed Jess.

She huffs and situates herself back in her chair. "Well, thank you for your clinical opinion, *Dr.* Collins. I'll be sure to take that into consideration. Oh, that's right, you're not a doctor," she says condescendingly. "You're telling me I should be ashamed, but you were at another woman's apartment last night! I do believe you're deserving of a healthy dose of shame as well. Or are you going to tell me you weren't, in fact, at her apartment?"

"No, I'm not telling you that I wasn't there because the truth is, I was." I admit. I feel terrible for what I'm about to tell her, but I have to be honest with her. "When you asked me to grab your keys, I saw her name on a folder and I took it. I made up an excuse not to stay over at your place and I went to see her instead. I was wrong to have taken the folder, and I was equally wrong for lying to you, but I had no choice in this. I *had* to go see her. You just don't understand, Vic, and you probably never will."

"Did you sleep with her? Did you cheat on me?" she says as she narrows her eyes and sits up a little straighter.

"No, and yes." Her eyes flare as she stares at me openmouthed and I quickly go on. "No, I didn't sleep with her, but I almost did. I would've if she hadn't stopped me." Maybe I didn't need to add that last bit, I can see it's upsetting her, but I won't deny my feelings for Jess now that she's back in my life.

She stands up abruptly, glaring at me with cold, hard eyes. "I can't sit here and listen to this any longer. For one thing, I'm not losing my license or business because you took that file and lost your mind. You need to get your shit together now, Jace Collins. You're a grown man. This is not high school anymore and she's not your sweetheart."

She starts for the door and then turns around, shooting tiny daggers at me with her eyes.

"She left you, moved on, and walked away, so just get over it. Get over her. I haven't spent countless hours on wedding preparations and sent out hundreds of invitations just so some petulant, mentally ill girl from your past can screw it all up. It's not like you're still in love with her after six years. You're in love with me! You're with me, so whatever this is, you need to rectify it now. My future isn't going to be ruined over some old high school crush of yours."

I look at her angrily and growl, "Don't talk about her like that."

"Why, J? Is it hard to hear the truth? She left you. The girl is mentally ill. She's also quite the bitch. I have no idea what you ever saw in her. She's not even that pretty. Figure this out, Jace, and screw your head back on straight, because this wedding is happening," she says. Then she storms out my door.

I lock up the office and head to my car. Victoria didn't come back to see me for the rest of the day. I have three missed calls from Mom, but I'm not calling her back. She's very close with Victoria, so I'm sure they've spoken, but I know how she is and I'm just not ready for the third degree right now. She never liked Jess, and I'm certain she'll be none too pleased with this recent turn of events.

I sit in my car, pondering what to do about everything. The worst part is that I don't feel guilty for what I told Victoria. I feel guilty for not feeling guilty, but that's it. Seeing Jess last night flipped a long-buried switch within me and I'm not sure I can flip it back off again. I'm not sure I *want* to flip it back off again.

I pull out my cell phone and dial her number. My heart races a little faster with each ring and I almost decide to hang up.

She answers.

"Why are you calling me, Jace?"

I sigh into the phone. "Can I see you?" I ask. I don't know what I'm hoping for, or what I even want. I just know I need to see her again.

"Why? We have nothing else to talk about. You're —"

I cut her off, not wanting to hear it another time. "Drop the I'm getting married thing. Yes, I'm engaged, but that happened way before I found you again, and I'm not married yet. So, can I see you or not?"

"Did you talk to the good doctor? Is she okay with you seeing me?" she taunts.

"Stop being such a child, Jess," I demand. She's acting so catty and I don't like it. This is not the Jess I knew.

"Wow, now that's a great way to convince me to see you," she answers. I want to tell her that she owes me, that she has to see me to make up for all those years I suffered without her, but I don't. I miss her too much to risk her hanging up on me.

"Jess, please just stop being so bitchy and guarded and talk to me. It's me. You don't have to put on this front for me. Are you at your place?

"Jace, this is just—"

"Yes or no, Jess?"

"Yes, I'm at home, but—"

"I'll be there in twenty minutes."

I stand outside her door holding two Sonic RT 44 Vanilla Cokes. She used to love Vanilla Coke; she drank gallons of the stuff from the Dairy Queen back home. I press the doorbell and hold my breath. A few seconds, which feel like long drawn-out minutes, go by before the door opens. Jess stands there with a low-hanging pair of gray baggy sweat pants on and a green T-shirt that says *I Think, Therefore We Have Nothing In Common*. Her long shiny black hair falls down over her shoulders.

She's beautiful.

I laugh at her shirt. "Some things never change. Did you wear that one especially for me?" I hold out the huge RT 44 drink to her as if it's a peace offering. She looks at the drink and back to me. A tiny smile graces her lips and I know I have her.

"Is it Vanilla Coke?" she asks.

"None other."

"Okay, fine, you can come in, but only because you brought Vanilla Coke," she says, opening the door for me. I walk in and smell something coming from the kitchen.

"It smells good in here. Are you cooking?" She lets out a huge giggle and says, "Absolutely not! It's Chinese take-out. I don't cook—ever—and trust me, you would not want to eat anything I attempted to cook. I'm awful at it."

"I doubt that. I'm sure you can cook just fine."

She walks into the kitchen and takes a large gulp from her drink. She reaches up into a cabinet to grab a plate and her T-shirt inches up exposing the soft skin of her stomach. I automatically feel the need to adjust myself.

Dammit! Jace, get those thoughts out of your head.

But she's sexy as hell, and all I can think about is running my tongue across that soft skin of hers.

"Jace? Would you like some of this lo mein, or would you like to continue eye-fucking me instead?"

I snap out of my trance and realize she's caught me staring.

Shit!

I'm an asshole. A pathetic, lovesick, horny asshole.

"Umm...damn. I'm sorry, but you just...you look sexy as hell, Jess, and that tiny T-shirt isn't nearly long enough for you to be reaching up into those cabinets," I tell her, and I'm sure she hears the appreciation in my voice.

"Why did you come here?" she asks, irritated. Not the response I was hoping for. "If you came here thinking you were going to finish what you started last night, you're wrong. Plus, I have a date in about two hours, so I won't be needing any of my womanly desires handled by you. Donnie manages to take care of that just fine." My fists clench immediately.

Donnie? Who the fuck is Donnie?

Jealousy and resentment sit just beneath the surface and the desire to reclaim her as mine rises with a powerful vengeance. Jealousy isn't something that I've ever really struggled with, but right now I just want her all to myself. I only had one night with her. *One night.* I hate thinking about all of the others that have been with her. Possessiveness wins out in my internal battle and I stare at her intently. I grit my teeth and try to convey the seriousness of the situation when she sets the plate down and glances back up at me. Hopefully my expression will leave zero doubt that I'm no longer here to talk.

Donnie will not be satisfying her needs tonight, or any other night. Fuck that and fuck him. I don't know who this guy is, and I don't particularly care. All I care about is showing Jess that she still loves me just as much as I still love her. She won't listen to my words, so I'll make her understand with my actions.

"Why are you looking at me like that?" she asks, genuinely bewildered. Then it hits her. "Don't tell me you're jealous. I'm not the one that's engaged, and yes, I'll keep saying it because it's true. You. Are. Engaged!"

I slowly set my drink down and round the counter, determined. Her eyes widen as I step into the kitchen and she counters my approach by backing up. She absently licks her lips and I fight back a grin, knowing she has no idea she just did that. Her words may be to put distance between us, but her body language tells a different story. My body thrums with sexual tension and want and I can feel my pulse thumping in my neck. I stop in front of her and take her in for a moment.

"I don't want her, I want you! You've been what I've wanted for over six years and that hasn't changed. I want you so badly right now that I can barely breathe," I proclaim in a low, guttural tone. Consequences be damned; I couldn't care less about any of them right now.

She stands there holding her drink and I step in closer yet again. I reach out to grab it from her hand and as I do, our fingers brush. The electricity sizzles between us and she flinches on a sharp inhale. It's still there and she feels it too.

That does it.

Our eyes meet as I lean in, closing the last bit of space between us. I grab her face between both of my hands and she stumbles backward up against the granite countertop. My pants grow tighter as I press myself firmly against her warm body. God, how I've missed her. She bites her lip and lets out a whimper as I thrust my hands into her long, sexy hair. Finally, I claim her mouth with a hunger of over six years. She's responding to me, and I know that every second my lips are on hers, her resolve crumbles a little bit more. I pull at the nape of her neck and suck her lower lip into my mouth, sinking my teeth into it slightly. She moans as she presses her hands into my chest. I move from her mouth down to her neck, and kiss my way back up to her earlobe. I nip and suck at it before whispering in her ear.

"I still love you, Jess. Let me love you." I lay more kisses on her as I let my hands wander over her. "Don't push me away, not again." Her breathing grows more ragged and I confess everything I've been thinking about since I saw her last night. "I want to rip every damn piece of clothing off your body and bury myself inside of you. I want to do that and never leave again." Her fingernails dig into my chest and she starts to speak.

"Jace," she says breathlessly. Before she can say anything else, I still, holding her, and whisper, "Say yes, Jessica. Say you want me as much as I want you. Tell me you still love me."

I pull back from her and look deeply into her eyes. She's flushed and her chest is heaving. Her nipples are taut, peeking through the thin material of her shirt, teasing me. Good God, I want her so badly. I want to feel her naked chest against mine, her smooth stomach against me. I search her eyes for an answer and she looks back and forth between my eyes and my arms, which have her trapped against the counter. She's thinking of running, I can tell, but I can't let that happen.

I lean in and cover her mouth with mine once again. I reach down, pulling on her hips, and then slide my hands down, firmly cupping her ass. She opens her mouth to me and while our tongues wind around each other in a fervent, heated dance, her arms clasp behind my neck. I swiftly grab her legs and position myself against her while wrapping her legs around me. Bracing her back with one hand, I turn and carry her toward the living room. I bump into an end table by the sofa and the lamp crashes to the floor. The movement startles her and she gasps, but I don't care—fuck the lamp! I'll buy her a new one. I lay her down on the sofa, following her body closely with mine. And that's when I know I've broken through. She's kissing me back excitedly, furiously arching her hips up to mine, and seeking my touch. Like she needs me just as much as I need her.

I flick my tongue across her top lip and trail heated kisses across her cheek down to her neck. She's practically panting and I'm so hard it's painful. I want every inch of it inside her, now. Her hands rake down my body leaving a trail of goose bumps in their wake. My body's on fire and the need to make her mine is ferocious. I've never felt so savage in my life!

We are hands and mouths and legs twisting, molding, and linking together. Years of want and need fill the space around us. I reach down and hook my fingers under the edge of her shirt, pulling it up to reveal her bare chest. Without hesitation, I suck her pert nipple into my mouth, hard.

She whimpers and it drives me crazy.

I circle the tight bud with my tongue softly, and then graze it with my teeth, mixing pleasure with pain. She starts fumbling with my belt and I know without a doubt that her feelings are in the driver's seat now. I move down her stomach and pull her hands away from my waist. I kiss just below her navel and look up at her. She's feverish, beautiful, and her chest rises and falls rapidly as breaths escape her full, pouty lips.

"You're mine, Jess, and I'm yours. I love you so much, but right now I'm going to make love to you. I plan on making love to you over and over again until the sun comes up. So you're going to have to cancel with that Donnie."

She sucks her bottom lip in and nods.

I pull the string of her sweatpants and the knot falls apart easily. I quickly pull them down and she instinctively reaches down, trying to conceal her scars. There are so many of them, so many more than there had been all those years ago. Worry shoots straight to my heart, but I push it away for another time.

I glance up at her and see the fear circling in her eyes. They gloss over as if she might cry and I quickly remove her panties, kissing and tracing the scars with my tongue, one by one.

I whisper against her battered skin, "I love you, Jess. All of you: the good, the bad, and the imperfect. I love it all."

She may be flawed, but she's all I want. I kiss her scars once more, rubbing her inner thigh with my fingers before sliding them between her legs. She's dripping with need and I want to taste her. My head dips down and her legs tense in response. Her hands weave through my hair and she moans, writhing against my face.

So much better than I remember.

The sound of her panting and pleasure, and the built-up tension between us is palpable, more than I can take for another second. I unbuckle my belt, shoving my pants and boxers to the floor. She reaches down and grasps at my shirt, fumbling with the buttons. She manages to unbutton three when I reach down, pulling it over my head, not giving a shit about the other buttons that pop off in response.

I move up and cover her body with mine. I kiss her hard, pouring all of the love, anger, sadness, and loneliness I've felt over the years into that one single kiss.

"I'm on birth control. I really am. The prescription is in the bathroom if you want to see it, but God, if you don't hurry up, I'm going to die. I need you inside me now."

I moan deep in my throat looking into her beautiful almond-shaped eyes. I love this woman with everything I have. Trying to suppress it, change it, manipulate it all these years was pointless.

I've been living a lie.

No more lies.

I allow my weight to rest on her and the heat of her skin fuses with mine. The puzzle pieces that were lost have finally been found. I push inside her with one hard, swift motion. She throws her head back and cries out my name, and it's the sweetest sound I've heard in six long years. Her slick heat envelops every inch of me and I fall into nirvana as I bury my face in her neck, inhaling the scent of her hair. She opens for me as I move harder and faster until our bodies are fully and completely merged as one. This is where I'm supposed to be. Here, with her.

What I'm feeling is unexplainable, almost painful in its intensity. My heart pounds and as we move together, something falls away between us. It's as if the years we've lost have disappeared and that space is being filled with nothing but love.

"Lies don't ruin relationships.
The truth does."
—Unknown

Jessica

I'M PANTING AND out of breath. My heart's racing and I feel light-headed. After six long years, Jace and I have had sex again. So many emotions are stirring around in my head, and I can't make sense of any of them. Jace looks at me with sincere, raw emotion burning in his eyes.

I'm speechless.

"I love you, Jess, so much," he whispers as he kisses my neck delicately.

I want to say it back, but the words literally catch in my throat. Just as I'm about to let my last wall down and tell him I love him too, someone knocks at my door, pulling us out of our lust-filled haze. The gravity of what we just did settles in my chest and I scramble to gather our clothes, trying to put myself back together.

"I have no idea who that could be. Unless...oh shit, I bet it's Donnie!" I exclaim. Jace looks annoyed at the interruption, and more than willing to tell Donnie to get lost. Great, this is all I need right now. How freaking awkward is this?

I pull on my sweats and T-shirt hurriedly while Jace puts his clothes back on too. We exchange uncomfortable glances and I pad through the apartment and over to the door, trying to smooth down my freshly fucked hair as I go. I reach out and open the door, trying to think fast to figure out what I'm going to tell Donnie.

But it's not Donnie. Never in a million years did I expect to see Dr. Ward standing at my damn door. My heart drops.

Holy motherfucking shit!

"Just as I predicted!" Victoria scoffs, both hands on her hips. She's glaring at Jace over my shoulder. The temperature in the room just dropped about five million degrees. She waltzes right past me into my apartment like she owns the place.

"I knew you'd be here. This is priceless, Jace, so classy of you. Have you officially gotten it out of your system now? Huh? I surely hope the hell so!"

Wow, this woman is a real piece of work.

I can't believe she's being so calm. She acts like he came over and borrowed some eggs or something. But by the flushed look on Jace's face and his disheveled clothing, which I'm sure mirrors my own, it's obvious we weren't baking in here. She has to know we just had sex. I feel half guilt, half smug as I take in the way she's eying Jace. I'd be losing my mind if I were her, but she's so composed. This woman doesn't love him. If she did, she'd be clawing my eyes out right now.

"Vic, what are you doing here?" Jace asks, running his hand anxiously down his flushed face.

"Well, I suppose I could ask you the same question, but it's pretty obvious what you're here for," she says, and she flicks her eyes at me contemptuously before continuing. "If you had your phone on, you'd know that your mother and I have been trying to get in touch with you all evening. She's very ill and has been admitted to the hospital. We need to get there as soon as possible, so your little charade with your high school tart will have to come to an end. Now."

What an emasculating little bitch. Surely Jace won't be going anywhere with this woman after what just happened between us.

Jace is looking at Victoria with panic in his eyes, as if at the mention of his mother being sick he's completely forgotten me and everything we just shared together. "What's wrong with her? Why is she in the hospital?" he asks nervously.

"They don't know. She fainted and the housekeeper called 911. They're running tests now, so we need to go," she insists.

He sighs, looking at me with defeat in his eyes.

God, he is. He's going to leave with her.

I feel myself start to withdraw from him, from the situation, from myself. I can't believe this is happening all over again. I'm losing him, except this time, it's his choice.

"Vic, can you give me a minute please? I'll meet you outside."

"Fine, five minutes and not a minute more. Say what

you need to say, and then say good-bye to her, Jace." I listen quietly, steeling myself for what I know is coming, as she orders him around like he's a small child. I wonder how the strong, confident man I knew ended up with a woman like her. "We are getting married; you need to stop this childishness. We are adults, not high schoolers," she spouts, and then sashays out the door in her designer suit and heels.

He looks at me and I turn my back to him so that he can't see how hurt I am. He did nothing to correct her, nothing to let her know that this isn't just some charade. He didn't tell her how important I am to him, that I'm not just some*thing* that needs to be worked out of his system. He didn't yell or scream, he just stood there and took it, and accepted it when she minimized all we are to each other.

I can't look at him. Tears that I refuse to let him see well up in my eyes. I feel his hand on my shoulder and I shudder.

"Jess, I'm so damn sorry. If Mom is sick I have to go see her. Please understand."

I tense at his touch and shrug his hand away, keeping my back to him.

"Just go. This shouldn't have ever happened. You're clearly confused about what you want. We blurred the lines tonight, but I see everything very clearly now. You're leaving me to go with her, the woman who just characterized me as something that needed to be worked out of your system. The same woman you didn't even correct." I laugh unsteadily, but nothing about this is humorous. "You could very easily go to see your mom alone, but you're not. That speaks volumes, and I'm not about to sit here and be your fucking piece of ass on the side. So please, just leave. I'm done with this, with you, with us."

Pain.

Loss.

Just block it out, Jess.

Numb.

"Jess, please don't do this," he pleads. "I just need some time, that's all. I don't want to lose you again and I want to be there for you through your therapy. Don't push me away again. I love you, I really do. That's never going to change."

My blood boils and I tighten my fists at my sides, turning around slowly to face him. I stare at him with ice-cold eyes.

"It doesn't matter! It hasn't mattered for six damn years, and it doesn't matter now," I shout, and ride my anger like a wave. "Whatever we had is lost, gone. You can look me in the eye and make all the promises you want, but it won't change the reality of this situation. You love me, but you need more time. You love me, but you want to fix me. Well, I don't care what you want anymore! I don't care what's best for you anymore! Go! Just go be with her, love her, care for her. I have to fix myself—love myself, Jace—and there's nothing you can do to fast-forward that process. No matter how deeply embedded we are under each other's skin, this will never ever work because together, we're broken."

I steady my voice and as the anxiety inside of me builds.

"Sometimes you just have to accept that some things can't be fixed, and that it's not about fixing what's broken, but about accepting what's lost," I say sadly, and I hope he understands that this is good-bye. "So please, just walk away and leave the pieces where they are. I'm tired of missing you. I'm tired of looking for something that will never be there. I've looked for it on the edge of a blade and at the bottom of a bottle. It's not there. It's just...gone."

His eyes grow dark and despondent as his shoulders fall. He silently turns and walks toward my door.

"I'm not going to force myself into your life, Jess, but what happened tonight was real. I can't just ignore it and neither can you. I'll call you after I make sure Mom is okay," he says. Then I watch him turn the knob and walk out of my life. Again.

I have to accept that this will never work because no one can be loved until they can love themselves, and I don't know if I'll ever be able to do that. I go straight to my room and pull out my journal, desperate to write and put my emotions down on paper.

Back to empty

Here's my cup, fill it on up

Runneth it over

Pour me something stronger

Don't want to feel this way any

longer...
Drown the me I can't let anyone see
Force it down
Swallow it all
Just pour me something stronger
than me...
It was enough
Once I could see
Carried to me
On the waves
Of a blue-eyed sea
I exhaled
I saw
I felt
To me, forever memories
To the sea, already forgotten
Turning the key
Again, locking it all away

I step back up
To the bar of life
Society and reality joining me
Holding out my glass
I say…
Just pour me something stronger
than me…

My eyes are puffy and my body aches. Waking up, I'm hoping that last night was a horrible nightmare, but I know it wasn't. Jace walked right out my door and straight to her. He might as well have taken my heart with him, because I feel nothing but hollow right now. All that's left is pain, fears, and vulnerabilities. I don't know if I'll ever really be able to feel good again. Years and years of therapy couldn't fix all that's wrong with me.

I swallow the pain of losing Jace, yet again. It tastes like morphine mixed with acid. It burns, but makes me feel numb all at the same time.

I have group again today and I'm not sure I even want to go, or if I should go after Jace's warning about finding another therapist and clinic. I have to fulfill my probation, though. Either way, this is the last time I'll attend this group. Hopefully, my request for a new placement has been received and I can go elsewhere soon.

Pulling myself out of bed, I shower and get dressed. Standing in front of the mirror, I look at myself and wonder: is this really all there is? Is this all that I am? All that I'll ever be?

My face is pale, and the circles under my eyes are pretty much permanent these days. I grab my makeup bag and do what I can to conceal the visible flaws. After blow-drying my hair, I give myself one last look in the mirror and see a pathetic, lost person in a flawed woman's body—a body marred with visible and invisible scars.

The ache in my chest is constant and never lessens. I know I have to let him go, but sometimes I think trying to forget someone that's touched your heart the way Jace has touched mine is as impossible as trying to remember someone you've never met at all. Moving on is easy, but leaving that someone behind is the fucking hard part.

I wish I knew what it felt like not to have this hole inside of me, this emptiness that never seems to go away. The only time I've ever felt like it was whole was when I was with Jace, but now I wonder if that's entirely true. I don't know what to fill it with, or even how to fill it. Ever since I can remember, I've felt a certain degree of emptiness, like something inside of me just wasn't there, wasn't pieced together right. When Jace came into my life, I felt less hollow, but each time I've had to endure losing him that hole has gotten bigger, wider, and so much deeper. I feel like all I've ever done is chase life, never catching it.

Walking into group, I feel less than enthused about

trying to find myself. After last night, I couldn't care less about anything. I know where Jace is, and who he's with, and that's all I can think about right now. Sometimes, my obsessive thoughts are so intense that they overwhelm everything I do.

I sit in one of the cold metal chairs and fidget with my sleeves as the others file in, babbling amongst themselves. The morose feeling that I'm submerged in feels heavy upon my shoulders and I just want to get up, go home, and drink, sleep, or cut. Instead, I have to be here listening to why I'm so fucked-up, why all these other fucked-up people are so screwed in the head too, and what we need to do to fix ourselves. It's really similar to alcoholics, I suppose. It's all vices, ways to cope.

"Hey, Jessica! Glad you're back. I wondered if you'd venture back here with us crazies or not," Mercedes chirps.

She's wearing tons of makeup and jewelry again, and her bright white teeth and that happy Lucky Charms smile of hers is working overtime today. How someone in this group can be so freaking happy, I'll never know.

"Hey, Mercedes. Yes, I'm back, but not by choice, I assure you," I mutter while rolling my eyes and sighing.

"Oh, it's not that damn bad! Just give it a chance, chica."

She takes the seat beside me and fumbles with her huge bag, pulling out her notebook and pen. Ms. Robin is setting up while more people take their seats. Out of the corner of my eye, I see him.

Kingsley.

He has on the beanie again, and small wisps of hair poke out around the edges. Simple gray Dickies and a black fitted T-shirt clothe his tall frame. He takes a seat at the far end of the group and glances up in my direction, briefly meeting my eyes. The edges of his gorgeous lips turn up into a smile, and I quickly look away, too emotionally exhausted to engage with him. Still...

He's really good-looking.

I try to reel in my thoughts before they run away from me. The last thing I need is to further complicate my already disastrous emotional state by becoming infatuated with some hot guy from my self-harm group.

I can feel his stare and, despite my internal reprimand, I can't help but look over again. He's leaning forward with his elbows resting on his legs, and when he sits like that, the bulge of his biceps is even more defined.

God, he's sexy in all the ways a girl wants a guy to be. He has this extremely unkempt ruggedness about him. Then, there are his eyes. They aren't your typical blue, no. They're an intense cobalt blue and they pull you in, whether you want them to or not.

I catch myself staring back at him, and when he grins that crooked smile at me again, I think I actually blush. I turn my attention back to the front of the room and try my best to breathe and slow my heart rate.

Ms. Robin starts the group by welcoming all of us and telling us what the group topic will be for the day. I pull out my pen and grab my notepad even though I won't be back again, so taking notes is pointless. Still, I might as well make some sort of effort.

"All right, everyone. If you're ready, I'm going to begin. Today, we'll talk about blame. There are many forms of blame. Many of us blame ourselves while some place blame on others. Regardless of what kind of blame you're dealing with, it's a negative judgment you're placing upon yourself or someone else."

I sigh and prepare myself for the next hour of slow and painful lecturing.

"We all have to stop making excuses for ourselves and for others. We have to understand that placing blame on ourselves, or on others, for our failures will accomplish nothing. It will only set us back when what we really want is to move forward. Blame is just another form of an excuse. When you make an excuse you're shifting responsibility and placing blame onto someone or something else. Can anyone tell me a time when they knew they were at fault for a bad choice, but instead they placed blame onto someone else?" Ms. Robin asks.

I hate when she throws questions out to us. I feel like I'm under a spotlight, even though I'm definitely not the only one sitting here. Nevertheless, It's still an uncomfortable feeling. Chris raises her hand and answers. I pretend to listen, but all I can do is think about Kingsley and his deep blue eyes that keep finding their way to me.

"I see that Mr. Hot and Mysterious keeps eyeballing you. What's up with that?" Mercedes whispers as she nudges me with her elbow. I glance over to see a smirk on her face.

"I have no idea what you're talking about," I lie.

"Suuuuure you don't. Uh huh, because you totally can't see that the guy keeps staring at you every chance he gets," she laughs quietly.

I roll my eyes and cut them back in his direction. He just grins again and looks back toward the front. I feel warmth sweep over my body.

What in the hell is going on with me?

This has to be due to the shit that went down with

Jace last night. I get excited over male attention all the time, but this feeling is a bit different.

He keeps cutting his eyes in my direction, and my eyes keep finding their way back to his. Each and every time, I feel this weird sense of recognition, a magnetism that I can't really explain. It's attraction, yes, but it's more than that too. I can't put a description on it, but it feels comfortable, familiar even.

"You two have got some serious vibes going on. I sense love in the air," Mercedes giggles.

"Oh no, you don't! Me and love don't belong in the same sentence, I assure you," I tell her sternly.

"Well, maybe you just haven't met the right guy. Have you ever thought about that?" she whispers as Ms. Robin drones on in the background.

I shake my head back and forth and roll my eyes. She has no idea what she's saying, or whom she's saying it to. I'm in no position to be falling in love—now or anytime in the near future.

This thing with Jace has me all twisted up inside, and the very last thing I need is another emotionally charged relationship in my life. If she knew my history with men, she'd never suggest I get involved with a new one.

"Mercedes, I can promise you the last thing I need in my life right now is another guy coming along, screwing with my head and emotions. Guys are only good for sex. The emotional bullshit can stay away forever, as far as I'm concerned."

"Well, just use him for sex, then. I mean, shit, look at him dripping with that I'll-fuck-you-senseless sex appeal," she says, giving me a mischievous wink. "He's all scruffy and rough-looking. Those ones are the best, right?"

"Yeah, no. I don't think so. Having a fling with a dude from a mental health group seems a bit crazy to me, no pun intended," I say quietly.

The session is wrapping up and his eyes continue to follow me. I gather my stuff while Mercedes keeps swaying her eyes back and forth between Kingsley and me. I feel a matchmaker moment hanging in the air. She really has no idea how bad of an idea that would be.

"Mercedes, I'm serious. I'm not interested in him."

"Okay. Whatever you say, chica!" she says, rolling her bright eyes as if she doesn't believe a word out of my mouth. "Looks like he's coming over here, though, so you better have your rejection ready."

Kingsley approaches us and my nerves seem to split in half. I have no idea why he makes me feel this way. Usually with guys, I feast on their attention, craving it with a hunger, needing it to fill that ever-present emptiness inside of me, even if I know it's just a temporary solution. But even with all those jumbled emotions, rarely do I feel anxious about it.

"Hey," he says in his low, raspy voice. The level of awkwardness between us is almost unbearable. Or maybe it's just me?

"Hi," I respond as our eyes connect. That odd but familiar feeling returns. I turn and walk toward the exit nervously.

"See yah next time, chica. Make sure to text me your number when you get a chance," Mercedes yells, and somehow I know she's going to want dirt on whatever's about to take place between Kingsley and me. For the first time, I consider that it might actually be fun to have a girlfriend. I turn and wave to her, deciding to give it a shot and text her later.

Kingsley falls into step beside me. "Umm, hey. You maybe wanna go grab some coffee with me?" he asks with that endearing, crooked grin.

He's so damn cute in such a disheveled kind of way. He's not all put together or clean-cut like Jace. He's got at least a week or more of growth on his face and he dresses like he couldn't care less what anyone thinks. He may be messy-looking, but he emanates sex appeal and confidence with every move he makes, and every word he speaks. I know I shouldn't go anywhere with him after all the shit that went down with Jace last night.

"I'll take your silence as a hint that you'd rather not go," he says as he holds the door to the parking lot open for me.

I look up at him as I pass and those eyes pull me in briefly, but I soon look away and snap out of the dangerous trance.

"It's not that I don't want to. It's just complicated. I'm complicated; trust me, you don't want to know me. I've got a lot going on," I hedge as I avoid his gaze.

"Good. Then we already have something in common. It's just coffee," he encourages. "How complicated can coffee be?" he asks.

Before I can tell him no, my phone rings and I look at the screen. It's Jace. I tap the ignore button and look up at Kingsley with a smile.

"Sure, why not? I'll have coffee with you."

To hell with Jace Collins.

I'm not pining over that man another minute.

"Great. Are you cool with motorcycles, or is that going to be a problem?"

"No, I don't have a problem with motorcycles. I especially have no problem with a Harley. But I do have a problem if you're a crazy driver of said motorcycle," I laugh. To be honest, the idea of straddling a Harley Davidson behind a man that looks like Kingsley Arrington certainly isn't something that I have any aversion to, regardless of his driving skills.

"I'm a great driver. Don't you worry, you're safe with me," he says while handing his helmet over. For some reason, his words resonate on a deeper level than I can really make sense of. I look at the helmet and back at him.

"Umm, you've had your sweaty head in this helmet. I'm not wearing this. I'll go without. If you're as good a driver as you say you are, then I shouldn't need it, right?" I give him a cocky grin and hold the helmet out to him.

"Listen, you stubborn woman, it's not about my driving skills. It's about all these other lunatics on the road. You're not getting on the back of my bike without a helmet on that pretty little head of yours, so stop with the prissiness and just put the damn thing on." With that, he pushes the helmet back at me.

Whoa! Where did all that come from? Kingsley just laid down the law to me and he doesn't even know me. If he's trying to impress me with his well-mannered ways, he's doing a terrible job.

"Well, geez you don't have to be an asshat about it! Do you always talk to ladies like that?"

He looks me up and down slowly, as if he's trying to come to some conclusion. Then he situates his stare right on my eyes.

"For some reason, I have a very strong feeling that you're far from being a lady. I can tell that you're feisty and stubborn as shit, and I could tell immediately that you're a hard ass, so I seriously doubt that you're offended by a few expletives. You're no shrinking violet. So shut up, put the sweaty helmet on, and get on the bike. Please." A big smile stretches across his sexy face and all my resolve starts folding.

I've never really had a guy talk to me like that. Sure, I've been disrespected, degraded even, but this is very different. He's aggressive, but not abusive. More like to the point, even a little playful. It's like he saw right through my bullshit and called me on it from the get-go. It's refreshing, and I have to admit, extremely hot. I think Kingsley can boss me around any time he likes.

"Fine, jerk. I'll wear the helmet, but my hair better not stink afterward," I joke as I pull my hair back out of my face.

He laughs, loving the fact that he has won this small battle. "Do you always talk to guys like that? I'm a very sensitive guy, Jessica. I'm wounded. I really am," he mocks.

"Ha, ha! Suuuuuure you are," I say as I fix the helmet on my head. "You have *sensitive guy* written all over you. Just like I have *lady* written all over me."

He straddles the motorcycle and starts it up. The unmistakable roar of the Harley's engine is loud, exhilarating. I swing my leg over the back of the seat and make myself comfortable. The heat of Kingsley's body combines with mine as he reaches around and grabs my hands one by one, placing them around his waist. I can feel the hardness of his abs and that heat between us creeps up to my cheeks, making me flush. He turns his head and gives me a smile that's sexy as fuck.

"Ready?" he asks.

"I guess so. You've already got me into your sweaty helmet and on your bike. I'm as ready as I'll ever be."

"Well hold on tight, then. Here we go."

He pulls out of the parking lot and onto the main road. As he picks up speed, the warm wind hits my face. I interlock my fingers in front of his waist and hold on for dear life. He lowers one hand to cover mine with his. It's a strange thing to notice when you're flying down the road on a Harley, holding on to the extremely trim waist of a hot guy you've just met, with the wind whipping your hair around the both of you, but his skin is rough and warm on mine. It's an amazing contrast to what I'm used to. After a gentle squeeze, he brings his hand back up to the handlebar and we speed down the road without a care in the world.

The breeze in my hair and the hot Texas sun beating down on me feels perfect. It's freedom, a feeling that I haven't felt in a very long time. I think getting on the back of this motorcycle may have been a very good idea after all.

Kingsley rockets up into the parking lot of a local Starbucks and parks. He's already kicking out the kickstand when I realize I still have a death grip on him. I quickly remove my arms from around him and start to take the helmet off.

"How was that? Not too bad, huh?" he asks.

"Nope, not at all. Even though I still could've done without the helmet." I joke, handing it back to him.

He hangs the helmet off his bike and motions toward the entrance. "Non-ladies first," he teases.

"You're such a smart-ass. I think we're going to get along just fine," I say, arching my brows with a mischievous grin on my face.

"I think you might be right."

"Sooner or later we've all got to let go of our past."
—Dan Brown

Kingsley

I HAVE NO idea why she had a change of heart—something to do with that phone call—but I'm glad she did. Ever since I saw this girl, I knew I had to get to know her. Yes, of course, the first initial reason I noticed her was because she looks so much like my Lily; that inky black hair reminds me of my Lily's hair. It's beautiful. She's beautiful. I can't keep my eyes off of her, and, for some reason, I feel like she's supposed to be in my life. As crazy as that sounds and as ridiculous as it may be, I know that this girl is someone that I really want to get to know.

The feel of her arms around me is amazing, but over far too soon. We pull up to the Starbucks and as her touch disappears, I feel a pang of loneliness shoot through me. I haven't been touched by a woman in nearly a year. That's how long it's been since Lily took her life while carrying our unborn son inside her.

No matter how many months go by, the sting, the pain, and horror of that day never subsides. I don't think I'll ever be able to fully come to terms with how she could be so selfish. I'll never understand how someone could fall so deep into the depths of hopelessness that they would choose to end their own life. I loved her, cared for her, and I was a good husband to her. Why she didn't come to me, or tell me she was feeling that way, I'll just never understand.

I go to open the door for her, but she grabs it before I do and walks on in like she owns the place. It's almost as if she's trying too hard, like she's trying to prove something to me or to herself, or both. There's such a hard exterior on this girl, but I get the impression that it's all a façade hiding something much deeper.

My eyes travel down to her tight little ass and I have to force myself to look back up. I can't go there with this girl; I can't treat her like some chick I just met in a bar or something. I've seen the pain in her eyes in group when she thinks no one's looking, and I can feel the tension that constantly rolls off of her. I certainly don't want to cause her any more, so I have to keep my hormones in check.

"You wanna grab us a table and I can get our drinks? What would you like, Ms. Jessica?"

"Oh no, I can buy my own drink, thank you. This is not a date. I've got mine, no problem."

Yep, here she is: Ms. Hard-ass, I can handle myself, independent woman.

"Whatever you say, I was just offering."

"Thanks, but I got it. No biggie."

She steps up to the counter and orders, firmly asserting her independence. God, she's cute.

"I'd like a venti iced passion tea, please, sweetened."

"Oh, are you not a coffee drinker?" I ask.

"Not particularly. My mom always drank coffee in the mornings and she liked to spike it with booze. That sort of ruined the idea of coffee for me, but I really like their Tazo teas here."

The tone of her voice changes drastically when she mentions her mother and she becomes even more rigid than she was before.

"Oh, well, that makes sense. I'm not a coffee drinker either. I just like their sweet, frozen drink things here," I laugh, feeling ridiculous for liking these froufrou drinks.

She giggles a bit and steps aside so I can order. All of a sudden, I'm feeling self-conscious about my choice.

"Um, yeah. I'll take a grande chocolate chip Frappuccino, please, with extra whipped cream," I say quietly.

I glance over at her and she has the biggest smile on her face. It's an actual real smile that meets her eyes. She's so beautiful; that smile should never leave her face. It looks so good on her and I find myself wondering why she never smiles. I hope I can keep putting it on her face. Maybe that'll be my new goal every time I'm around her.

She just doesn't know it yet.

We sit down at a corner table, and though she still has her guard up, I can see that she's nervous too.

"Do I make you nervous?" I ask her. I'm just a straight-to-the-point type of guy. I don't know how to be any other way.

My question seems to throw her off-kilter and I like it. She needs to loosen up a little.

"Um, no, you don't. Why would you ask me that? Do I look nervous to you? Or are you just arrogant enough to think you would be making me nervous?"

I can't help but laugh. Unfortunately, she's pretty pissed off at my reaction.

"Well, to be perfectly honest, yeah. You do seem nervous, and no, I'm not arrogant. There's not an arrogant bone in my body. Look at me, do I appear to be a guy that's in love with himself?" I say, quirking a brow at her and gesturing up and down my body. "I'm wearing a ten dollar Walmart shirt and Dickies. I'm the furthest thing from arrogant or self-absorbed."

She just has no idea who I am.

"What you appear to be is rude. I'm not nervous. You do not make me nervous. I'm cool, no nerves here," she replies as she crosses her arms and affirms the fact that she is, in fact, nervous.

"So, tell me why you're in that group. What's your story, Ms. Jessica?"

She hates me now. The look on her face is priceless. I can't help it; I'm struggling to hold back a laugh.

"You don't pull any punches, do you? That's a pretty damn personal question, Kingsley. Why don't *you* tell me why you're in group and we can go from there."

Obviously, I knew my question would ultimately lead to this question, but the reality of being faced with it is completely terrifying. I haven't talked to anyone about Lily since she died. I never attended grief counseling and I've never spoken at the group meetings. Until this moment, I haven't really had to deal with the whys of my behavior. I look up at her and I know that she can see the fear circling in my eyes, the uncertainty on my face, and feel the indecision hanging in the air between us.

"Never mind. Let's not talk about why we're in that group," she says, saving me from the demons of my past. Once again, I'm able to suppress it and push it all back to a safe place in my mind. I'm not ready to deal with it yet. Soon, but not yet.

"Okay, sounds like a deal," I tell her, and I can't hide the relief that's so obvious in my voice. I guess I can't really expect her to share her issues if I'm not ready and willing to share my own.

"Well, let me ask you a less personal question, then. What do you do? Where are you from and what do you do for fun?"

A little smile stretches across her face as she places a small strand of that shiny black hair behind her ear.

"That's more than one question," she says, tilting her head to the side, looking at me with those sad eyes. Her eyes rarely change, but in those rare moments that they come to life, it's something to see. Still, I want to know why she's so sad. For some reason, I really feel this need to reach out to her, to be there for her.

"I guess you're right. It is more than one question," I concede. "I can go first if you want me to. My answers aren't all that interesting, though. I'm a pretty boring dude," I tell her.

"Kingsley, I seriously doubt you're boring. You don't seem to be the boring type at all."

She thinks she has me all figured out: the arrogant bad boy who talks rudely to females. That's what she's got me pegged as, but she couldn't be further from the truth.

"Well, allow me to enlighten you to all of my excitement. I'm a welder by day and I do personal training in the evenings and weekends on the side." She smiles a little and I like that she likes what she's hearing. "I do the training more as hobby than anything else. I like helping people to be healthier and I love being in the gym. It's a win-win situation for me. I write and play acoustic guitar for fun. I'm not a good singer at all. Matter of fact, I suck. But I really love playing, it relaxes me and it's very therapeutic to write songs. Other than that, I pretty much keep to myself. I don't barhop or party it up. I'm just a simple dude living my life the best I can." I take a long drink from my straw before saying, "Like I said, soooo exciting!"

Her big smile is back and I fucking love it.

Fuck, get yourself under control, Kingsley.

"It all sounds pretty exciting to me. Sounds like you actually have a life. That's more than I can say for myself," she says, but her words trail off with her smile as she looks down at her tea. She twirls the straw around and I can almost see through that barricade she has herself locked up in.

"Why do you say that? Why do you say you have no life? I'm sure you have hobbies. Everyone has something that they like doing."

She doesn't look up, but shrugs her shoulders a little.

"I like to write too. Poetry. I like to write poetry. I guess that's my hobby, even though it doesn't seem like a real hobby to me. It's just scribbling in a journal. Nothing special."

She glances up at me as if she's looking for validation or something, but that's not fucking happening.

"Umm, are you joking? Writing is an art form,

whether it's music, novels, poetry, or news articles. Anytime you start with a blank page or canvas and create something from nothing it's art and it's beautiful. Of course, not everyone will agree because we all like different shit, but it's still art. It's your art and you should be proud of it even if it never sees the light of day. So don't ever say it's nothing special. That's just shit talk."

She stares at me intently as she tries to formulate a tough-girl response. "Kingsley, it's just a journal and some words. That's not art. You're taking what I said way too seriously. It's nothing artistic, really. I promise you."

"Do you play this *feel sorry for me* card with everyone or is it just me? You come off as this hard-ass woman who can take on the world, but then you sit here and act all defeated when talking about your poetry." I lean in toward her, undeterred by the scowl currently taking over her face. "Do you think saying it sucks makes me want to say it doesn't? Do you want someone to tell you that your writing has worth or that you have worth by putting yourself down? Because if that's the case, I'm not buying into it." I'm irritated that she's refusing to see her own strength. I know it's pissing her off, but I won't coddle her. "Okay, your poetry is shit. You shouldn't write another poem for as long as you live. There, feel better?" I say, looking at her dead on.

Yeah, it's a crude thing to say, but, for some damn reason, I feel like someone needs to snap their fingers in this girl's face, tell it how it is, and stop allowing her to put on this front.

"You know what? Screw you! I'm not going to sit here and let a guy I barely know talk to me like this. Who the hell do you think you are, huh? Let me tell you something, I spent a huge portion of my life letting people talk to me like I was shit and that's no longer something I tolerate. This," she gestures animatedly between us, "is done! This little coffee shop convo is over. I'm going to catch the bus and you can kiss my ass. You're a total douchebag, Kingsley!"

She huffs and puffs as she grabs her bag.

I don't move from my relaxed position in my chair. I lean back a little and grin at her. She's so pissed, but all I want to do is laugh. That was way too easy. She may have been able to hide from everyone all her life, but I'm not blind to what's beneath that hardened exterior that she seems to think she needs around herself.

I've been hiding for over a year inside myself. I know what it looks like to pretend to be okay, and she has red flags flying all around her.

"Are you really going to sit there with a smug smile on your face after pissing me off and disrespecting me like that?" she hisses as she stands up from our table.

"Yep, I am. I think you're pretty adorable when you're pissed off. I can't help but smile at you right now. You just need to calm the hell down, not take things so seriously, and learn how to take a compliment. No need for a hissy fit. And no need to run off. I can give you a ride home." I wait quietly while she mulls over my words.

She rolls her eyes and sighs dramatically as she drops down into her seat again. "Whatever," she says as she crosses her arms over her chest. "I guess I'll let you take me home, but don't expect me to invite you up when we get there. And I still think you're an ass," she huffs.

"Oh, I would never expect that. I wouldn't even ask," I tell her, holding both hands in the air in surrender.

"Okay, well let's go, then. I'm tired and I have to work tonight." She's still a little snippy, but I can see the worst of her tantrum has passed. I have to admit, I'm glad she didn't just walk out. For a minute there, I wasn't so sure.

"Oh, yeah? Where do you work?" I ask before sipping the last of my drink and chucking it.

"I work downtown at Rookies Sports Bar."

"I know Rookies. Been there a time or two, but I've never seen you there."

"Yeah, I haven't been there long. I don't really stick around most jobs too long."

We get out to the parking lot and I grab the helmet and hand it to her. She grabs it, grimacing as she does.

"Oh, hush and put it on."

"Are you always so bossy?" she asks.

"Yeah, pretty much. Don't worry, it will grow on you." I grin.

She rolls her eyes, but she's trying really hard not to smile.

I pull up to her apartment building and turn off the engine. I can tell that she's worried about me wanting to come up.

"Well, I hope I didn't scare you off too badly. We have to hang out again soon," I say without getting off the motorcycle. "Can I get your phone number by any chance?"

She eyes me and looks down at my phone as I hold it out to her. "I guess." She grabs the phone and punches in her number before handing it back to me.

"You're really not gonna try and come up?" she says, looking perplexed.

"No. You said you weren't gonna invite me up. It's cool, no worries," I say, putting the helmet on. What she doesn't know is I'm really not ready to come up anyhow.

She stands there, looking at me like she has no idea what to say. "I've never had a guy not want to come up. This is a first."

I secure the helmet strap under my chin and chuckle, "Well, there's a first time for everything."

I start up my bike and pull out onto the road. I look back and she's still standing there, just staring after me. I love that I've surprised her, threw her off guard, and showed her that not all guys are predictable. There's a lot more to Jessica than what I saw today, and for the first time since Lily died, I feel a desire to get to know another person. The feeling is foreign to me, but not at all bad. In fact, it's kind of exhilarating. We don't meet people by accident. They're meant to cross our path for a reason. Deep down, I know that she crossed my path for a big reason and I'm determined to find out what it is.

"Who I need is somebody that will eat up all my free time, my ego, my attention. Someone addicted to me."
—Chuck Palahniuk

Jessica

KINGSLEY IS ONE extremely baffling motherfucker. I have no idea what to think about the guy. I throw my keys on the countertop and go lie down on my sofa. I stare at the ceiling and think about our afternoon together. One minute he was sweet and sexy as hell, the next he was being a bastard to me.

Ugh, men are so damn confusing.

I look at my phone for the thousandth time. I'm furious with myself for not answering Jace's phone call earlier because now I'm torturing myself waiting to see if he'll call again. I know I said I was done with him, that we were over for good, and I meant it, but I decide to go ahead and text him anyway.

Because I'm weak.

Me: *Jace, I'm sorry I missed your call today. I do want to talk to you. Please call me if you can. I hope your mom is okay.*

Liar.

Truth is, I couldn't care less about his bitch of a mother. I abhor that woman and all her arrogant ways. I stare at the phone as if the harder I stare, the quicker it will make him respond.

God help me.

I decide to journal to try and keep my mind off of him and the weird day I've had with Kingsley. I swear, I have no idea why I need men so badly. They do nothing but piss me off and confuse me.

I get up, head to my bedroom, and flip on my lamp, grabbing my journal from my bedside table. I flick on my iPod and scroll to my Pink playlist. The music fills the quiet of my apartment and I let it fuel me, move me, inspire me. I flop down on my bed, reach over for the pen in my drawer, flip through my journal pages, and start to write.

Fleeting moments
Laughter bleeding
In between the lines of sin
Purged my soul from within
Stripped it all away
Gave it all to him

Freedom
Clarity
Air...
Breathe it in
Fleeting moments
Captured for only a short time
Never could be forever
But could've always stayed kind
Fleeting moments
Now floating away
On the wings of bitter good-byes
Why?
Misguided, missteps
Blurred lines
Faults at my feet
He deserves better than me

I keep staring at my phone's screen this morning, wondering if Jace will respond to my text or if this really is the end of us. I know I told him to go live his life, but the truth is I miss him. He's on my mind constantly. Common sense screams at me to just let him go. Too many years have separated us, too many bridges have been burned, and he has Victoria now.

But he's the first thought in my mind when I wake up each day, and the last each night when I close my eyes. Somehow, after all these years, he's come back into my life. It almost feels like we found each other again for a reason. Like we really were meant to be together.

At the same time, I know that I'm really in no position to love someone right now. My life is so upside down. I can't say that I even know how to properly love another person. I know how to hang on to someone, how to manipulate someone, how to lie and cheat and fool someone.

But love them? No.

Every time I look into that man's eyes, I see everything that I was, everything that I am, and everything that I can be. It's so hard to let go. You can't flip a switch; you can't push a button and banish the love you feel for someone.

My phone dings and I instantly feel a bolt of excitement inside my chest. I look at the screen and see that it's a number I don't recognize. Before I can open the text, I hear a knock at my door and hop up, pocketing my phone as I make my way to my peephole. It's Kingsley.

What the hell is he doing here?

I really hate people just showing up. It's so rude! I open the door and frown at him, letting him know that I'm not happy about this unannounced visit.

"What are you doing here, Kingsley?" And there's that grin. His laid-back, happy-go-lucky attitude makes me want to scream.

"Well, top of the morning to you too, sweet pea."

Sweet pea?

"Do not call me sweet pea! And again, what are you doing here?"

He's dressed in athletic pants and a Dri-FIT shirt with running shoes on. It seems he's hot no matter how he's dressed.

"I'm here to pick you up," he says confidently.

"Umm, when did we make plans for you to pick me up this morning? I don't recall such a thing being planned," I tell him, totally unsettled and taken off guard by this turn of events.

"I texted you."

His smile widens and it's all I can do not to return it. I'm determined to keep this guy at a safe distance because even though I'm beyond attracted to him, he scares the hell out of me. I can always predict guys. When they all want the same thing from you it's not hard to do. And I've gotten really good at staying disconnected from any guy I hang out with. But Kingsley is different. He gets under my skin and the last person to get under my skin like this was—

I cut off that thought before I have a chance to complete it. "Shouldn't you be at work or something?" I ask.

"Nope, it's Saturday. I don't work at the shop on weekends and I have no clients at the gym until later today."

"Okay, so why are you here?" I don't mean to be rude, but he did just show up unannounced on my doorstep.

"I'm here to take you with me to do my morning workout. So go put on some workout clothes and lets go!"

I can't help myself—I burst out laughing. He must

have had his brain altered by aliens in the course of the night or something. I don't go to the gym. The gym is like a magnifying glass for flaws. I've never been to one where I didn't feel like I was putting myself on display to be compared to the other women in there.

"Are you kidding me? There's no way in hell that I'm going to a gym. Why on God's green earth would you assume I'd agree to go work out with you? I'm not a gym girl, Kingsley. It's not my kind of thing."

He crosses his arms in front of his broad chest and smiles that fucking smile that kills me every time. I swear, I just want to suck those full lips right off his scruffy face!

"Jessica, I get the impression that you're a nothing-is-my-thing type of girl. I also get the feeling you rarely try new things, and I think you're dealing with a lot of stress. A workout is the single most effective thing for stress. Just come with me. If you hate it, we'll leave. I promise."

"Kingsley, I worked until two in the morning and I'm exhausted. The last thing I feel like doing is working out," I whine. He just stands there expectantly, staring at me. "Do you have a habit of showing up at girls' houses and dragging them to the gym? Why did you ever think I'd be game for this?"

As much as I hate to admit it to myself, I'm actually intrigued by the idea of spending the morning with him. But the damn gym? Ugh. I'm really not feeling it. But he's so damn persuasive, and sitting around this apartment all day being depressed over Jace doesn't sound very appealing. It suddenly occurs to me that I probably look like hell. I try, unsuccessfully, I might add, to straighten my hair with my hands without Kingsley noticing.

"Oh, who cares what your hair looks like? Go put on

some sweats, a T-shirt, and a ball cap and let's go. You look great just the way you are."

He's serious!

I look like shit and definitely need some time to put myself together. I know I must have dark circles under my eyes, and I can only imagine how washed-out I look without my makeup on right now.

"I look like ass. I cannot go out looking like this. I have to put some makeup on or something." And that's that.

Well, apparently that isn't that, because he just walks on into my apartment like he lives here and starts ordering me around!

"What'd I just say, Jess? Quit wasting time," he tells me, and from his tone it sounds like he may have been a drill sergeant in another life. "Go put on some sweats, a T-shirt, brush your jibs and hair, and let's go. You don't need freaking makeup. I hate that crap anyway. Women should just embrace their natural state. All that gloppy shit is unnecessary. You're beautiful—*you*—not some shit that you rub on your face. Now get a move on." He says, shooing me toward my room with his hands.

This guy is unfuckingbelievable. He just leans up against my wall, crossing his large, very tan biceps across his equally large chest, and stares at me.

"Well, what are you waiting for? Go!"

"Okay, okay! Geez, I'm going, I'm going! Don't get your man panties all in a wad," I say sassily as I turn my ass around.

He laughs at my comment and I catch his smile in the mirror as I shuffle off to my room. I swear to Jesus, that man has got to have the whitest teeth I've ever seen peeking out from the most sexually arousing mouth that I've ever seen.

Good God, I'm in trouble here. Big trouble!

He opens the gym door for me and I can barely force myself to walk inside. I feel completely exposed and vulnerable as I cross over the threshold and into the slightly musky, humid air.

"Umm, don't I have to have a membership or something to be here?" I ask, hoping there's a way—any way—to get out of this.

"No, you're my guest for the day," he says as he strolls up to the counter.

The petite blond behind the counter is gorgeous, and she's giving him her best fuck me eyes as she scans his key tag and hands it back to him.

"Have a good workout, Mr. Arrington," she swoons.

I roll my eyes and sigh.

Yep, this is exactly the place I want to be, I said NEVER.

"So, is that why you like it here? All the females swooning over you at every flex or squat?"

"What are you talking about?" he asks as I follow behind him through a sea of workout equipment to the back of the gym.

"That chick was totally eye-fucking you. You can't really tell me you don't get that all the time here."

He swings open a door to another room. "Actually, no, I don't. Plus, while I'm here, I don't pay attention to anything except what I'm here for."

I look around and take in the mirrored walls, which are just fantastic! They're really so far from fantastic that I can't even form the word on my lips. There's another F word I'd like to say right now, though. This room is like a little chamber of horrors to me.

I notice large ropes that are weighted down at the ends. Yep, totally a little shop of horribly painful-looking shit. I have no idea why we're in here, but I'm guessing I'm not going to like it one bit. Suddenly, all those machines on the other side of that door seem way more appealing.

He drops his gym bag and pulls out his iPod, plugging it into the stereo system. Music floods the air. Metallica. A smile spreads across my face.

At least there's one positive thing in here now.

"Okay, we need to get you warmed up first, so go out and hop on a treadmill for about fifteen minutes. Then, come back in here."

I look at him like he's crazy.

"There's no way you're throwing me to the wolves like that. I'm not going out there by myself to be on display like a freak. Why? So I can fumble with the treadmill that I don't know how to work beside people that I don't know? Not a chance."

Now he's rolling his eyes. He grabs my hand and proceeds to lead me out onto the main gym floor to what I suppose must be the cardio area.

"Listen, you've got to chill out a little. These people couldn't care less what you're doing. Look around, what do you see? They're all plugged in: earphones in, watching the TV monitors, or reading. They aren't paying attention to you."

I look around. He's right. No one's even looking in our direction. He leads me to an empty treadmill, punches a few buttons on it, and motions for me to get on.

"Right here," he points to a few buttons,

"you can control the speed that you want to go. And here," he gestures to a big red button, "you can push this to make it stop. You don't have to go really fast. Just get your heart rate up a little and keep it there for about fifteen minutes. Come back to the training room when you're done. You'll be fine, I promise." He gives me a reassuring smile and walks away.

I look down at the treadmill controls and turn the damn thing on. I set it at a speed I can handle without my heart exploding out of my chest.

Here goes nothing.

Fifteen minutes felt more like fifteen hours. I'm sweating and my heart's pumping like I'm on speed. I had no idea how out of shape I really was until right now!

"Kingsley, I'm done. That kicked my ass. I'm out of shape and I can promise you, there's no way I can do anything else," I say as he starts demonstrating how to use the big huge torturous ropes.

"Sure you can. You just have to push yourself. Push your limits some. I know you've got more than fifteen minutes in you. Just try these and then you can grab some water and take a break if you want. Don't be such a wuss."

I whip my head around and glare at him.

"You're an asshat, you know that? I'm out of shape. That's not being a wuss, that's being freaking out of shape!"

"Whatever. You're complaining either way. Stop your damn whining and get your little ass over here so I can show you how to do this. Only way to not be out of shape is to get in shape. So shut your trap and let's start getting you in shape. You're young, you're thin, and you shouldn't be ready to keel over from fifteen minutes on a treadmill. You should be able to do a lot more at your age. So, let's change that."

I sigh and roll my eyes. He's so bossy, so frustrating. In a weird way, I like it. I can't really explain why just yet, but regardless, I know that I feel stronger just by being in his presence. It feels good, even if he's a total smart-ass most of the time.

I'm leaning down to pick up the gigantic ropes when my phone buzzes in my pocket. I pull it out quickly and my stomach flutters when I see that it's Jace texting me.

Jace: *Jess, sorry I had to run off. Mom is really sick and I'm going to have to stay up here 'til we find out what's wrong with her.*

I read the text more than once, hanging on one word: *WE*.

Me: *Do whatever you have to do, Jace. You owe me no explanations.*

Jace: *Jess, don't be like that. We have a lot to talk about. This is just very bad timing. What happened between us did, in fact, happen and we can't just act like it didn't. My mom needs me right now. Please don't shut me* *out just because I can't be there with you.*

Me: *Are you kidding me right now? This is not about you being here or being there. This is about who you're there with! This is about you fucking me, and then leaving with her!*

Jace: *Jess, please try to understand that Mom needs to stay relaxed. She loves Victoria, and I can't just drop all of this on her while she's sick. I know I have to figure out what to do about my engagement, but now is not the time. Mother was so set on this wedding, and I can't tell her—while she's lying in a hospital bed—that I found you or that I'm still in love with you, not the woman that she sees me with in the future.*

"Hey let's get a move on. Get off your damn phone, woman, and get over here already," Kingsley says, and I vaguely register the smile in his voice.

I feel hot and my pulse races. All Jace cares about is making everyone else happy. He couldn't care less about me or my feelings. He just fucked me and left with that twat without a second thought. He is so concerned about his mother—if he only knew what that woman was capable of!

Of course she loves Victoria. Victoria is a mini version of her. Jace has found a woman to marry that's the cookie-cutter image of his stuck-up mother. A mother that never had a second thought about paying me off to kill her son's unborn child and never look back.

Don't do it Jess. Don't hurt him just to spite him. Just let it go; keep the secret you've always kept. Keep the secret that will crush the only man you've ever loved.

But I do it. I crush Jace with a single text.

Me: *Why don't you ask your dear mother how it feels to pay off the mother of her unborn grandchild? Why don't you ask your mom how it felt to watch you miss me and search for me? Why don't you ask your mom if she ever gave one fucking thought to a young, confused, terrified eighteen-year-old girl lying in an abortion clinic having her child sucked out by machines? Ask her that, Jace! I bet she'll hate knowing that you still love that girl despite all the trouble she went through in order to keep us apart! So, yeah, you're right. She'd never be able to handle knowing you found me again!*

I hit the send button. I know that I've intentionally hurt him where I knew I could hit him the hardest.

Now he knows his own mother betrayed him.

I shove the phone back into my pocket and fight back the tears. I walk with determination over to Kingsley and he hands me the rope contraptions.

"What's wrong, Jessica? You look like you're about to cry. What's going on?" he asks. Concern etches grooves around his eyes and forehead, but I ignore his questions.

"Just show me what to do with these. I don't want to talk about it."

"Do I need to kick someone's ass for you? Because I will." I can't look at him, but I hear the conviction in his words. "Whoever that was on your phone has you fucked-up all of a sudden. Are you sure you're good? Because you don't look good at all."

"Kingsley, I said I don't want to talk about it. I'm fine. Let's just get this over with, okay?"

"Okay, whatever you say, hard-ass. You know, one of these days it's all gonna crash down around you. You can't always be so tough. It's okay to drop the walls every once in a while."

He steps behind me and wraps each one of his arms around mine, grasping the ropes one by one over my hands. He leans in and I can feel the warmth of his breath on my neck near my ear.

"You don't fool me, Jessica. I know the game; I've played it every day for a long time now. Just know you can talk to me if you ever want to let it all out. Don't let the shit in your head control you. Scary things only go on in our minds if we let them. Monsters don't live under beds; in our minds is where they truly reside. Remember that."

I just nod, having no idea how to respond. He doesn't know that my monsters have infected my mind for so long that I no longer know where they end and I begin.

"All you wanna do is hold them tight and squat, just slightly. Then, just like this, you want to move the ropes up and down in fluid motions causing a kind of wave effect with them. Every time you bring the ropes down, you squat. Then you raise back up as you bring the ropes up. You want to slam the ropes down to the ground as hard as you can."

He has his front against my back as he guides me through the motions. I can feel his breath as he explains each part of the exercise, and even though I'm attracted to him, all I can think about is Jace.

This pisses me off!

I have this hot, great guy all up against me, but I can't stop thinking about the fucker that has my mind twisted up like a Texas tornado. Kingsley may not know what—or who—I'm thinking about, but he sure knows what I need to hear.

"Just think about something or someone that you hate and picture that on the floor. Crush it with these ropes," he says.

Now there's a concept I can work with!

He backs away and I raise the ropes and squat as I bring them down really hard. I slam the floor with them—it feels fucking great! I do it again and again. With each slam of the ropes, I picture Victoria, that bitch Mrs. Collins, and all of the girls in high school that tortured me for years.

I slam them down on the terror.

I slam them down on the sadness.

I slam them down on the fear.

I slam them down on the pain.

So. Much. Pain.

Tears start to spill down my cheeks as I picture Jace, and finally, myself. I hate myself the most. I hate myself most of all because no matter how strong I try to be, I know the truth. I'm weak. I'm fucking dirty. I'm used up. And no man will ever love me, because I hate me.

What I just did to Jace is proof that I'm a terrible, awful person. I hurt him because I felt hurt.

Hurt people, hurt people.

An eye for an eye, action before thought. That's me—a fucking impulsive, irrational ticking time bomb that never fully considers the consequences of my actions.

Suddenly, I feel arms around me and I'm shaking. My arms feel like noodles and my legs are trembling.

"Hey, whoa... That's good. Just drop them. Come sit

down and drink some water. It's okay, Jess. It's all going to be okay."

I wish I could believe him.

The wind is in my hair and the sound of the Harley's engine roars in my ears. My arms are wrapped around Kingsley and my head rests on his back. It's been two weeks since the day I broke down at the gym in front of him. He didn't pressure me into telling him what was wrong, and he hasn't asked about it since. Oddly enough, we've spent a lot of time together over the past two weeks working out, and not once has Kingsley made a pass at me. I keep waiting for it to happen, but nothing ever does. In a way, it's actually a relief.

Jace is still back with his mom and Victoria, I assume, and I haven't heard a single solitary word from him. The last communication we had was that hurtful text I sent him. He never responded. He never called.

Just nothing.

His silence is deafening. I know that I've ruined whatever chance I might have had with him. I've tried to keep busy, but I still think about him every day. Losing him all over again hurts, but I'm getting by, little by little, bit by bit. I work late shifts at the bar and I've kept up my Saturday morning workouts with Kingsley. To my utter shock and amazement, I actually enjoy going with him now. Mercedes and I have been texting some and we have plans to have drinks soon. I've avoided finding another group and doctor, but I know I'll have to soon.

We pull into my apartment complex and he turns off

the bike. "You working tonight?" he asks.

"Yep, Saturdays are my best tip nights." I tell him as I swing my leg over and off the motorcycle.

"What about tomorrow night?" I take his helmet—which I don't even bother arguing with him about anymore—off and hand it to him.

"Umm, no I don't usually work on Sunday nights. Why?"

"Well, I know you told me you never cook and that it's because you never learned. I thought maybe you could come over to my place and we could cook dinner together. I can show you how to make something. We can eat and hang out. Maybe watch a flick or something. If you're down for it, that is."

A giggle escapes me as I look up at him.

He's serious!

"You're funny. Do you want to burn your house down? I promise you that I can't learn to cook anything in an evening. I can't even make eggs, Kingsley!"

A hair falls into my eyes and he immediately reaches out, brushing it aside. I feel the warmth of his touch and a shiver runs down the length of my body. I force the feeling away and grin at him, sweeping my mussed-up hair back.

"My hair is a mess," I say, feeling a little shy all of a sudden.

"I love it. It looks great even when it's all jacked-up."

"Thank you, I think." We laugh together for a moment. We've been having a lot of moments like this lately: easy, carefree, comfortable.

"Okay, so it's a date! Come over tomorrow night around six o'clock and we'll make something simple. It's hard to screw up spaghetti. I promise, you'll be fine. I'll text you my address."

I haven't ever been to his house. He's never invited me over. He's been sort of elusive when it comes to his personal life away from the gym or my apartment.

"Sounds good. I'll see you then. If I can walk, that is," I say wryly. "Was it really necessary to do so many box jumps this morning? Good God, you're such an ass! You know how much I hate those things."

He laughs while he starts the bike back up, revving the engine a couple of times. He holds his hand to his ear as if he's trying to hear me. "Sorry, can't hear you. Hope you had a good workout. I know how much you looove box jumps!" Then he smiles that damned sexy-ass grin and drives off.

He's so bad! But I have to admit, I think I like his bad.

"They say monsters live under beds. They're wrong because our mind is where monsters truly reside."
—Kathryn Perez

Kingsley

STANDING IN FRONT of the door, I stare at the knob and try to regulate my breathing. Do I turn it and go in, or do I walk away again for the hundredth time?

I haven't been in this room since Lily died. It's been too painful, so I've gone on with life as if nothing happened, pushing it all down and keeping it all in.

But this fucking girl is making me feel again and it scares the hell out of me!

I see myself in her eyes: a scared person trying to hold it all together, trying to be strong, to be brave, trying to fool the world around them. I look at her and I see strength wrapped up in pain. I want to tell her to let it go, to let it all out, but I don't know if I'm wanting her to do that or wanting it for myself.

I don't know what her story is, or where her pain stems from, but one thing I do know is that pain is pain, sadness is sadness, and hurt feels the same to all of us, no matter how different we may be. What I know best is that pain can push some people to the edge, but I hope Jessica isn't in that place. I hope she never gets to that place. I know all too well what can happen when pain reaches the point of no return.

Slowly I reach out, turn the knob, and push the door open. The afternoon sun streams in, lighting the newly disturbed dust particles that bounce around the air in a flurry. I focus on them in a final last-ditch effort to delay the avalanche of emotions that are waiting to bury me. Finally, I look around, moving my eyes over each section of the room.

Her easel sits in the corner of the room near the window, and her old pink paint-splattered sweater—her favorite one that she said was so soft and warm—is still draped over her chair. It hangs there, waiting for her to slide it on again.

She never will.

Her oil paints are all lined up on her desk in perfect order. The paint brushes wait for her to hold them again.

She never will.

I walk over and run my fingers across her big oak desk. It's cold to the touch, and even though my fingertips are callused, I can feel the subtle ridges of the wood beneath them. I close my eyes and can see her perfectly in my mind, sitting here mixing paints, happy, smiling, surrounded by, and wrapped up in, her art. Her smile was so bright, but it never did seem to reach her eyes. I know that now, but why couldn't I see it then? Now I know the look of pain. But now, it's too late.

If only I had known she was suffering...

If only I had known she was hurting so deeply...

I might have been able to save her.

Why couldn't I see that even when she was here, she was already gone?

I pick up the sweater and bring it to my nose. I inhale, trying to capture any trace of her scent, but it's disappeared. Just like her. I drop down into her chair, gripping the sweater in my fists, tears filling my eyes and plummeting down my face. Tears that have never been shed finally break free. I've never cried for her, but today I will. It's time.

Time to face the loss.

Time to realize that my wife chose death over life because she felt she had no other choice.

Time to accept that she didn't reach out to me.

Time to accept that I may never know why.

Time to stop ignoring her death.

Time to face the reality of suicide.

I think about her all the time, but I never think about her death. I haven't been able to face it. Lily's always on my mind, and my thoughts can't move an inch without bumping into some part of her.

I cry for the life she lived.

I cry for the life she abandoned.

I cry for our child that was never born.

I cry for the woman that I loved and lost.

I finally mourn my Lily.

I've been lying to myself for so long that the lies became truth and the truth became a lie.

I look through my tears to the canvas in front of me

and run my fingers across the half-finished piece. Just like her life it's full of color, but at the same time so dark, only half-lived.

I slowly stand up and place her sweater back on the chair. I walk over to her desk, scanning the shuffled papers there. Pink lettering, peeking out from under a small stack of papers and envelopes, catches my eye. I reach down and move the papers aside, revealing an envelope with my name scrolled across it in curly, dark pink calligraphy. My heart skips a beat, and then begins hammering in my chest.

All this time, I've always felt so bitter that I had no real explanation, no final words, nothing but an empty house and a hollow heart. That's why I started going to group therapy. I just wanted to understand depression, suicide, self-harm. I couldn't understand how Lily could do this to herself. I thought that if I could listen to others who dealt with it, then maybe I could understand, have some clarity. But here I am, looking at a letter that may very well hold all of the answers to the questions I never asked when she was alive.

I pick up the envelope with trembling hands while fear of the unknown creeps around inside my mind. I shuffle through thoughts and worries, asking myself if I really want to know. Do I really want to see the last words she wrote to me? Can I handle the truth? More than that, can I handle her truth? I slowly open the envelope and pull out the letter.

K,

Words seem so insufficient, my love, but I know you, and I know you'll never rest until you have an answer to this huge question mark that I have placed in front of you. I can't begin to express how much I love you. First and foremost, please know that I never stopped loving you and you shouldn't blame yourself for my death. I've fought a losing battle for too long. One that I'm not sure I could ever make you understand. Unless you live through depression, you can never fully grasp it. It consumes my days and haunts my nights. And I'm tired, Kingsley. So tired.

I know you're asking yourself why I didn't come to you and all I can tell you is that I feel guilt. Guilt for not being better for you, for us, for our unborn child. Finding out that we were pregnant was the breaking point for me. I can barely hold myself together, much less care for a child.

I became a master of disguise, wearing a mask

for you and for our families; trying to pretend this poison wasn't eating away at me. I cut myself during the day to ease my pain, to control my world, and I always made sure the lights were off when we were in bed. I did all I could to conceal my pain. The thought of hurting you was more painful than hurting myself. You're a good man, K, and you took great care of me. Never doubt that. What's broken inside of me can never be fixed. It's deep and it's dark. The nothingness that consumes me every day burns and it overwhelms me to the point where I can hardly bear another minute of it. This dark cloud looms above me incessantly. But I'm finally ready to embrace it—it's become too much of a burden to shoulder any longer.

I know I smile for you and I know you're confused by it. But I smile for the world because my smile is my protection. It hides my pain, it hides my sadness, and it hides my fear. My smile gives you solace, it gives you assurance that everything's okay. It's my daily gift to you because you deserve all of my smiles and none of my sorrow. This infection within has taken my body, taken my mind, but I promise it never took my heart.

My heart will forever be yours.

I wish so many things for you, K. Please don't spend your days mourning me. Please don't lose yourself because I couldn't seem to find myself. Love again, laugh again, and create a family. You deserve all of those things that I stole from you. I spent so much time and energy trying to protect you from my pain and in the end, all I'm doing is hurting you more than anyone else ever could. I'm eternally sorry for that. I'm selfish and I know that. I'm a coward and a cheat. I'm cheating you out of the life you knew and I hate myself for it. I hope that one day you can learn to forgive me. Please, don't allow the past to steal your future. Don't allow my sickness to taint your future happiness. Just know that I'm no longer in pain, no longer scared, and no longer hurting.

Live your life for you and never stop being the wonderful, quirky, confident, amazing man that I know you are. Live for the moment—I know you can have so many beautiful ones.

Close this chapter of your life and start a new one. Turn the page and write your own story because this life is your canvas, Kingsley. It always has been. Please, go live it...

~L

I read the letter once. Twice. Three times, but no matter how hard I try to put it all together, the words just won't sink in fully. Anger and sorrow rip through me and I just want to hit something, break something; I want to hurt someone, something, anything! She had no right to make that decision for all of us. I'm so mad at her, at myself, at everything for this. I haven't cried, I haven't felt anger or pain since she died because I didn't want to face it. This is why! I feel fucking helpless and the absolute anger and hatred that I'm feeling right now hurts so bad. I don't want to hate her, I don't want to be angry at her. She took my heart with her and I want it back, I want my Lily back! I look up at the clock and I realize I've been in here longer than I thought. Jessica is coming over for dinner and here I am—a complete fucking wreck. I need to pull it together. I fold up the letter slowly, willing my hands stop shaking as

I do, and put it back into the envelope. I can't look at it anymore, so I place it in her desk drawer. I leave the room and close the door, closing up the room that holds all of my anger and loss.

After a quick shower, I throw on a pair of jeans and my favorite necklace. I wear it always. Lily gave it to me, so I only take it off to shower. Even though I'm angry with her right now, I have to wear it. I clean up a bit and check my pantry to make sure I have everything for dinner; then I grab my phone and send Jess a quick text with my address. It's only five o'clock, so I have about an hour before she'll be here.

Why do I feel so nervous?

This is not high school. I'm not a teenage boy falling over himself because of a girl. It's just dinner; no big deal.

But it is a big deal.

There hasn't been a woman in this house since Lily died. I haven't dated, and I haven't even remotely thought about dating until I met Jessica.

I look around the house to make sure it's all in order. Of course, it's all nice and clean. Lily was a perfectionist and the house was always spotless. Since her death, I've sort of turned into a clean freak myself, wanting to keep things the way she would have wanted them.

I pick up my guitar and decide to play for a while to calm my nerves. Playing always seems to center me when I need to relax.

"New beginnings can heal old wounds."
—Kathryn Perez

Jessica

I HEAR BEAUTIFUL chords from an acoustic guitar coming from Kingsley's house as I walk up his driveway. The windows are open and the evening breeze is blowing the diaphanous white curtains gently, causing them to sway back and forth. His house looks nothing like I expected. It's small, but quaint. There are hummingbird feeders among the flowerbeds spread out in front of the entryway, and a whimsical wind chime hangs on the front porch along with a white porch swing. I would've never pictured this as a bachelor's home. This house has a woman's touch.

Maybe his mom helps him out around here or something.

As I get closer to the porch and start up the steps, the breeze blows the curtains aside and I get a glimpse of him.

He's sitting shirtless on a sofa, playing the guitar. He's wearing a black cord necklace that has a flat, square silver charm on it. His shaggy hair hangs in his face, and his eyes are closed as he picks the guitar strings. He's so into the music that he looks like he's somewhere else completely, somewhere other than his living room. The ease with which he plays is soothing and incredibly sexy. I watch as his fingers deftly stroke the strings, and wonder at their agility.

I quickly reign in my thoughts and try to shake off the sexual attraction before pressing the doorbell. The music abruptly stops and I hear his footsteps as they approach.

The door swings open just as Kingsley is pulling on a shirt, and my eyes immediately fall to pants that are hanging oh so very low on his waist. That V, which is so extremely defined on this man, is practically begging for me to reach out and trace it with my fingers. The veins on his muscular body look like a road map to a heavenly place that I'd love to explore. Before my mind can race away with that thought, his shirt is on and hiding the abs of my affection.

Shit! Snap out of it, Jess.

"Hey, you're here!" He grins. "Come on in," he says as he motions me in the door.

I briefly scan the room. Again, I'm surprised. I'm in awe of how perfectly clean it is and it's so well decorated! Very artsy. Kingsley continues to surprise the hell out of me.

"Nice place. It's really cool here."

"Oh, thanks. Yeah, I like it. It's quiet and it's a good neighborhood."

Awkwardness looms as we stand in his living room. I

don't know what to say or do at this point. Thankfully, Kingsley saves me, breaking the tension in the room.

"Well, come on. It's time to get our cook on!" He reaches out for my hand. I look down at his skeptically and then back at him.

"Oh, come on! I swear you'll be fine. Not like you're gonna burn the house down; it's just pasta." He grabs my hand, laughing, and literally pulls me into the kitchen.

"Here, let me have your very large purse thing."

"Hey, I love my bag. Get up off it!" I say playfully.

"Yeah, well you can't cook holding that thing, goof-ball."

I hold out my purse to him and he hangs it on a small closet door in the hallway. He walks over to an iPod docking station in the kitchen and turns it on.

"Music always makes everything better," he says with a wink.

One Republic plays and he starts taking ingredients out of his pantry. He looks so comfortable in the kitchen as he moves around, pulling pots and pans out and setting everything up.

"Okay, take this pan and fill it up about halfway with water," he says, handing me a large saucepan.

"That I can do. See, if we keep it simple like this we may actually be able to eat what we're making tonight," I joke.

"Oh, hell no! You're cooking this shit tonight. I told you I'd teach you to cook something and that's exactly what I'm gonna do. You ain't getting out of it, darlin'."

Darlin'? What the hell?

He's never said that to me before. I think I like it, though. No, I think I love it!

"Okay, so we'll start the water to boil and start the meat. I personally prefer ground Italian sausage in my spaghetti, so that's what we'll use. Go ahead and grab it, crumble it up into this pan over here, and put it on a low to medium heat." He gestures around confidently, perfectly at ease in the kitchen, while I stare around nervously, like a deer in headlights.

I look at him, and then down at the sausage.

How hard could that be to screw up? It's just putting something in a pan, right?

"Alrighty, let's see if I can do that without burning it," I mutter.

He shakes his head back and forth as he pulls the pasta out of the box.

"You're such a dork, Jessica. This is not rocket science. Have some confidence! Own this motherfucking kitchen. Tell yourself that you're gonna make some good-ass 'sketti, and then be proud that you did it."

I'm still standing and so is the house! The sausage is done, the pasta is done, and all we have to do now is add the meat to the sauce. Garlic bread is in the oven and it smells great in here. I had no idea making garlic bread was so simple! I'm feeling pretty damn culinarylistic at the moment. And yes, that is a word. I just made it up, thank you very much.

"Here, you wanna taste it?" he asks as he dips a spoon into the sauce and holds it out to me.

I look at the spoon and an odd feeling sweeps over me. Him attempting to feed me something feels very personal, very sensual. I lean in toward him and open my mouth a little. He puts the end of the spoon inside my mouth and I get a small taste of the sauce. At that very moment—of all things to happen—I sneeze! Sauce goes everywhere! Everywhere on him and on me! I'm mortified. I cover my mouth with my hands, wishing I could dig a hole in the floor to crawl into.

"Oh my God, Kingsley. I'm so sorry! I'm so, so sorry!"

I look at him, expecting anger or annoyance, but he's smiling this huge, stupid smile, his face covered in pasta sauce. He starts laughing, like really laughing, and I start laughing too. I laugh harder than I have in a very long time. He reaches out and swipes some sauce off my cheek and licks his finger.

"Pretty good stuff, darlin'. I didn't expect to be wearing our supper, but hey, that's way better than burning the place down. I think you pass your first attempt at cooking."

I'm still smiling and laughing like an idiot as I reach out and copy what he did. I bring my finger to my mouth and taste the delicious sauce, closing my eyes to savor it. When I reopen them, our eyes lock. Suddenly, our laughter quiets and something very different fills the space between us. I lick my lips and he steps in toward me.

"Jessica, I know I've never made a pass at you, but I'm gonna kiss you right now if that's all right with you," he says while looking intently into my eyes.

What the hell am I supposed to say to that?

I'm not quite sure, so I don't say anything. I just nod. This may be a huge mistake, a very big mistake, but I close my eyes and let him kiss me anyway.

Kingsley kisses me; he kisses me like I've never been kissed before. It's more than a kiss, it's like he's starving for me, like he needs this kiss more than he needs air to breathe. He has his hands in my hair, holding my head, directing every move, every entwined motion of our mouths in a slow, steady, controlled pace. It's the most passion-filled kiss I've ever felt. I allow my body to relax into his and I let him kiss me, I let him kiss the living hell out of me and I love every second of it. It feels amazing and in this moment, I know things are changing, shifting for the better. Something very big is happening between us and I know our friendship will never be the same again.

He lets go of me and the kiss slowly ends. I'm not ready for the weird after-the-first-kiss moment at all.

"Damn, just damn!" he whispers, shaking his head slightly.

I look at him and feel heat creep across my face. I know I'm blushing and there's nothing I can do to hide it. He can see that I'm embarrassed.

"You're so adorable." He smiles before grabbing a washcloth and reaching out to clean off my face. The gesture is sweet, so endearing, so I don't move. I just let him do it. And it feels good.

Really good.

"This is Ruffino Chianti," he says as he gestures to the wine he's carrying. "It goes great with Italian food, but I probably should've remembered I had it while we were eating," he says while pouring me a glass of wine.

"That's okay. I wouldn't really know; I'm not a wine

drinker. I wouldn't think you'd be, either," I say.

He raises his eyebrows and smiles widely. "I'm full of cool surprises, don't yah know? I'm a cool fucking dude! But I'm not holding out my pinkie finger while I drink the shit. That's where I draw the line."

We both burst out laughing and I relish the moment, feeling freer than I have in such a long time. Being here with him, right here, right now, feels so natural, so comfortable. Like an old T-shirt I've worn all my life. It's full of holes and tears, but it's the most comfortable thing I own. I think Kingsley is my new favorite old T-shirt.

I take the glass of wine and he sits down beside me on the sofa. "So are you, umm, okay with what happened in there?" he asks.

Shit! Why does he have to ask? Why make it all weird?

"Uh, yeah it was fine," I say shyly.

"Just fine?" he asks with raised brows.

I roll my eyes.

Men!

"I mean the fact that you kissed me is fine. The kiss itself was much better than fine, Kingsley, but don't think I'm gonna help inflate your ego by going on about it," I reply dryly.

He smirks and reaches out, setting his glass on the end table. Then he grabs his guitar and props it up on his lap.

"That's what I like about you. You just say it like it is." He strums the strings a few times and shifts his eyes back to me.

"You ever try playing?" he asks.

"No, I have no idea how to play any musical instrument," I admit. Though I love music, I've never thought I'd be particularly good at learning how to play it, other than on my iPod.

"It's not so hard. I bet you'd take to it fast. You love to write poetry; I bet you could even write songs."

I shake my head and take a sip of the wine.

"Nope, I don't think so."

"Here, let me show you a few chords, see how you like it."

"Seriously, cooking and now the guitar? My learning curve is not that advanced."

"Oh, shut up! Here, take it. Just place it on your lap like this, and then hold here with your left hand. Now reach around from the back so your fingers are on the strings. Now, press down on the first string, the skinniest, with your ring finger here, just behind the third little metal marker—they're called frets. Now, reach with your first two fingers and put your second one on the fifth string at the second fret, and your pointer on the bottom string on the third fret, same as your ring finger."

He has got to be kidding! He's directing and pointing and gesturing as he imparts all this musical knowledge on me, but there is absolutely no way I'm following all that. He must sense my confusion because he scoots closer and puts his arm around me, covering my hands with his, showing me exactly how to do it. His body is warm and I tense a little at the sensation of his skin on mine.

"Here let me show you," he says softly.

He begins to play, we begin to play, and it's the sweetest, most amazingly erotic thing I've ever experienced. I can feel the vibration of the strings; hear the beautiful sound of the acoustic guitar. I soak it all in, including how incredible he feels pressed up against me. It makes for a very passionate moment. My breath hitches and I can feel my pulse start to kick up. Just when my heart starts to race, he pulls back. The music stops and my body nearly cries out at his absence.

"Sorry, did I do something?" I ask in defense.

He looks frustrated, but sad all at once.

"No, you didn't do anything wrong."

He drops his head and avoids my eyes. I have no idea what's going on, but I do know what makes most guys feel better. My need to please bubbles up, and I consider how my old automatic response could come in handy right now. So far, I've been able to keep myself in check with Kingsley, but tonight feels different.

Without a second thought, I reach over and gently rub his leg. I can feel how tense he is, so I rub my hand farther up toward the middle of his thigh. He instinctively moves his hand and covers mine with it. He squeezes my hand briefly and turns his head so we're eye-to-eye.

"Let me make you feel good, Kingsley. You've been so good to me, it's the least I can do for you."

I lean in toward him for a kiss, but he stands abruptly.

The bitter slap of rejection stings.

"What's wrong with you? You kiss me like it's the last kiss of your life, now you don't want me to touch you?" All at once, the feelings I've been trying to suppress about Jace start to rush in: doubt, fear, worthlessness, shame.

He lets out a huge sigh before responding. "Jessica, it's complicated. It's been a long time since I've been with a girl, a very long time."

"It's just sex, Kingsley. It's like riding a bike, you

aren't going to forget what to do, and, after that kiss, I'm pretty confident you know what you're doing."

He looks at me, dumbfounded.

"'Just sex'? Is that how you look at it? What on earth has transpired in your life for you to view the most personal act between two people as 'just sex'?" Though his words catch me off guard, there is no accusation in them, just genuine concern. I don't know how to respond, so I focus on my indignation.

"Yeah, just sex. Every guy wants it. Girls give it because we know it's how we get you. That's just how it works," I say, all sarcasm now.

He shakes his head and looks at me intently.

"Wow, I can't believe you just said that. If that's what you truly believe, then you really haven't ever had a real relationship. Sex is not how you get a guy, Jessica, and it's not how you keep a guy. Giving your body is not how you win someone over, giving your heart is how you get someone," he says kindly, and I can see the sympathy written all over his face, which just pisses me off more.

"Yeah? Well I tried that once and it got me nowhere but in pain. So fuck that," I say angrily.

He walks over, drops down, puts one hand on each of my shoulders, and looks right at me.

"I don't know what you've been through or what brought you to group therapy. I don't know what that pain in your eyes that I always see is from and I have no idea what inner battles you face daily. What I do know is you are worth far more than being 'just sex' to any man." His sincerity nearly breaks me.

I drop my head, feeling the tears fighting to fill my eyes, but I force them back. I refuse to be weak right now.

He places his forefinger under my chin and pulls my head up so I'm facing him.

"Listen to me right now. You deserve to have a man who falls in love with your mind, wants to undress your very conscience, and make love to your every single thought. You deserve a man who wants to see you slowly let down every wall you've ever built up.. You deserve a man that will work hard for you until you let him inside your heart."

It feels as if all the air in my lungs is being sucked out with every syllable that he speaks. I can barely breathe and I have the strongest desire to run. I want to leave and never turn back, but at the same time, I want to reach out and hug him. Hug him hard for saying those beautiful words to me. Instead, I stand here with a pained look on my face. He leans forward and kisses my forehead. His lips are warm and soft. Very slowly, he pulls away and brushes my hair out of my face.

"Talk to me, Jessica. Tell me what it is, who it is. Where does it come from, that pain in those beautiful, sad eyes?"

Is it that bad? So obvious that he can see it?

I can't handle this. It's too much, too damn heavy, and I can't do it. I have to get out of here.

"I have to go, Kingsley. Uh, I'm just... I'm sorry. I just have to go. I'll call a cab," I say as I get up, trying to collect myself.

"You don't have to go. I'm the one that should apologize. I kissed you like that in the kitchen because I wanted to, and, trust me, I want more, but it's not that simple. It's a big step for me to get involved with someone again. It has nothing to do with you at all." I hear him, but I don't really hear him. I'm too busy focusing on getting the hell out of here.

"It's okay, I understand. I still think I should go." I walk over to where my purse is hanging and sling it over my shoulder, starting for the door.

"Please, don't go. Stay." His husky voice breaks when he says "stay" and I have to look at him.

He's standing in front of the door with his hands in his pockets. His head is dropped a little and he kind of looks like a sad little boy. He's so strong and virile, but right now he just looks like a guy who doesn't want to be alone, a guy who's in pain. I know that look all too well. It's the same one I see every time I look in the mirror. He sees my pain and I see his. If I stay, we can sit together in our pain and be alone together, rather than alone and apart. I take a deep, cleansing breath.

I stay.

I put my purse down by the door, drop my arms to my sides, and look up at him. He cuts his eyes to my bag and then back to me. An uncomfortable silence situates itself around us while we both get ourselves together mentally.

"Thank you," he whispers. Holding out his hand to me, he gives me a small smile and I reach out and put my hand in his. He gives it a little squeeze and leads me toward the door, out onto the front porch.

"Let's sit a while."

We sit down on the white wooden porch swing and he stretches his arms out on the back of it—one arm around me—and it feels very comforting. We don't say anything at first and it's okay. It's okay just being still beside each other in the midst of the very loud wars that we both obviously have going on in our minds.

"I'm glad you stayed," he says.

"Me too." I lean my head over on his shoulder.

"This is nice," he says after a few minutes.

"Yeah, it really is."

"So, do you want to talk? Will you tell me why you're in group?" he asks hesitantly.

I let out a sigh.

"I guess," I tell him.

Now he'll run and run far after he sees what a freak I really am.

"Being honest with others empowers you to be honest with yourself."
—Kathryn Perez

Jessica

I CAN'T BELIEVE I just told him everything. Every freaking thing just came out like a dam bursting. Jace, my parents, that I have BPD. I laid it all out on the table. I don't think I even took a breath. My heart's pounding in my chest and my skin feels warm, my palms sweaty.

"Hey, it's okay. That was a lot of shit to get out, darlin'. Damn, I'm so sorry about all of it. That's rough. You're strong, though, you haven't given up, and you haven't let it beat you down."

He gently squeezes my shoulder and I shake my head.

"No, that's just it. I have let it beat me down. I'm a grown ass woman and I have nothing to show for my life. I have a shitty job, live in a tiny, shitty apartment, and have no car and no companion in my life. I have no friends to speak of and it's all because I let all of the bad things in my life determine my path. Anytime something good comes my way I mess it up. That's just what I do—I fuck things up. It's like I can't survive without drama in my life, like I need it to feed my impulsive jacked-up mind. It's just a vicious cycle that's on repeat. I let guys use me while I hang on to them for dear life, needing their attention. Then, the second it doesn't go my way I screw it up. I want them; I don't want them. I need them like I need food and water, and then I want them to leave me alone. It's an I-hate-you-don't-leave-me fucked-up cycle. I can't keep a job because I can't get along with my superiors to save my life. Same shitty cycle. All or nothing. That's the way my mind operates. I hate it, and even though I know why I am the way I am now that I've been diagnosed, it doesn't make it any easier to get through each day."

"What about therapy and counseling? You said they offered you a special therapy, that DBT stuff. Are you doing it?" he asks, seeming genuinely interested.

"No, I'm not. Since all the shit went down with finding out that the doctor bitch is actually Jace's fiancé, I haven't been back to any counseling of any kind. I've requested a new psychiatrist because Jace said it's a conflict of interest for me to stay there, but I haven't been given a new one yet. I'm supposed to get some letter or something once I've been assigned to a different one," I tell him, knowing that I'm dreading going back for individual sessions.

"Oh, I gotcha. Well are you gonna do it?"

"I guess I am. It's very intimidating though, you know? That DBT stuff is intense, very involved. I'm not sure I can do it."

"Of course you can do it. You can do anything; you just have to make a choice. Everything comes down to your choices."

If only it were that simple.

"I don't know. Most things don't feel like choices in my life. They feel like musts. Musts that are usually on the negative side of things. Knee-jerk reactions with lifelong repercussions. So, are you ever going to tell me your story?"

He sighs.

"I guess I sort of owe you that now, huh?"

"Yeah, but if you're not ready, it's okay." I tell him and I mean it.

"Okay, how about you come over again next weekend? We will cook a different meal and I'll tell you my story," he says.

It's getting later and a little chilly outside. I rub my hands up and down my arms, feeling cold.

"Are you cold? You wanna go inside?" he asks.

"Yeah, I guess so. But I really should go soon," I say.

"Nope, the night's young. Let's finish off that Chianti and play some Monopoly. Let's get all of that depressing stuff off your mind."

I just told him all my deep, dark shit and he wants to play Monopoly? Seriously?

"You want to play a board game that involves serious strategies while drinking?"

"Sure, sounds like fun to me!" he laughs.

"You're full of surprises, Kingsley. Never expected this night to end with Boardwalk and Park Place."

“You passed go, you collected two hundred dollars, and you royally kicked my ass, woman.”

We both laugh, and as I take the very last sip of my wine I realize we have finished off the entire bottle.

“Yep, looks like I did all right. I have got to go to the bathroom, though. Where is it?” I ask.

“It’s down the hall, past the closet where your purse was hanging.”

“Okay, I’ll be right back.”

I walk down the hallway, past the closet and there are three doors. I have no idea which one is the bathroom, so I just open the first one and flip the switch on the wall. Immediately, I know that it’s not the bathroom. It looks like an office or art room. Beautiful artwork adorns the walls and I’m drawn in by the splashes of color everywhere. I step in to take a closer look and see framed photos on a shelf of Kingsley and a beautiful black-haired woman. In one, they’re holding each other in a loving embrace; another has him kissing her on the cheek. Photo after photo of the two of them grace the walls, the desk, the shelves; every corner of the room features them, their love. My eyes land on one photo in particular with Kingsley kissing her belly, cupping it in what I can only describe as adoration. Her belly looks normal-sized but the way he’s touching and kissing it, you can tell what the picture represents. I’m suddenly confused, overwhelmed, and I know I’ve got to get out of this room. I don’t know what the hell I just saw, but I know I need to get out of here, now. I turn to go and just as I get to the door, I come face-to-face with Kingsley.

“What are you doing in here?” he asks tersely.

“Umm, I’m sorry. I didn’t know which door was the

bathroom. I opened—"

"So when you see this isn't the bathroom you just come on in here anyway and start looking at my private things?" he asks as he pierces me with his glare.

Is he crazy? I wasn't snooping. I didn't go through anything. I just saw some damn photos.

"I didn't snoop, Kingsley. Don't be an asshole. It was a simple mistake. It's just a room for God's sake."

I see his fists clench and I quickly realize that in my effort to defuse the situation, I said the wrong thing. He's really upset. I'm running all of the possibilities through my mind—who she is, where she is now, and what could've happened to her—but my mind is blank in the face of his anger.

"It's not just a room! It's my wife's art room. My dead wife's art room!" he screams at me. And in his scream I hear not just anger, but defeat, loss.

His dead wife?

Oh. My. God.

"Kingsley, I'm... I... I don't know what to say. I'm so sorry."

Not caring that I need to go to the bathroom, I push past him and make my way to the front door as fast as I can. I quickly grab my purse and bolt out the front door. I get my phone and scroll to the listing for the cab company.

"Jessica, wait, I'm sorry. Don't leave like this. Please, let me explain." He yells as he follows me down from his front porch.

I don't turn around. I just keep putting one foot in front of the other.

"Jessica, please! You can't leave upset. I'm sorry that I reacted so intensely." I can hear him closer behind me now, and even though I want to run away from him, from my mess of emotions, from this fucked-up situation, something stops me. That's what I always do—I run. Even if Kingsley and I are over before we've begun, I owe it to myself to stick this out. It's my choice, just like Kingsley said earlier. Besides, he heard me out earlier when I unloaded all my shit on him, the least I can do is give him the chance to do the same.

I pause and take a deep breath before turning around to face him.

"Kingsley, you don't have to explain anything to me. It's not my business. I'm not upset, okay? I just think maybe I should go."

He keeps walking toward me until he stops right at my feet. He's so handsome, but even his good looks can't distract me from the uncomfortable turn this night has taken.

"No, I want to explain. I want to tell you about her," he pauses, "about Lily."

Holy hell, this is some crazy, heavy shit.

Am I really up for this?

The wine has my head swimming and my emotions are bumping into each other at warp speed trying to figure out which way to go.

"I don't know. I had no idea you were married or that you had a family in that house. It just feels wrong or weird. I don't know," I say again, nervously fidgeting with my purse.

"You don't need to feel like that. I've never told anyone about her or what happened. I finally faced it all earlier today before you came over and, to be honest, you're the reason I did."

I look up at him in surprise.

"I'm the reason you faced it? What do you mean I'm the reason?"

"Listen, it's all pretty damn complicated and it's a long story, but spending time with you over the past few weeks has made me feel again. I haven't laughed or felt anything since Lily died. It's like I was living life, but looking at it from the outside in. It was just mundanely passing me by. Then, I met you and we've had a great time. For some reason, I'm drawn to you. I feel like we have a lot in common. I see your pain and the way you have all these defensive walls up—it's exactly what I do." His hands are on his hips and he shrugs, absently biting his lower lip before quietly continuing. "Today, I went in Lily's office for the first time since she died. I cried for her for the first time today, I cried for our unborn child for the first time today. I finally let all of my walls down and allowed myself to feel something about what happened," he says as he looks at me with sorrow in his blue eyes.

My eyes fill with tears and all I want to do is hug him. So that's what I do. I just reach out and hug him.

We are back inside, sitting on the sofa. He's just told me everything about Lily. Her suicide, the note he found today, and how he was looking for answers in the group. I'm heartbroken for him and his loss. He's spent the last hour telling me all about her and their life together. They were high school sweethearts. He told me about the letter and what it said, how he blames himself for her death, and how angry he is that she made such a huge decision for him and their baby. Of all the times I ever considered suicide I never took anyone else into consideration, just myself. Seeing how broken Kingsley is and how upset and confused he's feeling... Well, it's just really hard for me to reconcile how taking your own life affects others in such a big way.

"I think what we do to ourselves mentally can really give our minds the power to enslave us. We need to learn to let our mind empower us, and stop letting it throw us into the depths of misery and regret. Lily let her mind take over and it took her life in the process. I just wish I could've prevented it," he sighs.

He's such a deep thinker. Everything he just said is so very true. I think the bigger picture here is that you can't underestimate the pain in a person, because, in all honesty, everyone is struggling with something. Some people are just better at hiding it than others. But it's so hard to stop your mind from going to those dark places when you're lost in your depression and mental illness. That's what he doesn't understand. Until you've experienced depression, or a form of depression, you can't ever really know how strongly it controls you.

"I know you're angry at her and angry at yourself, but you have to let that anger go. It will poison you. I can tell you firsthand that Lily felt she had no other choice. I've been in that place so many times. It's dark, it's deep, and it has no sympathy for anyone. It's like having a blanket draped over you, enveloping you in darkness and despair. It's a black hole of pain and helplessness." I'm not sure my words will bring him comfort, but he needs to hear them, to have some frame of reference to understand what she may have been going through.

"The weight of it, the excruciating pain of it is hard to even put into words. That's why I cut myself. It is my only release. I know you can't really understand it, but I promise you, Lily felt she had no other choice."

I reach out and place my hand on his, looking at him with compassion.

"Her pain was so great that all she could do was seek out the one sliver of peace she knew—to no longer exist. That's not yours to own. She was sick, and her sickness killed her. Just like a cancer patient is killed by cancer, Lily was killed by mental illness."

He sighs as he tries to absorb the weight of my words.

"God, it's so comforting hearing you explain all of this. I've always wished that I could see inside her mind and find out what would make her do something so terrible. I've felt responsible for her death this entire time," he says, dropping his head into his hands.

"I know. You need to let it go. Let the guilt go because it wasn't your fault. She loved you the best she knew how, and even though it's hard to understand, she felt she was helping you by doing this. You're not responsible for her death, Kingsley." He may not believe it today, but I think he will in time. God, I hope he will.

He looks up at me, and his eyes are glossed over with impending tears.

"Thank you. Thank you so much for listening to me, for hearing me, and for helping me understand why she may have done it. I guess I just couldn't fathom it because my mind has never worked that way. Even dealing with her death and all the pain that's come with it, I've never gotten to a point where I felt I wanted to die."

"I understand. I'd do anything to have a mind that automatically works like yours," I tell him, smiling a little.

"Well, you have an answer, Jessica. That's why you have to do the DBT and stay in therapy. You're brave and your mind is a lot stronger than you give yourself credit for. You're beautiful inside and out. Just let that shine, let it grow, believe in it and see where that takes you. You've got this, Jessica. You just have to," he says, and I sense that his words are both a statement and plea.

He pulls me into him and I lay my head on his shoulder. I don't say anything because I know he's right. I know what I have to do, but knowing and doing are two very different things. The doing is the hard part.

"There are seeds of self-destruction in all of us that will bear only unhappiness if allowed to grow."
—Dorothy Brande

Jessica

FLIPPING THROUGH MY mail this morning, I find a letter from the clinic. I open it and read the letter saying that I've been reassigned to a new psychiatrist, Dr. Janice. Looks like I have my first appointment with the new doc next week. The next envelope is big and heavy and seems to be made out of a fancy paper. There's no return address, just a big silver *J & V* sticker stuck on the closure. Instantly, my head spins. It's a wedding invitation—I know it is. I quickly rip it open, revealing an intricate but elegant invitation. Silver calligraphy scrolled across the vellum overlay accents the lavender background. Stunning and classy.

It's everything that I'm not.

Victoria Loren Ward
and
Jace Sean Collins
Together with their parents
cordially invite you to share
in their day of matrimony.

I can't keep reading it. My eyes are blurry with tears and my stomach is whirling with nausea. Pain and regret flood every inch of my heart. I want it to go away, to stop.

I head straight for my room and yank open my bedside table drawer. My hands nervously fumble with the box, my box of freedom. Light funnels through my window and reflects off the blade as my heart rate kicks up. I need this relief, the relief that only exists when I cut. The shiny, cold metal gripped between my fingertips feels like an anesthetic ready to relieve the pain that hides inside me. Burning sensations sting as the blade penetrates the surface of my skin.

Inhale.

Exhale.

Inhale.

Exhale.

The deeper I go, the heavier my breathing grows. Blood oozes out in a crimson line and the high I'm so desperate for finally soars through my body. This is mine, all mine, and I'm in control. I control the length of the cut, the depth, and the level of pain. I etch the proof of my misery on my skin while trying to destroy the agony that festers within.

I click on Jace's Facebook page and scroll down and down. I click on every picture of them, torturing myself. Every photo looks so contrived, so fake. This is not him, not the Jace that I know. He's fooling himself. I click on Victoria's name and scroll through her timeline. She's the epitome of everything that I despise, so prim and proper. Looking at her life makes me want to puke. Her "About Me" section reads like a who's who of the field she's in. I come across a photo of her and Jace with him wearing a cap and gown; it's his Baylor graduation. I look at it for a long time. That's what I walked away for, so he could have that day. He had the day I gave him with her. I abruptly close my laptop, knocking over my glass of whiskey as I do. It's only noon and I'm three glasses into my bottle of Jim Beam.

Fuck it, I don't care.

I just don't give a shit anymore. My life is what it is. No sense in trying to stop the inevitable. I don't have to work tonight, so I'm going out. I need to let loose and stop wallowing in jealously and bitterness.

Fuck Jace Collins.

I don't need him. I don't need anyone.

I walk into Rookies Sports Bar wearing my tightest, most revealing dress. My sleek red dress accented by my thick black hair turns heads every time. Dark red lipstick accentuates my full lips and I'm ready to put them to good use tonight—anything to keep me from thinking about

Jace. I've been drinking on and off since this morning. It won't take much to get me feeling good tonight.

Kingsley has been texting me all day, but I haven't responded. I can't. He's too good for me. Plus, the guy won't even have sex with me. How could he possibly be interested in me and not want more? I just can't buy into that no-sex-because-I-care shit. Men do not operate that way. They just don't. I find a spot at the bar and slide onto the barstool.

"Hey, Jessica, what will it be tonight?" Kevin the bartender asks. I've been working here for a short time, but it's my night off. Rookies is where I was the night of my drunken car accident.

"Hmmm, 151, I think, Kev. Hit me with the hard stuff and keep it coming." He arches his brows and gives me an "oh shit" look.

"Didn't you learn your lesson a while back, woman? You're gonna find yourself in more trouble if you're not careful." I watch him pour the drink and contemplate his words, but only briefly.

"I'm not driving. I'm being a good girl. I took a cab." He slides the shot glass toward me and I throw it back quickly. I love the burn as it rolls down my throat and the warmth that spreads throughout my insides from the alcohol. It's another high, another form of numbing my shit hole of a reality.

"All right, doll, just be sure to take a cab back home too."

"Will do, Kev. Now hit me again."

I've had too many shots and too little food tonight. I'm wasted and not feeling a damn thing. It's bliss.

"Jessica?" I hear a familiar voice say. I turn my head in a rather slow drunken motion, enough to glance over my shoulder and bring Jace's face into focus. I twist my body toward him on the barstool and let out a huge laugh. I have no idea why, but it just barrels right out of my mouth. He stares at me, roving his eyes up and down my body with an obviously displeased look on his face.

"Well, well, if it isn't the former all-star quarterback of Jenson High School, the Baylor graduate, and soon-to-be-married Jace Collins! How fucking lucky are we here in this bar to be graced with your presence?" My voice gets louder and louder with every word. "Hey everyone," I shout, "this is Jace, he's my ex-boyfriend. I just fucked him recently, right before his lovely doctor wife showed up while his cum was still inside of me. Let's all have a round on Jace. He's fucking rich, he can afford it!" I raise my glass and laugh as he fumes with anger. I see his fists clenching at his side and I really don't give a flying fuck how mad he is.

"What the hell are you doing, Jess? You're drunk. I'm taking you home." I can't stop laughing. Tears form in the corners of my eyes, I'm laughing so hard.

"Sure, Jace. Like hell I'm going home with you! How did you even know I was here? You know what I got today? Never mind, don't try to think about it, I'll tell you. I got your beauuuuutiful wedding invitation." I gesture with my glass, spilling some of the liquid on the floor before taking a gulp and continuing. "How sweet of you to invite your dirty little secret to your special day."

"Shit!" He runs his hands through his hair, shaking

his head back and forth. “Damn, I’m sorry. I don’t know why she did that. Just let me take you home. You’re drunk and dressed like a streetwalker; it’s not safe for you here.”

“Ha! Not safe? Streetwalker?” I laugh again. “You didn’t answer my question, Jace. How did you know I was here? Maybe it’s not safe for me to be with *you*.” I mock, purposely looking to piss him off. That’s just the kind of mood I’m in tonight.

He huffs before answering. “I went by your place and you weren’t home, so I thought I’d try your work. I’m glad I stopped by, Jess. You really need to go home.”

“She’s not going anywhere with you. She’s coming with me, so back the hell up.” I lean to the side and see a very big Kingsley in his signature beanie with more scruff than usual. He extends his hand to me, “Jessica, come on. Let’s get you out of here. My bike is out front.”

God, do I have a GPS up my ass that these two are connected to?

Jace looks at me, then Kingsley, and then me again. “Is this who you’re with now? You’ve got to be kidding me, Jess.”

What the hell is that supposed to mean?

“Yes, matter of fact, this is who I’m with. Is that a problem? What is it? He’s not preppy enough, clean-cut enough, or cookie-fucking-cutter enough for you? Look at him. Go ahead and take a long, hard look because this is what a man looks like! Plus, you have no right to question who I’m with or not with. You’re getting married soon. Go home, Jace, go fuck your fiancé doctor bitch.” I slap money down on the bar. “I’m outta here, Kev. See you next time.” I stumble down from the barstool, trying to keep balanced on my black, high heels. Not easy after too many

151 shots.

"Here, take my hand. You need to get home and sleep this off." Kingsley takes my hand and guides me closely into his side, wrapping his arm protectively around my waist and helping me walk. I look over at Jace and give him the nastiest snarky smile that I can muster.

"No, Kinsgley, baby, I'm not sleeping when we get there, not at all, not with this sexy-ass body of yours. We are gonna play." My words sort of slur together and although I'm embarrassing myself, I just don't care. Jace's eyes say everything that his mouth isn't. I can see how my words sting and hurt him. I should be ashamed of myself, but I'm not.

I destroy everything good in my life, one impulsive choice at a time.

Kingsley turns toward Jace one last time and says, "Just leave her alone. You can't toy with her anymore. I won't let you. You made your choice, man. Go home to your woman. Jessica isn't yours anymore, she's mine."

I am?

Jace glares at Kingsley, studying him carefully, and I can see the anger and pain in his eyes, his stance—it radiates off of him. I should feel bad for him, but right now all I feel is anger too. He steps in closer toward Kingsley and I suddenly fear some sort of testosterone-filled face-off between the two of them.

"No, that's where you're wrong man. She isn't yours. She isn't a fucking possession. But I will tell you this—I love her and I've always loved her. You can lay claim to her all you want, but nothing you do will ever erase the fact that she loves me."

He shifts his eyes to mine and my mind spins a little

at his words. That, and all the alcohol running through my veins.

"I came here to tell you that I choose you. I choose to love you, Jess, to be with you. I came here to tell you that I'm breaking things off with Victoria and to tell you face-to-face that I have never for a minute stopped wanting you to be the woman by my side."

My mouth involuntarily falls open.

"Let's go, Jessica. He's just screwing with you and you know it. Let's just go."

I look over at Kingsley and I'm confused, still trying to process what Jace just said.

"I'm leaving, Jess. You can go with me or with him, if that's what you really want, but when you wake up tomorrow and remember tonight just know that I meant everything I said. All you have to do is say the word and I'll be there. We can figure this all out together and try to fix everything we've broken," Jace says. I want to believe him. It seems like he believes himself this time.

Kingsley takes my hand. "Come on, let's go."

I just nod and follow beside Kingsley as he guides me. I look back at Jace and say nothing. There's nothing to say right now. I don't trust his promises.

My head is pounding as I open my eyes, and the light flickering through the windows nearly blinds me. I groan, squeezing my eyes shut and rolling over to my side in a fetal position. My mouth feels like I've been chewing on cotton balls and my throat is like the Sahara Desert.

"Well, look who's awake. Rise and shine, hungover

one." He's talking entirely too loud and I just want to go back to sleep.

"Go away, Kingsley. I need more sleep."

"No way, get your ass up. It's nearly noon already and we have somewhere to be in an hour." He flips the lights on, which makes the damn room even brighter. "Go take a cold shower and I'll make you something to eat. No arguments from you either, especially after the shit I dealt with from you last night. You've got to be the worst drunk woman I've ever encountered, such a huge pain in the ass."

My head is spinning as I try to recall everything that happened last night. I remember the bar, Jace, Kingsley, and me making a complete fool of myself. After that, all I remember is holding on to Kingsley for dear life as he weaved in and out of traffic through the darkened city streets to my apartment.

Shit! I don't remember what happened when we got here.

"What did I do? God, I'm almost afraid to hear the answer. Did we have sex? Was it awful? Did I puke? What?" I ask frantically.

Laughter fills the room, rattling through my aching head, and I glare at him. He's standing at the foot of my bed in the same clothes he had on last night, only without the beanie. His hair is a mess and if he doesn't shave soon, he's going to have a full-on beard. You can barely see his dimples anymore due to all the scruff.

"What's so damn funny? Stop laughing at me," I pout.

"You really don't remember, do you?"

I carefully shake my head from side to side as I pull

my knees up closer to my chest, hugging them.

"You puked all over yourself, all down the front of that slutty red dress. Good riddance. I just threw it in the trash."

"You did what? Oh my God, Kingsley! I love that dress."

Suddenly, it occurs to me that I'm in one of my T-shirts and a pair of boxers. I look down and see *Er Mher Gherd* written across the front of my old shirt. I check out the floor and see my heels beside the black lacy thong I was wearing.

"You undressed me? You took off my panties too? What the hell, Kingsley! How embarrassing!" I can feel the heat coloring my face as I groan.

What the hell else happened last night?

He crosses his arms over his broad chest and continues on with that Cheshire cat smirk.

"Matter of fact, you took those off all on your own. To be more specific, you tried to do a little strip tease for me, although you could barely stand up in those ridiculous shoes." He arches an eyebrow and I die. "You kicked off the shoes, bent over, backside pointed right at me in that dress, ass all hanging out, and took the thong right off. You spun them around in the air on your fingertip, and then proceeded to puke all down the front of yourself."

Oh, God.

If I didn't feel sick enough before, I feel deathly ill now. If there were a nearby hole, I'd happily jump feetfirst into it. I quickly pull the comforter up over my face, mortified.

"Oh, hell no, you're not hiding from this. I cleaned your vomit, dressed you, and put you in bed. It is what it is. Get over it. I slept on the couch. So, to answer your question, no, we did not have sex and if we had I can promise you, it would've been nowhere in the realm of awful. Now get up, get in the shower, and get dressed, woman."

I hear my bedroom door shut and roll over to my side, kicking my feet like a kid throwing a tantrum.

That man is impossible.

I close my eyes and exhale. Jace's face flashes through my mind's eye. I sit up slowly and reach over for my phone. Four text messages from him. I'm scared to read them, but I swipe the screen anyway.

Jace: *You always do this. You always wreck us before there's any chance for redemption. Why? Why do you always do this? It's no different than high school.*

Jace: *I guess you aren't going to respond since you're with gorilla boy. I can't take this, Jess. My resolve is fucking cracking. Why didn't you just come with me last night? We could be together right now...*

Jace: *I love you, Jess. I always have and I always will. Thing is, you refuse to let anyone love you. I know I screwed up that night at your apartment and I know I should've had the balls to break things off with Vic from the start, but I didn't. I made a mistake. That's why I came looking for you last night; to apologize, to tell you I was going to leave her. But after the scene you made and seeing the destruction that breeds inside you I know that we will never work. You refuse to let love in. You destroy it. Until you get help for your disorder, you'll never change.*

Just like an alcoholic will never stop abusing until they get help, you'll never stop hurting yourself physically and emotionally until you get help and you'll keep hurting the ones around you too. I refuse to walk on eggshells around you. You're a ticking time bomb. Get help, Jess. Do it for you—not for him or me—but for you. I won't force my way into your life anymore.

Jace: *Good-bye, Jess.*

The truth hurts.

I read the last words and hurl my phone across the room. It hits the wall and shatters before crashing to the floor. My door flies open and Kingsley rushes through.

"What the hell was that?" He looks down and sees what's left of my phone. "Why did you just demolish your phone?" he asks carefully.

"I don't want to talk about it." My face is like stone. I refuse to cry a single tear over Jace Collins ever again. Emotion burns my eyes, but I fight it away.

"Are you okay?" he prods. "You look strange. What's going on, darlin'?"

"I said that I don't want to talk about it. I'm getting up, okay? I'm getting up and into the shower just like you asked. Please don't push me on this. It's just a phone. Who cares?" And with that, I'm up and moving into my bathroom, shutting the door on Jace and his self-righteous text messages.

As much as I didn't want to, I got up and got ready. I

grabbed a swimsuit, per Kingsley's request, but I have no idea where we're heading. I hope we aren't going too far; riding on this damn bike with a hangover is not an enjoyable experience at all.

"I have to change clothes so we're gonna stop by my place real quick," he yells over his shoulder.

A few more miles and we're at his house. I choose to sit on the porch and wait while he changes. I just don't feel comfortable in there, knowing it was where he made a home with his wife. The door opens, bringing me out of my daydreaming.

"Okay, let's get going." He's wearing workout clothes and I instantly feel argumentative. No way am I working out with this hangover.

"Where are we going, Kingsley? Please don't tell me that you expect me to go to the gym feeling like I do."

"Nope, we aren't going to the gym. Let's go. Stop your bellyaching."

"My stomach does ache, a lot. I just want to sleep, Kingsley. Why are you dragging me all over the place when I feel so horrible? Is this my payback?"

"Oh my God, woman, stop whining. You got yourself wasted, now accept the consequences. I don't feel sorry for you. I texted multiple times yesterday trying to set this up for today, but you chose to go out and destroy your liver instead. I want you to go with me to volunteer today."

"Volunteer for what?" I ask, puzzled.

"At the YMCA with kids. They're really great. I go a couple times a month. Lily used to teach an art class there. After she died, I started volunteering with the sports programs. I love it and I want to take you with me. I think you'll enjoy it too. The kids are awesome."

Kingsley constantly surprises me. I have no experience with kids, so I have no idea how I can be of any help.

"I don't know anything about kids, Kingsley."

"You don't need to. You just follow their lead. Adults learn far more from kids than kids ever learn from us. I think it will be good for you, yah know? Kids are everything that's good and pure. They can really bring a lot of things into perspective for a person. Every time I go, I leave feeling like a better person with a brighter outlook on life."

He holds out his hand and looks at me expectantly. I reach out and take it. It's warm and comforting, just like him. I look up at him and he smiles, pulling me in closer to his body. He wraps strong arms around me and squeezes. We take a deep breath together and sigh simultaneously as his head rests on top of mine. I feel myself relax as all thoughts flee my mind. All but one: I am so thankful for this man.

"Just trust me, okay?" he whispers. I nod into his chest and wonder how I got so lucky. I don't deserve him. Jace is right, I'll ruin this too, somehow, someway; I'll screw this thing with Kingsley up just like I do with every guy I meet.

"I know the phone throwing had something to do with him. I won't pry, but you have to move on from him, Jess. The situation is holding you hostage. You can't stay on that merry-go-round forever. It's already been six years too long."

He's right and I know it. I can't hold on to my high school love forever.

"I'm trying," is all I say. And again I'm thankful because he doesn't say anything else about it.

"Cry. Forgive. Learn. Move on."
—Steve Maraboli

Kingsley

"REALLY, I DON'T need you to take me to my appointment. It's so sweet of you to offer, but I need to do this on my own. Let's just hope this new therapist doesn't turn into a disaster like the first one did."

I'm disappointed, but I'm happy that she's trying and feeling strong enough to go alone. Watching her with the kids at the Y was amazing. I could see something inside her change for a few hours. The woman I knew existed within her was revealed. She's a natural in the water and the kids loved her instantly. She was so patient with them and she smiled the entire time.

"What are you over there grinning about?" she asks, while tying her shoes.

"You," I reply.

"Me, what?" She gives me a crooked little smile and I

can't help but want to take her face in my hands and kiss her right here and now. My need for her is relentless. Every moment we spend together it grows. I have to control myself, though. She's not ready. She still loves him and I'm pretty positive that if he came running back to her right now, she'd let him. I don't want half of her heart. I want all of it.

"I was just thinking about you volunteering with the kids," I tell her. "You really amazed me. You did a really good job and it was nice seeing you so happy."

She stands up and fidgets with her sleeves. She does that when she gets nervous. And she always gets nervous when she gets complimented. She's so used to being put down that a compliment is foreign to her. The sad part is that I think she's her own worst enemy. I think she puts herself down more than anyone else ever has.

"Hey, take the compliment. You were great. Own that shit and be proud of yourself."

She blushes.

Fuck! Why did she have to do that?

Brushing a few strands of her hair back from her face, my fingers softly graze her neck. She tenses a little, responding to my touch, and the sexual tension between us vibrates in an unsteady rhythm. I want her and I know she wants me. I want to do so much more than simply touch her hair. I want more of this woman, so much more. I want to erase that guy from her mind forever and firmly embed myself in her heart.

"You need to shave," she mutters, and then nervously turns and walks toward the kitchen. I scratch at my chin, feeling the growth of my whiskers. She's right; I do need to shave soon.

She grabs a bottle of water from the fridge and gets her purse. "I should go."

"Can I at least give you a ride to the bus stop?"

She smiles as she says, "Sure."

"Great. How about dinner tonight, my place?" I see her expression change and I know why.

"You can't keep being weird about coming to my house. It's okay. Lily would love you. I know she would. There's nothing wrong with me having a friend over. We can cook again." I wink and smile at her, trying to lighten the mood.

She gives me that look. The one where she's wanting to say yes, but feeling like the right answer is no.

"Say yes, Jessica," I prod.

"All right, but only if I don't have to cook anything difficult." She slings her purse over her shoulder and opens the door for us.

"How about breakfast for dinner? I can teach you to make eggs!" We both bust out laughing and I soak up the moment. It feels so damn good to laugh.

It just feels good to feel.

Part Two

RECOVERY

"I am my problem, but I am also my solution."
—Unknown

Jessica

STANDING OUTSIDE THE clinic, I take in a deep breath. The larger-than-life sign out front that reads *Mental Health Clinic* makes me feel like I should try to disguise myself as I go in. It just screams *crazy person walking*.

I go in, sign-in, and wait. The waiting is always awful in places like this. Sitting here, I'm scanning the room, looking at the others that are waiting, and judging them. They're judging me too. It's an unspoken truth.

Fifteen minutes inch by before my name is called. "Ms. Alexander, you may come on back," the receptionist says.

I enter a small office and as I look around I quickly realize that this therapist and Dr. Ward are polar opposites. Bookshelves full of unorganized books line the wall space and everywhere I look there's clutter. Nothing hangs on the walls except a clock and a quote decal positioned above the door. It reads *Talk to yourself like someone you love*. I can barely see a framed diploma leaned up against the wall on her desk with all the files stacked in front of it. I sit down on the blue-checkered love seat and take a cleansing breath. The door opens and in walks a short, middle-aged lady with shaggy, red hair, and a pencil pushed behind one ear. She's holding a Coke in one hand and a file in her other hand. She's wearing jeans and a T-shirt. My eyes make it to her feet to find that she's also wearing hot pink chucks. Interesting. Not what I expected in the least.

"Hi there! You must be Jessica. I'm Janice, your new therapist," she says in a friendly, upbeat tone. She extends her hand and I reach out to shake it before she takes a seat at her desk. Pulling a pair of eyeglasses out of a drawer, she puts them on and opens the file to give it a quick once-over.

"I've reviewed your file and records from the previous clinic as well as your hospital visit." She closes the file, placing it on her desk. She removes the glasses and leans back in her chair casually crossing her legs. "Thing is that I've read it and there's no need to go back over any of that information. I'm not going to give you any diagnostic questionnaires or sit here and ask you a bunch of textbook shrink questions. You have borderline personality disorder. That's pretty clear from all of the information you gave Dr. Ward. So, we know what the problem is. I'm not interested in the problem. I'm interested in a solution. So I'll ask you one very important question. How you answer will determine if you and I are right for one another in the sense of you getting treatment here."

She's very direct, but she's also not at all threatening. Her body language and tone of voice are welcoming, inviting almost. She has kind eyes and, for some reason, I don't feel as tense as I did before.

"Okay," I respond.

"Alright then. Don't answer quickly. Think hard about my question, and then answer. We can sit here as long as we need to. What I need to know from you is this—do you want to get better? Not the 'Yeah, I want to get better because I have to or because someone says I need to.' I want to know if *you*, Jessica Alexander, want to get better for yourself, by yourself, because it's what you and only you want in order to have a happier and healthier life. That if the judge said you could stop coming tomorrow you would still choose to be here. It has to be your choice, your decision and no one else's. Just know that everything in our lives is a reflection of a choice we've made. If we want different results, we must make different choices."

Choices. We all have them, just like Kingsley said.

I try to absorb everything she said. I stare into my lap and evaluate my thoughts one by one. A popping sound startles me when she opens her Coke. I readjust myself on the love seat and consider. I know that I can't keep living like I have been. I know that I want to be happy. I'm just scared, really scared that I might not be able to do it. I pinch the bridge of my nose, inhale then exhale. I look at her, forming my answer mentally before speaking.

"I do want to get better. I want to for me and that's the truth. The thing is, I'm terrified that I won't be able to succeed with this DBT stuff. It seems so daunting and I've never really completed anything in my life successfully. I think a better question is 'can I get better?'"

A smile spreads across her face, which confuses me. I assumed my answer wasn't good enough, but she looks pleased.

"Jessica, you were given this life because you're strong enough to live it. I have no doubt about that. Self-doubt can cripple a person faster than fear ever will. Self-doubt can kill dreams and rob you from your future." I listen nervously and try to breathe evenly. "One of the most crucial things that I'll want to hammer into your mind is that the way you talk to yourself is a key factor in your success. Our brains are big muscles. The more you work it the stronger it gets. At first it will be hard. You will fall down, you will make mistakes, and you will struggle. That's all okay." She smiles and I feel myself wanting to trust her. "What matters most is that you don't give up. You keep coming here and we keep fighting, together. I'll challenge you, push you, and basically put you in front of a mirror forcing you to face the deepest and darkest places within yourself. You won't like me some days and that's fine. I expect it. Tough love is my forte. Just know that everything I do is always in your best interest. You can do this. It's all in how badly you want it."

I don't know how to respond. She seems so confident about something that I have hardly any confidence in at all. I reach down deep within myself, calling on every ounce of bravery that I've ever had, and choose.

"Okay, I want to do it."

The words reverberate off the walls of my mind and I resolve to do this, no matter how hard or scary it may be. I want happiness and I want to love the person I am.

"Okay," she smiles at me, "I'm happy to hear that.

We will have one individual session and one group session with my DBT group per week. You can attend your other group one last time this week if you'd like. Starting next week you'll have all of your therapy sessions here. I'll send the necessary paperwork to the judge."

"Thank you," I say.

"You're welcome, dear. Be sure to pat yourself on the back too. Making the decision to take this step is all on you. It's your first victory and there are many more to come."

I look at her and smile. For the first time in my life, I think I feel a small sense of pride for the choice I've just made.

"Sometimes life will throw everything at you all at once. You can either catch it all or reach for the things that matter most."
—Kathryn Perez

Jace

"SHE HAS A brain tumor and it's extremely aggressive, Mr. Collins. We are going to perform surgery, but the tumor is located near a sensitive area of the brain, making the procedure very risky. We may only be able to remove a portion of the tumor, but it may help reduce her signs and symptoms. Then we can try radiation treatment for the remaining tumor cells."

Victoria squeezes my hand and I flinch. I haven't found the right time to tell her there's not going to be a wedding. I turn to her now, seeing her eyes glazed over with tears. She's really close to my mom and this is really hitting her hard. I take in a deep breath before I say anything.

"When will you operate on her, Doctor?"

"Today, Mr. Collins. Your mom has already signed all of the paperwork. She has requested to see you both before we get her prepped for surgery."

"Okay, we'll go on back now, if that's all right."

"Absolutely. We haven't moved her to the OR yet. She's still in her room."

Mother's quietly lying in bed, reading a magazine when we enter. The room feels cold, but flowers from all of her friends at the country club brighten every corner. She's covered up with the eight hundred dollar alpaca fur blanket that Victoria gave to her. She didn't even bat an eye at paying that much for a blanket for Mom.

"Mrs. Collins, I hope that blanket is keeping you nice and warm in here. This room is kind of chilly," Victoria says.

"Oh, it's perfection, my dear. You do have impeccable taste, Victoria."

Mom smiles and motions for us to come sit down.

"Sit, please, both of you. I wanted to speak with you before they take me in for surgery today. And before you argue with me, Jace Collins, just sit there and listen to your mother. Okay?"

I nod in agreement, but something feels off; and it's not just the fact that Mom is so sick.

"It's very possible that there could be complications with this surgery because of where the tumor is located," she starts. I have to focus on her words with a certain amount of detachment; otherwise I may not get through this. "I have had my attorney go over all of my estate paperwork along with my will. You know, dear, that I want nothing but for you to be happy and to have a fruitful life with a good wife by your side. Victoria has proven to be a loyal woman and I adore her. She loves you very much and she has your best interests at heart, as do I. Per the guidelines of my will, you'll be given everything in my estate upon the completion of your first year of marriage to Victoria. At that time, you'll be the full beneficiary of the estate," she says, deadpan.

Something inside of me begins to weaken. I'm looking at my mother, the woman that raised me, the woman that I have forgiven everything because a son loves his mother unconditionally. My struggle to stop myself from confronting her about the abortion rages just beneath the surface of my thin resolve. Her statement just now shouldn't shock me. More than anything it hurts, because no matter how hard I try to dismiss my mother's selfish, controlling ways, she never fails to push it right in my face. I look at Victoria and she's smiling. This angers me to no avail and the last of my resolve breaks away.

"Do you actually find this amusing, Vic? My mother gives me an ultimatum based on my love life and you smile?" I ask incredulously.

"Jace Collins, do not disrespect your fiancé. She's simply supporting her mother-in-law. Why is that a bad thing?"

"Mother, please do not speak about bad things or question me. I'm truly sorry that you're ill, and I'll pray every second while you're in surgery for a positive outcome. But you need to understand that your health will *not* be a determining factor in my personal life. It just won't. If you think your estate should go to me based on my personal decisions in my love life rather than the fact that I'm your son, then I don't want it."

I pause. What I really want to do is yell at her, but I can't bring myself to do that while she's sick in a hospital.

"I don't need your money, Mother, and I refuse to allow you to force anything upon me. I love you and want you well, but I have to draw the line here. I'm not sorry about taking a stand on this." Standing up to her is hard; I hate conflict where she's concerned, but enough is enough. Her face hardens and I prepare for the worst.

"Do you not see that I'm trying to do what's best for the future of this family? Why is this a problem, Jace? You're engaged to a wonderful woman and you're to be married soon. Why would you foresee my terms not working in your favor? Is this about that harlot from your senior year?" she hisses.

That's it, no more of this.

"Mother, Victoria, please excuse me. I'll be here when you come out of surgery, but I have to go right now. If I stay I'll regret my next words."

I push out of the chair and glare at Victoria, because I know she told Mom about Jessica and it pisses me the hell off. It wouldn't surprise me if Victoria were in on this estate shit either. I make my way down the hallway and out to the parking lot. I'm almost to my car when my phone buzzes. It's Victoria.

End.

I have no desire to talk to her right now, so I get in the car and just drive.

Of course this is where I'd end up. It still looks exactly the same as it always did. The water tower's a little rustier, but everything else is the same. I get out of the car and walk across the dusty gravel to the ladder. As I climb up, I do my best to shut everything out and focus on just putting one hand in front of the other, one foot in front of the other. I reach the platform and scan the area where Jess once wrote. Faded and barely there, I see it: *J & J always together, even if far away.* The day I left for college, she scratched that into the tower and put a big heart around it. I run my fingers across it and go back to that day. She was happy, we were happy. I miss her; I miss my hopes for what we could've been. Why do they say that time heals or that missing someone gets easier with time? Time is just a Band-Aid. It covers up the wound but the wound has to heal on its own.

I find myself daydreaming about her now; she haunts my dreams when I sleep too. There are moments when I miss her so much that I wish I could just pluck the memories from my dreams and relive them all over again. Finding and seeing her again immediately brought back all those long forgotten—or ignored—feelings along with the pain I'd felt when she left me. Should love hurt this much? Who knows? Maybe we are broken, maybe we don't belong together, and maybe we never did.

Thinking over all of it now, I try to pinpoint what drew me to Jessica Alexander in the first place. Was it that I saw Genevieve in her? Part of me recognizes that I've always wanted to save her from herself, from other people, from a fate like Genevieve's. But nothing I've done for Jess has brought my little sister back or lessened my guilt, and it never will. And, if I'm being honest, nothing I've done has helped the girl who took my heart away with her six years ago. Not one damn bit. Sometimes I think I actually made her life worse. But I fell in love with her. And ain't that just a bitch for me.

How the hell did I get here?

How did I get to a place in my life where every choice I have to choose from and every decision I make feels wrong? Minutes or hours go by, I don't know, and no matter how many ways I try to map out my future, I can't see Victoria in it anymore. Whether I'm with Jess or not, I know I don't love Victoria. And Jessica?

Jessica will always be my biggest "what if".

My phone buzzes again and I answer it, knowing if I don't she'll just keep calling.

"What do you want, Victoria?" I snap.

"Jace, it's your mom. There was a complication during surgery and I think it's bad. You need to get back here now."

"I'm on my way." I hang up and make my way down to my car as fast as I can. I put my hazard lights on as I speed to the hospital. "Don't die, don't die, dammit," I whisper. Tears burn my eyes and I go over and over the disagreement we had before I left. She's my mom, no matter how angry she makes me.

Just, God, please don't let her die.

I whip into the hospital parking lot, get out of my car in a flash, and run inside to find Victoria.

"Jace, over here," Victoria shouts.

"What's going on?"

"I'm not sure. A bunch of doctors and nurses rushed in, but they won't tell me anything."

I go to the nurses' station to find out.

"Excuse me, can you please tell me what the status of Ariana Collins is? She's my mother."

The nurse never looks up at me. She just continues on with her pile of paperwork and replies, "Sir, the doctor will come out and inform you as soon as he can. Please be patient."

My manners and rather calm demeanor just flew out the fucking window. "I want to know right now what's going on with my mom. I demand that you find someone who knows or someone who can find out! Do you hear me?"

She looks up at me with raised brows.

"Sir, you need to calm down. What's your mother's name again?"

"Ariana Collins."

"Give me one minute, but if you get out of control in here at any point you'll be removed by security. Please, try to stay calm."

She walks off down the hallway and I massage my temples, exhaling hard. I feel a hand on my shoulder and flinch at the touch. I turn to look at Victoria, only to see someone that I've lost any and all affection for.

"Jace, darling, I'm sorry. I'm sure she's going to be okay. We just have to hold on to that hope." She knows I'm mad at her, and lately, I have no idea if her words or intentions are sincere at all.

"Vic, just leave me alone, okay? Thank you for being here for Mother, but I just can't deal with how I'm feeling toward you right now."

Her eyebrows form a deep crease and I can see her jaws tighten.

"What's your problem? You've been intolerable lately. You've disrespected me, embarrassed me, and you've hurt me. How is any of that acceptable? I'm going to be your wife soon. That's no way to treat the woman you love."

Her expression never softens and with every word she speaks I wonder how I ever found myself in a committed relationship with her. She's nothing like me. We have almost nothing in common and her superiority complex is very unattractive. I used to think she was just a confident woman, but then confidence morphed into cockiness and she started looking down on people. I don't know if she changed or if she was always that way and I never saw it.

"Victoria, we can't get married," I tell her. "I'm calling the wedding off. You deserve my honesty, at the very least. I'm not in love with you. You're right; a man doesn't treat the woman he loves like that. I'm sorry. I should've done this a long time ago."

All of the color drains from her face and pure unadulterated fury rages in her eyes. I'm preparing for the verbal lashing that she's about to deliver when the nurse returns.

"Mr. Collins, your mother is okay. They had a rough patch during the surgery, but she's stable now. They have her in recovery. You should be able to see her soon." Relief settles over me and I send out a silent thank you. The good news has absolutely no impact on Victoria's glare.

"I'm going to see your mother and then I'm leaving. You, Jace Collins, are making a grave mistake. You will never find another woman as loyal, successful, or more dedicated than me. I would've carried on the legacy of your family's name in a manner that bestowed honor and dignity to it. You'll regret this. Mark my words. You are a fool!"

She turns and storms down the hallway, and I just let her go. I know this is the right decision. Deep down, whether she'll ever admit it or not, she knows it too.

"How are you feeling?" I ask. Mom looks tired and weak. Lying here in this hospital bed, she looks nothing like the hardheaded, strong-willed woman that I know.

"I'm feeling fine, son. Although, I am very upset with what you did to that poor dear Victoria. She's heartbroken, son. You have to go to her and fix it."

I shake my head in disbelief.

She just won't let it go.

"Mother, can you please focus on recovering and getting better? Please stop putting so much energy into my personal life."

"Jace, I really didn't want to do this and it may be a mistake, but I feel an obligation to you and our family to tell you."

"What is it? Just know that nothing you say is going to change my mind."

"I am doubtful of that. Victoria is pregnant."

Suddenly, my insides turn upside down and my thoughts are running into each other at record speeds.

I feel sick.

"Jace, are you okay? Honey, don't look so terrified. You'll be a wonderful father, just like your father was."

She smiles and pats my hand reassuringly.

"Mom, how do you know this? Why wouldn't she tell me? This makes no sense at all. I don't understand." I keep wracking my brain, trying to recall if there have been any signs of her being pregnant or hiding something from me, but I draw a blank. "This is crazy. She would've told me. I just called the wedding off. Why not tell me then? None of this makes sense, dammit."

"Jace, there's no need for foul language. She didn't tell you because she wanted to marry you knowing you were doing it because you wanted to, not because you felt an obligation to. Now, she's going to go off and raise that baby alone. Is that what you want for your child?" she asks, and my mind is spinning so fast I can't even form a response. "I know the idea of being a parent for the first time is scary, but you're a good man and you'll be fine. I don't want my grandchild being raised by a single mother. You need to keep the wedding on, Jace. Do the right thing by your child."

Something in me snaps at the mention of *her grandchild.*

"Really mother? You're concerned about the well-being of your grandchild now? Six years ago you had zero regard for your grandchild's life. You didn't care one single solitary bit about my unborn child. None!"

Her expression never changes. She's not even shocked by my accusation.

"I know what you did and I know how far you went to make it all go away, to cover your despicable actions. She was eighteen, Mom. Eighteen!" I shout. "She was alone and scared. You were the adult and when she was teetering on the edge of that cliff, you willingly and happily gave her a push. So please, do not tell me about what's best. You're deluded. I'm so glad that Dad isn't here to see the things you've done."

Her expression is cold now. There's no remorse, just nothing. She calmly tucks a piece of hair behind her ear and replies.

"I did what was best for my son, first and foremost. I have no regrets for protecting your future. The past is where it belongs—in the past. You'll go and make things right with Victoria. You won't tell her you know, because if you do, she won't go through with the wedding. You make her believe you made a mistake and you follow through with that wedding. You raise your child in a loving home and do what Collinses do. You hold your head high and be proud of yourself for all that you have and all that you are." She says all this as if she's reviewing the checklist for one of her parties, not laying out the plan for my life.

I stand up with no response and leave the room. I have nothing to say to her anymore. She is completely blind to how awful she was to a young girl and how badly it hurt me and Jess. She'll never see the error of her ways. Trying to argue with her is a waste of time.

"Jace, I love you, son. Please, do the right thing," she says as I close the door.

I have to see Jess and then I have to talk to Victoria.

"If you're brave enough to say good-bye, life will reward you with a new hello."
—Paulo Coehlo

Jessica

JUST BEFORE I knock on the door, I take in a deep breath. I raise my fist to knock and right before my knuckles touch the door it swings open. One of the sloppiest, most handsome guys I've ever seen stands in the doorway with a huge smile on his face.

"You shaved some," I notice. "Did you do that just for me?"

He scratches his chin and grins. "I cleaned it up a bit and you *may* have had a little something to do with that. You like?"

"I like."

"Well, I have a surprise for you, so I hope you like more than that." His eyebrows waggle up and down in a flirty way and his grin is killing me. His big, tough-guy persona mixed with his adorable good-guy ways is so damn sexy.

"What's the surprise? I thought we were cooking again?"

"I've given you a cooking reprieve tonight and I've done all the cooking for us."

I step into the house and my senses are attacked by an abundance of intoxicating aromas. Cinnamon, spice, banana, and caramel swirl through the air and my mouth waters instantly. As soon as I see the picnic blanket on the floor, I'm a goner.

"It's a carpet picnic. Breakfast for dinner on the living room floor. Super classy, right?"

My eyes try to take it all in at once, but they can't. Beautiful place settings sit on top of a red and white checkered blanket, candles are flickering throughout the room, a bouquet of flowers is centered on the blanket, and the most delicious-looking waffles I've ever seen are placed on pristine white plates topped with some type of bananas and sauce. It all looks so fancy. I never knew breakfast could look so elegant.

I look up at Kingsley, speechless.

"Is it too much? I just wanted to surprise you and I want you to like being here. If it's too much we can put the lights on and move it to the kitchen table."

"No, hell no! I love it, all of it. I love every single part of it. No one has ever done anything like this for me before. It's... I don't even know what to say, Kingsley. It's perfect." I'm so incredibly moved by his thoughtfulness.

A big smile stretches across his face, simple and sincere, and I know: I love him. I can feel it. Not the lustful, needy I-have-to-have-him kind of love or the I'll-die-without-him love. I love him from way down deep, from a quiet place that I rarely visit. I love him like a person loves the calm of a lake in the early morning hours when it's unmoving, still and peaceful. Kingsley is my calm. I don't love him because I want his love or because of some incessant need. I love him because he sees me and allows me to be me while never letting me forget who I can be. He never tries to fix me and he always, no matter how mad it makes me, forces me to see past my own bullshit. I love him in a way that I've never loved before. I love him unselfishly. For once, I don't need to have someone's affirmation or affections to know that they value me. For once, I feel love for the simplest and most authentic reasons. I love him because it's true. I know it and I feel it. It doesn't feel heavy or burdensome. It feels freeing and light. Love with no conditions. It's the most comforting thing I've ever felt in my entire life. For the first time, I love someone without expecting anything in return.

"Hey, where did you go? It's time to eat. I'm hungry as hell."

I want to tell him, but I can't. He wouldn't believe me if I did. For now, I'm just going to enjoy this night and not think about anything. I'm just going to step outside my mind for a little while and enjoy him and our time together.

"You have such a way with words, Kingsley," I laugh out.

"You know it, darlin'. I'm a refined dude through and through," he says with a mischievous smirk. He kneels down and starts pouring our drinks.

"These are mimosas, which I'm sure you are familiar with. I figured they were better suited to this food than wine."

"Yum, it all looks so good. Where did you learn to cook all of this stuff? I know breakfast is supposed to be easy, but this doesn't look like a typical breakfast at all."

"My mom is a great cook and I have three sisters. I was completely outnumbered growing up. I had no choice but to know my way around a kitchen. They never gave me a pass for being a boy. I guess it paid off."

"Do you see them often, your family?"

His face softens a little at my question.

"Nah, not really in the past year."

"Because of Lily?" I ask.

"I guess. I don't know. I just hated the pity and the looks. I'm still me, you know? But they all treat me like I need their pity or like I'm gonna break or some shit. That's why I like being around you. You treat me like me. Even after I told you about Lily, you never changed. You're still you and I'm still me; nothing changed. We just get each other. No bullshit, no games, no smoke and mirrors. I just hate the pity party shit. I don't believe in pity or self-loathing. That's why it irritates the hell outta me when you go down that road. When you talk down to yourself, it makes me nuts. You can't live like that. That's not living. That's living a rented life, wasting it by feeling sorry for yourself. I have felt pain and I've blamed myself for Lily. Of course, I fight that inner battle, but I'll be damned before I let it take over my mind completely. Accepting the ugly shit in life is just part of living. Pain tells us we are still here; it lets us know we've survived. When you really think about it, pain can free you, because without pain there is no pleasure in anything."

His words settle around us and I realize how unbelievably strong he is. I want to hug him, squeeze him, and tell him how happy I am to have him in my life.

"Kingsley, thank you."

"For what?"

"For being you. You're a gift. You make me see things in ways I never would otherwise. Oh, and you are an amazing cook! Thank you for that too," I joke, trying to make things less heavy. He smiles and takes a huge bite of his waffle.

"You haven't tried it yet. Go ahead, it's my take on bananas foster without the ice cream. It's just a bunch of good shit on top of fresh waffles. My sister got us a waffle griddle and I haven't used it in forever."

My plate is full of fluffy waffles and bananas swimming in a brown caramel sauce. And the smell is so freakin' good.

"Oh my! Jesus, Kingsley, this is amazing. Holy hell, I'm coming here for breakfast every day if this is what it's like."

"Score," he says, jokingly pumping his fist in the air.

"You're a nerd."

"Yep and you're a dork. We are perfect for each other," he laughs.

"Yeah, I think we might be," I say, looking down and feeling a blush sweep across my face. I look back up and he's unmoving. Our eyes connect, and somewhere in the midst of the laughter and jokes something changes. His eyes, rings of dark blue infused with an emotional fire, look into me. The room falls silent and not even the music coming from the kitchen can be heard as we stare at each other. If I'm completely honest with myself, I know that we want each other. He has tried to fight it, but it's here.

It's hanging so heavily in the air that you can almost reach out and touch the need, the want.

"Jessica."

"Yes?"

"Can I kiss you again after we eat?"

"Why do we have to wait?" My breathing increases as I watch him think about my question.

"We don't." His words are short and sweet, but absolute. Kingsley extends his hand to me and I reach toward him, intertwining our fingers before he pulls me to my feet. We sidestep the carpet picnic and he tugs me in closer to his broad chest. His scent wraps around me like a blanket, intoxicating and warm, comforting. When he lifts my chin, I'm mesmerized by the intensity of his gaze.

"Can I kiss you now?" he asks, and as I nod absently, I vaguely recognize that my words and my thoughts and my body and everything is no longer functioning properly now that I'm this close to Kingsley. "Keep your eyes open."

"Okay," I whisper hoarsely, my heartbeat thrumming in my chest. With a heat-filled glance, he lowers his head, caressing my lips with his, exploring their curves and contours tenderly. His soft tongue traces the lines of my mouth just before his teeth gently nip my lower lip, testing its fullness. On a soft exhale, the tension leaves my body and I melt into the magic of this moment, turning it from a mere kiss into a dance. Forward, backward, push and pull, we slowly move together and become one. My eyelids feel heavy as the pleasure of this kiss surges through me. I'm lost in this moment, lost in this man.

"No, keep them open," he implores, pulling away from the kiss for a moment. My eyes flutter back open and two large hands cup my cheeks. The callused pads of his fingertips graze my skin and he lowers his lips back to mine. He claims my mouth again, this time with more hunger, more need. The moans escaping him are sexy as hell, and I instantly give in as he pulls me closer to his hard body. I can feel his arousal, his need for me; it's the start of my complete undoing. Sparks fly through my body when his fingers weave through my hair, molding to my scalp, tugging just enough to make me release the sounds I've been holding back. His lips leave mine and he moves to my neck. One, two, three kisses as he licks a path to my earlobe. I can feel his warm breath as it glides across my skin. Chills fan across my body as desire rushes through my veins.

"I want you, Jessica." Kingsley's voice is low, his plea sexy and sinful, and I know without a doubt that I want him too—so much—but I'm terrified. I'm so scared and I don't even know why. Sex isn't scary to me. I know I want him, I want this, but something inside of me is fearful. He's different—we're different. Kingsley is the real thing and this isn't high school. I love him, but I love him differently than I have ever loved before. I don't know if I'm worthy of him, of this. How can I possibly live up to what he deserves? My head is at war with my heart and body. I can't make sense of any of it, especially with him holding me and kissing me like this.

"Get out of your head, Jessica."

"Kingsley, why? Why now? You said—"

"I know what I said. I also know what I feel. You can't tell me you don't care about me; I know you do, just like you know exactly how I feel about you. And if you don't, I'm sorry, but I'm here to set you straight right now.

I want you, all of you. I want to show you what sex really is, what it's meant to be. It's so much more than what you've known. God, I want to show you everything it can be. Let me show you love, Jessica. Let me show you what it's like to feel completely loved physically, mentally, and emotionally. I'm in love with you, Jessica. You've given me everything without even knowing it. I want to give every piece of me back to you."

I suck in a breath and abandon all my fears at once. He loves me? "I love you, too." Those are the last words we speak. His eyes grow wide and, in one swift motion, he scoops me up off of the floor and carries me down the hall into the bedroom. I feel weightless in his arms, safe surrounded by his love. A large four-poster cherry wood bed is centered in the room, and he carefully places me onto it. He pushes the stereo button on the bedside table and music fills the air.

"Do you trust me?" His voice catches on the question, as if he's unsure of my answer.

"Yes." I watch the tension ease from his body.

"Keep your eyes open." His husky voice has my skin tingling. "Don't even close them when you feel your body come apart around me." Pictures of my body unraveling under his pop into my mind, and my breathing speeds up momentarily. "I mean it," he says. Then he leans over and kisses me, reading my need and satisfying his own. "I want to see you, watch you watching me every second while I show you what love feels like."

I nod and brace myself for something completely unfamiliar to me. I'd say something but even the simplest words escape me right now. He reaches down to the edge of his shirt, pulling it up and over his head. His broad chest and smooth skin are magnificent. I let my gaze travel over his body, taking mental notes of each place I intend to touch. Shaggy hair falls into his eyes when he starts unbuttoning his pants. He kicks the jeans off and closes the distance between himself and the bed. His body is overwhelming, powerful. He's all man and the trail that disappears into the band of his boxers kills me. He reaches out, breaking my trance, and pulls me closer so that my feet dangle off the edge a bit. Our stare never breaks as he positions himself between my legs.

"This is going to take a while, so make yourself comfortable," Kingsley says with a promising grin.

I grip the comforter and try to breathe. He studies me intently as he traces his finger from my waist up to the top button of my flannel shirt. Ever so slowly, he unbuttons it, never taking his eyes off mine. My gut instinct is to look away, to avoid vulnerability.

As if he read my thoughts, Kingsley lightly grazes my jaw with the back of his finger. "Trust me, Jessica." And just like that, I do.

"I trust you," I promise as I look into his loving eyes, falling deeper and harder than I ever thought possible. His deft fingers undo my last button and separate the shirt, revealing my taut nipples beneath the thin material of my bra. I tremble as I lie here with my heart and soul fully exposed to Kingsley. He studies my body reverently, and the desire in his eyes robs me of any doubts I may have had. I know that he wants me just as much as I want him. His fingers trace down my sensitive skin to the button on my jeans, easily unfastening it and sliding them and my panties down together as he kneels to remove my shoes. I hear them drop to the floor before he removes my pants completely. Cool air from the open window makes me shiver as my body adjusts to being bare. Pulling my body closer to the edge of the bed, he kneels between my legs, gently pushing my thighs apart with his bare shoulders.

"You're so beautiful, Jess. I can't wait to taste you." My stomach tenses at his words and the fire already burning deep within me grows even hotter. I feel his lips on me and look down to find him still looking right at me. "I want you to watch me," he says as he lays another kiss on my sensitive skin.

Dear God, my body craves him. The intimacy of this experience is so unlike anything I've ever felt before. It's so personal, so intense, so...Kingsley. His hands slide up my legs and my body completely comes alive under his touch. All of my rough edges unfold and soften for him. Feelings of vulnerability and embarrassment tug at my consciousness as he looks at my scars, but his expression never changes. His eyes still tell a story of love and wanting. He leans down, placing one chaste kiss just above my pelvis, and then traces his nose lower. His eyes briefly close and then reopen as his tongue meets the warmth between my legs. He slides his hands up under my bottom and shifts my hips up to meet him. I release a shuddering breath, squeeze my eyes closed as I grip the comforter harder, and wrap my legs around him while he makes love to me with his mouth. I feel one hand move and then two fingers slide inside me.

"You're so wet, and you taste so damn good. I could do just this all night and be a happy man," he whispers against my sensitive skin. His fingers curl up and I whimper as they go deeper, reaching that spot. His tongue circles my small bundle of nerves while he pleasures me with his fingers. It feels incredible, too incredible, and I can feel myself reaching a precipice. My insides tighten around his fingers and my breathing is becomes erratic as my body winds tighter. Each of his strokes builds me up higher and higher until coherent thoughts are no longer within my reach.

"Jesus," he mutters. "You're so beautiful. You're killing me." The heat increases and I can't hold back. I'm going to come undone if he doesn't hurry up and give me more. I arch my hips up, practically begging for release. "Open your eyes," he demands. "I want to watch you fall apart for me. I want to look into your eyes when I make you come."

As if small weights are sitting on each lid, I struggle to meet his demand, inhaling deeply as I do. Our eyes meet as his fingers work me just right and his tongue abrades me, consuming me slowly, deliberately. Intense pleasure flows through me, igniting my body until nothing seems to exist but the feel of his presence in my universe. I'm not finished; I need more. I want him, all of him.

I push my head back into the bed as need runs through me. My mouth falls open and I moan loudly. "Kingsley, oh God..." He continues to stoke my flame into an inferno and I reach out for more, weaving my hands through his hair, gripping his locks tightly between my fingers. I've lost all semblance of control as I writhe before him. I'm his, oh God, am I ever.

"Look at me, Jessica. There is so much more to give you, but I'm not going to until you look at me," he orders. I snap my eyes open and bite into my lower lip. Just as our eyes reconnect, he brushes that spot with his tongue and curls his fingers up harder. Pleasure rips through me, surging hard down the center of my body, so hard it's almost painful. He doesn't let up, but catches me at my peak, bringing me even higher into a whole new realm of ecstasy. Crying out, I clench my fingers tighter in his hair, writhing against his face. Bliss crashes over my body in waves, easing away slowly, leaving me boneless and sated. I lie here panting, smelling the arousal in the air. My vision begins to come back into focus and I see Kingsley; he's smiling affectionately.

"Watching you come has got to be the most erotic thing I've ever experienced," he says in a low gravelly voice.

I exhale, trying to formulate a response, but the words won't come. My brain is on overdrive and I can't even speak. He rises up from his knees and hooks his thumbs under the waistband of his boxers, letting them soundlessly drop to the floor. My mouth waters at the sight of him. Kingsley's everything a girl could want and then some. Good God almighty! He climbs onto the bed from the bottom, sliding up my body. His skin sets small fires to mine every time we touch. We make our way to the top of the mattress, and my shirt and bra are removed quickly before he rests my head on the pillows. He brushes a strand of hair away from my face and then leans down, kissing me once on the forehead. That simple gesture represents everything that I know and love about this man. So much love.

"You're perfect. I can't believe you're here, with me, all mine." Ed Sheeran's voice sings "Kiss Me" as Kingsley lowers his body onto mine. For this moment in time we are stitched together, two hearts becoming one. He spreads my thighs wide with his knee and I feel him at my entrance, testing my desire. Just this light touch ratchets up my need for this amazing man, and my body zings with electricity as it readies for all of him.

"I love you, Jessica Alexander," he says, just before pushing into me. Any hope of responding is gone with his first movement. His hands find their way to mine and he intertwines our fingers, stretching our arms up above us. He pushes in farther, going deeper than I'm ready for, and a moan escapes my throat. He catches my lips with his, loving me with his eyes, his mouth, his body. He kisses me softly and loves me hard and slow. He moves passionately, with purpose, finding a smooth rhythm that feels like it may ultimately destroy me.

"Oh my God, Kingsley..." My fingernails dig into his hands and he holds me tightly. Sweat covers our bodies as we slide against one another, hips thrusting, meeting each other move for move. He groans against my neck and makes love to me in a way that's unique to him. I can feel the pleasurable sensations returning as I tense around him.

"Damn, you feel so good, Jessica. I just want to melt into you," he breathes. "I never want to leave your body. Tell me you're mine. Tell me I'm your guy; be my girl, Jessica. Let me love you every day, every minute, the way you deserve to be loved." Looking into the depths of his dark, ocean-blue eyes, I realize it's not just a statement in the heat of the moment. It's a promise, a plea.

"Yes, Kingsley, yes." I kiss him as tears fill my eyes. "I'm your girl, Kingsley, only yours." Every wall begins to fall, crashing down around me. Fears, pain, regret, lies, truths, hate, and the past break away and in their place is love, only love. His lips crush mine and he pushes into me as far as my body will allow. Time stands still as our bodies move together in perfect unison, like the winds move the waves of the sea. Our tongues caress one another, making silent promises with every touch. His taste, his scent, his words, they're mine—meant for me to hold on to. My heart swells with a feeling of love like I've never known before. I close my eyes and bright colors explode beneath the blackness of my lids as his name spills from my lips.

"Kingsley—"

"Let it all go, darlin'. Give it all to me. Just let go," he demands, and I do. A current runs through me as I undulate, pressing my body closer to his, holding him closer to me. The edge is so close; he's bringing me to it, whispering unintelligible words in my ear, loving me, guiding me, protecting me. I soar over it, losing myself in him, losing myself in his love. He thrusts hard one last time and I feel the full weight of his body upon me as he finds his release. We lose ourselves in the beauty of the moment and lie here together, unmoving.

"Here's a drink," he says as he walks back into the room and hands me some ice water. My skin in flushed and my body is liquid.

"Thank you. I am thirsty," I say with a wink.

I notice he's brought his guitar in with him. Between that and the white boxers he's wearing, he's a beautiful sight to behold. He really does take amazing care of his body. It's such a contradiction to the way he dresses and portrays himself. His hair is going in ten different directions and I love it.

"What's the guitar for? Are you going to play for me

while I fall asleep in a lovemaking coma?"

A lazy smile crosses his face and he sits on the edge of the bed next to me. "Something like that," he says cockily while scooting closer to me. I lay my head down and position myself so I can see him play.

"I haven't quite mastered this one yet. I just discovered this band last week on Spotify. I've been working on an acoustic cover of a song they do that reminds me of you."

He turns his head slightly toward me and gives me a sweet-as-sugar smile. He's so good; too good, really. He makes me feel whole and I haven't felt that way in so very long.

"Okay, here it goes. It's called "Bird With Broken Wings" by The Tyler Lenius Band. Don't laugh at my singing, either."

"I'm sure you sing just fine, Kingsley. I won't laugh, I promise."

He begins to play and the sound of his acoustic guitar fills the room. Watching him play, listening to the music while all wrapped up in his sheets after making love is some kind of beautiful. After a few chords, he begins to sing and my heart literally stops for a moment. He acted like he was a terrible singer, but his voice is unreal. It's raspy, raw and passionate. Hearing it now reminds me of the first time we met after group all those weeks ago. He glances over at me as he sings the lyrics. Every part of me is focused on every syllable.

You melt my heart
With one single kiss
If there's such thing as true love, it's this

And my whole world stops when you smile
Won't you be my babe for a while?

Without her I'm like a bird, with broken wings
Able to dream, but not to fly
So I spread my wings
And make wishes to the sky
That someday she'd be mine
That she'd be mine

My body tingles every time I feel your lips
When I'm holding you, I feel sparklers on my fingertips
This girl's gonna change my world

Oh, this changes everything
Without her I'm like a bird, with broken wings
Able to dream, but not to fly
So I spread my wings
And make wishes to the sky
That someday this girl would be mine

Without her I'm like a bird (like a bird, like a bird), with broken wings
Able to dream, but not to fly
So I spread my wings
And make wishes to the sky
That someday she'd be mine

The final chord of the song ends and he sets the guitar on the floor, propping it up against the bed before turning to me.

"Did you like it?"

I pull the sheets up against my bare chest as I sit up.

"Are you kidding me? Did I like it? I loved it, Kingsley! It was beautiful and perfect and incredible. I can't believe, for the life of me, that you think you can't sing. That was amazing. I could listen to you all night and never tire of your voice."

He gives me a rare shy smile. "Wow, thanks. I'm glad you liked it. Every time I hear that song, I think about you, about us," he says as he takes my hand. As he speaks, he rubs his thumb over my skin. "I can't really express how much you've changed my life in such a short time. You keep telling me how you need to fix yourself, but the ironic thing is that I'm the one who was broken. I was a shadow of myself and you've brought me back into the light. I can't even begin to tell you what you mean to me."

Tears well in my eyes as he leans forward. He places a chaste kiss upon my lips and lingers briefly before pulling back. We're eye-to-eye and smiling at each other. The love I'm feeling is mirrored in the softness of his gaze; it's comforting. He reaches up and brushes a wild strand of hair away from my face.

"Jessica, you're my here, my there, and my always everywhere. Together or apart, you've awakened a part of me that's been locked away for the past year. I love you and if loving you is wrong, then I don't ever want to be right."

"We are taught in life that love can heal wounds and rescind pain, but we soon learn that pain can often destroy the strongest of love."
—Kathryn Perez

Jace

"VIC, I KNOW you're there, so just pick up the phone." I keep calling her, but she doesn't answer. I try calling one last time as I pull into the parking lot in front of Jessica's apartment. Nothing.

I go upstairs and realize I haven't a damn clue what I'm going to say to her or why I'm really even here. I just know that I need to see her, talk to her. I knock and wait. My heart is in my throat and the seconds feel like hours. I knock again and nothing. I pull out my phone and call her, but it goes straight to voicemail.

"Dammit!" I lean forward, resting my head on her door, and I feel so damn lost. I turn around and slide to the floor, my head hung in defeat, and try to figure out how my life got twisted up so fast. Victoria's pregnant and I'm in love with someone else. I'm in love with someone that refuses to let me love her or help her and my mom is lying in a hospital bed barely escaping death.

Minutes, hours pass by. I sit outside Jessica's door, feeling like a fool, but I don't want to leave until I see her. I need to know if there's any chance of fixing anything that's left of us. I have to know. I can't move on until I know for sure. I rest my head on my knees and close my eyes.

"Jace?"

My neck is stiff and my ass is killing me. I open my eyes and see black chucks standing in front of me. I rub my hand over my face and try to let me eyes adjust as I look up.

"What are you doing? Are you drunk?"

It's her and she looks different somehow. Her hair is in a messy knot on top of her head and she looks tired, but there's something else about her that's different. It's her eyes. They're full of life, happy. I wonder why.

I stand up and crane my head from side to side, trying to work some of the stiffness out. "No, I'm not drunk, Jess."

"Well, then, why in the world are you asleep in front of my door at five o'clock in the morning?"

I run an anxious hand through my hair and try to come up with something that makes some kind of sense.

"Victoria's pregnant," I blurt out.

Real fucking good, J. Just blow shit right out of the water. She's really going to talk to you now! Fuck!

Her face hardens and she pushes past me. Her back is to me as she tries to find the right key for the door.

"Go home, Jace. I don't know why you're here to rub my face in this shit, but whatever the reason is, I'm not letting you do it. I just had the single best night of my life and I'm not allowing you to ruin it for me. Just go, Jace."

I grab her by the wrist and spin her around to face me.

"I need you to talk to me, Jess. Do you hear me? I. Need. You."

She stills for a moment, considering my words. Then she looks down at my hand wrapped around her wrist.

"Let me go, Jace," she says quietly.

"I don't know how," I whisper, and then release her wrist.

Our eyes meet and I can see her resolve weakening.

"Dammit all to hell, Jace Collins! Why are you doing this? Why, just why? This is not a game and I'm not a toy. Why are you doing this to me? I can't handle it." She covers her face with her hands and shakes her head back and forth.

"I know and I'm sorry. I'm so damn sorry! I'm confused and I don't know which way is coming or going anymore. I don't love her like I love you. How am I supposed to make a life with her and have a family with her if I love you? Tell me, Jess, how?"

She drops her hands to her sides and looks at me. I can't read her face as we stand silently. She inhales and looks up to the ceiling before fixing her gaze on me again.

"I can't answer those questions for you. I just can't. All I know is that nothing ever goes right for us. Something always comes between us and we're never able to stop it. If Victoria is pregnant, then you have to accept that. She is your fiancé. You have been with her for years. Us falling back into each other's lives, crashing into each other like atomic bombs hasn't done anything but wreck the life you were living. Don't you see that?"

"No, I don't see that. I see that I was slapped into reality. My life was a fraud, a fake. I got together with Victoria because it was easy, because she was there and she was persistent and she took my mind off of you. My mom liked her and she was the type of girl everyone said I was 'supposed' to be with. But I'm not in love with her. My mother had no qualms about pushing you out of my life and no thought about what I actually wanted or how I felt. She still doesn't. She has deceived me over and over again, and the woman that's carrying my child is a stranger to me. But when I look at you, all I see is home."

I step in closer to her, needing to touch her, to make her understand the truth of what I'm telling her, but she backs away from me. It's like a knife slicing through my heart.

"No, don't. Don't you dare come any closer to me, Jace Collins. I'm not letting you seduce me with all of your charm and smooth talking."

She's serious. I've never seen her like this before.

"What's the matter with you, Jess? You look different."

She fastens her eyes on me and cripples me with one sentence.

"I look different? Maybe that's because you don't know what I look like when I'm not in love with you."

The hallway suddenly feels smaller and the walls feel

like they're closing in on me.

"You don't love me anymore?" I whisper, stunned.

Tears roll down her face and splash to the floor.

"No, Jace, I do love you. I'll always love you. Nothing could ever change that, no matter what happens in our lives. But I can't hold on to a love that will never work. Being in love with you hurts and it's unhealthy. Being in love with you is like a drug with me. It's all wrong, regardless of how right it feels when we're together." Her chin quivers and all I want to do is reach out and wrap my arms around her. "Years have separated us and our lives have gone on. Even though some things have stayed the same, so many things have changed. I can't get better with you. I just can't. I know and recognize that now. You want to save me, to fix me, but I don't want a fixer." Her voice cracks, despite how strong she's trying to be. "When we were teenagers it was different. I'll never forget those days, but in the meantime life has happened and we can't erase it. I can't be your charity case girlfriend and you can't be my handyman boyfriend who's constantly trying to put me back together. Plus, I'm going to mess up. When I do, you won't like it. And, slowly but surely, you'll hate me. I don't want that for us."

Every word cuts deep.

"Are you in love with him?" I ask, even though I know the answer. He's the reason her eyes are happy.

"Yes," she says, so quietly I can barely hear her.

"Are you happy?" She looks at me and her face softens at my question.

"I'm closer to happy than I ever have been, I think."

My head is thumping and tears are burning my eyes. I try hard to fight them back, but I fail. One tear falls and she lunges forward, wrapping her arms around me tightly. I hug her back just as hard and we cry together. We cry for our past, for our lost child, for our lost love, and we cry for each other's pain.

"You're going to be an amazing dad, Jace," she sobs and sniffles into my neck.

I hold her tighter, trying to memorize the feel of her in my arms. I inhale the scent of her hair and try to imprint every detail into my mind.

"I'll love you forever, Jess."

I release her from the embrace and place a kiss on my fingers. I press my fingers to her soft lips and say, "Forever."

She doesn't say anything as I walk away. I can hear sobs echo throughout the hallway, but they get softer as I get farther away. It's over. Me and Jess are over. The finality of it wraps around my neck and nearly chokes me.

I'm sitting in the driveway at Victoria's house, completely at a loss for what to say to her. The last few weeks expand and contract in my mind, and I wonder if I'll ever be able to sort through everything I'm feeling right now. My phone starts to buzz and her front door swings open all at once. She's on her phone and I realize it's me she's calling. As soon as she sees me in the driveway, she hangs up. She's crying and looks frantic. I open the door quickly and go to her.

"What's the matter? What is it?"

"It's your mom, Jace. It's bad. They must've got our

numbers mixed up or something. They called mine looking for you. We have to go there now."

"Get in," I say.

I back up and whip out of the driveway as fast as I can. We sit in silence the entire way to the hospital. As soon as we pull in and park, we get out and rush in. When we reach my mother's room, the doctor stops me before I go in.

"Mr. Collins?"

"Yes, is my mom okay? What's the matter?"

The doctor's somber face says it all. I know. I can feel it. I push past him and open the door. Nurses are unhooking wires, removing IVs and shutting off machines. There's no more beeping. The room's quiet. I turn back to the doctor.

"What happened? I was just here yesterday and she was fine. How did this happen?" I plead.

"Her brain started bleeding, and we were unable to stop it before it was too late. This can happen with this type of surgery. I'm so sorry, Mr. Collins."

I look at a crying Victoria and picture our baby she's carrying. I look at my mother lying in the bed, cold, lifeless. It's all too much.

"I need some air." I bolt out of the room, walking down the hall as fast as I can before breaking into a full-on run. My legs can't carry me fast enough. I reach the exit, push past the doors, and keep running until I reach my car. My hands rest on the hood, which is still warm from our trip over here. I'm trying to catch my breath, but there are so many things rolling around in my head, overwhelming me; none of them make sense.

"Jace, are you okay? What do you need me to do?

Whatever you need, just ask."

I look up and it's Vic. For the first time in a long time, she looks kind and all of her hardened edges are softer. She really did care about my mother. I can see that now. I just shake my head. "I don't know. I just don't know." She gently places her hand on my shoulder.

"Let me help you. I know things are bad with us right now, but I still want to be here for you."

"Thanks," I say.

"Should we start making phone calls?"

"I guess so. Let me go back in and spend some time with..." I can't finish the sentence, but she knows what I'm trying to say. I gulp down some air and continue, "I'll see what they need from me here, and then we can go to the house and start making arrangements."

She nods in agreement and the thought crosses my mind that in one day, I've just lost the two most important women in my life.

It's the morning of my mother's funeral and I'm numb. I loved my mother, but I hate the way our last conversation went. I hate that we spoke our last words in anger. I also hate that I didn't respond when she told me she loved me. Victoria has been great and has helped with every detail, asking for nothing in return. She hasn't once brought up the engagement or the wedding. I want to ask her about the baby so badly, but haven't been able to bring myself to do it with everything else going on.

"Are you ready? It's time."

"Yeah, Vic, I'll be out in a second."

I check my tie and take a deep breath. I've been doing that a lot lately, taking deep breaths. It seems like the air in my lungs is the only thing keeping me going, the only sure thing I have left.

"Okay, let's go."

We drive to the funeral home and the parking lot is overflowing with cars. Everyone in town must be here.

I park and get out.

"Thanks for coming with me," I tell her.

"I wouldn't have let you do this alone, Jace. You know that."

She holds out her hand to me and I take it. Together or not, Victoria's strong and I need that right now.

"Live every minute as if it were your last."
—Unknown

Jessica

"KINGSLEY, THANK YOU for bringing me. I know you're against this," I say as I squeeze his hand.

"I just don't get why you need to go to his mom's funeral. You hated her. It makes no sense."

"He has been a big part of my life, and even though I know his mom was evil, I still feel like I should go."

"Okay. I just don't like it. That's all," he mumbles.

The drive feels like it takes forever. I hate knowing that Kingsley's unhappy about this, but I need to go. I just need to be there. Mercedes and I text back and forth throughout the drive, finally making firm plans to meet up and hang out. We're going to grab some lunch at some organic café she raves about. Taking a shot at a real friendship is a big step for me, but I'm feeling pretty optimistic about it. I guess I'm feeling a bit more optimistic about a lot of things lately.

As we pull into the cemetery, the memory of years ago when Jace brought me here floods my mind. I look around and see all the cars, all the people, and I'm suddenly afraid.

"God, everyone will be here. All the people that hate me are going to be here. I have no idea what I was thinking. This was a terrible idea." I feel the panic in my body and hear it in my voice, but I can't calm down.

Kingsley parks the rental car and reaches over, grasping my hand in his.

"Listen, I don't like this, but you're not going to not do something that you want to do because of people that hurt you in your past." He pulls my hand up and kisses it gently. "If you want to be here, then be here. They can't hurt you anymore. Do you hear me? You're a grown woman and you're stronger than you were then." Cupping my chin with his strong hand, he says, "You hold your head up high and go. I may be against this, but no way am I letting you back out because of them."

"You're right. They can't hurt me anymore." I reach down and dig through my purse. I shuffle through all of my junk and finally see it at the bottom. I pull out the little snowflake pin and dust it off.

"What's that?" he asks.

"It's my force field," I tell him with a small smile.

He looks confused as I pin it on my lapel.

"It's a long story. I'll tell you about it sometime, but not now. Are you coming with me?"

"No, I'll wait here. You can do this. You don't need me by your side."

I nod and don't argue, because, in reality, I don't

want to hurt Jace by showing up with Kingsley on my arm. I think Kingsley considered that too, which is why he's staying behind.

I am so damn lucky.

"Thank you." I give him a deep kiss and smile at him as I pull away.

I garner every ounce of courage I have and get out of the rental car. I'm wearing a simple black dress and black ballet flats. The graveside service has already begun, so I just stand quietly at the back and listen. I scan the crowd and almost immediately see Elizabeth Brant. She looks exactly the same. There's a little golden-haired boy tugging at her sleeve. He has braces on his legs and he moves in an odd fashion. She looks down at him, smiling, and shushes him quietly. Elizabeth Brant, a mom. What a weird thing that is to wrap my mind around. The little boy keeps pulling on her sleeve; then he grabs at himself with a scrunched-up look on his face. It's the pee pee dance. She reaches down, picks him up, and makes her way out of the crowd inconspicuously. My nerves are frazzled and the thought of coming face-to-face with her is literally terrifying. I plant my feet firmly on the ground and decide. I make the decision to face her, regardless of my fear or what may happen. She walks in my direction and the minute her eyes land on me they widen. The surprise is written all over her perfect face and she stops mid-stride.

"Mommy! I have to go to the potty bad," the little boy cries.

"Okay, okay, Junior, we're going."

She starts toward the parking area and just as she passes by me, she slows. It seems as if she's going to say something, but she doesn't. She just gives me an awkward smile and walks right past me. What in the hell just happened? She wasn't mean and she smiled at me. I step in closer to the rest of the guests and try to see past all of them, trying to catch a glimpse of Jace. As soon as I see him, I see her. Victoria and Jace hand in hand. She looks beautiful, as always, and he looks like Jace, just a very sad Jace. My heart breaks for him; I hate that he's hurting. Maybe I shouldn't be here. I certainly don't feel like I belong. I turn and start to walk back to the car when Elizabeth comes from around an SUV with the little boy on her heels. The boy wobbles past her and trips over his feet, falling to the ground right in front of me. He starts crying and I instinctively reach down to help him up just as Elizabeth gets to us.

"Mommy, I have boo-boos on my knees and they hurt," he cries.

"Oh, Junior, it's going to be okay. I have boo-boo medicine in my purse and SpongeBob Band-Aids too."

The little boy smiles through his tears and says, "Yay, SpongeBob Band-Aids."

Elizabeth picks him up and looks at me.

"Thank you for helping him up."

The millions of things I've wanted to say to her are stuck in my throat, held prisoner by years of pent-up anger and hurt. Before I can say a thing, her little boy breaks the silence.

"Mommy, is she your friend?"

If this kid only knew how very far from reality that is.

"No, honey, we aren't friends. But Mommy went to school with her a long time ago. Mommy wishes she would've been her friend, though."

What?

Elizabeth Brant has officially gone insane. For some reason, it pisses me off and I just want to slap her, but I can't because this is a funeral and she's holding her little boy.

"I won't disrespect you in front your child, but don't say things you don't mean just to smooth over the situation, Elizabeth. You never wished you were my friend and we both know that," I bite out.

I walk past her toward the car and she says, "You're right. I didn't then. I'm not that person anymore, though. All I'm saying is that I wish I would've made different choices. Having my own kid has changed my life and I'm sorry for the person I used to be. I'm sorry for everything."

I don't turn around. I can't. Forgiving her is just not something I can do right now. I get back to the car and get in.

"Let's go."

"Why? What happened?" Kingsley asks, and his deep blue eyes look me over with concern, like he's making sure I'm unharmed, safe.

"This was a mistake, that's all."

"Jessica, you didn't come all the way here just to turn around and leave."

I cross my arms over my chest and lean my head back.

"I know. It's just a lot and I didn't really think this through."

I notice people walking to their cars and leaving.

"Well, I guess it's over anyway," I say.

Kingsley starts the car and we wait as others leave one at a time. I stare at the faces of the people passing us by, some familiar, others not. Then I see him. Jace. He's talking to Victoria. She nods, hugs him, and walks away. He turns back toward the burial site and I watch as he passes it, kneeling by another headstone close by. It's his sister's grave.

"Kingsley, I know you'll hate this, but I want to go see him before we go."

He sighs and turns the car off.

"Fine, go ahead."

I lean over and kiss him gently on his stubbly cheek.

"I love you, you know that? You're amazing."

"Okay, okay, Jessica. Just go before I change my mind."

I walk out across the soft grass, hearing my heartbeat in my ears as I get closer. I'm nervous and scared and freaking out on the inside.

"Jace."

He turns around and his surprise at seeing me is all over his face.

"Jess?"

"Hi," I say simply.

He stands up. "What are you doing here?"

"I just wanted to be here. I don't know; I just felt like I *should* be here."

"Why?"

He looks so confused, and the tortured look on his face breaks my heart.

"I'm sorry. Maybe this was just a mistake." I start to turn around and he says, "No, don't go."

I stop and turn back around. "Are you sure?"

"I'm sure."

"Okay."

He holds out his hand and as soon as our skin touches, I'm transported right to the past. My mind might have been trying to forget, but my heart always remembers.

"Do you remember the day I brought you here?" he asks.

"Yes, of course I remember."

"I was just here the other day to bring flowers."

Beautiful purple flowers sit in vases at each side of the headstone.

"They're gorgeous."

He looks at me and the sadness in his eyes threatens to overwhelm me.

"Where did you get that?"

"Get what?" I ask, confused.

"That pin. The snowflake pin." He points to my lapel and I look down and touch it with my fingers.

"Oh, this? It was a gift."

"From whom?" He looks panicked, almost angry.

"Why, Jace? What's the matter? The little girl that lived next door to me in high school gave it to me."

"That's impossible," he says.

"Why is that impossible? You're kind of freaking me out."

"I gave that same exact pin to Genevieve a long time ago. She was wearing it when we buried her," he says, and he looks like he's seen a ghost.

Does he think it's the same pin or something?

"Jace, that's crazy. I'm sure that there are tons of these pins out there in the world. It's not like they only made one. You're just emotional and your mind is running wild on you. I can take it off if it bothers you."

His expression is pained and he shakes his head.

"I guess, I don't know. Maybe you're right. Maybe

I'm losing my damn mind." I've never seen Jace so broken before. I have to fight the urge to go to him, to hold him, to tell him everything will be okay. That's not my place. He has Victoria and I have Kingsley.

"Listen, I came because I wanted to tell you I'm sorry for your loss. I know your mom hated me and there was lots of bad blood there, but she was your mom and I know you loved her."

"Thank you, Jess. I really appreciate it."

His phone buzzes and he pulls it out of his pocket.

"Umm, I have to take this." He looks sorry, but it's just as well. I don't want to witness his pain any longer. I've said what I needed to say.

"No, go ahead. It's fine. I have to go anyway."

"Okay. Thank you, Jess, and please take care of yourself."

His words sound empty and I can see how hard he's trying to keep it together.

"Okay, bye," I say and walk away.

I get back to the car and Kingsley is wound tight.

"All right, we can go now."

"Okay, do you need to stop anywhere else while we're here? Are you positive you don't want to see your parents?" he suggests. We've talked about my parents a few times, and I've told him about our nonexistent relationship and why it's nonexistent, but I think he's still holding out hope for me. I love that he encourages me to have stable relationships in my life, but I'm just not ready to deal with them yet.

"I already told you, I don't talk to my parents. I haven't talked to them in years."

"Okay, okay. I was just asking." He holds his hands

up in defense before placing them back on the steering wheel and pulling out onto the road, but he takes a left toward town instead of a right.

"You're heading in the wrong direction, Kingsley."

"No, I'm not, Jessica," he mimics my tone of voice and I have to laugh. He always knows exactly what to do to put a smile on my face. "I have to get gas before we head back." He smiles at me as he grabs my hand and intertwines our fingers. We settle into comfortable silence as we make our way over the old winding blacktop roads.

Everything looks exactly the same. I feel some semblance of peace settle into my heart. I love Jace. He will forever be my first love, but I know I'm where I should be right now. Being with Kingsley just feels right. I roll down my window and take down my hair, relaxing in the warm Texas breeze that feels so good. Kingsley lets go of my hand and reaches down to turn on the radio. I hear the notes to Pearl Jam's "Last Kiss" before I see the truck barreling around the curve of the road into our lane.

"Kingsley!" I scream.

Excruciating pain.

Darkness.

It feels as if someone is hammering through my head and a dull throbbing has set up shop in my neck.

"Ma'am, you're okay. Can you open your eyes for us? Can you hear me, ma'am?" A muffled voice asks. It's a male voice, one I've never heard before.

I force my eyes open and the sunlight blinds me. I try to reach up toward the pain in my head, but someone stops me from moving. I'm disoriented and my vision is blurry.

"Ma'am, please, stay still. You have a concussion. We're getting you into the next ambulance so we can get you to the hospital with your friend."

My friend... Oh my God, Kingsley! My foggy mind starts to clear in the heat of panic and I remember. A pickup truck came around the corner into our lane and hit us head-on.

"Where is he? Tell me, is he okay?" My voice is raspy and my throat's dry.

"I don't know, ma'am. We'll get you transported soon and get you taken care of. Just stay calm. I'm sure everything's going to be okay with your friend too."

He places an oxygen mask over my face and I try to breathe. It's all going to be fine, it has to be. It just has to be. Kingsley is big and strong. If I'm okay, then he's definitely okay, right? I'm shifted onto a gurney and there's people hustling all around me. I'm hoisted up into an ambulance and they slam the doors shut behind me. Pain radiates throughout my head and I close my eyes, grimacing at the intensity of it. The shock and disbelief of the situation is second only to my injuries. All I want to do is get to the hospital and find out if Kingsley is okay.

"Listen to me, I want to know if Kingsley Arrington is okay. I'm fine! I have a concussion, okay, I get that, but I want to see my friend. Why won't anyone tell me how he is, dammit?"

"Ms. Alexander, please calm down. I'm Nurse Hamilton and I promise that I'll find out about your friend. You do have a visitor. If you're up to it, we can let your brother in."

"My brother?" There's no way he could get here that fast or even be notified yet.

"Yes, he's just out in the hallway. Do you want to see him?"

I just nod. I'm exhausted and have the worst headache of my life. If he is here, I'm sure he thinks this was another one of my drunken escapades.

"She needs to rest, so please make it short." I hear the nurse say, and then Jace walks in.

Definitely not my brother.

"Oh my God, Jess, I'm so glad you're okay," he says as he rushes over to my bed. The relief on his face is obvious. "We came upon the accident after the service and I saw them putting you in an ambulance. They only let family in, so I lied. Sorry," he says sheepishly.

"It's okay, Jace. I'm fine, really. Thank you for checking on me."

"Do you need me to contact your family? Do they know you're in the hospital?"

"No, they don't know and I'd rather they didn't. I'm fine. I'm sure I'll be out of here soon." Seeing my parents here, like this, after not seeing them for so long is the last thing I want. I still have way too much to resolve mentally and emotionally about my parents.

"Okay, I just thought I'd offer. Do you need anything at all?"

"No, I guess not. I'm waiting to see how Kingsley is and no one will tell me. That nurse is supposed to be finding out. I'm sure he's all right, but I want to know. I blacked out on impact and I don't remember much of anything."

He looks as if he's at a loss for words. It sucks. He just buried his mom and now here he is listening to me ask about another guy.

"Do you want me to go see what I can find out?"

"Jace, you've had a lot on your shoulders today. You don't have to do anything. You should go home and get some rest after all you've been through the past few days." I don't want to, but I ask anyway, "Where's Victoria?"

He sighs. "She's in the waiting area."

"Oh. Well you should definitely go, then. I'm sure this is the last damn place she wants to be."

At that moment, two police officers enter the room. I have absolutely no idea why they would be here to see me.

"Excuse us, Miss. We need to speak to you regarding the accident, if you don't mind."

"Uh, yeah sure. Why, what is it?" I ask nervously.

"Ma'am, the vehicle that hit you was being operated by a drunk driver. We just need to confirm a couple minor details for our report, that's all."

"Okay."

"Do you remember seeing the other vehicle?"

"Yes, I do, but it all happened so fast. I only really saw the pickup truck for a moment before everything went black. It swerved into our lane, but that's the last thing I remember."

"All right, thank you. We pretty much have everything we need, but we wanted to see if you had anything to add about what happened before impact."

The ER doctor walks in behind Jace and the police officers and she looks different, really different. Her face is somber and she won't make eye contact with me. This is bad. I know it.

"If all of you don't mind, I need to speak to the patient alone," she says.

My heart kicks up and I want her to stop. I don't want to hear whatever she's about to tell me. Why can't I just rewind time and go back? Something terrible is looming and I don't want to face it. Tears well up in my eyes and my chin starts to tremble before she even says the words.

Shut up.

Shut up.

Shut up.

Don't say it.

"Ma'am, I'm so sorry, but your friend was seriously injured. My team and I did everything we could, but Mr. Arrington didn't make it."

Now home from the hospital, I have a million unanswered texts from Mercedes. I drop the phone on the bed and open my nightstand with trembling hands. The tears won't stop pouring down my face. They remind me that I'm here, that I can cry, that I'm alive. I should be dead. It should be me instead of Kingsley. He should be here, living. He had purpose; he had a life.

The reality of his death continues to tear through me and all I want is to make it stop. I grab a razor and absently note how it gleams as I flip it between my fingers. Staring at the blade through tears, only seeing a blur, I squeeze my eyes shut. I don't want to live another minute in this life that I hate. I extend my left arm and see the veins laced beneath my pale, thin skin. Blood is pumping through them, begging to be released. I bring the razor's edge to my arm, pushing down until I feel the initial sting of my breaking flesh. The blood trickles out and adrenaline buzzes through my body. The sadness in my tears mixes with the relief in my blood. Every nerve ending is on high alert. I drag the blade slowly down the inside of my forearm toward my wrist. The farther I go, the harder I push down. The blood isn't trickling anymore. It's flowing out much faster, streaming in red rivulets down the side of my flesh, pooling on the floor below me. Suddenly, I feel like I'm floating and the sting starts to subside. The ache inside of me lessens; everything seems to be moving in slow motion. The blood keeps coming, but now all I see are spots, like a smoky afterimage of fireworks in a dark night sky. I'm so lightheaded and in a vague way, I realize that I've cut myself deeper than I ever have before. The blade drops to the floor, and, as if from far away, I hear the tiny piece of metal bounce off the ceramic tile. Grasping my arm, I try to squeeze the cut shut, but the bleeding doesn't slow down.

Fear.

I should feel fear. I should be terrified, but I'm not. Life is either about pressing the continue or quit button. I can't press continue anymore. My world slowly fades to blackness and I quit.

"The great thing in the world is not so much where we stand, as in what direction we are moving."
—Oliver Wendall Holmes

Jessica

Three months later…

DEATH IS A multi-dimensional thing and the many facets of dealing with it affect each human being differently. This morning, like every morning since that tragic accident happened, I wake up with an intense ache in my heart. How much time is enough before the ache goes away? I certainly don't know, but I really wish I did, because it hurts and it hurts deeply. I'm here in the present, trying to stop living in the past. I replay my days and little moments with Kingsley over and over in my mind. I'm so scared that I'll forget him. I'm scared of forgetting how he smelled, what his hugs felt like, or how bright his smile was. I find myself clinging to a moment, a memory, going over each and every detail carefully, because I don't ever want to forget. I'd do anything to have him walk in the door right now and say something completely crass just so I could argue with him. He'd be so angry with me for what I did after being released from the hospital that week. I would be dead if Mercedes hadn't come to check on me. After my suicide attempt, I was committed to this inpatient mental health facility. My therapist, Janice, says I get to leave next week, and though I should be happy about that, the truth is I'm beyond terrified. I've come a long way over the past three months and I know this was the best place for me to be. Hopelessness and debilitating sorrow crippled me after learning that Kingsley was gone. The worst part was learning the rest of the story. It was like a horror film unfolding in front of me. Looking back, the memory still moves in slow agonizing motion.

"Ms. Alexander, we are very sorry to inform you that the person who hit you in the accident was your mother."

Those words will forever be etched in my mind. My mother. She was drunk and driving, just like I've done so many times myself, and she killed a beautiful person that I loved. Trying to swallow that reality and face the hard truth of it isn't something that I've handled well at all. Therapy has been hard, really hard. Janice wasn't kidding when she said I'd hate her some days. I've hated her lots of days. Surprisingly, Mercedes has visited me every week without fail. I've never had a close girlfriend before and it's nice. She's hilarious and makes me laugh, even though laughing isn't something that I do often. She brings me books and although I've never been much of a reader, I'm totally addicted now. She brought me a book the first day she visited and I let it sit on my bedside table for two weeks. One day, I finally picked it up out of pure boredom and I didn't put it down until I'd finished. The next time she visited, I told her I had to have the second book of the series. She just laughed at me and pulled it out of her bag. Book two was just as good and I devoured every page. When I finished, I felt like a different person. The story was fiction, but the messages were not. During the hours I spent reading, I was given a reprieve from the pain of my reality. I felt hopeful and I'm sure I'll never look at books the same again. The girl in the book got schooled by a boy and I was completely schooled by the author of those books. They inspired me to live with an emphasis on life. A knock at my door rattles me out of my deep thoughts.

"Yeah, come in," I call out.

"It's phone call time. Do you want to make any calls today, Ms. Jessica?" Nurse Gail asks. She's a sweet older lady and I've grown to really appreciate her. I shake my head no.

"All right, Ms. Jessica, I just wanted to ask."

I never make calls. I have no one to call. Jace has written me many times, but I never write back. I don't know what to say to him. I've been dealing with so much hatred and fighting the never-ending voices in my head that I really haven't wanted to talk to anyone. I've been too busy facing demons. Jace holds so many reminders of my past that I don't know how to continue any type of relationship with him. I still love him very much and I know that no amount of time will ever erase who we are to each other. But he has his own life, he's moving on, and I have to respect that. I can't continue to hang on to something that I lost long ago.

I've decided to talk for the first time in my DBT group today and I'm nervous, really nervous. I stand up and make my way to the podium set up in front of the semi-circle. My palms are sweaty and if my mouth gets any drier, I may not get one word out. Janice gives me an encouraging smile and I take a deep, calming breath.

"Hi, I'm Jessica, and I have borderline personality disorder. I'm here for a suicide attempt and I'm a cutter. Three months ago, I lost someone who loved me in spite of all these things. He loved me for me, and for the first time in my life, I loved someone back for the simple reason that it was how I felt. I didn't want to gain anything from it and I didn't try to manipulate it. His name was Kingsley," I swallow before going on. "He was a sarcastic asshole a lot of times and I loved that about him. He never let me bullshit him and he never allowed me to pity myself." I pause, needing to take a moment before I break down. Retaining my composure, I continue. "He encouraged me, empowered me, and supported me, always reminding me of the possibilities and choices each day presented. He was a beautiful person and even though it hurts like hell missing him, I'm so glad I knew him. I've been on such a terribly unhealthy cycle with men all of my life. Honestly, I never knew what a healthy relationship was until Kingsley. Sex and drama were all I really knew. My emotions always drove me to dark places, and every relationship I'd ever had ended because of my bad decisions. The constant belief that I need a man in my life to complete me has haunted me for as long as I can remember. It's something that I struggle with every day. Needing someone to love me and want me has always driven me to the brink of madness." I straighten my shoulders and shift my weight from one foot to the other anxiously before I try to get the rest of my words out.

"The past three months have opened my eyes to so much. I know I have a really far and tough journey ahead of me with my therapy, but where I am today is so much closer to wellness than I've ever come before. This morning, I stood in front of the mirror. The reflection staring back at me was still a damaged girl, but I know her better than I ever have before. Knowing yourself after being a stranger to who you are all of your life brings a lot into focus. I've always seen a stranger looking back at me, but today, I didn't." I make eye contact with Janice and she's smiling proudly.

"Just like many of you, I've always blamed the world around me for all of my pain, but I've learned in DBT that I have control over many things in my world, like my choices. It's scary to take responsibility for my actions after always acting before thinking, but I'm determined to follow the skills I've learned here." Everyone's eyes are on me and the room is completely silent. I keep talking and it feels damn good to get it all out.

"I'm so very tired of being held prisoner by my own mind. As I looked in the mirror today, I saw a woman that's been through hell and back, but a woman that's survived her past. I know that I can do this, and I refuse to let anything stop me. Life can push me, pull me, and beat me down, but it's not going to break me. I've been broken before, I've been bound and I've survived. There's a me that has hidden beneath pain all my life, but no more. And I have to say, I kinda like the girl I saw today. She's stronger, she's a fighter, and she doesn't need a man's love to validate her. She doesn't need people to like her to let her know she matters, because she does matter. She can love herself. And until she can walk through each day knowing these things absolutely, with pure faith in herself, having a guy in her life isn't a priority." A few people wipe tears from their eyes and I know that my story is hitting home for them.

"I saw me today, and today, I don't hate me. It's time that I get to know the girl staring back at me in that mirror better. It's time to have a love affair with myself, time to live my life for me for once. No longer can I allow my mistakes to dictate my future. Janice told me once that life begins at the end of your comfort zone and I'm prepared to live my life, no matter how uncomfortable it may feel." With every word I speak another bar breaks in my mind. It's a prison I've waited a long time to escape.

"I don't remember who said it, but a self-proclaimed quotaholic friend of mine shared one of her favorite quotes with me recently. It talks about what lies behind us, before us, and within us. It really made me think about what I've learned over the past few months. I've learned that what lies in front of me is all that matters. What has been left behind is nothing compared to the strength that lies within me. A part of me died that day with Kingsley, but I think sometimes something in us has to die completely for there to be a rebirth. I'm ready. Today, Jessica Alexander starts to live, learns to love herself, and begins to shed the ghosts of her past."

"Life can't be divided into chapters...only minutes."
—Colleen Hoover

Jace

One year later...

SITTING HERE IN front of a therapist for the first time in my adult life feels strange, but it's necessary. Explaining everything that's happened over the past year and a half to Dr. Brenner has actually felt refreshing. I know I work in the mental health field and all, but up until recently, I really didn't think I had any reason to need to talk to anyone. Therapy was just something "those people" needed, but never me. I was above it all. What a load of shit that was. It took everything falling apart around me for me to realize that I needed some help. Today, my divorce will be final and the new reality of my life is going to take some getting used to.

"Wow, that is a lot," Dr. Brenner says.

He's a tall, lanky man with small, wiry glasses and a receding hairline. As he takes notes, he hunches forward over his desk. Though he scribbles in an almost frantic fashion, his demeanor and voice are quite calm. I've heard he's the best in the area.

"I can see where you'd be overwhelmed and need someone to talk to. How are you feeling about what you have to face today?"

"Well, I want the divorce, so I'm glad that it's going to be final today. Though I was looking forward to being a dad, it's kind of a relief that Victoria lied about being pregnant. I haven't cared for her in a long time and I can't imagine raising a child with someone that I feel no emotional connection to." I take a breath and go on. "What I'm having the hardest time with is finding out that our relationship was a complete sham from the very beginning."

I lean forward and clasp my hands together, slightly dropping my head as I sigh.

"I loved my mother despite all the vindictive things she did. But now? I just can't stop feeling angry with her. Finding out that she planted Victoria in my life after maneuvering Jess out of it...it's more than I can take. I just keep looking back over my college years, even the time after college, and thinking about what a complete fool I was."

"You weren't a fool, Jace. You were a young man and a beautiful, strong-willed, intelligent woman came along—planted or not—into your life at a time when you were tremendously vulnerable. There was nothing wrong with that. Loving someone isn't foolish. I know it taints the memory of the relationship, but it doesn't make your part of it a lie."

I do feel foolish. I feel like a dumbass. Dr. Brenner keeps talking, and though I want to believe his logic is correct, right now it's just hard to wrap my mind around.

"You've expressed that you know you were never really in love with Victoria. Why did you allow the relationship to get to such a serious place if you knew you weren't in love with her? Have you explored that at all?" he asks, and I wonder if my embarrassment is showing on my face the same way his curiosity shows on his.

Yeah, I've explored that. I've also explored what a coward I was to let Jessica leave my life so easily. It's constantly in the back of my mind. But I don't want to waste another minute thinking about anything having to do with Victoria. I'm so tired of beating myself up for all the mistakes I've made, all the chances I've missed.

"I have, and the answer is it just happened that way. She was comfortable and our relationship was easy. We had fun together. Eventually, we spent more and more time with one another and it became routine. The next natural step was getting engaged; it just seemed like the normal thing to do."

I lean back, running a hand through my hair. Talking about all of this isn't easy for me. I usually hold things in, or, even worse, completely ignore my own feelings. My whole life I've always kept it together and been the good guy that never fell apart. I'm the guy that fixes things. It was me that had to put Mom back together when Genevieve died. I figured it was my fault that she died, so I had to fix everything that her death affected. I needed to prove the best way I knew how that I could help make it better. I did the same thing when my dad passed away. With Jess, I was too late to save her from being beaten up by Elizabeth and her friends. I was too late to save her, but I could still help her, be her friend, and prevent it from happening again. I just wanted to help fix what had been broken inside her. But in the process, I fell in love with her. I realize now that I never learned how to find a balance between helping her and truly loving her. She needed someone to stand with her, not hold her up.

"Once the pain of losing Jess started to ebb, things gradually got easier and easier with Victoria. She always made a point to focus on trying to keep me happy and distracted from any kind of stressors. She was one of the most helpful people to me in college. I swear, sometimes I'm not sure if I would've passed some of those exams if it weren't for the long nights of her grilling and studying with me."

Dr. Brenner slides his glasses up the bridge of his nose as he continues to take notes with the other hand. He looks back to me periodically when he does this to make sure I know he's paying attention.

"So, you did have good times with her," he confirms in his easy tone. "You can't just dismiss the entire relationship as a failure. You shouldn't view yourself as an idiot just because your mother secretly orchestrated the two of you meeting. I think you should cut yourself some slack where this situation is concerned. What about the other woman? Jessica? Where is she now?"

Under my skin, inside my heart, and constantly on my mind.

I inhale deeply and the picture of the last time I saw Jess comes into my mind.

"Nowhere," I say, and try to keep the disappointment out of my voice. "Like I told you, I haven't heard from her in a year. I tried and tried contacting her, but she never responded. She's on social media; I try and keep up with how she's doing that way. But she doesn't communicate with me directly. I'm pretty sure she never will."

"She was in an inpatient unit with mental health concerns for a while, though, correct?" Dr. Brenner asks as he flips back in his notes.

"Yes, she was. I wrote her while she was there but, as I said, no response. She was there for three months. I do still hold out hope that one day I'll connect with her again."

Dr. Brenner glances at his watch then back to me.

"I think we're off to a good start here. We've run over our hour quite a bit, but we can pick up right where we left off next time." He smiles as he places his pen down. "Make sure to schedule next week's session with Grace before you leave. And Jace," he starts, "today will be fine," he assures me. "We'll talk all of it over next week. If you need anything before then, don't hesitate to call."

We both stand up and he makes his way around his desk to shake my hand.

"Thanks, Dr. Brenner, I really appreciate it. I'll see you next session."

Victoria glares at me from across the conference table as her attorney slides the documents over to me.

"You're giving everything up. I hope you realize that. You'll get nothing from your mother's estate now," she sneers, and I wonder if she remembers that we've been over this a million times. I sign my name on the dotted line and look back up at her.

"Yes, Victoria, I'm aware of that. Money isn't worth staying in a marriage with someone who worked with my mother to manipulate me." I can feel the muscles in my neck tense, but I'm doing all I can to keep my cool. "When I asked you about the pregnancy, you didn't even flinch. You just happily went along with my mother's ploy, just like you did from day one. The one thing I haven't been able to figure out is what the hell was in it for you, Vic? The money? You have yours and your family's money. Me? You're way too into yourself to care about whether I'm beside you or not, so that's not it." I wait to see if she'll finally give it up. No such luck. "Your lies have caught up with you, Vic. Screw you and screw the money. It isn't worth living a lie."

Her glare intensifies and her expression grows thunderous. I glance over at our lawyers who, surprisingly, look uncomfortable with the screwed-up situation. You'd think after all the divorces they've worked on they would've seen everything.

"Have it your way! I've been loyal to you. I've given you years of my life and you're just throwing all of that away." Her eyes narrow and her voice drops to a dangerous level. "If that tramp hadn't walked into my office and back into your life, we'd be married and happy right now and you'd be none the wiser."

I place the pen back onto the table and straighten my shoulders. She's trying to goad me, but I refuse to fight with her anymore. Her persistence, her arguments, and her petty jealousy...all of it's exhausting, she's exhausting; I just want to move on with my life. It's time to face my issues and start living for me. I've spent my days helping others and in the process, I've completely lost my sense of self. Looking back on my life, I'm ashamed by my constant need to appease people and mitigate situations. To the outside world, I appeared to be a confident, take-charge kind of guy, but I let those closest to me walk all over me. I know I have to face the fact that I allowed my mother to convince me that I couldn't be my own man. Along the way, I lost a love that I'm pretty sure I'll never find again. I should've fought harder for Jessica. I see that now. Only it's too little, too late.

I slide the documents back over to Victoria's attorney and, before the ink even dries, I feel better. My eyes meet hers and pure disgust is painted on her face. I know I don't have to set the record straight, but I also know that these are some of the last words I'll ever say to Victoria. Might as well make the best of them.

"Jessica has nothing to with this. You are who you are. Just because I never saw it before doesn't change that I see it now. You're self-serving and self-righteous and I never really loved you. I couldn't, because you never really loved me. Love isn't selfish, ever. Love gives, love forgives, love empathizes, love has no conditions and it always remains constant through the ups and downs. You and I were never in love. I've been in love once in my life and until I find that kind of love again, I'm not going to fool myself with a cheap imitation. Just accept this for what it is. Move on. If you can, find real love with someone that will love you in return. One day, you'll thank me for this."

She shoots up out of her seat, throws her Chanel bag over her shoulder, and stomps toward the door, leaving me with a few choice words.

"Screw you, Jace Collins. I hope you're miserable for the rest of your life," she shouts. "One day, you'll be begging me to come back to you."

The door slams behind her and it's done. Finally. I'm officially divorced and prepared to start over. I've taken the last month off to try and figure my life out and my new practice, back in Jenson, opens next week. My new house on the lake is small and quaint and it suits me just fine.

My lawyer interrupts my internal musings. "It may not seem like it right now, but you dodged a bullet with that one, son," he says as he stands to put the paperwork in his briefcase. On the other side of the table, Victoria's lawyer meets my eyes. Though he can't comment, he just nods quickly in agreement before grabbing his coat and briefcase and leaving the room.

"Good luck," he says, and I smile for the first time all day. New beginnings are ahead.

I flip open my laptop and check my Facebook messages. Nothing. No surprise there. I've been messaging Jessica on and off over the past months, holding out hope that she'll reply, but she never does. I don't know why I keep trying. I miss her, I guess. I want to be in her life in some way and I hesitate to push her, but I refuse to give up completely. The little icon by her name turns green.

She's online.

I take a deep breath and a chance...

Jace Collins: *Hi, stranger.*

I wait.

And wait.

And wait.

Ten minutes pass and the little flicker of optimism I felt begins to dim.

Jessica Alexander: *Hi.*

She replied! I say a silent "thank you" to myself and reply with a huge smile on my face.

Jace Collins: *I'm so glad to hear back from you. It's been a while.*

Jessica Alexander: *Yeah, it has. How are you?*

Jace Collins: *I'm okay. Lots of change lately, but it's good change. I took some time off work and my new practice opens next week. I'm excited about it.*

Jessica Alexander: *That's wonderful! I'm sorry about the split with Victoria. I saw some posts about it.*

Jace Collins: *No, it's fine. I'm more than okay with it. How are you doing? I see you're in school. I'm proud of you.*

Jessica Alexander: *Well, all that matters is that you're happy. I'm glad you're okay. Yes, school. Hmmmm... That was a huge step. Some days are better* *than others. School isn't something that I've ever really enjoyed, but college is different. There are some things I've grown to like. It's just daunting when I think about how long I have to go before I get to stand in front of a classroom and teach. But I keep focusing on how important that day is to me, no matter how long it takes.*

Jace Collins: *You'll be an amazing teacher. How is your mom? I saw the pics of you two. That is such an enormous step for you. She looks really well.*

Jessica Alexander: *She's good. She's been out of the Jones Substance Abuse Corrections Facility for about a month now. We are attending joint counseling sessions to work through our issues from the past. It's not easy.*

Jace Collins: *Jess...*

Jessica Alexander: *Yeah?*

Jace Collins: *I miss you. This is nice. Thanks for replying.*

Jessica Alexander: *I miss you too. Things are just complicated for me right now. I'm sorry about not responding before. I hope you can understand. I'm still trying to cope with my past and the person I never want to be again.*

Jace Collins: *I know, and I do understand. It may be too much too soon, but when you're in town next time to see your mom, could we grab some lunch or something?*

Just to talk. Friends? I'm not asking for anything more than a lunch date. No pressure. Just two friends getting to know each other again.

This time she doesn't reply immediately. Maybe I shouldn't have asked. I'm an idiot. Why couldn't I have just enjoyed the moment and let it be? But down deep I know why. I want her in my life and I'm prepared to fight for it this time.

My messenger dings.

Jessica Alexander: *Sure, I guess we could do that. I'll be there this Saturday for the day. What time and where?*

I'm reading the message over for the second time, feeling like I'm in high school all over again. My heart beats hard in my chest; I feel like I just scored a date for prom. My fingers fly across the keyboard as I type out a cool, simple message.

Jace Collins: *How about noon down at Marina Café?*

Jessica Alexander: *That works. I'll see you then. Make sure you order me a Vanilla Coke* ☺

I love that she's being lighthearted and joking.

Jace Collins: *Done deal. See you then Jess, and thanks.*

Jessica Alexander: ☺

I log off and exhale. I have a lunch date with Jess. It's just lunch between friends, but I'm so damn excited that I can hardly contain myself. The smile on my face feels like it may be permanently plastered there.

I'm sitting in the outdoor seating area, looking out over the water. The weather is perfect—not too hot, not too cool—but I'm so damn nervous that I can feel sweat forming on my forehead. A waitress brings over the Vanilla Coke I ordered for Jess and a Stella beer for me. I need to chill and a beer will help relax me a bit. I check my watch for the hundredth time just before I see her from the corner of my eye. I look up and smile, facing her for the first time in over a year.

So. Beautiful.

Jess. She's here, with me. The reality of it is strange, but the feeling I get while looking at her punches me right square in the face. I love this woman. No amount of time, heartache, or bullshit has changed it and it never will. I love her and somehow, someway I will get her back. I don't care what I have to do to make her mine again. She looks happy and strong, like the Jessica I always knew was hiding under all that pain and suffering. She shines like a star. My pride for her swells; she beat the hardest battle a human being ever fights—a battle of the mind. Even though she struggles daily, I can clearly see that she's doing it by herself, for herself, and she never needed to be fixed by anyone else. She's done an amazing job of that all on her own.

"Hey," she says. Her tentative smile warms me from within, and the thought crosses my mind that inside I've felt cold for a long time.

The moment is awkward for both of us. I feel like I should say something charming or witty, but I don't.

To hell with it.

It's time to have some courage and take a risk. There's nothing left for me to lose and if I don't try now, I'll always regret it. No more passing up the important moments in life; small moments like this one are what I've failed to embrace in the past.

I take a few steps toward her and reach out to hug the living shit out of her. She gasps and starts to giggle as she hugs me back; I laugh right along with her. This feels so incredible. Right.

This is my Jess. Always has been, always will be.

"Hi," I whisper as I inhale the fruity scent of her thick hair.

"Hi back."

I slowly release her from my bear hug and she's smiling, really smiling. No more of that unsure, nervous smile, no. This is the most perfect smile a girl could ever smile.

"Sorry, I just went with my gut. I couldn't help myself," I tell her, trying to contain the excitement exploding inside my heart.

"It's okay, but only because you've got my Vanilla Coke waiting for me," she says, gesturing toward the table.

We both laugh and I pull out her chair for her before I sit down myself.

"You look good, Jess, real good."

She blushes a little and tries to keep a straight face.

"Janice says I should say 'thank you.' I'm still working on the accepting compliments thing. So, thank you, Jace. You look nice yourself."

Beads of condensation drip down from her glass as she takes a drink. Every gesture, every movement she makes has my complete attention. The curve of her neck, the bend of her elbow, and the way her hair rests on her shoulders...I take it all in, memorizing it, savoring it. After not seeing her for so long, I just can't look away. I wouldn't want to.

"So, have you decided what subject you want to teach yet?" I ask her, wanting to keep the conversation flowing.

"I'm thinking of English or Language Arts. I'd really love to be a swim coach too. I don't know, though. I have a long way to go." She looks out across the water and rests her chin on the heel of her hand. A calmness settles around her, one that I've never seen before, and I observe the moment silently, in awe of the girl before me. "I love it out here. It's really beautiful," she sighs.

"Yeah, it really is," I say, my eyes never looking away from her.

She glances up at me, and the blush from before flares up again, even pinker than the last time.

"Stop it, Jace. You're gonna embarrass me," she responds shyly.

"What? I was just agreeing with you."

"Uh huh." She grins and swirls her straw around in her drink before taking a sip.

"I bought a little house on this lake, you know?"

Her eyebrows shoot up. "You did?"

"Yep, I moved in a couple days ago. I still have boxes

everywhere, though. I hate unpacking."

She's grinning from ear to ear.

"That's fantastic! Well, you shouldn't be here with me. You should be unpacking. Your practice opens next week too. You have tons to do. I don't want to take up your time."

I shake my head at her. "Jess, it's fine. I'll work on it this afternoon. Trust me, unpacking is something that I can procrastinate on for a long time."

She's contemplating her response as I look on, and I can see the exact moment when she makes up her mind.

"I can help you, then. I'm here all day. I already spent the morning with Mom. I bet we could knock it all out today. Then you wouldn't have to worry with it next week."

Jess...in my house. Us...together all day. Yes and yes.

"Are you sure? I certainly won't turn that offer down."

She claps once as if she's just won a dispute.

"It's a deal, then. Let's eat and get to it, Mr. Collins. I'll just follow you over in my car when we leave here," she states.

"I hope you're up for some work because there are tons of boxes that I haven't unpacked yet."

"If you unpack as well as you swim, I know we've got our work cut out for us," she quips with a wicked grin, "but I'm up for it."

Damn, I love this girl.

We finished our meal and left. Now Jess is pulling into the driveway at my new house right behind me. I still can't believe she's here. I kind of want to pinch myself, but I refrain. I get out and she meets me up at the door.

"Jace, this place is so great all tucked out here by itself. It's beautiful and peaceful."

"Yeah, I love it. It's small but it has a ton of character," I respond as I unlock the door and gesture for her to follow me in. "Come on in. Welcome to my little house of boxes," I joke.

She steps inside and scans the space. "Wow, for a small place, these high ceilings really open it up. I love the skylights."

She's in my house. Again, I'm trying to convince myself that this is actually happening.

"Thanks, I like that touch as well."

She sets her purse down by the door. "So, where do you want to start?"

I look around aimlessly at all the boxes and throw my hands up. "I guess it doesn't really matter. Let's just pick a box and go with it."

"All right," she agrees.

We both kneel down and pick up different boxes. I hand over a box cutter and we simultaneously open them up.

"Jace, these boxes aren't even labeled," she scolds with a smile.

"Um, yeah I know. I'm really bad at this moving stuff. Sorry."

She shakes her head at me and digs into her box. "Well, this is all clothes. Which room is your bedroom? Or would you rather do the clothing yourself?"

"No, no, it's fine. My room is the last one on the left."

I point toward the hallway.

"Okay," she says, getting up to carry the box back to my room. Trying to resist the urge to follow her back there and throw her on my unmade bed is physically and mentally taxing, but I stay put and focus on the box of stuff in front of me.

Get it together, Jace. You don't need to mess things up right when she just came back into your life.

A few minutes later, she returns to the living room as I'm digging through old photo frames and picture albums. I don't look up until I hear her clear her throat. I snap my eyes in her direction and there she is, holding up my old *Music Makes Me Horny* T-shirt. It's faded and worn from years of use, and I wonder if she remembers when she gave it to me, how she called it "Jace blue." I know I sure do.

"You still have this after all these years?"

I stand up and walk over to her, reaching out for the T-shirt. "Of course I do. Why do you look so surprised?"

"Um, I don't know. I just didn't think you'd still have something from that long ago."

If she only knew...

"Jess, there are many things from back then that still remain. That T-shirt is only one of them," I say seriously.

I'm not sure if she gets the subtext, but I think she does because her eyes soften. I can tell she's feeling nostalgic just like I am. Only it's more than nostalgia. It's a permanent memory of thoughts, words, feelings, and moments that never disappeared with all of the bridges we burned.

Just before I say something else she quickly snaps out of the moment and walks past me.

"Okay, what box is next? Let's get crackin', Collins. Let's get this done."

I lay the T-shirt down and smile.

"Yes, ma'am. I guess you can help me hang some of these frames and stuff."

She joins me on the sofa and we start sorting through photos. She holds one up from my Baylor graduation. It's me and Trent in our caps and gowns.

"How was it on that day? How did it feel to accomplish that?"

"It was good," I assure her. She looks contemplative, but I can't tell what she's thinking. "You'll know that feeling soon enough."

She sets the picture aside and reaches out to turn over an upside-down frame. As soon as she flips it, she pauses and takes a moment before picking it up slowly. She pulls it in to take a closer look; the expression on her face is strange. Her brows crease and she glances over at me, confused.

"Where did you get this, Jace?"

"What do you mean where did I get it? It's mine. Why? What's wrong? You look weird, Jess."

She stands up, gripping the picture, still staring at it intently. "Who gave this to you? How do you know my old neighbor?"

Her old neighbor? She's definitely mistaken.

"Jess, that's not your old neighbor. That's Genevieve, my little sister."

All at once, the color completely drains from her face, and she glares at me with confusion and dismay. She shakes her head back and forth hurriedly.

"No, no, it's not. It can't be. This is Vivvie. She lived

next door to me in high school."

She turns the picture to face me and points right to Genevieve's face.

"This is her. I know it. She's even wearing the same purple jacket and pin she gave me in this very picture. This can't be your sister, Jace."

The pin. The purple snowflake pin... Jess was wearing one at Mom's funeral. I don't even know what to say. She has to be confused. This is insane.

"Jess, that *is* my sister. Look, here are my photo albums; you can see for yourself. And Genevieve's nickname was Vivvie."

I hand her the photo album and she takes it, dropping to the sofa. She desperately flips through page after page of family pictures. Tears form in her eyes and slowly roll down her face. Her hands are trembling; she's really starting to scare me.

"Jess, what's going on? How did you know her nickname and why did you think she was your neighbor? She's been gone for a long time. I don't understand. Make me understand."

She looks at me with a blank stare. Her lips start to move as if she's going to say something, but she stops short of vocalizing her thoughts and presses her lips into a hard line. Her head tilts down toward the album once more before she gets up. She walks quickly to her purse, brings it over to the sofa, and anxiously starts digging through it. Moments later, she removes her hand from the purse and displays Genevieve's pin in her open palm.

The purple snowflake.

She points to the picture of Genevieve again and says, "She gave this to me. I've kept it with me always. She saved me one day. She's the reason I didn't go through with my first plan to kill myself after I had the abortion. And when I was in the hospital after Kingsley died, after my suicide attempt, I almost didn't make it, but she was there again."

Tears well in her eyes. She's looking at me as if I can solve this crazy mystery, but I'm just as confused as she is.

"I was dreaming or something. Kingsley was in my dream and he was happy. He'd been reunited with his wife and son. I don't know...it was all so strange." Her brows draw together in a pained expression and I have no idea what to say. "But I remember that Vivvie was in my dream too. That dream has haunted me because she looked the same. She had on the same clothes and was still a little girl, even though six years had passed since I met her in my backyard. In the dream, she spoke to me. She told me it wasn't my time to go yet and that I had to fight. She told me that I had things left to do, that I'd do great things one day. She told me that I was going to make a difference in people's lives, that love would find me again, and that I had to open my eyes and live so that I could do all of those things."

She pulls the photo in toward her face again and studies it closely. "She said teaching would be my life's purpose, my gift, and that, like she told me before, it's rude not to accept the gifts you're given. Then she smiled and was gone. All I remember after that is waking up in the hospital. When I got better and went home for the first time, I went next door to find her. I wanted to thank her and see how she was doing after all this time, but no one was there. My mom told me the house had been empty for years."

Tears are streaming down her face and her hands are trembling, causing the photo she's still holding to shake in her grip. I focus on that, because the realization of what she's just told me is starting to soak in and my mind can't comprehend it all at once.

It's too much.

"Why did she give you the pin, Jess?" Everything in me is pleading with her for some reasoning.

She looks at me through her tears and says, "She said it was my force field. She said her brother gave it to her because she was special and it was a special pin with special powers. She said it would protect me. I tried to tell her I couldn't take it, but she insisted."

I said those things. I gave Genevieve that pin. Those are my words. I can't make sense of this. My palms are sweaty and my mind is racing a million miles a minute.

I have to stop trying to analyze any of this right now. At this point, I need to let my heart guide my reaction because explaining the unexplainable is impossible. I reach down and take the pin from her palm, pinning it to her shirt just above her heart.

Our eyes lock onto each other and the ledge I'm standing on seems to get smaller beneath me. But now, I'm no longer afraid of falling.

So I jump.

I cup her chin gently and look into her beautiful, confused eyes. "She was right, Jess, about all of it. This is for someone special, someone that I love with all that I am. You *are* going to do great things in this life," I whisper, gently placing a kiss on her forehead.

I wrap my arms tightly around her and rest my chin on her head as she hugs me back and cries into my chest.

For the first time since Genevieve died, I feel like a weight has been lifted, and I'm seeing clearly, like maybe there is hope for me, for Jess, for us. And, somehow, I have my little sister to thank for that. Because although Genevieve is there, she's also here, with us. I don't know what there is like, but here has never been so promising...

THE END

Epilogue

"Everything has beauty. Even the ugly. Because without the ugly, there would be no beauty. Because without beauty, we would not survive our pain, our sorrow, and our suffering."
—Madeline Sheehan

Jessica

One month later...

WALKING ACROSS THE cemetery, I know I should feel something like anxiety or sadness, but mostly I feel a sense of serenity. The warm Texas breeze has the tree branches swaying and the sounds of rustling leaves and birds chirping are peaceful. The smell of freshly cut grass moves through the air and reminds me of the happy days I had as a kid. I hold my journal under my arm as I make my way to Kingsley's grave. His headstone is simple and the engraving his family chose is perfect. Everyone always focuses on the dates but all I can see is the dash. His birth and death aren't what mattered. The life he lived is what truly mattered most.

KINGSLEY JAMES ARRINGTON
HUSBAND, FATHER, AND FRIEND.
HE LIVED AND LOVED HARD.
BLESS HIM FOREVER AND ALWAYS.

My chest tightens and my heart feels a small spasm of pain. I swallow down the lump in my throat and push away the tears that want to come. I won't be sad today. It's been over a year since I lost him, but I can't continue to grieve for him. He would hate that. I wish he could know me today. He would be so proud of me. I think back to something he once told me; something I never understood until now.

"I love you for you, Jess. Your past doesn't define who you are. Biography isn't destiny."

I kneel down as his words finally resonate. The soft grass meets my knees and I open up my journal. I flip to the last page where my newest poem is. My mind rewinds back to the precious moments I had with Kingsley and I smile. He was one of those people that came into my life and shone a bright light on it, showing me everything I never saw in myself. He opened me up to the endless possibilities of who I could be. He planted the seeds that slowly grew inside my heart, bringing me hope and love. Kingsley was one of those once-in-a-lifetime people that can never be forgotten because his impression upon my life and the world will always be there. I tear out the poem and fold it into a small square. I reach out and prop it up against the headstone. The sky is bright blue today with crazy deep blue hues surrounding the fluffy clouds; it reminds me of his eyes. I close mine to get a clearer picture of him in my mind, the words of my poem running through my head. I titled it "Rafters Above."

Walls had been built
Fears birthed from unrelenting
self-doubt
Seated alone within the confines of
my mind
Peeking out
I captured a glimpse
There you were

I saw you

Looking closer
Looking through my defenses

You saw me

Step-by-step
You traveled the emotional miles
You pushed
You magnified
Standing me in front of myself
A bright light
You shined upon me
You forced me to see it

The real me

Seeds that you watered
Never once taken for granted
They grew
Implanted

Inside my heart
Branching out into my soul
Breaking
Destroying

Each boundary deploying

Every bridge burnt
Rebuilt by a carpenter of love
A creator of hope
Now resting upon rafters above
A once-in-a-lifetime person
A friend
An infinite impression

I bring my fingers to my lips, placing a kiss to them before reaching out and pressing them against his engraved name on the stone. I whisper two words, "Thank you."

The tears start to come and I quickly stand up, brushing off my knees and taking in a deep breath. I pick up my journal and look at the headstone, but I know he's not there. I look up to the sky and smile once more.

"Good-bye Kingsley," I tell him. Then I turn and walk away.

Jace and I have been dating for a month now, but we are taking things slow. He's been incredibly patient, but he's also been persistent in making sure I know that he's in this for the long haul. School takes up a lot of my time and he's really busy with work. Oddly enough, we've decided to start going to a few joint sessions with his therapist to sort through some of our demons from the past. Our first session together is today. Seems strange to be in counseling with your boyfriend, but I think, knowing our pasts and how upside-down our lives have been, it's a positive thing for us. Everyone needs a little therapy at one point or another in their life. We're trying to do better now that we know better. I love Jace, and his undying love for me is something that I never thought I could accept, because I never believed I deserved it. Therapy has taught me many things about myself. Believing that I *am* worth it is the hardest lesson of all to fully absorb. It's still a daily struggle, but it's a battle I gladly face because it's a fight worth fighting.

I have a ton of homework piled up in front of me. Jace is coming to pick me up in a bit, so I need to get on it, but I bought myself a new journal yesterday and I'm dying to put a few words in it. I reach down and pull it out of my purse, opening it to the first page. I run my hand over the crisp, white, blank page and try to think of a title. "Therapy", which seems pretty fitting, sounds good.

Pain and hurt
They move quickly inside you
Stripping away layers of self-worth
Crashing through your thoughts
Rearranging your ideas

Sifting through your soul
Dragging you along

Love and hope
They take their time
Tip-toeing through your mind
Rethreading the frayed edges of time
Giving you signs

Love will always show up
It wants in
Open the window to your heart
Let. It. In.
Love will see you
It saw me
I see it too
Self-love
It's my THERAPY.

Please check out Kathryn's website
www.Kathryn-Vance-Perez.com
for more information on her books, upcoming events, signed paperbacks, the THERAPY playlist and more.

For more information on The Amanda Todd Legacy Foundation or to make a donation please visit:
www.amandatoddlegacy.org

For more information on The Tyler Lenius Band, their music, show dates, merchandise and more please visit:
www.tylerleniusband.com

If you would like to learn more about borderline personality disorder you can visit:
www.bpdresourcecenter.org

NOTE FROM THE AUTHOR

DEAR READER,

This is a very personal story for me and I can't tell you how appreciative I am that you gave it a chance. The topics I wrote about in this book are ones that I hope one day will no longer have any stigma attached to them. Our young people are suffering in silence because they're ashamed. It is my hope that someday soon, we'll live in a world where bullied teens and those that live with mental illness can live outside the box of shame and fear. If you're one of those people, please reach out and ask for help. Asking doesn't make you weak; it makes you strong. Helping yourself is the most courageous thing you will ever do. I am a suicide survivor and I'm thankful each and every day for those that have been a part of my journey to healing. It wasn't an easy journey, but I get out of bed each day knowing it was worth the miles traveled. Loving who I am is still an everyday struggle, but I choose each day to try. I was diagnosed with borderline personality disorder in my early twenties and entering therapy was the best and scariest decision I have ever made. Dialectical behavior therapy and the work I did in that program saved my life. I truly feel that I wouldn't be here today if it weren't for the amazing therapist that provided me with the tools to live a happier, mentally healthier life. The hard work was worth every painful and scary step.

Just like Jessica, I had to face my emotional baggage and learn to make a new path in my life, to find my passion. After roaming aimlessly through life trying to find it, I found writing. Or maybe writing found me. I wanted to write Jessica's story because I believe that there are many others out there who have traveled a similar path, and I wanted to shine a bright light on topics that are usually kept in the dark. I openly talk about my past because we should embrace our mistakes and our dark times, because without them we'd never have the lessons and the light.

Live everyday with the hopes of becoming more. Dream big and take chances. Never regret the risks you took and always strive to love yourself first. When it gets hard, put on a force field and face the pain and the fear, because you are stronger than you know. We all need a force field some days.

Stay Strong,

Kathryn.

ACKNOWLEDGMENTS

I HAVE NO clue how to even begin thanking people that were involved with this book. No amount of words will ever do them justice. Their dedication, compassion, and inspiration goes beyond any expectations I could ever have had.

To my children, you're the most amazing little humans in my world. I love you with all that I am and you make me so very proud. I'm in awe of you every single day. Your patience during my long hours at the computer is something that I know was hard for you. I am more thankful than you'll ever know.

To my husband, through many challenging times you have been there and you continue to be there, no matter what. This book would've never been possible if it weren't for your unwavering support of my dreams. Thank you for believing in me when I didn't want to believe in myself. Thank you for picking up the slack around the house when I was spending countless hours working on this story. Thank you for being both mom and dad some days. Thank you for being you. I love you so much.

To my mother, you're my biggest cheerleader and I couldn't be more thankful for you and your continued support of whatever I am doing in my life at any given time. I love you to the moon and back. Thank you for all the times you've kept the kids so I could work, done my laundry when it piled up, or cleaned up for me. All of those little things are more helpful than you'll ever know. I promise to have more time to spend with you now that this book is written. Well, until I jump into the next one anyway. ☺

To the KVP Street Team members and the group sponsor, Whirlwind Books Blog, wow, what an amazing group of people you are. My gratitude for you is boundless. Abby, Aimee, Amanda, Amy, Brandi, Carmen, Carol, Chelle, Chris, Denise, Elizabeth, Felisha, Fern, Fred, Gail, Heather, Jasmine, Lena, Megan, Michelle, Nancy, Pamela, Sally, Sonia, Teresa, Tiffany, Toni, Danielle, Heather Vanessa and Yara, I love you all so much and I am so honored to have you on my team! You're all my purple snowflakes!

I am also thankful for many of my fellow authors. One of my favorite things is when we pull together, helping and supporting one another. Each one of the following people had an impact on me during the process of writing this book and I am thankful for each and every one of them: Cassia Leo, Laura Dunaway, Molly McAdams, Kelly Elliot, EL Montes, Tina Reber, Karina Halle, Katie Ashley, Mia Asher, Claribel Contreras, SL Jennings, Elle Chardou, Leslie Fear, HP Landry, Kelsie Leverich, Trudy Stiles, Gail McHugh, Toni Aleo, Heidi McLaughlin, and Jasinda Wilder. Sarah Dosher, I am also eternally grateful for you and for the friendship we have had from day one over a year ago. I'm so happy to have traveled this path with you and I know we will continue to do so far into the future. Love you lots girl! KA Robinson and Jessica Prince I am ecstatic to have made such good friends with both of you. The conversations here and there, funny texts and a smile on a frown type of day that you give me when it is much needed is priceless. Lisa N. Paul, your help with the steamy scenes will certainly be appreciated by the readers. That's for sure! Thank you so much for your help and support. Aleatha Romig, your class and humbleness sets you apart and I am honored to be in your circle of friends. Thank you for your continued support and valuable advice. Christine Zolendz, thank you so very much for allowing an excerpt of Therapy to be in the back of your novel, Brutally Beautiful. That was such an honor.

One author in particular who puts up with my incessant ranting and self-loathing on a regular basis is one, Madeline Sheehan. I am happy to call you a friend and I can't tell you enough how grateful I am for you. Thanks for always being there and for always encouraging me. Thank you for talking me off a ledge many times and for pushing me to be a better writer. You make me laugh and you always help me to see things from a better perspective. Love you lots! Babe, yeah. ☺

It takes a lot of input, research, and thought to put a book together. Without all of the vital roles each person plays, an idea would never become a polished, complete story. To my beta readers, Gail Charnick, Amanda Penrod, Chris Thompson, Megan Kapusta, Jenn Hall, Chelle Northcutt, Kaci Buckley, Beth Rustenhaven, and Murphy Rae. Thank you so very much for spending so much of your free time helping me fine-tune Jessica's story. You're invaluable to me. Never forget that! Chelle, Megan K, Chris and Gail I want you to know how very much your one on one encouragement and support means to me. I couldn't have done this without you. You're truly amazing!

I also must thank Chase Glover for helping me better

understand drinking and driving laws. To the wonderfully talented musician, Tyler Lenius, I have to say how excited I am to share your music with my readers. I am so honored to have one of your songs within the pages of my book. Music makes everything better!

To my editor, Megan Ward, nothing short of AMAZING can describe how I feel about you. Your professionalism and dedication to this story will forever mean the world to me. The countless hours on the phone, texting, emailing, and working with me on this book far exceeded my expectations. I can never tell you enough how appreciative I am of all the hard work you put into this story.

To Aimee Emerick, Megan Simpson, Brenna Weidner, and Lena Ampofo, thanks for being there in the beginning of Jessica's story. I hope you are happy with how it turned out. Denise Tung and Fred Lebaron, no words are adequate enough for the support you have given me over the past year. I love you both. Thank you.

To my cover designer, Sarah Hansen of Okay Creations, I want to thank you for bringing my vision to life in this stunning cover. Not only did you practically read my mind, you blew my mind. The back is equally as beautiful as the front. Your talent is always worth the wait. And yes, I'll keep saying it, you are always right!

To Julie Titus of JT Formatting, thank you for making my words look pretty on everyone's e-readers and within the pages of a paperback. Your talent and dedication to your clients is nothing short of exceptional.

To every blog that has supported me, I am eternally grateful for your continued support of new indie authors. Your dedication to this community is tireless and I am so very appreciative of you. I would like to especially thank

Whirlwind Books and The Indie Bookshelf for all that you have and continue to do to support my work.

To Amanda Todd, a snowflake up in heaven, your memory lives on through many and I'll never stop advocating for others that struggle with the challenges you struggled with. May God and his angels forever wrap their love around you and your family. You'll never be forgotten.

To the WDDR writing group, thank you ladies for your invaluable advice and for being a place to go when I need to find answers or just let off some steam. Y'all are amazing!

Lastly, but certainly not least, I want to thank Colleen Hoover. Without you I would've never been inspired to follow my dream to write the stories I had in my head. You motivate me to be better, do better, and to never quit. Your kindness and generosity amazes me. I can't tell you how honored I am to know you, and to have you as a mentor and friend. I can never explain to you how much you have changed my life in both small and big ways. Thank you for believing in me. I and Love and You.

ABOUT THE AUTHOR

KATHRYN LIVES IN her small East Texas hometown with her husband and two children. She is a music infused writer and self-proclaimed book junkie. When she isn't listening to music, writing or reading you will probably find her watching her favorite sport, UFC.

Kathryn is also an anti-bullying advocate and avid supporter of mental-illness and suicide awareness.

You can follow Kathryn on Facebook at
www.facebook.com/kathrynvanceperez